"I hate

Brooke looked uncomfortable.

"What?" Jonas asked.

"Your son had a dead woman's cell phone in his room. Do you think he had anything to do with her death?"

Jonas stepped back, her words hurting more than if she'd slapped him. "What? No. Of course not." He raked a hand through his hair, hating the flash of doubt that raced through him. "No. I mean my son has been getting in some trouble lately, but he'd never hurt—kill—someone over a stupid phone."

She held up a hand. "Just had to ask."

The anger fizzled as fast as it had flamed. "I understand why you might ask that, but no. It's not possible."

"Then how did the phone wind up under his mattress two months after its owner was found murdered?"

Lynette Eason
and
USA TODAY Bestselling Author
Margaret Daley

Danger Trail

Previously published as *Trail of Evidence* and *Security Breach*

◆ HARLEQUIN® LOVE INSPIRED®CLASSICS

LOVE INSPIRED BOOKS

Recycling programs
for this product may
not exist in your area.

ISBN-13: 978-1-335-08184-1

Danger Trail

Copyright © 2018 by Harlequin Books S.A.

First published as Trail of Evidence by Harlequin Books in 2015 and Security Breach by Harlequin Books in 2015.

The publisher acknowledges the copyright holder of the individual works as follows:

Trail of Evidence
Copyright © 2015 by Harlequin Books S.A.

Security Breach
Copyright © 2015 by Harlequin Books S.A.

Special thanks and acknowledgment to Lynette Eason and Margaret Daley for their contribution to the Capitol K-9 Unit miniseries.

www.Harlequin.com

Printed in U.S.A.

CONTENTS

Lynette Eason is a bestselling, award-winning author who makes her home in South Carolina with her husband and two teenage children. She enjoys traveling, spending time with her family and teaching at various writing conferences around the country. She is a member of Romance Writers of America and American Christian Fiction Writers. Lynette can often be found online interacting with her readers. You can find her at Facebook.com/lynette.eason and on Twitter, @lynetteeason.

Books by Lynette Eason

Love Inspired Suspense

Wrangler's Corner

The Lawman Returns
Rodeo Rescuer
Protecting Her Daughter
Classified Christmas Mission
Christmas Ranch Rescue
Vanished in the Night
Holiday Amnesia

Family Reunions

Hide and Seek
Christmas Cover-Up
Her Stolen Past

Rose Mountain Refuge

Agent Undercover
Holiday Hideout
Danger on the Mountain

Visit the Author Profile page
at Harlequin.com for more titles.

TRAIL OF EVIDENCE

Lynette Eason

This means that it is not the children of the flesh who are the children of God, but the children of the promise are counted as offspring.
—*Romans 9:8*

Dedicated to my Lord and Savior, Jesus Christ.
Thank You for giving me the passion to write
and to write for You.

ONE

Veterinarian Jonas Parker jerked from his slight doze and lay still in the recliner where he'd crashed only a few minutes earlier shortly after midnight. He'd spent the night treating a longtime client's Doberman, who'd gotten hit by a car. A few lacerations and a couple of broken bones later, the dog now rested in the kennel at the office and Jonas had come home to get some much-needed rest. Only now he was hearing things. His ears honed in on the noises of his house and he frowned, wondering what had awakened him.

Silence echoed back at him.

Annoyance rushed through him. He'd just gotten re-laxed enough to maybe fall asleep, and his house set-tling had disturbed him. He snorted. Earplugs might be a good investment. He closed his eyes and let out a low breath.

Crash.

Jonas shot into a sitting position as his blood pounded through his veins.

That wasn't the house settling. Someone was *in* his house. Upstairs.

Felix! He had to get to Felix, his thirteen-year-old son. He froze, his thoughts scrambling. No. Wait. It was

Saturday night. Felix was sleeping over at a friend's. A flash of relief, then determination made his heart kick up speed.

Who was it? What did the intruder want? Money? Jewelry? Moving as silently as possible, Jonas rose from the recliner and stood, fingers clenching and unclenching at his sides.

A weapon.

He needed to be able to defend himself.

Where was his phone? He had to call for help. And get out.

The stairs creaked. He stopped at the edge of the room.

To get to either the front door or the back, he would have to go through the kitchen. Which meant passing the stairs.

While his adrenaline pounded, Jonas thought hard. His cell phone was on the kitchen counter. He didn't have a landline.

Soft footfalls on the steps reached his ears as though someone didn't want to make a lot of noise, but wasn't very skilled at being quiet.

Jonas grabbed the nearest thing he could use as a weapon from the built-in shelf. Felix's track meet trophy, his son's pride and joy. Hefting it in his left hand, he decided to bolt for the kitchen, grab his phone from the counter and keep going out the back door. He'd avoid a confrontation if at all possible but he needed to get help on the way.

Grab the phone, get out and call for help. A good plan. He slipped past the bottom of the steps, praying the darkness hid him from whoever was on them. In the kitchen, moonlight filtering from the window over the sink illuminated the way.

The floor creaked behind him.

A hard hand centered itself in the middle of his back and a hard shove propelled him into the kitchen table. Jonas bounced, stumbled and crashed into the refrigerator. Felix's trophy tumbled from his fingers. Fury boiled through him and he spun, striking out, praying to hit something. He landed a hard fist on his attacker's face.

A hiss of surprise and a curse reached his ears.

Jonas managed to grab the trophy once more. Then the feel of something hard and cold against his left cheek froze him. "I have a son," he whispered. "He needs me."

"Give me the phone."

"What phone?" Jonas clutched the trophy, his mind racing.

"Give me the phone!"

The weapon moved, slipping from his cheek. Jonas brought the base of the heavy trophy up and moved sideways at the same time. He connected with the attacker's stomach, heard a whoosh, then the gun clattering on the floor. The man cursed, swept his hand out and grabbed the gun. Jonas swung the trophy once more, connected. The intruder gave a harsh cry and bolted for the door.

Jonas panted and rose to go after him. Then thought of his son and stopped.

He grabbed his cell phone from the counter and dialed 911.

Brooke Clark pushed the laptop away and rubbed her gritty eyes. One in the morning and she was on her laptop? She needed to be sensible and get some sleep. But her adrenaline was still high even though her eyes longed to shut.

She'd just walked in the door an hour ago from a

crime scene where Mercy, her very skilled K-9 golden retriever, had done her job well. She'd recovered some key evidence in a bank robbery and once testing was done on the glove, Brooke knew the DNA would put the criminal away.

Unfortunately, sleep would have to wait. She groaned, settled into the recliner and decided to keep working on the case that had caused her and her team no end of frustration.

Congressman Harland Jeffries continued to pound home the fact that his son's murder still wasn't solved. Late one night two months ago, someone had killed Michael Jeffries. Michael wasn't just the congressman's son, but was also a well-respected lawyer. The congressman had come upon the scene, his son on the ground, shot, and the murderer standing over Michael's body. The killer had turned the gun on the congressman and shot him, leaving him for dead. Only Harland hadn't died. He'd lived to tell the story and demand justice for his son. Unfortunately, darkness had prevented the congressman from seeing the murderer's face, so the hunt was still on to find the person responsible.

She and the other members of the Capitol K-9 team wouldn't be granted rest until the case was solved. Brooke loved her job, but frustration built at the lack of progress when it came to finding answers. She flipped the page in the file. Rosa Gomez, Congressman Jeffries's housekeeper, was also connected to the case. Shortly before the shooting, Rosa had been found dead at the base of the cliffs in President's Park. "Which hasn't been technically proved to be murder. It could have been an accident," she told Mercy. The dog yawned, then gave a low whine and nudged against her hand. The animal's affection made her smile and run her hand over Mercy's silky soft ears.

Mercy, her sweet—and super smart—golden retriever. Highly trained, Mercy and Brooke were partners in the elite Capitol K-9 Unit based in Washington, DC. Mercy specialized in retrieving evidence. Brooke sighed. She wished there were some evidence to be retrieved in either Michael Jeffries's murder or Rosa Gomez's death. "It's all right, girl. Just because I'm up doesn't mean you have to lose out on a good night's sleep." Mercy heaved a sigh and settled at Brooke's feet. Then rose to pad to the door and back.

"You're restless, too, huh?" Brooke got up from the recliner and went to open the door for Mercy. The dog bounded into the fenced yard, and Brooke stared out into the dark night. She shivered at the chill. March was a cold month in DC, and Brooke hadn't grabbed her coat. She watched Mercy sniff and weave in and out of the bushes lining the fence. The trees beyond offered a sense of privacy and security, one of the reasons Brooke had purchased the home.

She pulled the door shut behind her and sat on the cement steps, wrapping her arms around her middle. Maybe the cold would revive some of her dead brain cells. Her thoughts were like a dog with a bone. She couldn't keep her mind from gnawing on the Jeffries case.

Harland Jeffries was about to push Gavin, her captain, over the edge. Gavin was a good man, a professional in every sense of the word. Brooke respected how he had managed to hold on to his temper when it came to the congressman's incessant demands on Gavin's time. She stood. "Mercy, come."

The dog bounded over to her and sat at her feet, ears

perked. Brooke gave those ears a good rub and let the dog back into the house. Poor Gavin. He was really torn. She knew he was between a rock and a hard place. He had a lot of respect for the congressman. Harland had been a mentor to Gavin, and Gavin loved the man like a father. It was tearing him up not to be able to give him some answers.

She forced herself to head to bed. She'd count sheep if she had to. Or review the case notes while snuggling under the warm down comforter. Maybe then she'd doze off.

And maybe pigs would start flying.

Jonas shut the door as the police officers headed toward their squad car. He appreciated the fast response to his 911 call, but the officers had basically checked out the scene, taken a few pictures of the dumped drawer in Felix's room, then told him to be thankful he wasn't hurt and nothing was missing. Oh, and to call if anything else happened.

Right.

He sighed and reached back to massage the area at the base of his skull. He needed a vacation. A stress-reducing getaway. But Felix was in school for another three weeks before his spring break.

Maybe then.

He trudged up the stairs to Felix's room and took another look around. The drawer on the floor, the unmade bed, an unfinished 3-D puzzle of the capitol building. He sighed and picked up Felix's favorite sweatshirt and tossed it across the footboard of the bed. A pair of jeans and a hoodie joined the sweatshirt.

His eyes caught on the picture on his son's nightstand. Felix had been about two years old. He was laughing up at Shannon, his mother and Jonas's ex-wife. It had been a happy time in his young life, Jonas's life, too. Neither Felix nor Jonas had known the trouble that would come just a few short years away. Trouble brought on by Shannon and her commitment-phobic ways.

Jonas sighed, flipped off the light and headed to his own room. He crawled between the sheets, forcing his muscles to relax, his mind to drift into prayer. Until he remembered the crash he heard. The drawer to Felix's nightstand had been yanked out and dumped. His heart thudded. The officers had come to the same conclusion he had. The intruder had already been in his house when he'd arrived home. Either the man hadn't heard him come in and drop into the recliner—or he hadn't cared and just continued his search.

Jonas debated whether to get up and clean up the drawer or wait until later.

It would wait. He drifted. Sleep beckoned.

At least until the strange beeping jerked him awake again.

Jonas sat straight up, his adrenaline spiking once more. Heart thundering in his chest, he grabbed the baseball bat he'd placed on the floor near his bed and swung his legs over the side. He stood and padded on bare feet to the door.

The faint beeping sounded again. Then all was silent.

Jonas's fingers flexed around the bat. He grabbed his cell phone with his left hand and shoved it into the waistband of his knit shorts.

More beeping.

Jonas followed the sound into his son's bedroom two doors down from his. He stood in the doorway and listened.

Nothing.

And then he heard it again. Louder this time. He was definitely closer.

Jonas flipped the light on and blinked against the sudden brightness. When his eyes adjusted, he dropped to his knees on the hardwood floors and scanned the area under Felix's dresser. Finding nothing, he rose and moved to his son's bedside table. The drawer still lay on its side. He grabbed the small flashlight and went to his knees once again.

Jonas flashed the light under the bed. The beeping sounded right next to his ear. He lifted the mattress, separating it from the box springs, and froze, puzzled. A cell phone? He snagged it and dropped the mattress back into place. Fingers curled around the phone, he lifted it up to study it. "Who does this belong to?" he muttered. One of Felix's friends? But why would Felix have it hidden under his mattress? Had he stolen it?

Jonas snapped the light off and carried the phone into his bedroom. He flipped on the lamp and sank onto the bed, his eyes still on the device. Low battery. Hence the beeping.

He touched the screen to bring the phone to life. A picture stared back at him. A woman holding a baby. He frowned as recognition hit him. He knew that woman. He'd seen her on the news, hadn't he? And in the papers. He got up and strode into the kitchen to grab the newspaper from the counter.

There. Right on the front page. Housekeeper for Congressman Harland Jeffries, Rosa Gomez had been found at the bottom of the cliffs in President's Park approximately two months ago and the investigation continued to make front-page news as new evidence came to light. The Capitol K-9 Unit had been working the case and the story had stayed hot, the media constantly re-minding everyone that this case hadn't been solved yet.

And someone had just broken into his house look-ing for a phone. He stared at the device. Could he have been looking for this one?

His thoughts went immediately to Brooke Clark, a Capitol K-9 Unit team member who was working the case.

An officer and a beautiful woman. He pushed aside the personal thoughts and focused on what to do about this phone. Right now, he couldn't worry about how Felix had gotten ahold of it, he had to turn it in.

And he knew just the person he wanted to give it to.

Brooke jerked out of the light sleep she'd managed to fall into sometime between her last sip of warm tea and a prayer for divine help in solving her case. She rolled to grab her phone from the end table. "'Lo?"

"I woke you up. I'm sorry."

Sleep fled. She sat up. "Jonas Parker?" Her heart stuttered. Just saying his name brought back a flood of memories. Both wonderful and...painful. Along with boatloads of regret. The same feelings that rushed through her every time she saw or spoke to him. Which hadn't been too long ago. Maybe a month? Amazing that she had no trouble pulling the memory of his voice from the depths of her tired mind. But then why would she? She often dreamed of him, their past times together. And they hadn't even dated. Not once. She blinked. "What's wrong?"

"You're working the case about the congressman's son's death, aren't you?"

"Yes. Michael Jeffries." She cleared her throat. "You called me at four o'clock in the morning to ask that?"

"No, I called to tell you that I think I found something that you might need for your investigation."

"What?"

"A phone with a picture of Rosa Gomez and her two-year-old son as the wallpaper."

Fully awake now, Brooke swung her legs over the edge of the bed. At the foot of the bed, Mercy lifted her head and perked her ears. "Where did you find the phone?" she asked.

The fact that Rosa's wallet and phone hadn't been found with her body had raised a lot of questions. Like had her fall from the cliffs been an accident or murder? And if it had been an accident, where were the items? And if it had been murder, had the murderer stolen them?

Another question: Was Rosa's death connected to the shooting of her boss, Congressman Jeffries, and the murder of his son? So far, they had few suspects, one being a senator's daughter, Erin Eagleton. She'd disappeared the night of the murder and her starfish charm, engraved with her initials, had been found at the scene. Brooke was glad that Rosa's child was now in the custody of his aunt, but so many questions remained. Maybe the phone Jonas had would answer some of them.

"Ah… Well, that's the problem. And one of the reasons I called you."

"Come on, Jonas, tell me."

"I found the phone under my son's mattress."

TWO

Brooke threw the covers back, wide awake now. "You found it where?" Surely he hadn't said—

"Under his mattress."

He *had* said it.

"And that's not all," he continued. "Someone broke into my house tonight and demanded I give him 'the phone.' Of course I didn't know what he was talking about at the time, but now I'm feeling quite sure he meant the one I'm holding."

Brooke struggled to process everything. "Are you all right? Is Felix okay?" Pain shafted through her. She pushed it away. When she'd met him, Jonas was working as a vet at the K-9 dog training facility. He'd been divorced, with a young son. And he hadn't made any secret of the fact that he found her attractive. She'd felt the same spark but had smothered it as best she could. Jonas had also never made any secret of the fact that he wanted a houseful of children.

Children she could never give him thanks to a hysterectomy at the age of eighteen. The car wreck that had killed her parents had also killed her dream of being a mother. She swallowed hard and pushed the thoughts away. She'd dealt with this, and she didn't need to dwell on it or rehash it. What was done was done. She'd moved on. And so had Jonas. And yet—

Over the course of the past eight years, they'd run into each other, but had never exchanged more than a few pleasantries. She'd climbed the ladder in law enforcement and had landed her dream job with the Capitol K-9 Unit when it had been formed a few short years ago. For some reason tonight's call stirred up old longings and questions about what might have been. And the guilt that she'd never explained why she'd run from him.

"Felix wasn't here," he said. "He's spending the night with a friend."

"But you weren't hurt?" She blinked away the past.

"No, I managed to chase him off."

Relief hit her. "Good for you." She bit her lip. "All right. I'll come over and get the phone."

"Now?"

"I don't want to take a chance on whoever you scared off coming back. We need to get that phone into the right hands so it doesn't fall into the wrong ones."

He paused. "I hadn't thought about that. Bring your dog. Maybe she can pick up the intruder's scent."

Of course he knew about Mercy. Just like he knew she worked for the Capitol K-9 Unit. So. He'd been keeping up with her, too. Interesting. "She'll be with me." She glanced at the clock. "It should take me about ten to fifteen minutes to get there."

"I'll be waiting."

Brooke hung up, her mind spinning. Jonas Parker had called her. Jonas needed help and he'd called *her*. Just the thought of seeing him again on more than a passing basis made her palms sweat and her pulse beat a little faster.

Mercy whined and hopped to the floor where she sat,

head cocked, ears lifted. Her tail thumped the floor as though to say, "I'm ready when you are."

Brooke dressed in record time, popped a K-cup in her Keurig and pulled her travel mug down from the cabinet. Time for the strong stuff. While the coffee brewed, she gathered her bag and Mercy's leash.

Ten minutes later, she was in her truck and headed for Jonas's house. A fact that continued to make her blood hum and stir the memories of a time she'd tried to forget. She'd been a rookie with the DC police department's K-9 unit and he'd been interning as a vet at the dog training facility. They'd crossed paths often enough to strike up a friendship. When Jonas had expressed an interest in being more than friends, she'd spooked and run, canceling out on a date at the last minute and then finding excuses not to see him alone again. She hadn't handled it well, too caught up in her own insecurities and hurt to really consider how her actions would affect him. He'd been embarrassed and hurt and they'd parted ways.

And yet he'd called her about finding evidence in the case she and the Capitol K-9 team were working so hard on.

The pressure was on to find Michael Jeffries's killer and Congressman Jeffries's shooter—most likely the same person. Tension was thick, but Brooke had no doubts about her team. They were the best. They'd find the killer. She just hoped it would be before he struck again.

Jonas paced the den, his heart pounding, his palms slick. What was he thinking?

That he wanted to see Brooke Clark. Vaguely he wondered if he should feel guilty for being secretly

glad he'd had a legitimate excuse to call her. Then he
pushed the guilt away. His divorce had been final ten
years ago. He'd mourned the loss of his marriage, but
finally, with the help of a recovery group at his church,
realized he'd done everything he could to keep his marriage together. The fact was, it had ended and it was
time for him to move on.

Why his heart had settled on Brooke Clark was
something that had him stumped. But she'd been the
reason he'd sought out the recovery group in the first
place. He'd needed someone to tell him it was all right
for him to find companionship. Date again.

And then Brooked ditched him. She'd simply can-
celed their last date and had avoided him until he gave
up trying to get in touch with her. And he'd never figured out why. Maybe it was time to get some answers.
Even if they were ones he didn't want to hear.

A car door slammed.

He tensed and went to the window to push aside the
curtain so he could see out. As always, his heart did that
funny little beat when he saw her. A petite woman in
her early thirties with short black hair. She still looked
the same. Slightly older, but not much. And definitely
still beautiful.

Brooke. She was here. Her golden retriever, Mercy,
leaped to the ground and shook herself, her brown eyes
on Brooke, waiting for instructions. Jonas had followed
her career and watched her climb the ranks in law enforcement. He was proud of her.

He opened the front door. Brooke looked up and
caught his gaze and Jonas blinked. He hadn't forgotten
how blue her eyes were. On the contrary, he remembered every detail about her. But those eyes always ren-
dered him speechless when first making contact. For a

moment they just stood and stared. Then she smiled and walked toward him. "Hi, Jonas. Good to see you again."

Jonas took a step and, in a bold move, wrapped her in a hug. Her scent surrounded him, old feelings rushed back. And she didn't push him away. He took a deep breath. "It's really good to see you, too, Brooke. Come on in."

Brooke swept past him and he heard her give the dog a low command. Mercy sat. Jonas stepped inside and shut the door behind him.

She looked around. "So what happened?"

Jonas pinched the bridge of his nose. "It's a bit of a story. Would you like to go into the den and have a seat?"

"I'd rather not. Did the intruder leave anything behind? Touch anything that his scent would be on?"

So. It was going to be all business then. All right. He could take a hint. Jonas tightened his jaw then relaxed it. She was here to help, not socialize. The fact that she hadn't pulled away from his embrace encouraged him. First things first. "I was in the recliner in the den when I heard a crash. It came from my son's room. The intruder had pulled out one of the drawers from Felix's nightstand. It was on the floor when I went in."

"Then let's start there."

"Of course." Jonas led her into Felix's bedroom, once again giving thanks that his son hadn't been home at the time of the break-in.

She focused in on the drawer on the floor. "I guess I don't have to ask which drawer."

"No. Guess not. I just left it alone. Once I decided to call you, I didn't want to cover up any smells." He paused. "I also hit the guy with Felix's trophy so his scent may be on there, too."

She shot him an admiring glace. "Good job. Okay, we'll see what we can do."

Jonas stepped back and let them go to work. He watched, marveling at the team, how well they worked together. "You're very good at what you do, aren't you?"

She turned. "We're one of the best." She said it in all sincerity, without a hint of boasting or pride. Just stated a fact. He liked that about her.

"You didn't ask for my address."

She blinked, then cleared her throat. "Excuse me?"

"You didn't have to ask for my address. You already knew it."

"I looked it up in the police database."

"Of course." Now he felt embarrassed. "For a moment there, it gave me hope."

"Hope?"

"Hope that you'd thought about me. Hope that… I don't know, that maybe we could be friends again."

"We never stopped being friends."

He shook his head. "Of course we did. Friends do stuff together, hang out, enjoy each other's company. We went from friends to acquaintances that shared a nod of acknowledgement whenever we ran into each other. That's not friendship."

Brooke bit her lip and turned away. "This isn't what I came over here for. Let me just do my job."

Disappointment flooded him. He'd pushed too hard, too fast. He was coming across desperate and it wasn't that; he just had questions. Questions that would have to wait. "No problem."

Once she finished going through the house, she let Mercy out the door the intruder had exited. Mercy trotted down the street, nose alternating between the ground and the air. She stopped several houses down and sat.

Brooke called to her and Mercy hurried to her side. "She's lost the scent. Most likely the guy had a car waiting right where Mercy sat down. He climbed in and off they went."

He nodded. He'd expected as much. He handed her the phone. "The battery is at two percent. It won't last much longer. There may be a charger in his room. I didn't think to look."

She studied it. "It's fine. Chargers are easy to come by." She looked up. "Did you find a wallet belonging to Rosa?"

"No. Just the phone."

"I hate to ask this, but…" She looked uncomfortable.

"What?"

"Well, Rosa's wallet was missing, too. Do you think Felix could have hurt Rosa to get her phone and wallet?"

Jonas stepped back, her words hurting more than if she'd slapped him. "What? No. Of course not." He raked a hand through his hair, hating the flash of doubt that raced through him. He lifted his chin. "No. He's a thirteen-year-old boy, he's not perfect. And I mean he's been getting in some trouble lately, but that's just because he's never gotten over his mother's leaving, never truly accepted the fact that she would do that. He'd never hurt—kill—someone over a stupid phone." Anger flared.

She held up a hand. "Just had to ask. And I didn't necessarily mean that he killed her on purpose. It could have been an accident and he was too scared to tell anyone what happened."

"No, no way. Absolutely not." She nodded, her eyes on his. The anger fizzled as fast as it had flamed. "I

understand why you might ask that, but no. It's not possible. If something like that had happened, Felix would
have come to me." Wouldn't he?

"Then how did the phone wind up under his mattress two months after its owner was found murdered?"

The question hit him hard. He swallowed. "I don't
know, but I know we have to find out."

"We need to talk to Felix."

She held the phone up. "We need to turn this in, too."
She headed to the bedroom door when Jonas heard a
loud roar and felt the house rock beneath his feet.

Mercy barked. Brooke fell to her knees. She thought
she heard Jonas calling to her just before something
struck her shoulder, her leg, her cheek. Pain lanced
through her. "Get out! We have to get out."

Jonas's hand wrapped her upper arm. She realized
he'd fallen, too; he'd just recovered faster than she.
Smoke seared her lungs, but nothing felt hot.

"Are you all right?" Jonas coughed as he pulled her
toward the door.

"Fine. Mercy, heel!" The dog slunk on her belly to
Brooke's side. She pulled her shirt up over her nose
and mouth. Jonas did the same. She grabbed one of
Felix's shirts from his bed and wrapped it around the
animal's mouth and nose, leaving it loose enough for
her to breathe while filtering the smoke.

"Smoke is rolling in fast," he said.

"Do you see any flames?"

"No. Let me lead you, I know the layout." He
coughed and together they made their way down the
stairs, ready to turn and flee back up at the first sign
of fire. Finally, they hit the bottom of the steps. Jonas

led her toward the door. Mercy hugged her side and she kept one hand on the head of her faithful friend.

Jonas opened the door and she yanked him back in to slam it. Her shoulder throbbed with the movement.

"What are you doing?" he asked.

"Do you have a back door?"

"Yes."

"Let's use that."

She could barely see his puzzled expression, but gave silent thanks that he didn't argue with her, just kept his firm grip on her good arm and led her toward the back of the house and into a sunroom. Her leg throbbed, but nothing was broken and she moved through the house with minimal pain.

Smoke still filled the air, but she could breathe much better here. He opened the door and they stepped out into the night. Fresh air hit her and she sucked in a deep breath even as her mind spun. She pulled her arm free, then slid her hand down to wrap her fingers around his. "Come on," she croaked.

They raced away from the house, her leg protesting the movement, but nothing bad enough to stop her from getting to safety. Sirens already sounded and Brooke suspected one of the neighbors had heard the blast and called 911. Jonas had a nice fenced-in yard that backed up to his neighbor's. They moved to the edge of the property.

Brooke turned to see smoke billowing from the den window, but no flames. "I'm going to see if I can spot anyone trying to get away from the house." She took off with Mercy at her heels. Jonas's protest registered, but she needed to see. Rounding the corner of the house, she stopped and looked up and down the street. Neighbors stood on their porches and some in the street as they watched the commotion. The first fire truck screamed to a stop at the curb. Brooke's gaze bounced from person to person. Curiosity and concern graced the faces of the onlookers. No one seemed particularly satisfied.

Jonas stepped up beside her. "See anything?"

"No. Do you see anyone who shouldn't be here? Anyone you don't recognize?"

"I'm...um...probably not the best person to ask."

"Why?"

"Because I'm a lousy neighbor." He gave an embarrassed shrug. "I work and I spend time with Felix—when he lets me anyway. I hate yard maintenance so I hire someone to do it."

"Which means you're not working in the yard and talking with people out for an evening or weekend walk."

"Exactly."

She nodded and approached the fire captain. "We were in that house. We're fine. There's no one else inside."

The man turned, his concerned gaze landing on the two of them. "Are you sure?"

"Positive."

One of the firemen stepped out the front door and motioned to one of his buddies. "Captain?"

"Yeah."

Jonas and Brooke moved closer. Mercy stayed by her side. Brooke wanted to hear what was said.

"It was a Molotov cocktail. When it was tossed through the window, it landed in the fireplace." The man shook his head. "Never seen anything like it. There's a lot of smoke, but not any fire damage to speak of. Looks like it wasn't meant to burn, just cause a lot of smoke."

Jonas breathed out. Brooke laid a hand on his forearm. He looked at her. "You're right," he said. "They came back."

Brooke pulled the cell phone Jonas had found from her pocket. "I think it's time to ask Felix where he got this phone and who knows he has it." She switched to her business phone. "And we're going to get someone to watch your house tonight. I don't think we were smoked out by accident. Whoever threw that in there knew what they were doing. It's possible they plan to come back and search the place."

"So then I'm not sleeping here."

"Not with the smoke and the danger. You're going someplace safe."

THREE

Brooke sat in the SUV next to Nicholas Cole, a fellow Capitol K-9 member, and kept her eyes on Jonas's house. It looked empty and deserted. Just the way they wanted it to look. If someone planned to return to the scene of the crime, she and Nicholas would be waiting. "What time is it?"

"Five minutes later than the last time you asked," he said.

"You sound like my grandfather."

"You sound like a five-year-old. It's 4:45 a.m. An hour of the night that should have me in bed dreaming of a vacation on the beach, not conducting a stakeout."

She snorted and swung her gaze back to the area around the house, looking for movement, a flash of light. Anything. And got nothing.

She could hear the dogs breathing behind her. They were suited up, their protective vests on and ready to go. And so was Brooke. She itched for a break, a chance to go after someone who could give them a break in this case.

Instead of going after Felix to question him about the phone, they'd simply sent an officer to watch the house where he was staying. Felix was safe for now and if the person who wanted the phone came back and they caught him, Felix would never have to know how fortunate it was he chose to spend the night away from home. Talking to the boy could wait until morning. Catching the person who wanted the phone was priority. The sun would be up in a couple of hours, but Brooke just had a feeling something was going to happen.

Her heart, protected by the Kevlar vest she'd donned earlier, thumped a heavy rhythm. Anticipation swept through her. It was about time something good happened.

General Margaret Meyer apparently thought so, too. The Capitol K-9 Unit existed because of her. Her current position as the White House Special In-House Security Chief gave her a lot of power and leeway. Gavin reported straight to her and she expected top-notch results from her team. Which they gave her. When Gavin had presented her with the need for some manpower due to a possible break in the case, she'd been more than happy to spare Nicholas from his current duties at the White House to help Brooke track down the lead.

"So who is this guy?" Nicholas asked. He sipped on a drink they'd picked up from the local gas station.

"What guy?" Brooke knew exactly who he meant, but she needed to buy some time to figure out just how much she wanted to reveal about Jonas. Then again, it wasn't like there was that much to say. Nicholas simply lifted a brow and she shrugged. "We met about eight years ago. He was doing an internship and I was a rookie K-9 cop."

"And you hit it off?"

"We did."

"Was it serious?"

She hesitated. It had been serious. Too serious. "We

were friends. We had a lot in common and spent some time together, but—" she shrugged "—it just didn't work out."

"It just didn't work out, huh? Let me guess. He wanted more and you ran away." She sucked in a deep breath and shot him a sharp look. Nicholas shrugged. "Sorry if I struck a nerve, it's just what you do to every guy who shows interest in you."

"I do not."

"Do too."

Brooke snapped her lips shut. She would not get into some juvenile argument with him. Because they both knew he was right.

Her phone rang. She lifted it to the ear that didn't have the earpiece she'd use to communicate with Nicholas should they get separated. "Hello?"

"Hi," Jonas said.

"Hi." Did she hear footsteps? "Are you pacing the floor?"

A short, humorless laugh filtered through the line. "Yes."

"Well, you can stop. Nothing's happening—" A shadow to her left caught her attention. She nudged Nicholas who nodded. He was already watching him, tracking him with his eyes. The dark SUV blended into the nighttime surroundings. If they opened the doors, the interior lights would stay off. Even her cell phone was on the dimmest setting. There was no way the guy now approaching the back of Jonas's house would know they were watching him. "Gotta go. Someone showed up. I'll call you in a bit." She hung up on his protest and opened the passenger door. Nicholas was already approaching the house, his weapon drawn, his dog, Max, at his side.

Brooke pulled her own gun, let Mercy out of the back and went in the opposite direction of Nicholas. She rounded the corner of the house just behind Mercy. The dog barked and made a beeline for the figure at the back door.

"Police! Freeze!" Brooke called.

Nicholas started to close the gap. "Don't move!" The man turned, raised his hands. Instead of deciding he was caught, he spun and darted for the back fence that separated Jonas's house from the neighbor behind him. The dark-clad figure scaled the fence and dropped to the other side. Nicholas went after him. Brooke called to Mercy and together, she and the dog went another route.

Back around the side of the house, Brooke was just in time to see the would-be intruder bolt down the street. Nicholas let Max go with the command to stop the flee-ing fugitive, so Brooke kept Mercy beside her. Max cut loose with a low woof and loped off in pursuit, his strides long and even. Brooke lost sight of him as she and Nicholas raced to catch up. The guy was fast.

Brooke figured Max was faster.

Until she and Nicholas almost slammed into the tall chain-link fence when they turned the next corner.

She'd hung up on him. Jonas glared at the phone as though the blame lay with the device. He growled and stomped out of his temporary bedroom at the veteri-nary office.

Brooke had hung up on him because someone was near his house and probably trying to break in. Their surveillance plan worked, but would she be in danger now? He paced to the door. Two officers sat in the park-ing lot. He knew another one was parked at the back.

And one was at the Fuller household where Felix was spending the night.

Not that he expected that someone would be able to figure out where Felix was if they were looking for him, but he had to admit knowing an officer was watching out for his son made him feel better. He and Brooke had discussed picking Felix up and bringing him back to the office for the night, but they decided not to. Brooke argued that he was probably safer where he was at this point. It wasn't the Fuller house that had been bombed or the Fuller house that had been broken into. They'd come looking for the phone, not Felix.

He appreciated the fact that no one was taking any chances with his safety, but now Brooke might be in danger.

But that was her job. She was probably in dangerous situations all the time. That was what she did, right?

Yes, but it didn't make it any easier for him to deal with. Not when she was in danger because his son had taken a phone that didn't belong to him and the wrong people had tracked him down.

He had to know she was all right. He walked to the front desk and grabbed his keys. His car was in the first parking spot. He paused for a second. What if he went to find her and just got in the way?

But he wouldn't. He'd drive past his house and see if anything was happening, make sure everything was under control. Jonas headed out the door and walked over to the police officer who was exiting his vehicle.

"Sir? You need to go back inside."

"I'm going to run an errand." He switched directions and headed for his car, his worry pushing him and spurring him to move faster. "I'll be back shortly."

"I don't advise you leaving on your own."

"I wouldn't if it wasn't an emergency."

"Let me call it in and see if they want someone to tail you then."

"I don't have time to wait, but I'm going to my house for a few minutes. You can send someone there." He slid into the driver's seat, cranked the car and backed from the parking spot. As he pulled to a stop at the edge of the lot, he glanced in his rearview mirror to see the officer speaking into his radio and heading for his car.

He was probably going to follow him anyway, but Jonas didn't care. He wasn't going to sit around and wait for someone to figure out what to do with him.

Brooke was at his house and might be headed into danger. He couldn't just sit around twiddling his thumbs waiting to hear that she was okay.

Brooke hauled herself over the fence of the old textile office building. Backup was on the way, but there was no time to wait. The man they were chasing would be gone. And he was a link to the case. A case she very much wanted to solve. She'd beat Nicholas to the fence so he'd just have to stay with the dogs unless he could find another way in.

Her feet pounded against the crumbling asphalt parking lot. The building had been up for sale for years and each year it seemed to erode even more than the last. She caught sight of movement around the side of the building and took off after it, whispering her location to Nicholas.

She rounded the corner with caution, weapon held in front of her. Nothing. Except an open door.

Had he gone in or simply opened the door to head around the building? She pressed her finger against the earpiece. "Are you inside the fence?"

"Just now. Had to cut my way through. You get him?"

"Not yet." She kept her voice low, her back to the side of the building.

A screech came from inside the building. Guess that answered that question. "He's inside. I think he pushed open one of the steel doors at the back. I'm going after him."

"Backup will be right behind you. Max and I are on the way."

Brooke gave him her location and slipped through the door into the dark. She stopped just inside to the right, making sure she didn't make herself a target in the open doorway. She let her eyes adjust, but she still had trouble seeing anything. Too dark. Easy for someone to sneak up behind her. She needed a light, but didn't dare take the flashlight from her belt.

The good thing was if it was dark for her, it was dark for him. As her eyes adjusted, she could make out shapes so it wasn't pitch-black. She had to be careful to stay in the shadows. Again, if she could see a little, so could he.

She moved softly, her steps cautious, her ears tuned to the area around her. Her neck and back tingled. She expected a bullet to slam into her at any moment. The vest she wore would offer some protection for her torso, but nothing for her head. She hadn't seen a weapon on the man running from Jonas's house, but until she saw otherwise, she'd treat him as armed. And dangerous.

"Where are you?" she whispered.

"Max, Mercy and I are coming inside."

She heard a scrape to her left and spun, her weapon ready, hands steady in spite of the adrenaline pumping through her.

A light flashed then disappeared. Footsteps on stairs.

The sound still coming from her left. Brooke moved toward the noise, still cautious, but determined to stop him. Shadows danced around her, light from the half moon filtering through the dirty windows. And the blue lights now flashing, offered even more light. "Up the stairs," she whispered. "To the left of the door about twenty feet." She placed her foot on the first step, then started up.

"Got it. Backup's outside."

"Saw the lights."

A loud scrape from the top of the stairs made her pause. The windows along the second floor offered very little light. She could make out shapes, but nothing moving. She took another step, which put her about halfway up the staircase.

A large shadow appeared at the top of the stairs. An object teetered on the edge of the highest step. She blinked, her brain trying to discern the image.

Then the thing wobbled once again. A head appeared around the edge. A grunt reached her ears.

Brooke finally registered what was happening and turned to flee as a loud rumble came from behind her and whatever was at the top of the step slid toward her. She gasped as her foot turned on the last step and she fell to the floor. She rolled and looked up to see a large upside-down desk a split second away from crushing her.

FOUR

Jonas's drive past his house resulted in nothing. But the police cruiser that zipped past him as he turned back on the main highway caught his attention and he followed it to the old textile office building. Police tape ran the length of the fence. The K-9s and their handlers were out and the air crackled with law enforcement energy.

He couldn't get to the fence due to all of the emergency vehicles so he parked and stood on the hood of the vehicle. He scanned the faces, looking for the one that he most wanted to see. Not there. One of the officers to his right on the other side of the fence pointed to the building and said something into his phone.

Was Brooke inside the building? Or was she just lost in the crowded chaos?

Gawkers from the nearby neighborhoods had come to the line to see what was going on and officers held them back. Jonas could go no farther either. He would have to wait. His fingers curled into fists. He forced them to relax. *Don't get anxious until you have something to be anxious about.* The order didn't work. He scanned the fence line and looked for a way in.

Hopelessness coursed through him as he realized

he was in for a wait. There was no going through and no going around.

A car pulled up beside him. The vehicle had the Capitol K-9 logo on the side. The officer climbed from the vehicle, a frown on his face. He flashed his badge at Jonas. "Are you Jonas Parker?"

"I am."

"I'm Chase Zachary. I got a call you went AWOL."

"Something like that," he muttered. "Brooke called me and had to hang up because she was on surveillance and someone showed up. I had to make sure she was okay."

"You might want to leave that to us. Now would you please get back in your vehicle? I'll follow you home."

Jonas had great respect for law enforcement, for the officers who put their lives on the line every day for him. If it had been anyone else in that building besides Brooke, he might have followed the order. Instead he shook his head. "I'm waiting right here until I know she's safe."

Chase lifted a brow. Then he narrowed his eyes and gave Jonas a closer once-over. Whatever he saw must have convinced him arguing would be futile. "She means something to you?"

"Yes." Jonas didn't feel the need to elaborate.

"Right. Then sit in my vehicle at least. We don't need some sniper trying to take you out while you wait."

Jonas blinked. "Sniper?"

"You've had two incidents tonight. A break-in and a Molotov cocktail through your window. Seems someone's after you."

Jonas nodded. Without another word, he opened the passenger door to the K-9 vehicle and climbed in. He slammed the door, his gaze on the building. "Can you get us through?"

"Of course I can. No reason to, though. It's being handled." A dog nudged his ear and without thought, Jonas reached back to scratch his ears. "Who's this?"

"Valor."

"He's beautiful." The Belgian Malinois butted up under Jonas's hand again. Jonas complied with another ear rub.

"He's a great partner."

Jonas looked at the building again. He knew the situation was being handled but that knowledge didn't stop him from wanting to be closer. "She's in there, isn't she? She went in after him."

Chase nodded. "She and Nicholas Cole, another K-9 team member. And the dogs. They'll get him. There's no way he can get out of there without someone grabbing him."

"What if he decides not to come out? What if he decides he wants to make one last stand?"

"Then it could get ugly. But Brooke and Nicholas are trained. They can handle him. They'll get him."

"Of course they will." Because if *they* didn't get him, whoever they'd chased inside might get *them* and Jonas didn't think he would survive that. *Don't let her die because of me, God, please.*

Brooke clasped Nicholas's hand and rose to her feet with a grunt. She swayed and took a moment to get her footing and catch her breath. "Thanks."

"You okay?" he asked. He looked pale and a little shaken himself.

"Yeah." She looked at the mangled pile of wood and

steel. Nicholas had pulled her away at the last possible second. "How much do you think that weighs?"

"More than you want slamming on top of you." She shuddered and Nicholas patted her shoulder. "Don't think about it."

"I'm not." But she was. If he hadn't pulled her out of the way, she would be dead or seriously injured. "This guy is playing hardball," she muttered. She maneuvered around the part of the desk that blocked the stairs and started up. Nicholas stayed right with her. Barking reached her ears.

"I hear Max," Nicholas said.

"Yeah, I do, too. He's already up there?"

"I sent him up as soon as I pulled you out of the way. Mercy's just inside the door downstairs waiting like a good girl." He radioed in that they were still in pursuit. Brooke led the way down the hall, her footsteps echoing on the bare concrete that once had probably been covered in carpet.

The barking continued. "He's got someone cornered."

"Or he's trapped and can't get to the person," Brooke agreed.

Brooke and Nicholas came to the end of a hall. And a closed door. Nicholas gave the command for Max to sit and be quiet. Brooke held her weapon ready. Nicholas reached around her and opened the door. Brooke swung in. Max darted ahead and up another set of stairs. She followed him to the next level.

"Roof access door," Nicholas said.

They played the same dance and she breathed a bit easier when no gunshots came her way. Max pushed through and out onto the roof. Nose to the ground then in the air, he darted to the side of the building. And sat.

Brooke rushed over. "Fire escape."

"The guys would have seen him. Where did he go?" He tapped into his earpiece. "Did you see him come down the north side of the building? Down the fire escape?"

Brooke heard the negative response and took in the area. She stepped out on the fire escape and tried to think like a desperately fleeing fugitive. "He didn't go down."

"What?"

"He went over." She nodded to the overgrown trees lining the back of the building, just on the other side of the fence. "He grabbed that limb and shimmied down that tree. Or even crossed over to the next one. They're so close together, he could have been three or four trees in before he climbed down."

Nicholas shook his head. "You've got to be right. He never set foot on the ground or our guys would have nabbed him."

She slapped a hand against the wall. "Which means he got away."

And would live to come back and strike again.

Jonas breathed a sigh of relief when Brooke walked out of the building, Mercy trotting at her heels. She was a good distance away, but he'd recognize her and her dog anywhere. "Where's the guy who tried to break in my house?"

Chase shook his head. "I'm guessing he got away. We'll find out soon enough."

Jonas frowned and reached for the door handle as several law enforcement vehicles spun out of the parking lot. Nicholas and Max went with them. "Where are they going?"

"The suspect may have been seen in a different location and they're going after him," Chase said. "Nicholas will see if Max can pick up his scent."

For the next several minutes, Jonas watched the organized chaos. Brooke and Mercy disappeared back into the building. "Where's she going now?"

"To see if Mercy can find anything."

A short time later, Brooke and Mercy appeared once again. She moved closer to the fence. Closer to Jonas. He could finally see her clearly. "I'm going to guess by the look on her face she and Mercy didn't have much success."

Chase sighed. "I'd say that's a good guess."

"Yeah." Jonas's sigh echoed Chase's. "May I go talk to her now?"

Chase nodded. "She'll have a bit of paperwork to do for this one."

Jonas stepped out of the vehicle and walked to the edge of the fence then along the perimeter until he came to the gate. Brooke spotted him and her brow rose. She clicked to Mercy and walked toward him. "What are you doing here?"

He drank in the sight of her. Safe, whole, alive. "You hung up on me."

That brow rose higher. "Seriously?"

"Seriously. You scared me."

Brooke's jaw dangled slightly before she snapped it shut. "Sorry about that."

"I know it's your job, Brooke," he said softly. "It's just going to take a bit of getting used to when you're called into a dangerous situation."

"Getting used to?" she repeated.

He supposed that statement did make it sound like he planned to be around for a while. Then realized that was exactly what he planned. Now if he could just convince her.

Her expression softened. "I get it, but you really should have stayed put. You're going to have to trust that I can do my job. That I'm good at it and I take precautions, not risks."

He nodded. "I'll remember that."

"Good."

A man in khakis and a blue polo shirt headed toward them. He held a hand out to Brooke. "Officer Clark. You want to tell me why the Capitol K-9 Unit is involved in this one?"

Brooke shook the man's hand. "Detective David Delvecchio of the DC police department, meet Jonas Parker. It was his house the guy was trying to break into. We had a stakeout going on, but unfortunately, as you can see, he got away."

The detective eyed Jonas, then turned his gaze back on Brooke. "You want to tell me a little more?"

"Jonas's son found some evidence linking to the Rosa Gomez case, which of course is also related to the Jeffries shooting."

"I see." His eyes flicked back and forth amongst the three, Brooke, Chase and Jonas. He finally settled back on Brooke. "How did he get away from you?"

She rubbed her forehead. "He went out onto the fire escape on the second floor, jumped into one of the large trees across the fence line and climbed down. At least that's what we think."

"So it's time to expand the search." Chase finally broke his silence.

"Yes."

Jonas pulled his keys from his pocket. "I guess I'll head back home…er…to my office, I mean."

"I'll take you to your car then follow you," Brooke said.

Chase nodded. "I'm going to check in with Gavin and Nicholas and see what I can do to help."

Detective Delvecchio nodded. "I'll fill my officers in. Keep me updated, will you?"

"Of course," Brooke said.

Brooke said her goodbyes and motioned for Jonas to go ahead of her. She'd parked not too far from his own vehicle, just outside the fence. He turned to her. "I'm glad you're all right."

"I'm sorry you were worried."

He shrugged. "Maybe it was stupid of me to come out here, but I just couldn't sit at the office. I'm the one who should be sorry."

"It wasn't exactly smart after the fact there have been two violent incidents against you tonight, but I get it."

"So you're not mad?"

"No. I'm frustrated. I wanted to catch that guy."

He nodded. "I wanted you to catch him, too."

She patted his arm. "It's not over yet."

He had a feeling truer words were never spoken. "Meaning he'll be back?"

She drew in a deep breath and let it out slowly. "Probably."

Sunday morning, Jonas slipped from the cot he'd spent the past couple of hours tossing and turning on. It wasn't the cot's fault. It was actually pretty comfortable. He just couldn't shut his mind off. He stepped into the bathroom and looked into the mirror, gave a grimace and averted his eyes. He'd definitely had better mornings.

In the early days of his divorce, he'd often slept at

his office. He'd finally had the bathroom installed when things had lagged in the courts and he'd gotten tired of showering at the YMCA. When the dust had settled she'd gotten the house, he'd gotten five-year-old Felix, and his practice. And Jonas was fine with that.

He'd purchased the house he and Felix lived in now and they'd made a good life together. At least he'd thought so. Over the past several years, each time he ran into Brooke stirred his restlessness, though. She made him long for things he'd thought he'd left in the past. Things he'd refused to allow himself to hope for.

Now he found himself looking forward to the day simply because he was going to see Brooke again. The only thing that marred that sweet anticipation was the fact that someone had bombed his house last night. Okay, that and the fact that Felix was still having issues no matter how hard Jonas tried to help him. If it wasn't a fight, it was grades.

He sighed and mentally recited his to-do list. Call his home owners insurance company was number two. Find out where Felix had gotten the phone was definitely number one.

And learning if anyone had managed to capture the guy who'd returned to his house last night. Brooke had followed him to his office, and they'd planned their next move. Get Felix from his friend's house and find out where he got the phone. Usually, he and Felix attended the local community church. He wasn't that active, but he couldn't seem to completely tear himself away from his faith. In fact, at this point in his life, he knew he should be reaching out for it with both hands. So today would be a different kind of Sunday. He paused. "I guess I should be mending my fences with You, shouldn't I, God?"

Silence echoed through the bathroom and Jonas sighed and went back to his morning routine. Maybe God was tired of listening.

He'd just finished brushing his teeth when he heard his assistant arrive. Then voices reached him. He stepped into the lobby to find Claire Simpson and Brooke introducing themselves. Brooke hadn't wasted any time getting back to his office this morning. "Good morning," he said.

Brooke nodded. "Morning."

"I see you two have met."

Claire nodded. "I was just telling her what a beautiful dog she has."

"Claire loves anything with four legs," he told Brooke. "Let me just leave a few instructions for her and we'll head out."

He could see the curiosity in Claire's narrowed eyes, but didn't want to take time to explain Brooke's presence in addition to the other things he needed to tell her. He glanced at the clock on the wall. Eight forty-five. He'd told the Fullers he'd pick up Felix at nine-thirty. Plenty of time to cover the morning's work with Claire. He looked at Brooke. "You get any sleep?"

She shook her head. "Not much. I finished the paperwork and closed my eyes for a few minutes."

Jonas rubbed a hand down his freshly shaven chin. "I can't believe you were right. The whole smoke bomb thing was just to get us out of my house so someone could search the place."

"It looks like it."

"Should have set it up so an officer was inside my house and could have just grabbed the guy when he broke in."

"Maybe." She gave him a soft lopsided smile. "Mercy

and I'll be in the car," Brooke said. "Nice to meet you, Claire."

"You, too, Brooke."

They left and within minutes Jonas had finished up with Claire and was climbing into the passenger seat. Mercy sat in the back in her special kennel. "So tell me more about who Felix spent the night with?"

Her question grounded him, brought all of his worries surging to the surface. "He's a friend from school and the track team. His name is Travis Fuller." He gave her the address, and she entered it into the GPS and pulled out of the parking lot. "I can tell you how to get there," he said, amused.

"I don't want to have to worry about it. You said Felix had been getting into trouble."

Jonas sighed. "Yes." He shook his head. "He's been getting in fights lately. His grades are circling the drain, and his attitude is getting hard to tolerate." His hand fisted on his thigh. "I'm up to my ears trying to keep my practice going since my partner quit three months ago."

"Working a lot of hours?"

"Too many," he admitted.

"And Felix is taking advantage of your distraction."

"In a big way. I know it, I see it, but I feel trapped. I can't ignore my work or I won't be able to keep a roof over our heads, but I can't ignore Felix either or I'm going to be visiting him in juvenile detention." He didn't know why he was baring his soul to her, but he had to say it felt good to share it.

"I'm sure you do the best you can. It can't be easy being a single parent."

"It stinks." He gave a soft laugh. "But I love that kid more than anything."

"Yeah," she whispered. "I can tell."

He reached over and snagged her hand to squeeze her fingers. His throat tightened. "I've missed you, Brooke."

She sucked in a deep breath and shot him a glance out of the corner of her eye. "I've missed you, too."

He blinked and she laughed. "What? You didn't expect me to admit it?"

"No."

She shook her head. "The past is sitting like a weight between us, isn't it?"

"Yes."

She tapped the wheel and made a left turn. "I don't know what to tell you, Jonas. I thought I was making the right decision at the time when I chose to keep all distractions to a minimum and focus on my career."

"So it was strictly your career that was keeping you from being willing to talk about us having a future together?"

"It was part of it."

"What was the other part?"

A sigh slipped from her and she gave a small shrug, but didn't answer the question. He relished the fact that she hadn't pulled her hand from his yet and continued to watch her as she drove. "I thought we had something, that we could have been good together. I never did understand why you wouldn't give me a chance. As you can imagine, all kinds of things ran through my mind. Was it because I was divorced? Because I had Felix?"

She seemed to think about it. Then slipped her fingers from his. He grimaced. He wanted to kick himself. He'd moved too fast. Too much too soon. She'd been back in his life for just a few hours and he was already scaring her away.

But this time she didn't run. "No, your divorce didn't have anything to do with it. And Felix is a precious gift. He never factored into why—" She fell quiet and he hoped she'd elaborate. She didn't. "When we were friends," she said, "you never really talked about your ex-wife. I mean never. Like not one word. And when I brought her up, you changed the subject. Mostly to talk about Felix."

"Really?"

"Yes."

He thought about that. Was she right? Maybe. "What do you want to know about her?"

She shrugged. "What happened with you two? Why did you split up? Or is that too personal?" she asked.

"Not too personal. It's not a secret. She had a problem with commitment."

"Ah."

"She found someone else who suited her 'live and let live' lifestyle better than I did." He shrugged.

"What? So she left you? Why would she leave *you*? Is she *crazy*?"

Jonas barked a short laugh. "Well, those questions just did more for my self-esteem than anything else I could think of."

She flushed and it endeared her to him. She also looked uncomfortable. He let her off the hook. "I miss what could have been, but I don't miss her now."

"But Felix does?"

He sighed. "No, he doesn't remember her. He misses the idea of her."

"He wants a mother."

"He does, but when she left us, she left. Like I have no idea where she is or what she's doing now."

"You've had no contact with her at all?"

"None. After I signed the papers, she disappeared from our lives."

Brooke pulled to the curb of the Fuller home and cut the engine. "I'm really sorry about that."

"I was too at the time. But it is what it is and I've moved on." He looked at the house. "And now I'm ready to get some answers from my son."

"You want me to go with you?"

"No. I'll get him. I don't want to say anything in front of his friend."

"I'll wait here."

He nodded and climbed from the car. He walked toward the front door and drew in a deep breath. Trouble and Brooke had re-entered his life without any warning. He prayed the trouble was resolved fast and left as quickly as it appeared.

He just hoped Brooke didn't go with it.

FIVE

Brooke watched him walk up to the front door and ring the bell. She admired his broad shoulders and strong back. He'd always kept himself in great physical condition, and that hadn't changed. His love of all things sports kept him fit.

She glanced in the rearview mirror, wondering who'd thrown the bomb in Jonas's house last night. Who had they chased and lost? She'd never had a glimpse of his face. His dark clothes disguised his build, and the baseball cap had hidden his features. The darkness had definitely worked in his favor.

A young teen stepped outside onto the front porch. He had a black backpack slung over his right shoulder. Brooke would have known he was Jonas's son had she spotted him in a crowd. A miniature replica of his father, he had sandy blond hair and a lanky build. She'd seen him as a young child about five years old and he was now just an older version of the child she remembered. She knew that he had Jonas's light brown eyes, too.

The sullen expression was all his own, though.

He shoved past Jonas then lifted his head and saw her sitting behind the wheel. He stopped, his frown deepening. He turned and said something to Jonas, who nodded. Jonas shook hands with the man still standing in the doorway then the two of them headed toward the car.

Jonas slipped into the passenger seat. His son slumped in the back next to Mercy's kennel.

Brooke took a deep breath and let it out in a slow silent whoosh. She caught Felix's eye in the mirror and he looked away. "Hi," she said. "I'm Brooke."

"Hi," he mumbled.

He didn't ask who she was or seem to care that she was there. "You hungry?"

He perked up at that question. "Yeah, I didn't have time to eat breakfast." He shot his dad an accusing look.

"Hey, it's nine-thirty. You had plenty of time to eat."

"I'm a teenager, Dad. I sleep in on Sunday morning. Or I do when I'm spending the night with a friend and we plan to get breakfast at church."

"The whole breakfast thing might be my fault, I'm afraid," Brooke said. "I insisted on getting you early. Hence the offer to feed you."

"Oh." The defiant look fell away and he actually gave her a curious look. "Okay. Sure. Where are we going?"

"What's your favorite breakfast place?"

"The Original Pancake House on M. Lee Highway." He and Jonas spoke at the same time and she smiled.

"Sounds good to me." She glanced in the rearview mirror and waited for the dark vehicle coming up beside her to pass. It slowed and she tensed, her mind flashing to the night before, her hand moving to her weapon. When the car passed, she let out a slow breath. *Not everyone is after him,* she reminded herself. But someone was and she'd take all precautions to make sure Jonas—and now Felix—stayed safe.

She pressed the gas and pulled away from the curb. Fifteen minutes later after several failed attempts at conversation with Felix, she parked and they climbed from the vehicle, Mercy trotting obediently at her side.

Once seated with Mercy at Brooke's feet under the table, they ordered and silence fell again. Jonas caught her gaze. She nodded. He cleared his throat. "Felix, someone broke into our house last night."

The teen's head shot up and for the first time that day, he met his father's gaze. "What? Why? Are you okay? Did they catch him?"

"Yes, I'm fine, thanks." Jonas's jaw worked. She could see he was touched at his son's concern. "The house isn't so fine, but we are." He explained what happened and that they would have to stay at his office until the insurance company could give an appraisal on the damage. "But I've got friends in high places. We'll get it taken care of pretty fast."

Felix looked dazed. "So who are you again?" he asked her. Finally something other than defiance on his face.

"I'm Brooke Clark. I work for a law enforcement organization called the Capitol K-9 Unit." Felix's eyes flicked toward Mercy, who sat under the table, her head the only part of her body poking out. Brooke answered his silent question. "Mercy and I are partners. Your dad called us last night after the break-in."

"Why you?"

"I found this." Jonas pulled the phone from his pocket and slid it across the table.

Felix's eyes went wide, and he clamped his lips together.

Brooke's senses tingled. "Where did you get it?" she asked him.

Felix crossed his arms and looked away, the defiance back in spades. Jonas gave a huff of frustration. "Tell me, Felix. This is important. A picture of a dead woman is on this phone, and we need to know what you know."

Felix swallowed and a flash of fear crossed his face, but he refused to comment. Jonas's face began to darken, and his eyes turned thunderous. Brooke laid a hand on his arm. He sat back, and she could tell he was putting good effort into gaining control of his temper. "Felix, do you mind if I tell you a story?"

He jerked and shot her a confused look. "About?"

"About a little boy who no longer has a mother."

Felix's fist tightened around his glass and for a moment Brooke wondered if he was going to pick it up and throw it. "Sure," he gritted. "What about him?"

"About two months ago, a woman named Rosa Gomez was killed. Even though it hasn't been proved to be murder yet, we believe she was pushed off the cliffs at President's Park. She had a little boy who's only two years old. The good thing is that Rosa had a sister named Lana. Lana now has custody of little Juan, but losing his mother shouldn't have happened. We want to catch the person who took her away from him."

Felix flicked a glance at his father. "He doesn't have a dad either?"

"Not one that wants to be in the picture," Brooke said. "At least that's the impression we've gotten so far since no one has come forward to say he's the father."

Felix took a swig of his drink, then set the glass back on the table with a thunk. The waitress delivered the food and a lull rose. Jonas thanked the woman, who nodded and left.

"Do you mind if I say the blessing?" Brooke asked.

"No, go ahead," Jonas said. Felix looked a little uncomfortable, but didn't protest.

Brooke prayed over the food and asked God to continue to keep them safe. They ate in silence for the next few minutes. "What's going to happen to him, to Juan?" Felix asked.

"Right now, he's with his aunt, so he's being taken care of, but his mom is gone and we want to find who killed her so he doesn't have to grow up wondering." Felix looked ready to burst into tears, but Brooke hoped her words would get the boy to tell them what he knew. She didn't like being so manipulative, but every word she spoke was true. "We've tracked down every lead we could get, but lately, it seems the trail has grown cold. Until now. Until your dad called to tell me about the phone. This is a huge deal for us, Felix. Would you please tell us what you know about the phone?"

"I found it," he blurted. "On the cliffs, buried under the rocks near the police tape. I didn't know it belonged to a dead woman. I didn't know, I didn't."

"Okay. I believe you." Brooke felt Jonas tense beside her. She spoke quickly before he had a chance to interrupt. "Would you be willing to show us where you found it?"

"Yes. I'll show you." Now that Felix had confessed, he couldn't seem to get the words out fast enough. "I didn't mean to steal it. I thought someone had just lost it. I knew once I got it charged, I could connect to the internet to play games with my friends. That's all I wanted it for."

"How'd you get—and keep—the battery charged?" Jonas asked.

He shrugged and looked down at the table. "I couldn't charge it until the day before yesterday. Travis finally found an extra charger and brought it to school for me." He lifted his head and jutted his chin. "If you'd let me have a cool phone like all the other kids, I wouldn't have felt the need to keep the one I found."

"So this is my fault, huh?" Jonas asked, the thread of anger back in his voice.

Felix swallowed and offered another shrug.

Brooke's heart ached at the tension between the two. They needed each other, they just didn't know what to do about it. "Okay, here's the plan—"

"He chased me," Felix muttered.

"What?" Jonas asked sharply.

"When I found the phone," Felix said, "there was a man out there. He, uh, saw me, I guess, and chased me."

Jonas leaned in. "Who was it?"

Felix lifted a shoulder. "How should I know? Some old dude. Like about your age, I guess." Brooke barely managed to smother her snort of laughter at the look of consternation on Jonas's face at his son's comment. She looked away and processed Felix's words. But he wasn't finished. "I thought he was a cop and if he caught me he'd put me in juvie or something for being behind the crime scene tape. I ran fast and hid. He looked for me for a while, but I was faster and smarter."

"Good for you," Brooke said. "I'm glad he didn't catch you. He could have been a dangerous guy."

Felix shivered. "I didn't think about him being dangerous, I just didn't want him to catch me."

"When did you find the phone?" Jonas asked.

"A couple of months ago."

Brooke glanced at Jonas, her mind spinning with possibilities. Sometimes deduction was a "what-if" game. "Okay, so you found the phone a couple of months ago. You get it charged up day before yesterday. Felix, last night the person who broke into your house demanded your dad give him 'the phone.'"

Felix flinched. His gaze jumped from his father to Brooke then back to Jonas. "Are you sure you're really okay?"

"I'm fine, but I don't think the timing is a coincidence."

"I don't either," Brooke said.

Jonas rubbed his eyes. "You think whoever is after the phone has just been waiting for it to come back online?"

"I do." She nodded and took the last bite of her food. "And tracked it via the GPS."

"Exactly." She nodded to the phone. "I can't believe the thing still works. I mean, you didn't find it the day she died, did you?"

"I don't think so. I remember that it had rained that day. I was throwing rocks into the puddles to see how high the water would go. There was a big puddle behind the police tape, so I ducked under. I moved one of the rocks and found her phone." He shrugged. "It had a LifeProof case on it," Felix said. Brooke nodded. The case would have protected it against the elements. "The battery was dead when I found it," Felix said. "I took the case off to make it easier to play the games once I got it charged. I didn't know someone would be tracking it." He dipped his head and studied his fingers. "I guess I should have turned it in to someone when I found it, huh?"

Jonas sighed. "Yes, you should have, but there's nothing to be done about that now. The important thing is that you're telling the truth now."

Brooke drew in a deep breath. "Absolutely. Thanks for telling us this, Felix. I appreciate it."

"I'm sorry," he said, his voice low, eyes on the table once again.

Jonas reached across the table to cover his son's hand when the window over the booth behind them ruptured.

SIX

Jonas registered the bullets riddling the side of the restaurant, the glass falling, the screams surrounding him. All he could do was wrap one hand around Felix's wrist and the other around Brooke's arm and yank them to the floor.

He covered Felix with his body as best he could while he scrambled to think, to picture a way out. What if they came inside? Terror slammed through him. He had to keep Felix safe. He stayed still, feeling Felix's heartbeat slam against his own. "Be still, don't move," he yelled above the screams, the chaos.

The roar of an engine, then the squeal of tires spinning against the asphalt reached his ears.

Were they gone? He stayed put for another few seconds, waiting, listening. When nothing more happened, Jonas lifted himself away from his son. He ran his shaking hands over Felix's face, his arms, chest, checking for blood. And found nothing. Felix stared at him, freckles looking 3-D against his white face. "Are you hurt?" Jonas asked him.

"No." Felix blinked. "I don't think so."

Jonas turned. "Brooke? You okay?"

"Fine." Her fingers trembled, but she pushed away

from him and scrambled to her feet. She checked the dog, then glanced out the window. "He's getting away. Stay here and stay down! I'm going to see if I can get a plate." She and Mercy bolted through the restaurant. Jonas grabbed Felix to him and held him as he searched the restaurant for anyone with injuries. Sirens sounded in the distance.

Was the shooter really gone? Had they just lived through a drive-by?

"Dad?"

His son's shaking voice cracked.

"Yeah?"

"Are you okay?"

"I'm okay." He pulled Felix to him for a hug, and the teen didn't resist. He held him for a brief moment and then the chaos escalated a notch with the arrival of law enforcement.

Brooke came back in, her face tense, jaw set. She probably didn't get a plate. She beelined for them as more cops and paramedics swarmed the restaurant. Brooke must have told them it was all clear. Which meant the shooter got away. Brooke motioned for them to follow her. Jonas gripped Felix's arm and led him away from the scene. The noise level rivaled that of a jet plane. Once outside, Brooke turned to say something and stopped. Her eyes went wide. "You *are* hurt."

"What?" Felix frowned.

"Who?" Jonas asked.

"You." She reached for his arm. He looked down to find it bleeding. The low throb of pain finally registered with him.

"It's just a scratch."

"We'll let the paramedics make that diagnosis. Come on over here."

"I'm a doctor, remember?"

Felix snorted. "You're a vet, Dad. Let a real doctor look at it."

"Thanks so much, son. Nothing like keeping a person humble," he muttered. But he saw the worry in Felix's eyes and nodded. "Fine, if it will make you two feel better."

Brooke led him over to one of the ambulances. While the paramedic patched him up stating, "It's only a scratch, you're a fortunate guy," Brooke and Mercy dove into the fray of the investigation. He watched her put Mercy to work, the dog sniffing, looking for any evidence that might help them discover who had just shot up the restaurant.

And why.

Jonas decided not to let denial take over. There was no doubt in his mind that this shooting was related to the other two incidents from last night. What scared him was that whoever was after the phone didn't seem to care if he hurt someone else in the process to get it. Innocent people could have been seriously injured or killed in this latest episode and that scared Jonas to the bone.

Mercy didn't seem to find anything to interest her. The crime scene unit moved in and an officer approached him. "Do you feel up to giving your statement?"

"Sure." His arm throbbed, but he'd refused the painkiller offered. He needed a clear head. His glance slid back to Brooke and he watched her nod at one of the other Capitol K-9 Unit members as she walked toward him. She'd called for reinforcements.

Which meant she'd come to the same conclusion he

had. Everything was related. He just hoped they managed to live long enough to figure out the connections.

Brooke tried to rub the grit from her eyes. She was used to going with very little sleep sometimes, but that didn't mean she liked it. She walked over to fellow team member Nicholas Cole. A former navy SEAL, he stood tall, military written all over him. He'd left his K-9, Max, in his vehicle but she hadn't called him to the scene for Max's help. She wanted to give Nicholas the phone to pass on to Gavin, their boss. She knew the two were meeting in a couple of hours and she wasn't sure how long she'd be tied up at the scene. "Thanks for coming."

"No problem." Concern knit his brow. "You sure you're all right?"

"Shaken, but I'm fine. Grateful to be alive."

"Was anyone hurt?"

"A few scrapes and cuts, but fortunately no one was killed. The bullets hit the window of an empty booth just behind where we were sitting. I tried to get out fast enough to see a license plate, but I was too slow." Frustration at her failure bit at her.

He shook his blond head and focused pale brown eyes on her. "What's going on?"

Brooke pulled the phone from her pocket and handed it to him. "Do you have a charger in your car? I have a different kind of phone so mine won't work."

He looked at the bottom of the phone. "Yep, mine will work. Come on."

Brooke followed him with a glance over her shoulder. Jonas appeared to be finished with the paramedics. He caught her gaze and motioned for Felix to follow him. The two headed her way. She turned back to Nicholas.

"What's on it?" he asked.

"Rosa Gomez's picture."

He shot her a sharp look. "Where did you get it?"

She gave him the short version of the story. He plugged it in and the phone beeped to indicate it was charging.

Jonas and Felix drew closer. "They're escalating," she murmured to Nicholas.

"What do you mean?"

"The smoke bomb was meant to get us out of the house maybe." She nodded toward the mangled restaurant. "This was different. This was meant to kill."

Jonas stepped up beside her, and she shut off that thread of conversation. Felix hung close to his dad, still looking pale and shaken. She nodded at Jonas's arm. "Are you okay?"

His lips quirked, but his eyes remained serious. "It's just a scratch."

She smiled. "This is Nicholas. Nicholas, meet Jonas Parker and his son, Felix. Felix is the one who found the phone and was gracious enough to tell us everything he knew about it."

Felix's brows shot up and Brooke winked at him. His shoulders relaxed a fraction and he shot her a grateful look.

The two men shook hands and Nicholas gave Felix a fist bump. "Good job, kid."

"But I—" Felix started. Brooke held his gaze and he finally shrugged. "You're welcome, I guess." He swallowed. "I have the case at home if you want it, too."

"We do, thanks." Nicholas powered up the phone and gave a low whistle when the screensaver appeared. "That's her and that's her son, Juan."

Nicholas scrolled through the other pictures. "Most of them are of the boy."

Brooke leaned in. "Wait a minute, scroll back. What's the last picture she took?"

Nicholas went back to it. "This one? It's fuzzy, but it's a man."

"And they're out on the cliffs. See the outline?" Brooke pointed.

"Yes. And the date is the day she was found dead."

Brooke met his gaze. "I think it's possible Rosa took a picture of her murderer."

"It hasn't been proven to be murder," Nicholas reminded her. "It could have been an accident. This guy could be anyone."

"True," Brooke agreed, "but the fact that her wallet is still missing…"

"Could be someone have found it like Felix here found the phone."

"Okay, that's possible." Brooke pursed her lips. "But she's still connected to the Jeffries home where there was a murder. And then there was all that trouble at the children's home after it was discovered one of the children may have seen the murder…" Several weeks ago, the All Our Kids foster home had been targeted. The children and staff had been moved to a secure location until authorities were sure they were safe. Unfortunately, they wouldn't be until they discovered which child had snuck out during the night and witnessed Michael Jeffries's murder and the congressman's shooting. None of the kids would admit to being near the Jeffries home.

"You don't believe Rosa's death was an accident, do you?" Jonas asked.

"No. Not for a second. Do you?"

"No," Nicholas said. "I've made no secret that I think it's homicide. We need to keep digging for the evidence to prove she was murdered."

Brooke pulled in a deep breath. "We also need to have a meeting with the rest of the team and figure out the best way to determine who that man in the picture is."

He pulled his phone from his pocket. "I'll set up that meeting and get this phone to Gavin. I'll text you when he gives me a time. In the meantime, quit getting shot at."

"I'll do my best."

Brooke had slept fitfully last night, worried about Jonas and his son. She worried Felix would have nightmares about the shooting. She'd also been concerned that whoever was after the phone would come back again, not realizing Jonas had turned it over to the Capitol K-9 team. She knew Gavin had arranged for a protection detail on Jonas and Felix, who were staying at the veterinarian office until his home could be aired out, but she'd been unable to put the duo's safety from her mind.

And now she worried she'd be late for the eight o'clock meeting Gavin had called to discuss the new developments in the case. Mercy lay at the foot of the bed and watched as Brooke rushed to get ready. Brooke had finally fallen asleep around four in the morning and of course she'd overslept. She clicked to Mercy and she and the dog rushed out the front door to the vehicle. Mercy hopped in the back. Brooke paused to see her neighbor, twelve-year-old Christopher Denton, swinging his wooden bat. "Nice form, kiddo!"

He grinned and gave her a salute. "I had a good teacher."

She saw the balls at his feet. "No broken windows, huh?"

"I'll do my best. I'm just hittin' grounders."

She could only hope his grounders didn't turn into fly balls. Brooke had taught him how to swing a bat and connect with a baseball about two weeks ago when she'd seen him struggling. His single mother worked two jobs so Brooke looked out for the boy when she could. "Is your mom home?"

"Yes, ma'am."

"Good deal. See you later." Brooke climbed into the SUV and slammed the door. She backed out of her drive, keeping a careful eye on the surrounding area, then headed down the street to the stop sign.

Fifteen minutes later, she walked into headquarters and bolted for the conference room. The last one to arrive, she slid into her seat and let out a slow breath. "Sorry." Mercy slipped under the table with the other K-9s. Nicholas sat to her right, Gavin stood at the head of the table next to a whiteboard. Adam Donovan, a former FBI agent, leaned forward and gave her a friendly nod.

Isaac Black smirked. "They make alarm clocks, ya know? You see, you plug them into the wall and they have these buttons where you can set the time you need to wa—"

Brooke flashed him a fake smile. "Zip it, Black." Chase Zachary, a former Secret Service agent, shot her a grin and she rolled her eyes. But she truly didn't mind the good-natured ribbing; she figured it was called for. No matter how determined she might be to be on time, something usually happened to have her running at least five minutes late.

Gavin rapped the table. "Listen up, we've got some new developments in the Jeffries case. Brooke, you want to fill everyone in?"

Brooke took a deep breath and launched into an explanation of everything that had happened since she'd been awakened by Jonas's phone call.

She ended her narration by holding up a picture they'd printed from the phone, "And this is the picture of the man we saw on Rosa's phone. We need to find him. He's either the one who killed her or he knows something about her death."

"Anyone have any suggestions on how we want to go about looking for this guy?" Gavin asked.

"Let's get his face on the news and put some flyers up," Adam said.

"Good idea. Anyone else?"

For the next hour, they bounced around ideas and finally decided on the flyers. Chase stood. "We'll get them made up and start posting them around the area. Hopefully, someone will recognize him and call us."

Gavin looked at Nicholas. "Are you still working with Selena Barrow?"

"'Working with' might be a slight exaggeration. If that's code for listening to her expound on the fact that we haven't found her cousin yet, then yeah, I'm still working with her." Serena was employed as the White House tour director. She was also Erin Eagleton's cousin. Erin's charm had been found at the murder scene and she'd been missing ever since. Serena was convinced her cousin was in danger and often showed up at the office to request an update on the case. Nicholas seemed to be the one who ended up fielding her questions more often than not.

Nicholas leaned in. "But I can handle her. That's not what's weighing on me the most. I've been doing some more digging into the congressman's business dealings." He glanced at Gavin and Brooke could see his hesitation. She knew exactly what was going through his mind. He didn't want to say anything negative about Gavin's former mentor and yet he had information he felt the team should have.

Gavin stiffened. "Go on."

Brooke bit her lip.

"You're not going to like it, but hear me out, Gavin, all right?"

"Of course."

"I'm not a big fan of the congressman," Nicholas said. "I've made no secret of that. I respect what he's done with the children's home and how he took you under his wing. He's done some good things, I'll admit that."

"But?" Gavin raised a brow.

"But I suspect that things aren't completely above-board with him. I'll also admit it's more suspicion and speculation than anything. I don't have any solid proof."

Gavin placed his fists on the table and leaned toward Nicholas. "If you can't prove it, don't say it. Think long and hard before you open your mouth and slander a good man."

Nicholas met Gavin stare for stare. "It's not slander, Gavin. I'm not sharing this with anyone but the people in this room."

"Then get proof."

Nicholas sat back and crossed his arms. "Right."

Gavin held his gaze a moment longer, then looked

over the very still and quiet team members. "That goes for all of you." He paused and homed back in on Nicholas and his expression eased a fraction. "You're not often wrong, Nicholas, I'll grant you that." He paused and frowned. "I just think you are in this case, so tread carefully." Gavin gathered his phone and other things and headed out of the room. The others trickled slowly behind him.

Brooke got up and Nicholas touched her arm. "Hang on a sec, would you?"

She paused. "Sure."

When it was just the two of them left in the conference room, Nicholas shut the door. "Gavin's too close to this. He doesn't want to hear anything negative about the congressman."

"Yeah, I got that."

"But I'm telling you, there's something not right about him."

"What have you found out?"

He motioned for her to sit down. She did and he sat next to her, his shoulders leaned in, face tense. "I was at the White House the other day doing some snooping. I found out that Congressman Jeffries had a young aide, Paul Harrison, who quit unexpectedly. The source I talked to said he didn't know the details, just that the guy was there one day cleaning out his desk. When my source asked him what was wrong, he wouldn't say, but he was scared."

"Scared of what?"

"That's just it, I don't know and I couldn't find out."

"Which is why you didn't tell Gavin this. Have you found the aide?"

"No, not yet. Mr. Harrison disappeared shortly after he quit working for the congressman." Nicholas clasped his hands in front of him. "This whole thing stinks, Brooke. I think the congressman is dirty. I just need help proving it."

Brooke blew out a breath and leaned back in her chair. "That's going to be quite a job."

"I know. We're close, though, so close I can almost taste it. I want to put this guy away."

"If he's guilty."

"He's guilty. I've been digging into the congressman's history and activities. Especially those close ties to Thorn Industries."

"Thorn Industries is coming up a lot lately—and it's not good stuff." She pursed her lips.

"Exactly. If he's guilty of some kind of corruption, I think that would make him extremely paranoid and nervous."

"Nervous enough to kill?" Brooke narrowed her eyes as she considered her own question.

"I don't know."

"What if Rosa knew something? Or saw something?" she pressed.

"And he had to kill her to keep her quiet?"

"Maybe."

"It's possible of course, but pure conjecture."

"Which might be pure truth. I'm also going to see if I can track down the aide whose sudden departure has me curious."

Brooke stared at him for a few seconds, then gave a reluctant nod. "Okay then. If you're right, then we're not going to need just proof, we're going to need airtight, *irrefutable* proof. Like a confession kind of irrefutable proof."

"And we're going to need to watch each other's

backs. There's no telling how far he'll go to protect his name."

"If you're right, we already know how far he'll go."

Brooke pursed her lips. "All right then. Let's get those flyers up and see if we get a hit on anyone. If we do, we can immediately see if that person has any kind of link to the congressman."

"Good idea." He glanced at the closed door. "And keep this between us, I guess. I don't want to stir up Gavin's wrath any more than I already have."

"I understand." She frowned. "It's going to be hard for him if your suspicions are proven true."

"I know, but we don't have a choice. We have a dead woman who deserves justice."

"And a single dad who has a killer after him and his son."

SEVEN

Jonas hung up with the insurance company and sighed. He looked around his office and just prayed Felix was staying out of trouble while at school today. He'd been grumpy and snappy and nothing Jonas had said or done this morning had been right. Not only that, Felix had complained his toast was dry and the cereal soggy. He'd walked out the door without a look back.

Jonas rubbed his tired eyes and glanced at the clock. It was only eight-thirty in the morning, and he had a full day scheduled. The first patient would be arriving any moment and Jonas couldn't get himself together. Yesterday had been surreal and he still wasn't sure it hadn't been just one more nightmare to add to his repertoire.

He picked up the stress reliever ball from his desk and started squeezing it. Squeeze, release, squeeze, release. He threw it across the room and watched it bounce. That helped.

Claire poked her head in the door. "Mrs. Boyd is here with Chester."

Jonas forced a smile to his lips and stood. "What is it today?"

"She thinks he ate a bowl of gummy worms her grandson left on the coffee table." Chester, the big golden who ate anything he could sink his teeth into. Whether it was meant for him or not.

Jonas shook his head and headed for the door when his cell rang. "Tell Mrs. Boyd and Chester I'll be right there." He pressed the answer button. "Hello?"

"Hi, Jonas, it's Brooke."

Just hearing her voice made his day better. "Hi. How's it going?"

"Busy. We're moving full speed ahead on trying to track down the man in the picture on Rosa Gomez's phone. We're putting flyers up all over town. Since someone tossed a smoke bomb in your house two nights ago and then shot up the restaurant yesterday, we're going to put some around those areas, too. Do you mind if I bring some to your office?"

"Of course I don't mind." He glanced at the clock. "Would you be free for lunch around noon?"

"I think I could do that."

"Good. We'll talk about where to eat when you get here."

"How was Felix this morning?"

His mood soured. "Don't ask."

"Ouch. I'm sorry. He'll come around."

"Yeah." Maybe.

"See you in a few hours." She hung up.

Jonas stared at his phone. As much as he loved his job and his patients, he knew the next three hours and fifteen minutes were going to drag by.

When Brooke finally walked in the door with Mercy trotting at her heels, Jonas smiled. Then frowned. She looked so serious, with her tight jaw and set shoulders, but he was still happy to see her. "I thought noon would never get here."

At his words, her petite frame relaxed and her blue

eyes gave him a glimmer of a smile. "I felt the same way. I'm starving."

"Do you think we could eat somewhere that won't get blown up or shot at?"

Her nostrils flared at the reminder and for a moment he was sorry he'd brought it up. Then she smiled. "Sure. I have the perfect place." She handed him several fly- ers. "Do you mind handing these out to your clients?"

"Of course not." He placed them on the front coun- ter. "We'll post one on the door, too."

"Great, thanks."

"So. Lunch?"

"Why don't I drive?"

Claire's attention had been bouncing back and forth between the two of them. "So, I guess I'll just stay here and man the phones while you two enjoy your meal."

Jonas froze for a second before turning to Claire. She held his gaze for a moment then laughed. "I'm kidding. Enjoy yourselves."

"Are you sure? You're welcome to come with us. I could lock up for a couple of hours."

Claire waved a hand. "It was a joke, Jonas. Go on. I've got enough here to keep me busy for a while and I want to finish it before five." She picked up the tape and grabbed one of the flyers. "And I'll put this in the win- dow right now." The phone rang. "Or I will in a minute. Go." She answered the phone with a smile.

She really had been kidding. He shook his head. He'd never been very good at picking up vibes from women and it didn't look like his skills had improved since his wife had left.

Although, he had to admit, he picked up on Brooke's vibes pretty well. And they confused him. She seemed like she wanted to get closer to him. The look in her eye, her body language. All of that confirmed it. But then when he'd try to respond, she'd get skittish and throw up a wall that left him bruised and battered when he slammed into it.

He followed her out to her vehicle and she opened the back door for Mercy. The dog hopped in and settled herself in the special area designated just for her. Brooke slipped into the driver's seat and Jonas watched her fasten her seat belt. "So do you like burgers or chicken?" she asked.

He shrugged. "I like both."

She slid him a look. "Which one do you like today?"

"Burgers."

Brooke started the car and pulled from the parking lot. "There's a little place not too far from here. Hopefully, I'll get to finish a meal. I'm waiting to hear back from Nicholas about visiting Congressman Jeffries sometime today."

"Why him?"

"We think he may have some more information about his housekeeper's death—and his son's."

"Do you think he had something to do with either?"

Brooke pulled into the diner's lot and parked. She looked over at him. "I can't say whether he did or not. But my other team member and I feel like it wouldn't hurt to talk to him again."

Jonas nodded and stepped from the car. He looked around, trying to see if anyone had followed them. He noticed Brooke doing the same. "Do you see anything?"

"No. And I was watching while I was driving. I never saw anyone suspicious behind us."

They walked into the restaurant and Brooke led him to a corner booth that had no windows. Brooke slid in and Jonas took the seat opposite her. They ordered and then Jonas looked at her. Intently. She took a sip of water. "What is it?"

Time to start tearing down some walls. "I've just wondered about you. Running into you, seeing you occasionally only made me wonder more."

"Wonder what?"

"Do you mind if I ask you a personal question?"

She didn't answer right away. Instead, she tilted her head and met him stare for stare. Finally, she shrugged. "You can ask. I won't promise I'll answer."

"Fair enough." The waitress interrupted with the serving of their order. When she left, he looked back Brooke. "Why haven't you ever married?"

Brooke froze. Well, he'd said it was a personal question. She cleared her throat. She didn't want to lie, but she didn't want to just lay the truth out there either. She offered what she hoped was a casual shrug. "I think I'm a career girl, Jonas." She looked up and met his gaze. "I've spent the past fifteen years of my life preparing, training, learning and working. I've known exactly what I wanted to do ever since I saw an old rerun of Lassie rescuing Timmy." She smiled. "I guess I just haven't let things like romance and marriage distract me." Which was all true. It didn't mean she didn't wish things were different every once in a while, but she'd accepted that her lot in life was to be alone. No man wanted damaged goods.

"I think you were pretty tempted to be distracted way back when we first met," he teased softly.

Thank goodness the waitress chose that moment to bring their food. Brooke ignored his statement and the only thing she could think to do was to bow her head to say a short silent blessing. And plead for a change of subject. She looked up to find Jonas's eyes on her. "Well?" he asked.

"Well what?"

"Come on, Brooke, admit it. You felt something for me years ago. Why did you push me away?"

"Why are you *pushing* this now?"

He hesitated. Then sighed. "Like I said, because I've always wondered. When we first met, we hit it right off. We became best friends and then when I wanted more, you threw up a wall and took off."

"It wasn't you," she whispered.

"I know. Or at least I do now. You said it was you, but at the time all I knew was you were crazy about me, too. Your rejection threw me for a loop." He gave a short, humorless laugh. "I never would have had the guts to put myself out there and tell you how I felt if I hadn't been 100 percent sure you felt the same way. So why would you push me away?"

Her palms started to sweat. She really didn't want to have this conversation, but could tell he'd been waiting a long time to say these things. She glanced at the door, wanting to run, escape the memories, the what-might-have-beens had the car wreck never happened. Of course she might never have gone into law enforcement if not for the wreck. Then she never would have met Jonas. She swallowed, then cleared her throat. "I—"

"You broke my heart," he said softly.

Brooke winced. "I—"

He shook his head, looked at his food then back at her. "Every time we'd bump into one another, I'd want to stop you and ask you these questions. I'm sorry I'm just blurting all this out. But seeing you again has resurrected all those old feelings, and I just want to know if this time could be different."

...

Her phone rang, and she couldn't move. "Nothing like putting a girl on the spot," she finally said. "You never did beat around the bush, did you?"

"No, not much. Still don't." He gave a small smile as her phone rang again. "After being shot at and almost blown up these past couple of days, life has come into startling clear focus for me. Answer your phone and we'll finish this conversation after you've had a bit of time to process it." He stood and wiped his mouth. "I see a client whose Boxer is scheduled to have surgery next week. I'll be right back."

She grabbed the phone, knowing he was giving her some time to think and privacy to take her call. His thoughtfulness warmed her even while his words terrified her. For a number of reasons. Nicholas's number flashed on the screen. "Clark here." Jonas walked away, his back straight, broad shoulders hinting at his strength.

"Hey, Brooke."

"What's up?"

"We've got an appointment to talk to Congressman Jeffries in thirty minutes. Can you meet me at his house?"

"Of course. I'll leave now."

"See you there."

She hung up and caught Jonas's eye. He kept his conversation with his client brief, then moved toward her while she pulled some bills from her wallet. Most of their food sat untouched and she didn't have time to have it boxed up. It would take her every minute of the thirty allotted minutes to get to the congressman's house. "I've got to go," she said. "Do you mind riding with me and waiting in the car?" She explained the call from Nicholas.

"I'll get Claire to pick me up," he said. "You don't need me along."

"You're sure?"

"I'm sure."

"All right, thanks." She snapped her fingers, and Mercy joined her at her side. She could feel Jonas's eyes on her all the way out the door and knew their conversation wasn't over. A ball of dread settled in her stomach that had nothing to do with finding a possible murderer. She'd rather face down a killer than talk about why she would never marry. That thought alone almost stopped her in her tracks. But she kept walking and thinking. And she realized she really hadn't dealt with her anguish over her inability to have children. She drew in a shuddering breath. She didn't have time to deal with her issues. She had a killer to catch.

EIGHT

As soon as Brooke climbed into her car, Jonas's phone rang. His heart dipped when he saw the number. "Hello?"

"Dr. Parker, this is Grace Hale with Falls Church Middle School."

Grace Hale, principal and disciplinarian. "Hello, Dr. Hale." He couldn't help the resignation in his voice. "What's Felix done now?"

"We caught him skipping class."

"Skip—" Jonas closed his eyes. "All right. I guess you're going to suspend him?"

"No, I think it would be best if we didn't. His grades are suffering enough. Suspension isn't going to do anything positive for him." A principal who cared. Jonas sent up a silent thank-you. "He's going to have two days of in-school suspension where he will be closely supervised while he works on material that will get him caught up." A slight pause as though Dr. Hale were weighing her next words. "I'm also going to recommend he talk to one of our counselors here."

"I see. His mother left him—us—when he was young. He's never given up hope that she would come back. Lately I think his hope is gone and that's why the surly attitude and acting out. I think he's finally come to understand that she's not coming back. You understand?"

"I do." The woman kept her tone soft, without accusation or contention. Jonas appreciated that.

"Would you trust your child's emotional well-being with the counselor you want him to talk to?" he asked.

A slight pause. "One of them, yes."

"Then that's the one he can talk to."

"Thank you, Dr. Parker."

"Dr. Hale?"

"Yes?"

Jonas cleared his throat. "Thank you for not suspending him."

"He wasn't doing anything, just sitting in the bathroom on the floor staring at the wall. I think he's hurting."

"I think he is, too." His heart ached for his son, but he just didn't know what to do for him. Maybe the counselor would help. He cleared his throat. "At least he wasn't fighting."

"Indeed." Another pause. "I heard Felix was there when someone shot at the restaurant."

Jonas flexed his arm at the reminder. It still hurt when he moved wrong. "Yes, but we talked and he seemed to bounce back."

"Sometimes appearances can be deceiving."

Very true. "All right, he can talk to your counselor, and I'll talk to him when I see him this afternoon."

He hung up with the principal and called Claire, who agreed to pick him up. He had a caseload that he needed to focus on. And he had to figure out what to say to his son. His phone rang as he was slipping it back into his pocket. A glance at the caller ID had his black mood lifting. "Hi."

"Hey, I forgot to ask you one thing," Brooke said.

"What's that?"

"Do you think after Felix gets out of school, you and he could go with me to the cliffs and he could show us where he found the phone?"

"Ah, yes, we can do that."

She paused. "You okay?"

"Not really." He told her what happened with Felix skipping class and the principal's recommendation for a counselor.

She was silent for a brief moment. "I'm here and I need to go in, but I'll just say a counselor can help. A good one anyway."

"I know. Thanks, Brooke."

"Sure thing. Talk to you soon."

He hung up. His son needed to see a counselor. Again. Jonas sighed. He'd thought Felix had been doing better. They'd been talking and hanging out and then Christmas had come and gone and Felix had started shutting him out once again. He shook his head and as Claire pulled to the curb, Jonas decided he needed to take a serious look at praying again. He had a lot to talk to God about if God was interested in hearing about it. Jonas decided it was time to find out.

Brooke stepped out of her vehicle and told Mercy to stay put. The dog gave her a mournful look, but settled down in her kennel with a sigh. The day wasn't hot, but it wasn't cold either. She left the rear windows down and the screens up with the fans blowing so Mercy would be comfortable during her wait.

Nicholas climbed out of his matching K-9 vehicle

and did the same for Max. "Did you tell him what you wanted to talk to him about?"

"No, I didn't want to give him a reason to refuse to see us."

The congressman had agreed to meet them at his house. She supposed he didn't want to have to answer questions about their presence at the Congressional Office building, although most would probably just think they were working his son's murder.

Nicholas rapped on the door and Brooke took a good look around. The house had a classy, stately air about it. The door opened.

A young woman smiled up at them. "You must be the officers who wanted to speak to the congressman."

"Yes ma'am. Is he here?"

"I'm afraid not. He had to leave suddenly. Something about a forgotten doctor's appointment. He asked me to let you know."

Brooke sighed, frustration zipping through her. "Guess we could show up at his doctor's office."

Nicholas shook his head. "It's all right. Thank you very much."

"Of course." She shut the door and Brooke turned around to stare out across the estate. "You think he's avoiding us?"

"I don't know. We'll catch up to him eventually."

She shoved a stray piece of hair behind her ear. "You'd think if he was as interested in solving his son's murder as he says he is, he'd make himself available."

Annoyance stamped itself on her team member's handsome features and he nodded his agreement. "Do you have any other ideas?" he asked.

They headed toward their vehicles. "We've got the

flyers going up, we're still examining the phone..." She shook her head. "Any luck on finding the aide?"

"Fiona thinks she may have tracked him down in Maryland working at a gas station slash convenience store. He changed his name, but did a sloppy job of running. He even used his credit card. She had a local officer snap a picture of him to verify, but warned him not to spook the guy." He pulled the picture up on his phone and turned it so she could see the clean-cut young man in his late twenties. The next picture was of the same young man with longer, shaggy hair cleaning the glass door that led into the convenience store.

"He looks different, but it's definitely the same guy."

"That's what I think."

"That's quite a career change."

"He didn't want to be found, but doesn't have the skills to stay hidden. Like I said, he used his credit card early this morning."

"Are you going to talk to him?"

"Yes, are you up for a road trip tomorrow if I can clear it with Gavin?"

"Of course." Her phone rang. She glanced at the caller ID. "Speaking of Gavin."

His brow lifted. "Great. Maybe he's got something for us. Put it on speaker, will you?"

She did. "Hi, Gavin."

"Brooke, I know you're with Harland, but this is pretty important."

"Actually, the congressman wasn't here."

"What?" She could hear the frown in his voice.

"He decided he had a doctor's appointment at the last minute. Guess he forgot about it."

"He's been under a lot of stress, you know that." Now reproval echoed back at her.

She pursed her lips. "I know."

"He'll probably call you to reschedule."

"I hope so."

"So let me get to the reason I called. Cassie called me a few minutes ago. She said she may know which kid snuck out the night of the shooting." Cassie Danvers, the director of the All Our Kids children's home. And also Gavin's fiancée.

"Who was it?"

"Tommy Benson. He's been waking up with nightmares about a tall man with a gun."

"A tall man with a gun. Could be our shooter?"

"Could be. I think it'd be a good idea for you to go by there and talk to him."

"We've talked to him before and gotten nowhere."

"Be creative. You're a female. Maybe he'll feel more at ease talking to you since he's been living with Cassie and gotten pretty attached to her."

"And you."

"Yeah."

She smiled at the sudden gruffness in his voice. He'd definitely fallen for the kid. "All right, I'll talk to Cassie and find a good time to come by and see Tommy."

"Sounds like a plan. Keep me updated."

"Of course. One more question before we hang up."

"Yes?"

She explained the need to drive into Maryland to speak to the aide.

Gavin hesitated. "This has been a crazy case," he finally said. "You go and take Nicholas with you. When do you need to leave?"

"First thing tomorrow morning?" She looked at Nicholas and he nodded. "It's just about an hour over the state line into Maryland."

Gavin gave her the green light. "Keep me updated."

She hung up and looked at Nicholas. "This is a step in the right direction. Talking to the aide and finding out who the blue mitten belongs to. That little mitten found at the scene has been bothering me since the beginning. We've suspected all along one of the children from the home snuck out and saw something. Now one of them is having nightmares about a tall man with a gun."

"Sounds promising."

"I hope so. I'm feeling slightly desperate. I'll take just about anything at this point."

"Yeah. All right." He paused, then gave a short nod. "You talk to Cassie and the kids again. I'll see what time we can leave in the morning and come by and pick you up."

"Great." She thought she might give Jonas a call and see if he had any furry friends that might like to accompany her to the children's home.

Jonas sat parked at the school, in line to pick up Felix. He'd called Claire and told her not to get Felix. Jonas wanted to pick him up himself. While he waited, he checked his email and made a few calls. In the midst of checking his messages on his home voice mail, Jonas's phone beeped at him indicating an incoming call. When he saw that it was Brooke, he switched over, his heart picking up a little bit of speed. "Hi there."

"Jonas, do you have a moment?"

"Of course. I always have time for you, Brooke." She went silent and he wondered if he was too forward. Probably, then decided he didn't care. "What can I do for you?"

"I was wondering if you could get your hands on a couple of puppies."

"Mercy isn't enough?"

She gave a low chuckle. "I need to get a seven-year-old boy to trust me in record time."

"Ah, I see. One puppy would probably do it. Two would cinch it." He smiled. "I have a client whose German shepherd had a litter about five weeks ago. She's probably still got them. Want me to give her a call?"

"Absolutely. I know we were supposed to go out to the cliffs, but do you think you could get the puppies and Felix and meet me so I can take the puppies out to the foster home?"

He glanced at his watch, then at the school. "Sure. I can do that. Felix should be getting out pretty soon. Do you want me to meet you there?"

"Noooo." She drew the word out and Jonas lifted a brow.

"Okay, what's the deal?"

"You can just give me the puppies. The foster home is in a safe house until the threat to the children and Cassie is over. The location of the safe house is secret right now."

"I understand. I still want to go."

"I could take you, but I'd have to blindfold you," she joked.

"You don't trust me?"

"It's not that." She sighed and turned serious. "It's just that these kids could still be in danger. If someone finds out where they are, it could be tragic. When this case broke a couple of months ago and it came out that one of the children possibly saw something at the congressman's house, someone was desperate enough to set fire to a foster home. A *foster* home, Jonas. We just can't take any chances with their lives."

Jonas knew she was absolutely right. "I get it. So blindfold us."

She didn't speak for a moment and Jonas figured he'd caught her off guard. "Really?" she finally asked.

"Sure. I'd love to have a hand in helping the kids. Their lives have been disrupted enough already. Let Felix and me come." He cleared his throat. "It might do Felix some good, too. He hasn't exactly had a perfect life with his mom leaving, but regardless of what he thinks, he's got it pretty easy." She didn't say anything for a moment. "I hope your silence means you're thinking about it."

"Actually, I am. You just gave me an idea. Do you think Felix would be willing to help us?"

"What do you mean?"

"He's the same age as some of those kids in the home. If he comes in with the puppies, they'll swarm him. Little Tommy Benson might be more willing to talk to a thirteen-year-old than an adult."

"Felix'll do it."

"Are you sure?"

Jonas closed his eyes. Would Felix be willing or would he just have on his attitude? "No, but I'll ask him."

"Okay. While you're doing that, I'll have to call my boss and tell him what we're thinking. I'm guessing he'll be all right with it, but I still need to get his input. I'll also have to let Cassie know what's going on and clear it with her, too."

"Get permission and I'll work on Felix and the puppies."

"Please tell me you're being careful, taking extra precautions."

"I am. That's why I'm in the carpool line. No more

riding the bus for Felix until this is all resolved. I think there's an officer keeping an eye on us, too."

He heard her sigh. "I hate that it's necessary, but I'm concerned about Felix being a target."

"I share that concern. I've asked the principal to keep a close eye on Felix and warned her that there might be trouble."

A slight pause then, "That was smart. You're starting to think like a cop."

Realization hit him. "You'd already called the school."

"Yes, but I'm glad you're staying on top of things."

"Where do you want us to meet you?"

"At your office. I'm on my way."

"See you soon, Brooke."

She hung up and Jonas got on his phone. He knew just who to call so he wasn't worried about getting the requested pups. He just prayed he could do it without getting shot at or blown up.

Please, God, keep us all safe.

NINE

Brooke arrived at Jonas's office. While she waited, she scanned the area, looking for anyone who shouldn't be there. Satisfied she hadn't been followed, she called Gavin and received permission to take a blindfolded Jonas and Felix out to the children's home/safe house. "Sounds like a good idea. It's worth a try anyway."

"Great. Do you want to call Cassie and let her know or do you want me to?"

"I'm more than happy to call Cassie." Gavin's voice took on a warmth every time he said the woman's name.

"I kind of thought you would be."

Gavin's low chuckle made her smile. Once they hung up, her smile drooped. Would she ever have what Cassie had with Gavin? Even Adam Donovan had managed to fall in love during the investigation, with Lana Gomez, Rosa Gomez's sister. Adam's love for Lana had lit a fire under him in regards to finding out the reasons behind Rosa's death.

But unless Brooke allowed herself to open up and trust someone about her inability to have children, the possibility of finding love was nil.

What would Jonas say if she told him? He loved his son and she knew he would love to have more children.

Eight years ago he'd told her his dream to be married with a houseful of kids. It had been during one of their last conversations before she'd shut him out completely. She shook her head and shoved the painful memories aside. Or at least she tried to. The truth was, every time she was with Jonas, she couldn't help but long for what could have been. Or what could be now. She knew he was interested in picking up where they left off, but she could tell he was a bit leery of her, too.

She figured he wasn't real keen on setting himself up for another broken heart and she couldn't blame him. She knew she was giving off conflicting signals, but didn't seem to have any control over it. But if there was going to be hope for the two of them, she'd have to overcome her insecurities and fears.

His car pulled into the parking lot and she could see Felix in the passenger seat. He actually had a smile on his face, German shepherd puppies tucked under his chin. Felix and Jonas climbed out of the car and Felix juggled his armload. Jonas's eyes met hers and he gave her a slow smile. "Thanks for this." He blinked and she thought she saw moisture before he cleared his throat and looked back at his son.

The puppies licked and squirmed but Felix kept a firm yet gentle grip on them. His gaze met hers and his smile faltered. Then one of the puppies nipped his nose and he yelped, sounding a lot like his new friends. Brooke laughed and motioned for them to get in her vehicle. Mercy sat in the backseat in her kennel, her interest in the puppies clear yet controlled. Jonas opened the back door for Felix and he settled himself in. "Here's their box," Jonas said as he passed the cardboard through the door.

"I can hold them," Felix said.

"That's fine, just put your seat belt on, okay?"

The teen placed the puppies in the box while he fastened his seat belt. Brooke opened the kennel door and let Mercy investigate. The dog took her time sniffing and examining the squirmy canines. She gave them both a lick and settled back into her kennel, satisfied. Brooke shut the door and climbed behind the wheel. She started the car and pulled away, heading for traffic.

"Did your dad tell you what we need you to do, Felix?" she asked.

"He said you wanted me to use the puppies to get the kid to talk about what he saw the night that lawyer was killed."

"Right."

"But use some tact, will you?" Jonas asked. "Don't mention that night unless Brooke motions for you to say something. She's the one who's going to be asking the questions, okay?" Jonas asked.

"We already went over this. I'm not stupid, Dad."

"I know you're not, son." Jonas's sigh was heavy.

"I'm going to be close by," Brooke said, "so if I start talking, you kind of just focus on the puppies, all right?"

"I got it," Felix huffed. But Brooke could tell his attitude wasn't quite as hard as the first time she'd seen him. He fell silent during the short drive to the edge of town.

She pulled over to the side of the road. "Can you open the glove compartment and pull out those two blindfolds?"

Jonas did as she asked and passed one back to Felix. "Seriously?" he asked.

"Seriously," Brooke said.

The boy shook his head but didn't argue, just slipped it over his eyes. "So this is kind of like undercover work, isn't it?"

He wanted to sound bored, but she caught the thread of excitement in his tone. She smiled. "Yes, it is. You're going to go in, get Tommy's trust and help us get information. All you have to do is work with the puppies."

Felix sighed and she figured they were repeating themselves a bit much. She just didn't want anything to go wrong or for the whole plan to backfire and alienate Tommy instead of getting him to talk.

"Sorry, Felix," she said softly.

"Thanks," he said just as soft.

Jonas reached over and curled his left hand around her right. And she let him.

Until she noticed the vehicle staying steady just behind them. She snagged her phone and dialed Gavin. "I need some backup."

Jonas whipped off his blindfold. "What is it?"

"Behind us. No one followed me to your office, I'm sure of it."

"Maybe it wasn't you."

"What do you mean?"

"I mean what if someone followed me from Felix's school?"

He had a point. "I think it's time we got you and Felix some twenty-four-hour protection."

"What?" Felix blurted from the backseat. "No way. I don't want someone following me around all day. It's bad enough the school resource officer won't let me out of his sight and now you want to make it a full-time thing? No way. Dad, tell her no."

Brooke ignored Felix. She understood his concern,

but right now, she was growing more anxious by the second as the car behind her closed the distance.

Jonas could see Brooke's worry as her gaze snapped back and forth between the road and the rearview mirror. "Is help on the way?"

"Yes, but we may have to take care of things ourselves until it gets here."

"Take care of things how?"

"Hold on tight," she muttered. The car sped up. "He's going to try to run us off the road."

Jonas's adrenaline shot to maximum levels as he turned in the seat to catch Felix's frightened gaze. "Hang on, son." Felix nodded and held his precious cargo.

Jonas tried to get a glimpse of the driver, but the man had a mask on. The car crept closer. Closer. Jonas held his breath and gripped the door. He wanted to throw himself into the back and cover Felix with his body, but there wasn't room—or time.

And then the car following them tapped the rear bumper. The only reason they didn't spin out was because Brooke surged ahead.

"Grab something and hold on tight," Brooke shouted. She slammed the brake and spun the wheel. The car's back end swung out. Felix yelled and puppies yelped. The vehicle on their bumper flew past. Jonas caught a glimpse of it, then spinning trees.

Then they were stopped. An abrupt halt that jerked him against the seat belt. "Felix? You all right?"

The boy didn't answer. Jonas whipped his head around to see his son hovering over the two puppies.

Mercy had been knocked around, but stood and shook herself. "Felix?"

Felix looked up and Jonas flinched at the blazing anger in the teen's eyes. "I'm fine. Who is doing this? And why?"

"Hold that thought," Brooke said. "They're coming back."

"What?"

Sirens sounded and the black sedan slammed on brakes before reaching their vehicle, backed up and did a one-eighty turn. It sped off and Brooke sucked in a deep breath.

Nicholas pulled up beside her. Two other police cars swept past them and gave chase. She rolled her window down. "Pretty fancy driving there," he said.

"Maybe. I'm glad you showed up when you did."

"Did you get a plate?" Nicholas asked.

"No. I tried, but couldn't catch it."

"I think I caught the letter *X* and maybe the number 3," Jonas said.

Brooke looked at him, admiration glinting in her eyes. "Nice job."

He shrugged and glanced back at Felix. He'd released the puppies back into their box and sat with his arms crossed, the glare in his eyes not having lessened. "What is it, son?"

"They can't get away with this."

"They're not," Brooke said, her tone grim. "That's why we're doing everything we can to stop them." She sighed and rubbed her forehead. "All right, let me call Cassie and tell her we're going to have to do this another day—"

"What? Why?" Felix demanded.

Jonas frowned at the boy's tone, but Brooke lifted a brow. "You don't want to go home and chill out a little? You got knocked around a bit."

"I'm not hurt and in case you forgot, my home is a veterinarian's office right now, thanks to these people. And no, I'm not interested in chilling out. I want to find the dude that ran us off the road and tried to shoot us at the restaurant. If we don't find him fast, these things are just going to keep happening. We need to help so those kids can go back to living in their home and feel safe."

Jonas couldn't help his sagging jaw. This was his son? His surly, attitudinal teen who only thought about himself most of the time? He shot a look at Brooke, who looked more amused than anything. She gave a slow nod. "All right then. You're on. Let's get going." She looked at Nicholas. "Will you make sure we're not followed?"

"Absolutely. Officers are in pursuit as we speak."

"Good. Call me if you need anything else."

He nodded. "I talked to Jeffries and rescheduled our meeting. We're on for tomorrow morning first thing. At his house again."

She lifted a brow. "Is he going to be there this time?"

"He says he is."

Jonas watched the two converse and wondered if there was anything between them besides work. At first, jealousy flared, but then faded. He didn't get that from them. He got a sense of deep respect and friendship, but nothing more. He wanted to disregard the relief flowing through him, but couldn't. He also couldn't ignore the fact that Brooke was important to him. And the more he was around her, the more that grew. He wanted to find out if they had a chance this time around but was leery about getting his heart trampled on again.

She looked at him. "Blindfold, please."

"Seriously?" Felix asked from the back even as he did as asked without hesitation.

"Seriously."

TEN

Brooke glanced at Felix in the back and noted he still wore his half angry, half determined expression. Below the blindfold, his jaw jutted. As he grew, he would look more and more like Jonas. Not a bad thing in her opinion.

Jonas reached over and grasped her fingers once again and she let him. She needed the human contact, the reassurance that they'd survived yet another attempt on their lives.

He held her hand until she turned onto the mile-long drive that would lead to the safe house. Guard dogs patrolled the area and she had to show her ID at three different stops along the way. Finally, they reached the gate. A tall fence surrounded the property and she hoped the kids didn't have to stay there too much longer. They needed to be back in their original location near the Jeffries mansion in Flag Heights. For some of them, it was the only home they'd ever known. "You can take your blindfold off now."

"Wow, what is this place?" Felix had his blindfold off and his eyes bounced from one end of the complex to the other.

"The children's home," she said. "Are you ready to meet some people?"

"Yes." He still had determination stamped on his face, but now there was excitement present. He glanced at her. "Is the boy you told me about here?"

"The one that lost his mom?"

"Yes."

She shook her head. "No. He was for a little while, but then his aunt Lana was granted custody of him."

Felix pressed his lips together and took another look around as she parked. "Oh. I'm glad he has a mom again."

"Yeah, me, too," she said, wondering what was going through his young mind.

"My mom took off."

Jonas inhaled, but didn't say anything.

"I know," Brooke said. "I'm sure that hurts."

"Sometimes." He shrugged then nodded. "But I'm over her. It was her choice and if that's the kind of person she is, I'm probably better off without her. I'm ready." He stepped out of the car and grabbed the box with the puppies, balancing it against his stomach. Brooke told Mercy to stay. She didn't need her companion for this trip.

Together the three of them approached the front door. She saw the conflict in Jonas's eyes even though she thought he might be trying to hide it. He was processing his son's words and might need a minute. She moved slowly, taking in the area.

The home now sported a large play area with a swing set and other items necessary for a child to cut loose and have fun. Brooke raised her hand to knock, but before she connected with the wood, the door swung open. Cassie smiled her greeting. Brooke decided she was probably the only one who noticed the stress in the smile. "Hi, glad you could make it," Cassie said.

Brooke made the introductions. Felix ducked his head and studied the puppies until Jonas nudged him. He glanced up. "Hi."

"Welcome. Come on in and I'll introduce you to the troops." She led the way through the lobby and into a large area that had been converted into a den. Several children sat at a picnic table playing checkers. Four others who looked between the ages of eight and fourteen stood on a mat in front of the large-screen television and jumped up and down as a cart raced over a rail track. "That's good exercise," Brooke said.

"Fun, too," Jonas agreed. He rubbed his right shoulder and Brooke frowned.

"Are you all right?"

"Caught my sore shoulder against the door during your fancy driving." He shook his head. "I'm fine."

The puppies scrambled to get a foothold on the side of the box only to slide back to the bottom. Cassie peered over the edge and hooked one under his chubby belly. "Children, look who's come to visit."

Felix set the box on a side table and picked up the other pup.

The children gathered, their oohs and ahhs filling the room. Brooke scanned the room looking for the little boy she'd seen a couple of months ago. Her gaze landed on a brown-haired boy about seven years old. He stood back from the group, his face pale, eyes haunted. He blinked and started to leave. Brooke made her way to Felix and whispered in his ear. "There by the door."

Felix nodded and slipped through the children. Brooke wandered behind him. Jonas helped with the other puppy and children, but she could feel his gaze on her back. Felix held out the puppy to little Tommy. "Wanna hold him?"

Tommy's eyes went wide. "Me?"

"Sure. You looked like you wanted to."

"Why don't you sit on the couch?" Brooke asked. "Then you can hold him in your lap."

Tommy scooted to the sofa and climbed up. His little legs stuck off the end, the laces of one tennis shoe dangling toward the floor. He held up his hands. Through the side window, Brooke noted that Cassie and Jonas had managed to lure the other children outside. They all sat in a circle, legs spread to allow the puppy to run from one child to the other. Laughter floated through the screen door in the kitchen.

Brooke parked herself on the edge of the other couch and let Felix and Tommy talk. Felix chatted, keeping up a running monologue about all kinds of different things. The one Tommy seemed to respond to the most was football. The minutes passed. She didn't want to rush them, but when the puppy fell asleep in Tommy's lap, she nodded to Felix. Felix cleared his throat. "Hey, Tommy, I hear you're having some trouble sleeping at night."

Tommy froze. Brooke flipped through a magazine and pretended not to pay attention.

"Yeah." Tommy's soft whisper reached her ears.

"When my mom left, I couldn't sleep at night either."

"She left?"

"Uh-huh. She left when I was about three so I don't remember much about her but I keep thinking she's coming back." He glanced away. "I don't think she is, though."

"I'm sorry," Tommy said.

"Me, too." Silence hung between the two boys. She

wanted to jump in, but held herself still. She could see Tommy struggling with something, trying to make up his mind about whether or not he wanted to let the words out.

"My mom and dad died in a car wreck and I didn't have anyone else who wanted me to come live with them."

"That's tough."

Brooke thought her heart might simply shatter at the pain being shared by the two boys. She blinked away the tears and drew in a steadying breath. She had to keep it together.

Felix scratched the puppy's head and he wiggled awake, yawning. "Is that why you're having trouble sleeping?"

Tommy swallowed and lifted the puppy to his face. He spoke to the animal. "No, it's cuz of my dreams. I see him in my dreams."

"See who?" Felix asked. He scratched the puppy's back.

Brooke trembled. Finally. Felix met her gaze, his eyes wide. Brooke gave him a thumbs-up and he straightened his shoulders a bit before leaning closer and settling a hand on Tommy's shoulder. "You can tell me, Tommy. Who do you see?"

Tommy drew in a deep breath. "What's the puppy's name?"

Felix wilted a fraction, but Brooke gave him an encouraging nod.

"He doesn't have one," Felix said. "You want to name him?"

"I'd name him Buster if he was mine," Tommy said.

"His name is Buster then."

Tommy finally looked at Felix. "In my dreams, I see

the man with the white hair. He's big and scary and I don't like him. He had a gun and I'm afraid he's going to come get me and shoot me."

White hair? She couldn't take it anymore. "It's okay, Tommy, you don't have to be afraid of him," Brooke soothed as she moved over to sit beside the boy. The puppy stretched to lick Tommy's nose then scrunched back down to nibble on his fingers.

Tommy gave a low giggle that faded as fast as it appeared. He looked up at Brooke. "I don't?"

"No way." She pulled out her badge. "See this?"

"Yes."

"You know what it means?"

"It means you're a police officer?"

"That's right. Do you remember we talked once before?"

"Uh-huh."

"We're here and we're going to protect you so you don't have to be afraid. Can you tell me a little more about the man with the white hair?"

Tommy clamped his lips together and shook his head.

"Okay then, if I get someone to come, could you help that person draw a picture of the man you saw?"

Tommy shrugged. "Maybe. I mostly saw his back. In my dream, I mean."

"Right. In your dreams." Brooke pulled up a picture of Congressman Jeffries on her phone and showed it to the child. "Was this the man with the white hair?"

He studied the picture, his forehead creased. Then lifted his shoulder again. "I don't know." He looked away and swallowed hard.

Brooke slipped to her knees to look the little boy straight in the eye. She cupped his cheeks. "I want you to know that I'm very proud of you for telling Felix about the man with the white hair. You can go to sleep without worrying about him. He can't hurt you, okay? Even if you see him in your dreams, you can tell yourself that he can't hurt you." Tears filled his eyes, and he blinked until they ran down his cheeks. Brooke swiped them away and he leaned into her arms, the puppy squirming between them. "Okay?" she pressed.

He nodded against her shoulder. "Okay."

Brooke reached over and grasped Felix's fingers and squeezed. He returned the pressure and she looked up to see a glint of pride in his eyes.

She turned to find Jonas staring at them and thought she saw a hint of moisture in his eyes before he blinked and leaned down to pick up one of the children that had attached herself to his leg. Brooke hadn't heard them come in from outside.

The little girl was about four years old. She patted his cheek and stuck her thumb in her mouth. Jonas held her like a pro. Like a natural father. A wave of pain swept through Brooke so strong and so great it nearly knocked her to her knees.

He was a good father to Felix and deserved to have more children. As many as he wanted. And she could never be the one to give him that. She really needed to remember that.

Brooke straightened and cleared her throat. "All right, Tommy, thank you very much."

"Can I play with the puppy now?"

"Sure. Most of the other children are outside with his brother. You want to take him to join the fun?"

Tommy nodded and she helped him off the couch, the canine clutched in his little arms.

"You did great, Felix," Jonas murmured to his son. Felix let a smile slip across his lips before he managed to get it under control. He gave a careless shrug, not fooling anyone in the room with his nonchalant attitude. "I'd better go make sure they don't hurt the puppies." He sauntered out the door, but Brooke thought his back seemed straighter, his head held higher.

"Wow," Jonas breathed. "Was that my kid?"

"Yeah, he did great. Now I need to call Gavin and fill him in and get a sketch artist out here to work with Tommy." Nicholas stepped through the door. Brooke lifted a brow. "Everything all right?"

"I'm just here to make sure you get home safe."

"Great. I was just getting ready to call Gavin." She motioned him to follow her into one of the back rooms. "I don't want the others hearing this, but I want to put it on speaker so you can listen in."

The phone rang twice before Gavin picked up. "Gavin here."

The snap in his voice made Brooke pause for only a second. "Hi, Gavin. I've got an interesting development. Tommy said that the man he saw in his dreams not only had a gun, but white hair."

"Okay."

She drew in a breath. "The congressman has white hair."

Nicholas frowned at her boldness, but she just waited.

The silence from Gavin made her shift, her nerves tightening as she wondered if she'd gone too far. Then Gavin cleared his throat. "Right. He has gray hair, not white. And don't forget, he was shot, too. And it wasn't self-inflicted."

"I know, Gavin, I just…"

"So let's keep our focus where it needs to be."

"What if the congressman's son shot him?" Nicholas asked.

"What?"

"What if Michael was trying to defend himself against his father? What if the senator shot Michael, but Michael managed to get a shot off, too?"

Gavin went silent again and Brooke wondered if he was going to hang up. "Where's the gun, Nicholas? The weapon was never recovered, remember? Harland was lying in a pool of blood, practically unconscious when help arrived. The crime scene unit searched the scene. Law enforcement searched the scene. Your very own team members searched the scene. Are you suggesting that all of those professionals missed finding the weapon?"

Nicholas sighed. "Of course not, but—"

"And what about the car that was seen speeding away?"

Nicholas shook his head and Brooke could tell he wished he'd kept his mouth shut.

"It still could have been Erin Eagleton," she said. "Her necklace—with a charm with her initials—was found there and she's disappeared. She was Michael Jeffries's girlfriend. She's still a viable suspect."

"Yes, she is," Gavin agreed. "And there may be others we haven't discovered yet." He paused. "Look, I'm not as close-minded as I'm coming across. If Harland is involved in something, I want to know it. I just have a hard time believing it and don't want to miss finding the real killer because we're distracted and focused on the wrong trail."

Or we miss Harland being the killer because we're distracted and focused on the wrong trail, she thought. But decided against pointing it out. Nicholas met her gaze and she knew he was thinking the exact same thing.

* * *

Jonas watched out the window as the children and their guardians romped with the puppies. They looked happy and well-adjusted. Someone looking in from the outside wouldn't know the turmoil these kids had already experienced in their young lives.

When Brooke had hugged little Tommy and let him rest his head against her, a fierce longing had gripped Jonas. He wanted Brooke. Not just as a casual friend, but as a lifelong partner, someone to walk through the ups and downs of life with him. Someone to share more children with. Jonas headed down the hall to the room where she and Nicholas had taken their conversation.

Her low voice drew him to the door. "Yes, he's sure. White hair." She listened then shrugged. "I know the congressman has gray hair, and not white, but combine the other factors of a moon and it being at night, maybe his gray hair looked white to Tommy. I'm not trying to put words in his mouth, but maybe he's just not using the word *gray*, but that's what he means." She paused and her gaze met his even as she listened. He started to leave, not wanting to butt in where he shouldn't, but she held up a hand to stall his departure. "I get that, Gavin, but it's still possible Tommy is describing Jeffries. Could you set it up with Cassie to have a sketch artist work with him?" More silence, more pacing. "All right. Any word on Erin Eagleton? I still think she may be the key to solving this thing." A heavy sigh slipped from her. "Okay. Thanks." She hung up and turned to Jonas. "Well, we'll see what happens."

"Is he going to send a sketch artist?" Jonas asked.

She nodded. "As soon as he can set it up."

"You really think you'll get an accurate picture of the man Tommy saw that night?"

"I don't know, but I think it's worth a try."

The clamor of laughter and children's high-pitched voices reached them. "They're coming back in," Jonas said.

Felix held the two puppies. "It looks like it's going to rain."

Brooke nodded. "It's time for us to leave." Tommy raced forward and wrapped his arms around her waist. Brooke seemed startled for a split second before she dropped to her knees to hug him. "I'll come back soon, all right?"

Tommy nodded and Jonas thought Brooke might break down and cry. He took a step forward, but she blinked a few times then smiled at Cassie. "Thanks for letting us come."

"Of course. Anytime. Stay safe."

Tommy went to Cassie and she picked him up and planted a kiss on his cheek. Tommy smiled and leaned his head against her shoulder.

Brooke led the way out.

Felix climbed into the back of the vehicle, the box clutched closely to him, the playful puppies worn out and sound asleep. Brooke let Mercy out to take care of business. In short order, she was back at the vehicle. She jumped into her special spot and lay down, her head between her paws.

Jonas glanced at the clock. He'd been gone from the clinic a good while. "I'm going to check in with Claire."

"Sure. Just put your blindfold back on. I'll let you know when you can take it off." She glanced into the backseat at Felix, who rolled his eyes, but complied with a small smile. She didn't think he was terribly annoyed. Her phone buzzed and she glanced at the text. "Nicholas and Chase are going to escort us back to your office.

They're working in conjunction with the local police to set up a 24/7 guard."

He nodded. "All right. I'm not going to fight the idea. Felix might not like, it, but I'll do whatever I've got to do to keep him safe."

A groan came from the backseat. They ignored him. "And yourself," she said.

"Right." Jonas dialed his office's number and got Claire on the second ring as Brooke aimed the vehicle down the long drive.

"All is fine here," Claire assured him. "Slow, but fine. We had a couple of people who wanted to come in, but I explained you had an emergency."

He sighed. "I'm going to have to find someone to help out."

"Do you want me to put a call out for resumes?"

"Yes. And then start checking references. I need someone fast."

"What about Graham Brown? He called last week asking about an interview."

Jonas pictured the son of his father's best friend. "Is he back in town?"

"He is." Claire went on to list a few other possibilities and Jonas listened with half an ear. His mind kept circling back to the side mirror and wondering who could be behind the attacks on them. "Jonas?"

"Right. Sorry. I'm here. Just…call whoever you think best and set up interviews with me. I'll take it from there."

"All right, I can do that."

Jonas hung up, and peeked through the bottom edge of his blindfold to see the screen and dialed his home to check his voice mails. Three hang-ups. One from his mother who lived in Richmond, Virginia. Two from his sister who wanted to know what happened to his house.

He deleted those and went to the next message.

"Give me the phone or your kid is dead."

Click.

ELEVEN

Brooke heard Jonas's indrawn breath and looked over to see the part of his face beneath the blindfold drain of color. "What is it?"

He shook his head and hung up the phone. "Nothing. Not here," he said in almost a whisper. She glanced in the backseat. Felix had his head against the window, the blindfold covering his eyes. He gave all appearances of being asleep, but that didn't mean he was. She nodded. Whatever Jonas had heard on the phone he didn't want to repeat in front of Felix.

Nicholas and Chase had fallen in with her about ten minutes ago as she'd pulled onto the highway. One in front and one behind.

"Are the police going to be waiting when we get to the office?" Jonas asked, his voice low.

"Yes."

He nodded and she saw his Adam's apple bob. "Good."

"You checked your messages?"

"I did."

She looked in the rearview mirror. She thought maybe Felix really was asleep. "Felix?" He didn't move. "You can take off your blindfold now." Still no response. "You can take yours off, too, Jonas." He did. She glanced at his phone. "Do I need to take a listen?"

"Yes."

"Pull it up for me and hand me your Bluetooth." She put the device against her ear and Jonas played the message. "Give me the phone or your kid is dead."

She blinked. "Is that the only one?"

"Yes. There were some hang-ups before that."

"We'll see if we can trace the number," she said. She handed him her phone and his Bluetooth device, replacing it with hers. "Dial number 1 on speed dial." He followed her instructions, then handed the phone back to her. "Gavin. I need you to get a subpoena for the Parker residence phone records." In a low voice, with frequent glances at Felix in the backseat, she explained the threatening phone call.

"I'll get Fiona on it. What else?" Fiona Fargo, a whiz with any kind of technology, would have what they needed within a few hours. If that long.

"That's it for now." She started to hang up. "No wait, Gavin?"

"Yes?"

"I think we need to wear our Kevlar vests 24/7, Jonas and Felix included." She ignored Jonas's sharp look.

"It's come to that, has it?"

"I just want to be prepared."

"I'll have some waiting for you when you get to the office. We'll pass them in and they can put them on before they get out of the vehicle."

Sounded like a good plan to her. "Our ETA is about five minutes."

"Slow down and take your time. It'll be a little longer than that before I can deliver the vests."

"Got it." She lifted her foot from the gas. "See you soon." She hung up and told Jonas the plan.

"Vests?" he asked quietly.

"I think it's a needed precaution."

A sigh slipped from him and she couldn't help reaching out and patting his hand. "I'm sorry, I know it's an imposition."

He grasped her fingers before she could pull them back. "Yes, it is, but we'll manage. I just want Felix safe. That's the most important thing."

"You're a good dad, Jonas."

He tilted his head then turned to look in the backseat. "He's really in a deep sleep."

"Yes. He zonked out a few minutes after we left the children's home."

"I don't think he's been sleeping well. I hear him get up at night sometimes. If I ask him if he's all right, he says he's fine and gets back in bed, but I don't know. I don't know what to do for him."

"It's a tough time right now."

"Very." He paused. Then, "As for me being a good dad, I'm not so sure about that."

"I am."

He fell silent as he studied her. She resisted squirming and concentrated on driving.

Ten minutes later, Brooke followed Nicholas as he turned into the parking lot of the veterinary office. Chase swung in behind her. In the rearview mirror, she noticed Felix rubbing his eyes and looking around. Two squad cars took up two spaces. Jonas tensed and rubbed a hand down his face. "I guess this is where it all begins?"

She nodded. "You'll have full coverage from this point on."

"Oh man," Felix said. "Say hello to Big Brother."

"Stop," Jonas said mildly.

Another car pulled in beside them. Brooke tensed as the officers threw open their doors and walked toward the new vehicle. An arm extended out the window. The hand attached to the arm held a badge. Brooke relaxed a fraction. The badge disappeared back into the vehicle and two vests appeared. One of the officers took the vests and brought them over to Brooke. She passed them to Jonas and Felix. "Put these on."

"Seriously?" Felix uttered a disgusted sigh, but complied. "This is getting totally out of control, you know."

"Yeah," Brooke said. "I agree." She looked at the officer. "Any sign of unwanted visitors?"

"No. We've been canvassing the area and the property, doing perimeter searches and everything. It's been quiet."

"Well, we're here now so that's liable to change."

He lifted a brow. "Yes, ma'am. And we're ready."

Jonas and Felix had the vests on. Felix settled the puppies in his lap. He tapped the vest. "These are really going to help with that head shot. I'm impressed."

Jonas shot his son a frown. Brooke would have laughed if the situation hadn't been so serious. She caught Felix's eye in the rearview mirror and realized he was using sarcasm to deal with the stress. "You'd make a great cop, Felix. You're a natural."

He rolled his eyes, but not before she caught a flash of surprised pleasure.

With the other officers surrounding them, the vests not as much protection as she would have liked, they escorted Jonas and Felix into the building. Claire's eyes went wide and her mouth formed a silent O. Jonas gave her a sheepish look. "Hi, Claire."

"What is going on?"

"It's a long story."

"Obviously."

Brooke stepped forward. "Have you had any trouble while Jonas has been gone?"

"No, not a bit." She paused. "Then again, what do you mean by trouble?"

"Anything out of the ordinary? People coming in who shouldn't be here?" She glanced at Jonas then back to Claire. "People calling and leaving messages that make you uneasy?"

Claire frowned and shook her head. "No, nothing like that." Another pause. "Except maybe the guy who came in right after lunch."

"What about him?"

"He said he was an old friend of Jonas's and wanted to talk to him."

"What was weird about that?"

"When I told him Jonas wasn't here, but he could leave his name and number, he waved me off and said he'd find him later."

Brooke leaned in. "Can you describe him for me?"

She shrugged. "Around six feet tall, dark hair, dark eyes. Nothing that really stood out to me. Just an average-looking nice guy." She snapped her fingers. "Oh, and he had on one of those muscle shirts. He had a tattoo on his right shoulder."

"A muscle shirt in March?"

"The cold didn't seem to bother him."

"Do you have security cameras in here?" she asked.

"Yes."

"Let's look at the footage."

Ten minutes later, Jonas worked the mouse and brought up the video of a man entering the front door.

He walked up to the desk and Claire greeted him. They talked for less than a minute, then he turned and left. She looked at Jonas. "Do you recognize him?"

"No."

"I do," Felix said. She turned to find him staring at the monitor. He looked up and caught her gaze. "That's the guy that was out at the cliffs the day I found the phone."

Jonas shook his head. "This is getting beyond crazy."

Brooke nodded. "I won't argue that statement. Can you zoom in a little more on him?"

Jonas did and she stepped back. "Nicholas, take a look. Do you recognize him?"

"No. You?"

"No."

Nicholas and Chase both moved closer. Nicholas narrowed his eyes. "So the guy on the cliffs and the guy who came in here are one and the same," he said.

Jonas turned to look at Claire. "You didn't recognize him from anywhere? Ever seen him before?"

She paled. "No."

"Did he see the flyers on the desk?"

Her eyes shot to the stack of flyers still stacked. "I don't think so." She swallowed and gave a nervous groan. "I got so busy answering the phones, I never put the posters up."

"It's all right," Brooke soothed. "It's probably a good thing. If he'd seen the poster in the window and recognized the man in the picture, he might not have been so cordial." She pursed her lips and looked at Nicholas and Chase. "I think we need to really up the security around here."

"Or move them to a safe house," Nicholas said.

"No," Felix said. "I don't want to move to some safe

house. I've got school." Felix flashed them all a hard look and turned to head to the back of the office. Probably to their temporary room to sulk.

Jonas pressed his fingers against his eyes. Moving to a safe house would severely hamper his business—although being dead wouldn't do it much good either. And Felix's safety came first, of course.

He sighed. He didn't have a partner. He'd have to close down and that would put Claire out of work for however long it took to solve this. "Is there any way you can just keep us safe here? I think Felix would be all right at school, especially if he stays on campus and doesn't go anywhere alone." He shot his son a questioning look. Felix nodded, his expression earnest.

Brooke and her two coworkers exchanged glances. "It's possible," she said. "It would just be easier at a safe house."

"I understand that, but…"

"But?" Brooke asked.

"Ah! I don't know." Jonas ran a hand through his hair. If he made the wrong decision his son could be killed. "Give me a bit to think about it."

Brooke nodded. "Fine, just don't take too long."

Jonas paced, his thoughts swirling. He wanted to do the right thing by Felix. Had to do the right thing. As hard as it might be. Ten minutes was all it took to figure out what he needed to do. While he thought and paced, Brooke and Nicholas discussed the case and outlined several alternatives that might work to keep him and his son safe. For now…

Fine. A safe house. Or… He looked at Brooke. "Excuse me. I'm going to talk to Felix. I'll be right back." He walked to the back and found Felix sitting on the cot, eyes glued on the screen in front of him. "Felix?"

His son didn't hear him. Or was ignoring him. Jonas gave him the benefit of the doubt and walked over to tap the kid's tennis shoe. Felix pulled the earbuds down. "What?"

"Sir?"

"Sir?" Felix dutifully repeated with a miniature roll of his eyes. Jonas thought about snatching the Kindle from his hands and demanding an apology. But that would only add fuel to the fire. He controlled his impulse. He didn't have time to get into a power struggle with his son. "We need to make a decision and I want your input."

"I already gave my input. I'm not going to a safe house."

"Even if it means keeping you alive? Keeping me alive?"

That seemed to catch his attention. "Are you in danger because of me?"

"No. No, I…well, I don't know. It doesn't matter the reason behind the danger as far as this decision is concerned. What matters is keeping us safe." He sighed. "Will you think about it for a few minutes? And I mean put aside what you want and think about the danger, about being willing to do whatever it takes to stay safe."

Felix shook his head. "I'm not going to some dumb safe house. I'll run away."

Jonas wanted to hit something. Sometimes Felix's stubborn streak was enough to send him over the edge. "Think about it, Felix." Jonas got up to give his son some space. Give himself some space.

He returned to the front office to find Brooke and Nicholas still talking. When he stepped into the area, she lifted a brow at him. He shrugged and pinched the bridge of his nose. An idea formed. "What if I sent Felix to live with my parents for a while? What if we just removed him from the equation?"

"No way!" Felix said from behind him. Jonas spun to see that his son had come into the room. Now Felix moved backward, toward the door again. "I'm not doing that."

"Felix, your life is at stake here!" Jonas couldn't help the shout. He drew in another deep breath and closed his eyes, praying for some control. "You don't want to go to a safe house, I get that. This might be the best alternative. And it would get you out of the area."

"But—"

"I don't like it either, but we may not have a choice."

Felix glared. "You just want to get rid of me. Abandon me the same way Mom did."

The words stabbed dagger sized holes in his heart. His son knew exactly how to push the buttons that hurt the most. He stared at Felix, refused to let his son look away. "You know that's not true."

"All I know is that you want to send me away. I'm not going." He pushed open the door that led to the back, where the exam rooms and their temporary living quarters were. "Something good finally happened today and I felt—" He continued his backward walk and shook his head. "No. I'm not going. Why can't we just go home? I want to go home."

"We can't—"

"I know that." Felix's fingers curled into tight fists. "I know." He disappeared and Jonas bit his tongue on the words he wanted to fling at his son's back. Not words of anger, words of love, promises to never abandon him. But now wasn't the time. Not with the silent onlookers.

He sighed. "I'll talk to him again." As soon as his

blood pressure settled down. "If we go into a safe house, how long would we be there?"

"Unfortunately, there's no way to tell."

Jonas nodded. He shoved out of the vest and set it on one of the waiting room chairs. "Claire, why don't you go on home? I'll take care of the rest of the day."

His assistant glanced at the clock. "Not much day left anyway. I'll see you tomorrow?"

He hesitated. "Call before you come, all right?"

She frowned then shrugged. "Sure." She left with a wave.

Nicholas and Chase pulled Brooke to the side and another intense conversation ensued. Jonas figured Felix had had enough time to cool off and went to find him. His heart ached at his son's pain and he had to fix it. Not that he really believed he could actually "fix" it, but he had to try and do *something*. Convince him that going to a safe house wasn't an act of punishment, but an act of love. Brooke had told him he was a good dad. Now he needed to put those words into action and stand firm in his decision.

He glanced in at the two cots that formed an L-shape. His under the window, Felix's on the adjoining wall. No Felix. With a frown, he looked to the bathroom. The door was cracked. "Felix?" He crossed the room and peeked in the bathroom. "Hey, where are you?"

When he didn't get an answer, he opened the door to expose the whole bath area. Shower to the right, sink straight ahead, toilet and linen closet area to the left.

But no sign of his son.

Panic started to creep in, but before letting it grow further, Jonas wanted to check the rest of the building. He started with the exam rooms, then his office, the storage area and out through the swinging door connected to the kennel. Nothing.

He froze, his brain spinning. He turned to the door that led out to the back and found it unlocked.

He never left it unlocked.

A wave of nausea swept over him.

Felix was gone.

TWELVE

"Felix is gone," Jonas said from behind her. Brooke spun to find him standing in the doorway that led from the back.

"What?"

"He's gone." He rubbed a hand over his face, his weariness palpable.

"There's no way anyone could have taken him," Brooke said.

Jonas shook his head. "I don't think anyone took him. I think he left on his own. I'm pretty sure he slipped out the back door."

"That door doesn't sound the alarm when opened?"

"Not if the alarm is cut off. Felix knows the code."

She looked at Chase, who bolted for the door. Nicholas spoke rapidly on the phone, then hung up and followed after Chase.

"We'll search around here, you start calling friends," Chase said. He shut the door behind him.

Brooke snapped her gaze to Mercy who lay near a line of waiting room chairs. "She's not a search and rescue dog, but she's had some training. I'll see if she can pick up his scent."

"Felix slept on the cot in the back last night, the one on the left as you walk in the room."

"Good. Mercy, heel." The dog leapt to her feet and rushed over to plant herself at Brooke's side. Brooke led the way to the back with Jonas and Mercy at her side. In the room, she stopped at the cot, snagged the pillow and held it to Mercy's nose. "Find him, girl." The dog sniffed, nudged it and sniffed again. Then her nose went to the floor, back into the air. She darted out of the bedroom, down the hall and to the back door.

Brooke pushed it open. Mercy darted out. Her nose quivering, she led them to the edge of the property that backed up to another building. Here she stopped, whined, sniffed the ground, tested the air then sat. "She lost the scent."

"What does that mean?"

"Felix could have gotten into a car. Do any of his friends drive?"

"None that I know of. He's thirteen. If he's got older friends, they'd be from school and I don't know about them." He paused. "Actually, some of the guys on the track team drive, but he doesn't hang out with them."

"That you know of."

"Yes." He paced three steps then back. "What if he was picked up by the people after him? What if they were watching, just waiting for a chance to grab him?"

Brooke hated that he voiced her thoughts. She'd been hoping he wouldn't think about that. "Let's just pray he contacts you soon or that we find him." She looked around. "Your security cameras won't reach this far, will they?"

"No."

Brooke led Mercy back to the office and let her inside. "We need to find him," Brooke said to Jonas.

"Would you call the friend he was with the night some-one broke in?"

"Of course." He reached for his phone, his face pale, jaw tight. She figured he might be experiencing a wide range of emotions. Anger for Felix for leaving, fear his decision would result in tragic consequences. Indecision about what to do next.

Brooke frowned and set out a bowl of water for Mercy. The dog lapped it up.

While Jonas spoke on his phone, Brooke called the local PD and requested a BOLO be issued. It was a long shot, but sometimes they got good response from a Be On the Lookout order. She snapped a picture of the framed photo on Jonas's desk. Felix stared at the camera, a half smile on his lips as if he had secrets to share, but wasn't interested in doing so. She sent that to Fiona. "Get this to all the officers and tell them to be on the lookout for him, will you?"

"Consider it done." Fiona disconnected without both-ering to say goodbye.

Jonas hung up and shook his head. "They haven't seen him."

"Can you think of where else he would he go?"

"No. I don't know." He started his pacing again, from one end of the office to the other. "I can't think. Travis is the only friend he really hangs out with. They're on the track team together and while he and the rest of his teammates get along, they don't do much together. He has some acquaintances from the youth group, but he's not close enough to any of them to go to one of their houses. At least I don't think so." Guilt flashed across his features and he came to a stop in front of her. "And that's my fault. The lack of friends at church."

"Don't go much?"

"No. Not much."

"We need to call them anyway, just to be sure." He nodded. She remembered his strong faith back when they worked together at the kennel and the fact that he always said the blessing before meals. His faith wasn't totally gone. "What happened?"

He gave her a sad smile and a shrug. "Life." He clasped his hands between his knees and looked down. "I think I need to reassess that, though. Make God a priority in my life again." He looked up. "And not just because trouble has found its way into my house. I've actually been thinking about it for a while, feeling… convicted might be the right word."

"I understand that." And she did. She struggled every day with questions for God. Some she asked, some she ignored. Some were just too painful. But she refused to shove Him aside, instead choosing to believe His promises that He had a plan for her future. If she didn't believe that, she wouldn't be able to function on a daily basis. But that didn't mean she couldn't understand what Jonas was saying. Feeling.

"Only now I may have waited too long and Felix is going to suffer the consequences," he said.

"I don't think God works that way. Felix isn't in trouble because you put God on the back burner. He's in trouble because of his choices—and the choices of those after him."

Jonas looked thoughtful and worried all at the same time. "Yes, I know you're right. It's hard not to let those thoughts intrude, though."

Jonas stayed quiet, then pulled his phone from his pocket. "I'll call the school and ask the principal to get a list of any older kids that Felix has been seen hanging around with."

Before he could punch in the number, Nicholas opened the front door and stepped inside. Jonas hesitated, waiting, his eyes hopeful. "Anything?"

"Nothing."

Chase brought up the rear and shut the door behind him. "We took the car and searched up and down the road. No sign of him, I'm sorry."

Jonas slumped against the wall and stared at his feet.

"Hey, do you need to sit down?" Brooke asked.

He lifted his head, his eyes weary, face drawn. "No. I need to find my son."

"We'll find him, Jonas." She stepped forward and rested a hand on his arm. "Chase, could you call the school and get any information about students Felix may have hung around with who have cars?"

"Of course." Chase stepped outside to make the call.

"We've got to have more coverage on this place," she said to Nicholas while Jonas held the phone to his ear and paced the floor. He went to the window every other pace and looked out only to resume his going-nowhere journey of back and forth.

"You know as well as I do it's a manpower issue, not a willingness issue," Nicholas said.

"I know that, but we're talking about people's lives. If this is related to Michael Jeffries and Rosa Gomez's deaths and the congressman's shooting, then we know they won't hesitate to do whatever it takes to get rid of them. The thug who is after them has already set fire to a children's home, Nicholas. He's desperate." She paused. "Or just has no conscience. Or both."

"I know that," Nicholas said, "but we're going to have to get Gavin's, maybe even Margaret's, clearance on it." He ran a hand through his blond hair. "That phone call I got before we went to look for Felix was from Harland Jeffries. He's ready to talk to us first thing in the morning."

She noticed Jonas had hung up and was listening in. "I'll have to go, Jonas," she said.

"Of course you will. You can't babysit me 24/7."

"I don't consider it babysitting," she said and frowned. She didn't want him to think she felt obligated. "I care about you. I want to make sure you're safe." His eyes warmed and he cleared his throat but didn't look away from her. She was the first to drop her gaze as heat started to rise from the base of her neck. She could almost see Nicholas's amusement at her discomfort. That was fine. He could be entertained as long as he kept his mouth shut. "There will be cops all over this place, watching out for you and looking for Felix."

He nodded then straightened as his eyes sharpened. "Wait a minute. Felix said he wanted to go home."

"What?"

"Right before he walked out. He said he wanted to go home. What if he did?"

Brooke frowned and shot a look at Nicholas. "It's possible. You only live about a mile from here, right?"

Nicholas nodded. "Absolutely. Let's go."

They made their way to the cars and headed to Jonas's house. Less than two minutes later, they pulled to the curb and climbed from the vehicles. Brooke placed a hand on Jonas's arm to keep him from bolting to the house. "Give me the keys and stay in the car, will you?"

"You think someone else might be in there besides Felix?"

"I don't want to take a chance."

He fished the keys from his pocket and handed them over to her. "I don't like this," he muttered. "I don't like it at all. You could get hurt. I should—"

"I have the training and the gun. It's better this way."

He almost smiled through the tension and worry over his son—not to mention the fact that it appeared someone wanted him dead. "Right. But I'm staying behind you."

She started to protest, saw the look on his face, the set of his jaw, and stopped. "Stay behind, close but not too close."

He nodded. She walked up the front steps and handed the keys to Nicholas. She could hear the huge fans blowing on the inside. The restoration company had come and gone. She and Nicholas positioned themselves on either side of the door and had their weapons drawn. She could feel Jonas behind her. Still, tense, desperate to find Felix safe. Adrenaline pounded through her. *Please let him be here, God.*

Nicholas unlocked the front door and twisted the knob. The door swung in. Brooke stepped over the threshold, weapon ready. The smell of smoke still hung in the air, but it wasn't overpowering. At least she could breathe. The foyer was clear. Nicholas stepped around her and headed up the stairs. Concerned, she watched him, knowing the roar of the fans would mask any sound an intruder might make. Then again, they would hide their arrival, too.

She looked to the left. To the right. Nothing so far. Jonas slipped inside and moved to stand with his back to the wall.

She waited for Nicholas's call as she moved into the kitchen. Neat, orderly, nothing disturbed. She backed out and moved into the den, noticing Jonas still in the same place, hands clenched, a muscle in his jaw jumping.

In the den, the smell was stronger. Cleaning solution and old smoke. She ran a hand over the couch. Still slightly damp.

"Clear!"

"Clear!" Brooke echoed. "Did you find any evidence of Felix?" She shouted to be heard.

"No." He came down the stairs. Brooke slid her weapon into her holster. "You?" he asked.

"No," she sighed, worry ramping her pulse back up. "He's not here."

"Nothing?" Jonas asked.

She turned to face him as he stepped into the den. "No. Sorry."

He blew out a sigh and shook his head. "Okay, I'm staying here tonight."

She frowned. "I don't know if that's such a great idea."

"Felix wanted to come home. He may wait until nighttime to do that. I'm going to be here in case he does."

She narrowed her eyes. "Fine, but you're not staying here alone."

Nicholas rubbed a hand over his chin. "I've got him covered. I'll take the night shift."

"Good," Brooke said. "Because I think we may be dealing with more than one person. We've got Tommy's white-haired man with the gun and the person who broke into Jonas's house."

"I agree. It's definitely more than one person."

"And unfortunately, I don't think the people causing all of this trouble bother to sleep."

THIRTEEN

Brooke was ready to go by seven the next morning. Harland Jeffries had called to cancel, citing an emergency meeting. She wasn't happy with the man, but decided that worked with their schedule a little better. They planned to track down the missing aide. She'd checked in with Nicholas after a restless night's sleep, worrying about Felix and Jonas.

"Felix called his dad about three hours ago. He told him he was sorry for all the trouble, but he wasn't going to let his dad send him away and was sorry for causing all the trouble and worry."

Brooke sighed. "He doesn't get it, does he?"

"Nope. But I'm glad he's just a runaway at the moment and not a pawn in this deadly game."

"I'm glad, too. I just hope he either comes home or the good guys find him."

"We had officers looking for him all night and no one reported any sign of him. Overall, it was a quiet night, but I'm not holding my breath that the calm is going to last."

Brooke agreed. She just figured it meant the people after Jonas and Felix were busy plotting their next move. The idea set her nerves on edge.

She climbed into her vehicle and Mercy hopped in the back. Nicholas would leave Max behind with Jonas. She drove to Jonas's house, which was only about fifteen minutes from her own. When she pulled to the front curb, Nicholas was standing on the porch waiting. She rolled down the window. "Ready?"

"Yep. We have an extra passenger, though."

Brooke frowned. "Who?"

"Jonas is going with us."

She lifted a brow and felt a twinge of happiness race up her spine at the thought of just being in his presence for most of the day. "All right. Why?"

He walked out to stand next to her car. "I don't feel comfortable leaving him here." He shook his head. "He didn't get much sleep last night. He's worried sick about his kid."

"I don't blame him. I'm worried, too."

"If he stays here, he's going to think and brood about it. Might even take it upon himself to do something stupid like go looking for him."

"Thereby making himself a target," Brooke murmured.

"Exactly."

She nodded. "Can't hurt for him to come along. And we'll be one of the first to know if something happens with Felix." Good or bad, but she left that part out. She glanced in the back. "There's room."

"It's just an hour or so. Pull up tight to the garage and we'll get him in. He can ride in the front with you. I'll make myself at home in the back with the dogs."

"You sure?"

"Yes. I'm going to grab a nap on the way there. Chase is going to tail us to make sure we're not followed and there aren't any more incidents like yesterday's."

"Sounds like a good plan." Brooke pulled to the garage. Jonas must have been watching. The electric door opened and she pulled all the way in as he had his car parked on the far side. Jonas slipped around to the passenger seat and Max and Nicholas settled themselves into the back with Mercy. "Good morning," she said.

"Morning."

He looked so tired. Her heart went out to him. "I won't ask if you slept."

"I kept thinking the phone would ring. Or Felix would walk in the door." He shook his head. "Or something."

She wanted to hug him, to reassure him. "I'm sorry."

"Thanks."

She glanced in the rearview mirror and caught Nicholas's eyes. "Does he know we're coming?"

"No. Didn't want to give him a chance to run."

Brooke nodded. With each passing mile, she was more and more aware of the presence of the man beside her. Nicholas dozed off about fifteen minutes into the drive and a silence fell between her and Jonas.

She noticed he kept looking at his phone and figured he was hoping for a call or a text either from Felix or *about* Felix. Chase stayed with them all the way, sometimes falling back, but never letting her lose sight of him. Her nerves stayed stretched tight. After everything that had already happened, she expected another attempt and stayed on guard, waiting for it to happen. She knew Nicholas would be awake and ready to act. All she would have to do is call his name. This case had them all learning to snag rest when the opportunity presented itself and to be ready to be alert and in action within the blink of an eye.

"We're almost there," Jonas said.

"Yes. Not too much longer." She glanced at him. "There are officers on your house. If Felix comes home, someone will be there to protect him."

"I know. I feel a bit guilty that I'm not there myself. Or at the office. Or out looking for Felix. That's really what I should be doing."

Nicholas had called it. "Your safety is our priority. You have to stay safe and be there for Felix when he comes home."

"Right."

Brooke pulled to an intersection with a four-way stop. Nicholas stirred in the backseat. "Guess nothing happened."

"Not yet."

He grimaced at her fatalistic response.

She checked the GPS and turned right, then the next left. The gas station sat tucked at the far end of the parking lot. Two people pumped gas. One car sat in front of the front door. "Kind of slow on this Tuesday morning, isn't it? Hope this guy is working," Brooke said.

"He's working," Nicholas said. "I called and said I had a package to deliver. I asked if someone would be there to sign it. The person said Jake would be."

"I take it Jake is the former aide's new name?"

"Yep. According to Fiona."

"God bless Fiona."

Nicholas smiled.

Jonas nodded to the entrance. "You're right when you say it's pretty slow, but people are here."

"Stay here, all right?" Brooke asked.

"I'll be a good boy." He growled the words, making Brooke wonder at his sincerity. She frowned at him and his face softened. "I will. I won't do anything stupid, I promise. I'll just stare at my phone and pray Felix calls me."

Brooke reached over and tucked his hand into hers for a squeeze. "I know it's hard, Jonas. Just don't give up or stop praying."

"I'm not."

Brooke nodded. Nicholas was already out of the car and waiting. "We'll leave the dogs here and be right back. Hopefully this won't take too long."

Before Brooke shut the car off, Jonas rolled the window down. Brooke cut the engine, slipped out of the driver's seat and shut the door. He checked his phone and sighed at the screen. He knew wishing Felix would call wouldn't make it happen, but he couldn't seem to help himself. He looked up to see a young woman carrying a toddler come through the double glass doors. "Don't bother going in there," she said with a roll of her eyes. "Whoever's supposed to be working must have decided he didn't want to anymore. It's a shame leaving the store open like that. Stuff's going to get stolen if the owner doesn't do something fast."

Brooke flashed her badge. "Do you know the owner?"

"No, I'm just passing through. I paid for my gas at the pump, but wanted to get a couple of drinks. I hollered for someone to let 'em know they had customers, but no one came out." She shook her head and walked to her car.

Brooke frowned, not liking where this was going. She caught Nicholas's eye. "I'll check out the store."

Jonas straightened, his attention on the three people, their words filtering through his mind. Where was Paul Harrison aka Jake?

Nicholas waved to Chase, who'd parked at the edge of the lot near the entrance.

"What's up?" he asked.

Brooke explained. Chase pulled his weapon. He and Nicholas entered the store. Over the next several seconds, two more customers filed out. Brooke talked into her phone. Jonas opened the car door, thought about getting out, then shut the door without moving. He'd promised to be a good boy.

"What's going on?" he called to Brooke.

She walked back over to the car. "They're doing a sweep of the store."

Jonas nodded but frowned. "It seems like trouble is following too close or is one step ahead."

"Yes," she murmured. "It does."

She opened the back door and let the dogs out. "Heel."

They sat at her side, eyes on her face, waiting for the next order.

Jonas waited, too. Nicholas finally appeared, weapon holstered and shaking his head. "I didn't find a body. Found some blood on the wall and the floor." Chase came out after him.

Brooke nodded. "Let the dogs search."

Nicholas nodded and Jonas stepped out of the vehicle. Brooke shot him a frown. He leaned against the door and paused to see what would happen next. Brooke led Mercy to the door of the convenience store. The dog shifted impatiently, quivering with the excitement of the hunt that was about to begin. Brooke opened the door. "Seek."

Mercy shot into the building. Jonas moved closer so he could see.

Nicholas let Max loose and also commanded the

dog to seek. Nicholas followed him. Chase held his K-9 back. After a second of sniffing and getting his bearings, Max took off around the side of the building.

Jonas wanted to help, to do something besides just wait. He slipped around to watch Max, who went straight to the Dumpster at the back of the store.

Brooke kept an eye on Mercy, who was doing her best to find something. In the store's back room, Mercy sniffed the blood spatter on the floor, then the wall. She went to the exit and sat. Brooke opened the door and let the dog out. Mercy bounded into the sunshine, her nose quivering, hind end wagging.

Brooke spotted Nicholas at the Dumpster. Max sat and barked three times. Mercy stayed on her trail, straight to the Dumpster. She sat next to Max and barked.

Brooke's gaze met Nicholas's. "We need to look in there."

"I'm afraid so."

She grimaced. "I'll do it." Jonas came around the corner and Brooke's heart clenched at the lines on his face. "You should have stayed in the car," she told him.

"Maybe." But he didn't move.

Brooke grabbed two wooden crates that had been set next to the Dumpster. She stacked one on top of the other and then climbed up.

"You want me to do that?" Nicholas asked.

"I've got it." She'd been with the team long enough that she no longer felt she had to prove herself by taking on some of the more distasteful aspects, but Brooke had promised herself when she started, she'd never back down from doing whatever it was that needed to be done. She knew Nicholas would do the Dumpster diving if she asked. She also knew he knew she wouldn't ask.

"Be careful," Jonas murmured.

Brooke shoved open the lid of the Dumpster. The smell hit her and she jerked back with a grimace. The crates wobbled and she grabbed the edge of the bin to steady herself. Jonas reached out and gripped the wooden piece, righting it and holding it. Nicholas did the same.

"What is it?" Nicholas asked.

She shot him a dark look. "It stinks. Hand me the gloves, will you please?"

She reached down to snag the gloves Nicholas held up to her. She snapped them on, then turned back to the trash. With one finger, she pushed aside the large piece of cardboard that covered the heap. And stilled. She looked down at the men. "I found Mr. Harrison," she said.

Jonas sucked in a deep breath, but still didn't budge. "What happened to him?" he asked.

"Shot. Once in the chest, which probably explains the spatter on the wall and the floor inside. And, if the evidence beneath him is any indication, once in the head after they dumped him in here." She grimaced and climbed down. "I'm guessing whoever killed him didn't want him found too quickly and this was a handy spot to stash the body."

Nicholas shook his head and pulled out his phone. "Should have cleaned up the blood if they didn't want someone looking for him," he muttered. "I'll get a crime scene unit here."

"How did they know?" Jonas asked. "How did they know you'd come looking for him?"

"I don't know," Brooke said, her heart aching for the loss of the life of the young aide. It was wrong. Needless. If only he'd asked for help, told someone what had him so scared. Instead, he'd run away and now he was dead. "However, what I do know is that it's time to catch a killer before someone else dies."

She saw sheer fear sweep across Jonas's face and knew he was thinking of his son—a thirteen-year-old boy, out there by himself being chased by people who didn't hesitate to kill to get someone out of their way.

And Felix had definitely gotten in their way.

She pulled the gloves off and trashed them. "What now?" Jonas asked.

"Now we wait," Brooke said as she pulled a bottle of hand sanitizer from her pocket and used it liberally.

Thirty minutes later, two black vans pulled into the parking lot. "The crime scene unit's here."

"So is the medical examiner," Nicholas said.

Brooke nodded. "We'll let them take over for now."

"I think it's time to ask the congressman about his missing—and now murdered—aide," Chase said.

Nicholas turned to Jonas. "I think it's time you got back in the car. We're going to be here awhile."

Brooke shook her head. "We need to get this case solved or we're going to wind up with one crime scene after another."

FOURTEEN

Jonas took the bag of groceries from Nicholas. "Thanks." It had been a long day. He was wiped out from the fact that he'd been there when they'd found the aide, compounded by the worry that wanted to eat through his heart about Felix. He should have just crashed into the nearest bed. Instead, he found himself cooking dinner.

Nicholas shrugged out of his coat. "I didn't want you out and about going shopping. This is much safer."

"Anything on Felix?" Nicholas took the bag into the kitchen and set it on the counter. He'd turned the fans off for the moment. He'd turn them back on when he didn't have to carry on a conversation.

"No, he's dropped off the radar." Nicholas frowned.

Brooke stepped into the kitchen and grabbed a head of lettuce and a knife from the block near the sink. "I'd suggest that we put his face on the news and bring the public into it, but I'm afraid that would only alert the people after him." She started chopping the lettuce and Jonas grabbed a bowl for her to put it in. "Let's see if the cops can locate him first."

"I'm hoping he comes home," Jonas muttered.

"Yeah." She stopped her chopping and shot him a

sympathetic look. He shook his head and looked at his phone. Something he'd been doing on a regular basis even though he had the ringer turned up to maximum volume.

Together they worked and soon had a good meal on the table. Nicholas joined them, but left to monitor the perimeter with Max after cleaning his plate. Mercy lay on the kitchen floor, ears flicking, nose twitching.

Jonas took his last swallow of tea and set the glass on the table. "Felix is upset, I get that, but to take off like this when he's in danger..." He shook his head.

"He's definitely upset," Brooke said. She reached across the table and snagged his fingers.

He pulled his chair around next to hers. Close enough to allow their shoulders to touch. "I need a different topic of conversation."

"Okay. What do you want to talk about?"

"Tell me what I did wrong. What made you just decide to quit seeing me?"

She stood, her agitation clear. "It wasn't you, Jonas, it was me. Me!" Mercy rolled to her feet, her eyes on her mistress. Jonas didn't move. Brooke paced from one end of the kitchen to the other. Mercy watched her and whined. Brooke stopped and dropped her head, her chin resting on her chest. She took in a deep breath.

Jonas blinked at her distress. "I'm sorry, Brooke, never mind. It's not important, I guess."

"You're an amazing father. You have a depth of love in your heart for Felix that I can only imagine."

"What does that have to do with anything?"

"Do you want more children?"

"Of course. One day." He paused. "Why?" Then his eyes went wide and before she could answer, blurted, "You don't want kids?"

"I want them, I just can't have them."

He froze at her quiet whisper. "What?" She still didn't look at him. He went to her and placed a finger under her chin to lift her eyes to his. "You can't have children?"

"No." A tear slid down her cheek. "I had a hysterectomy when I was eighteen. I was in the car wreck that killed my parents. I was bleeding, they had to do surgery and…" She shrugged away from him, crossing her arms across her stomach, turning her back to him. "I can't have children."

"So you pushed me away because of that? Why didn't you just tell me?" Anger surged through him and he fought to control it, to keep his tongue from releasing the words trembling on the edge. "Do you know how I agonized over what I could have done to send you running?"

"Jonas—"

"I lay awake at night wondering."

"I didn't—"

"I racked my brain trying to figure out how I'd offended you." He stared at her. "Did you really think so little of me that I would reject you because you couldn't have kids?"

"Why not? That's what Carl did."

He went quiet. Then sighed. "Who?"

"My boyfriend at the time of the accident. He was nineteen. I was eighteen. We were in love, you know, going to get married and have a houseful of kids." She rolled her eyes and shook her head. "I came to in the operating room to find out my parents were dead. My grandparents were devastated, but they assured me they would be there for me and we would all get through this."

"I remember your grandparents and how close you were."

"Are. We still are."

"But?"

"But they didn't know that Carl was coming to visit me. He overheard them talking about my hysterectomy and how they were going to tell me that I would never have a child."

Jonas closed his eyes. "And he told you."

"Yeah." She sniffed and swiped her eyes. "He tried to be gentle about it, of course, said he was sorry about my parents, sorry I'd been hurt, but he couldn't be my boyfriend anymore because who knows where we might end up. He wanted to be with someone who could have kids one day. He kissed my forehead and walked out."

Jonas rubbed his eyes. "I'm so sorry, Brooke. But I wasn't Carl, not then and not now."

"I know," she whispered. "I know, but the hurt was just too deep, the scars too many. The day I walked out of that hospital, I swore off relationships. I loved dogs, I loved the law." She glanced at Mercy, who'd dropped back to the floor. "I loved my job. I couldn't let you distract me. I'm sorry. When I realized how you felt—"

"You ran."

"As hard and as fast as I could go." She sighed. "A few months later, I almost worked up the courage to tell you."

"But?"

"But when I came back to talk to you—"

"What? When? You never came back."

"I didn't approach you. I was talking to your former partner and he told me a little about what you were doing. Like the fact that you were continuing to build your life and your career and raising a young son." She shrugged. "I told myself you didn't need me upsetting your apple cart again. So I left before you got back to the office, threw myself into my job and told myself to forget about you."

"And did you?"

She swallowed hard, but didn't look away. "No."

"He never told me you were there."

She shrugged. "I didn't tell him not to say anything. He probably just forgot."

"Well I didn't forget about you. I loved my wife." He frowned. "At least I thought I did. I did my best to be a good husband to her, a good father to Felix, but…" He sighed. "I don't know what went wrong, to be honest. I worked a lot of hours building the vet business. She got lonely and found someone else. After she left, I told myself no more relationships. No more falling in love." He gave her a crooked smile. "But I couldn't seem to help it. I found myself thinking about you. How I'd let you go without too much of a fight and I regretted it."

Her eyes bounced to his mouth then back up. A flush worked its way into her cheeks. He lowered his head and touched his lips to hers. At her response, he moved to deepen the kiss.

And guilt hit him.

He stood and shoved his chair away. "I'm sorry."

She blinked and looked away. "No. I am."

"I need to focus on Felix. I can't—"

"I understand, Jonas. Stop. It's okay."

He nodded and raked a hand through his hair.

Brooke buried her face in her hands and blew out a sigh. When she looked up, he tried to decipher the expression in her eyes, but couldn't figure it out. Anger? Sadness? Resignation? Regret? She stood. "All right. It's time for me to get out of here. There's an officer on the curb. Nicholas has done several sweeps and it's clear for now."

"I feel like I should be out there looking for him. I don't know if I can handle sitting around and waiting." When he caught himself looking at his watch again, he grimaced.

Brooke walked to the door. "You really don't have a choice, Jonas. I understand your conflict, but what if Felix comes looking for you?"

He nodded. "I know. I'll stay put." For now.

She hesitated, her hand hovering over the knob. She looked as though she might say something, then just gave him a weary smile. "Good night, Jonas."

"'Night."

She slipped out the door, her words now echoing in the stillness. *I can't have children.* He walked to the window and spotted the officer on the curb. Brooke pulled away and disappeared down the street. Jonas felt his heart go with her.

FIFTEEN

Brooke let Mercy into the house after a short run around the block. Her mind spun in an endless loop, replaying the "almost kiss" over and over until she wanted to bury her face in her pillow and scream. Why had he done that? What had he seen in her expression to indicate she wanted him to kiss her?

She nearly laughed out loud at that last silent question. She knew exactly what he'd seen. She might as well have stamped *Kiss Me* written across her forehead.

She groaned and dropped onto the couch. It was going to be a long night. She should have volunteered for Jonas's guard duty. At least that would have given her something to do besides stare at her walls and wish she'd grabbed Jonas and given him the kiss of his lifetime. But she hadn't done that.

And frankly, she was glad she hadn't. Sort of. She understood the guilt that he'd been feeling. His son was out there, angry, upset—and a target. He couldn't be having a romantic moment while that was happening. She got that. Not only that, but she kept pushing him away. Only tonight they'd almost kissed. Well, they had kissed. A light kiss that could have been so much more.

She rubbed her eyes. How confused he must be with

her words and actions contradicting each other. She sighed. She wasn't doing it on purpose, she was just as conflicted with herself as he probably was.

Her gaze fell on her grandmother's Bible. It sat in its usual spot in the center of the coffee table. Her grandparents had loved her. Had raised her to love God and to seek His will for her life. But every time the subject of her and marriage and children came up, bitterness accompanied it. Since she didn't want to be bitter, she often just refused to think about it.

But now she had to.

She'd told Jonas why she'd pushed him away almost eight years ago and he'd been angry. Hurt. Betrayed. Had she been wrong to keep that to herself and not explain her actions?

Definitely.

She picked up the Bible and let it fall open. Her grandmother's handwriting jumped out at her. Right before Brooke's grandparents had moved to Florida to retire, her grandmother had placed the Bible in Brooke's hands just before they'd pulled away from the closing at the lawyer's office. "Read it, Brooke. Let God be your comfort."

Be my comfort, God. Show me how to lean on You and not be bitter.

She closed the Bible, stood and walked to the window to glance into the yard. Mercy went to the door and whined. Brooke let her out and stepped onto the back porch steps to watch the animal roam the yard, sniffing, tail wagging. She snagged something from the bushes and trotted to drop the neighbor kid's baseball at her feet. "Thanks, Mercy. I think I've created a monster." She picked it up and made a note to return it. One day, one was going to go through her window.

Her phone buzzed. She snagged it and found a text from Gavin. This is what Tommy and the sketch artist came up with.

Brooke zoomed in on the computerized composite and gave a disappointed sigh. She texted back. It could be Jeffries or not.

I know. It's inconclusive. I spoke with Tommy myself. He still says he never left the home that night.

Still afraid he'll be in trouble if he says it.

Yes. So right now we have nothing on Jeffries.

She was sure he was relieved over that. Brooke still wasn't convinced Jeffries was innocent. Great. Thanks.

Welcome.

She shoved the phone into her back pocket. "Come on, Mercy, we'd better get some sleep while we can. No telling when the phone will ring again."

Mercy started to trot back toward Brooke, then turned and froze, her attention suddenly focused on the area behind her.

The night air seemed to quiver, then go still. Brooke frowned and rose, rubbing her arms against the chill that was only partially due to the weather. "What is it, girl?"

Mercy glanced back at Brooke then started toward the back of the fence. A low growl escaped her and Brooke's adrenaline kicked into high gear. She reached for her weapon.

The one that wasn't there.

She'd left it on the end table next to the recliner. "Mercy. Come!"

The dog immediately stopped, but kept her focus on whatever had captured her attention. She whined and Brooke knew the dog wanted to obey, but also wanted to go after whatever was near the fence. "Mercy. Come."

Mercy barked, but obeyed. She came to Brooke's side and sat, her entire body tense. Brooke looked toward the bushes and the trees that lined the other side of her fence. For the first time she worried that someone could climb one of the trees and drop into her backyard. "Come on, girl, I'm not liking this. Inside. Now."

Brooke forced the dog through the door, followed her inside and went to retrieve her weapon from the end table. She then spun on her heel and went back out the door, shutting the dog inside. Mercy barked at her, but Brooke wanted to know what was bothering the animal so much. And she wanted to make sure nothing happened to the dog. If someone had a weapon, they'd go for Mercy first, most likely, take her out of the picture. And since Mercy didn't have her vest on, Brooke wouldn't take the chance.

She walked through her backyard to where the waist-high bushes met the back of the fence. "Is anyone there? Hello?" The tree rustled above her and she swung the weapon up. "Come down. Now."

A dark-clad figure slipped from the tree, landed on the other side of the wooden fence and ran.

Mercy's barking reached a frenzied pitch from inside the house.

Brooke raced for the gate, threw open the latch and headed in the direction she thought her would-be intruder might have gone. Her shoulders itched. She didn't have her vest on but knew if she took the time to get it the guy would be long gone.

She exited onto the street and came to a stop. From the trees in her backyard, the only direction to go was over the neighbor's fence directly opposite hers or through the small area of woods onto the main street.

She figured he'd go for the street.

Only she didn't see him anywhere. The faint sound of a car starting straight ahead spurred her on. Her tennis shoes pounded the asphalt. Taillights blinked ahead and she stopped, knowing it was a futile chase. With a frustrated slap of her fist against her thigh, she turned and made her way back to her house. She moved back through the trees, walked through her gate and opened her back door. "Mercy, come." The dog didn't need to be told twice. Brooke swept her hand out toward the backyard. "Search." Thirty minutes later, Mercy had come up empty and Brooke was exhausted. She led the way back into the house and called Gavin. "I just had an intruder at my house. Mercy let me know he was there in a tree just over my fence line. When I confronted him, he ran. I tried to chase him down, but I lost him."

"What? You went after him without calling for backup?"

"I didn't have time."

"That wasn't a smart move, Brooke."

She sighed. "What would you have done in my place, Gavin?"

He cleared his throat and didn't speak for a moment. "I'm glad you're all right. Lock your doors and I'll let the local PD know they need to do some frequent drivebys at your place tonight."

"Great. Thanks."

"You sound tired."

She gave a small laugh. "There's a reason for that. I'm going to bed. See you in the morning."

She hung up with Gavin and walked into her bedroom with Mercy at her heels. "'Night, Mercy. Wake me up if anyone tries anything, will you?"

Mercy settled herself at the end of the bed. Brooke crawled beneath the covers and closed her eyes.

Then opened them. Then got up and locked her bedroom door.

Jonas couldn't sleep and it had nothing to do with the fans sounding like freight trains blowing though his home. Frustration nipped at him. He knew he needed to get some rest, but knowing that and shutting off his mind were two very different things. Hence his vigilance at the front window of his house. He'd left the porch light on in the front and turned on the back lights in case Felix wanted to come in that way. The officer was on the curb. Every so often, he'd get out of his car and do a perimeter scan.

Under police escort, Claire had gone back to the office to take care of the animals. The officer had seen her safely home so at least he didn't have to worry about her or work tonight.

He just had to worry about Felix.

Be anxious for nothing.

The verse ran through his mind. "How do I do that, God? This is Felix we're talking about," he murmured. "Please take care of him, wherever he is."

He wouldn't blame God for not listening, but Jonas figured Brooke was right and God wouldn't hold his absenteeism against him. "Thank You for that," he whispered. But it was time to change that and put God back where He belonged. As a priority. No matter what happened with Felix.

He took another look out the living room window and noticed the police cruiser sitting empty. A shadow disappeared around the corner of the house and he figured the officer was doing another safety check. Jonas had to admit the man was thorough, attentive and alert. Jonas appreciated that.

He glanced at his phone. *Call me, Felix. At least let me know you're all right.* For the first time since his wife had walked out, Jonas felt like letting a few tears flow. He wondered if that made him weak.

Then he wished Brooke were there with him. She wouldn't find him weak; she'd probably offer him her shoulder. He blew out a sigh and shook his head. This was getting him nowhere, but he just couldn't get away from the anxiety clawing at his throat.

He turned away from the window, then stopped and looked back at the police car. The officer hadn't returned yet. Jonas frowned. He'd been watching, hoping to catch Felix walking up the street and as a result, he'd seen the officer come and go over the past two hours.

In all of his patrols around the perimeter of the house, it hadn't taken him this long to return to his car. Uneasiness started to build. Jonas wanted to chalk it up to paranoia, but the events over the past two days wouldn't let him. Had the officer run into trouble? Found something? He picked up his phone and dialed Brooke as he went through the house turning off the loud fans.

"Hello?"

The fact that she answered on the first ring said a lot about her own state of sleeplessness. "Hey, do you have the number for the officer outside my house?"

"No. Why?"

"I've been watching him for the past couple of hours. Well, watching for Felix, but noticing the officer making his rounds around my property. He walked away from his car about ten minutes ago and hasn't come back yet. He's never taken this long."

"Sit tight. I'm on the way."

"What? Why?"

"I'm concerned. I had an intruder—I think. A would-be one anyway. It's possible he went straight from my house to yours. Make sure the doors are locked. I'm on my way and sending backup."

"I don't know if that's necess—" He stopped. A low creak from the front of the house reached his ears. "Wait a minute."

"What is it?" He heard rustling in the background like she was moving, getting ready to leave her house.

"I think someone's in my house," he whispered.

"Get out."

"It could be Felix trying to sneak in." Hope flared. Caution ruled. He wouldn't call out until he knew for sure. He slipped his feet into the loafers he'd left in front of the recliner, then moved to the foot of the stairs. The noise had come from the front of the house, maybe the stairs. Could Felix have crawled through a window? Not likely. Jonas had double-checked them and they'd been locked.

"Jonas? You need to get out of the house until you know for sure who it is."

"What if that's the purpose? Get me out of the house then kill me?" He lowered his voice and looked out at the squad car one more time. Still no sign of the officer. Should he leave? He could make it to the front door. Or should he hide? The feeling of having lived this once before swept over him.

"Good point," Brooke said. "What if you got in your car? Lock the doors and hunker down until help gets there?"

The idea didn't sit well with Jonas. He wanted to confront whoever had the audacity to break into his house with a police car sitting right outside. Then he thought about Felix. What would happen to Felix if Jonas did something stupid and got himself killed?

He went to the back door and looked out into the garage. The moon filtered through the windows and he could make out the shape of his car. He heard Brooke talking in the background. Probably calling for help.

Making up his mind, he opened the door and stepped into the darkness of the garage. He shut the door behind him and glanced back into his kitchen through the glass paned door. Nothing yet.

"Are you there, Jonas?" Brooke asked.

"Yeah," he whispered. He heard the worry in her voice. Where were his keys? In his pants pocket hanging over the chair in his bedroom. He changed into sweats when he'd gotten home.

"What are you doing?"

"Getting out." Standing in his kitchen with his phone pressed to his ear, Jonas saw the shadow of a man, his weapon raised.

"Help's on the way. The officer isn't answering his phone."

Jonas paused only for a second before deciding against hiding in the car. He pressed the garage door and flinched at the low rumble. Would the guy in the kitchen notice? He moved to duck under the door and felt something slam into his back. The concrete rushed up and he threw out an arm to break his fall.

Pain shot up from his wrist to his elbow. He lost a

few layers of skin, but figured that was the least of his problems as he rolled to his back only to stare up at the man standing over him, gun trained on his face.

SIXTEEN

Brooke raced through the streets as fast as she dared, siren blaring, lights flashing. Mercy sat in her area in the back, but Brooke could feel the animal's tension reflected in her own. The dog knew something was up and was ready to work.

"Jonas? Are you there? Jonas?" Silence answered her. But he hadn't hung up. "Jonas?"

"Where's the kid?"

Brooke jerked the phone from her ear then shoved it back. "I don't know where he is. We're all looking for him."

"I said where is the kid! Answer me or I'll blow your head off!"

Brooke realized the person wasn't talking to her. He was talking to Jonas and he had a gun on him. Chills swept through her and she pressed the gas a little harder.

"He's missing. He left last night. We're all looking for him." Jonas spoke, his voice low, a thread of steel-laced anger vibrating through the line.

"You're a liar."

"I'm not!" Brooke heard the snarl and prayed he wouldn't do something stupid like attack the guy with the gun. "He got scared and took off. No one knows where he is."

She turned on the road that would lead her to Jonas's house. "Hang on, Jonas."

Through her handset, she heard sirens.

"Let's get out of here!" Another voice.

"What do we do with him?"

"Shoot him."

A gunshot cracked through the line. She flinched and her terror level shot up. There were two of them. And one of them had shot Jonas. "Jonas! No, no no. Please no." A thud and a grunt came through the line. She heard scuffling and running footsteps. "Jonas!" *Oh please, God, don't let him be dead.* She turned the next corner and screeched to a halt in front of Jonas's house. She bolted from the vehicle to find Jonas on the ground, officers chasing two fleeing suspects. Mercy hopped to the ground, her nose working the area around her.

Brooke wanted to take Mercy and follow the officers in pursuit, but her first concern was Jonas. She dropped to her knees beside him and started patting his chest, his arms. "Are you okay? Are you hurt? Where are you shot? You're bleeding!"

He grabbed her hands and sat up. "I'm fine." He glanced at his arm. "That's nothing."

"I heard a gunshot."

"Yeah, but he didn't shoot me." He stood and winced, clasping his injured arm. "One of the officers shot at the guy who had the gun on me. It stopped him long enough so I was able to knock the weapon away from him."

"Did the officer hit him?"

"I don't know."

She nodded to his arm. "You're bleeding," she said again.

"I'm getting used to it." He grunted. "When I came out of the garage, one of them knocked me to the ground. I broke my fall with my arm."

"Is your arm broken?"

"No, just scraped and painful."

She noticed two of the officers who'd been chasing the intruders returning. Their frowns didn't tell a happy ending to the pursuit. She led Jonas over to them. "They got away?" she asked.

"Yeah," the larger officer said. "They had a car waiting. No license plate, but I've got a BOLO for the vehicle. It's a gray Ford Taurus, paint scraped off the right rear bumper."

"How's the officer who was watching the house?" Jonas asked. "I never saw him come back to his car."

"We found him around back. He's out cold. They hit him hard. Ambulance is on the way."

She winced and nodded, then glanced down the street to the right. Then the left. She looked at Jonas. "I think you might be getting to know your neighbors before too long."

He followed her gaze. "At least they don't hide away and ignore trouble in the neighborhood." He shook his head. "They'll probably blackball me from the home owners association."

"Or charge you double dues."

He gave her a tight smile, neither one of them really interested in finding humor in the situation right now. She cupped his chin. "Are you really all right? When I heard that gunshot—" She bit her lip and fought the surge of emotion.

"I'm really all right." He pulled her into a loose hug with his good arm and she pressed her forehead into his chest. She relished the feeling of being in his arms even as she told herself to pull away. He was a case, his son was missing and she had to keep herself at a distance in order to stay objective.

Right.

She looked up to find Nicholas eyeing her with a raised brow. Thankfully he didn't say anything and didn't even give her a funny look.

He did appear concerned. She slipped away from Jonas and put some distance between them so she could think. She gestured to Jonas's arm. "You might need to have that checked."

"By a real doctor?" His lips quirked in a side smile. "Like I did the bullet graze?"

"Touché." She nodded to the house. "Let's get you back inside. I don't think those guys are coming back, but why take chances?"

They made their way back into the house via the front door. Jonas led the way to the den, flipping lights on as he went. The tension in his shoulders was noticeable. Chase and Valor followed behind.

Nicholas looked at Chase. "I think you should stay here. Inside."

Chase nodded. "I was thinking one of us should."

"Brooke's going with me in the morning—" he glanced at his watch "—in a few hours to talk to Congressman Jeffries."

"Then I'll stay," Chase said.

Brooke hesitated. *She* wanted to stay. To make sure that Jonas was all right and that no one tried to break in again. She glanced at Chase. A small smile played around the corners of his mouth and Brooke straightened her spine. "Fine. Sounds good to me."

She told Mercy to heel and headed out the door, knowing no one bought her nonchalance. She was terrified for Jonas and Felix and knew the others were too. Because as much as she might want to deny it, the old feelings from years past weren't so old anymore. They were new and exciting and frightening. And if she didn't find out who was targeting Jonas and Felix, she might be attending funerals, instead of the wedding that kept jumping to the forefront of her mind.

Jonas watched Nicholas and Brooke drive away. He turned to find Chase watching him. Chase's dog, Valor, sat at his side. The Belgian Malinois yawned and settled his big head on his paws. "Sorry you got babysitting duty," Jonas said. He went into the kitchen and opened the fridge.

"I'm a former Secret Service agent. I'm used to it." The man was young, in his midtwenties and tall. His green eyes held life—and a wisdom that came beyond his years. Jonas had a feeling Chase had quite a few stories to tell. "And I don't mind. It's different from what I'm usually doing so the change of pace is nice."

"You said former. Why get out of the Secret Service?"

Chase shrugged. "Search and rescue is my passion. I liked my time in the Secret Service, but when I was offered this position, I jumped at it. This is where I belong."

Jonas nodded, his mind on his son. It helped having someone there to talk with, but he couldn't stop wondering if Felix was safe. For the first time, Jonas regretted not getting Felix a phone.

"Are you sure you want to stay here tonight?" Chase asked.

"Yes, Felix may come back home." He looked around. "The worst of the damage was in here. The kitchen and bedrooms are fine now that the smoke is gone. However, I do need to run back to the office and take care of the animals that are there."

"I'll take you."

Jonas nodded. "All right." He looked around the house, the stark emptiness of it slashing his heart. What would he do if Felix never came home? He pulled in a shuddering breath and ordered his mind not to go there. Felix would come home. He had to.

"Someone will find him, Jonas."

He looked into Chase's kind eyes. "Yeah, but will it be the good guys or the bad guys?"

The sun was high overhead when Brooke and Nicholas pulled up to the congressman's front door the next morning. Brooke was breathing a bit easier after the rest of the night passed with no more attempts on Jonas.

The large mansion should have been overbearing and monstrous. And while it was big, it was more classy than ostentatious. At least in Brooke's opinion. That fact probably had to do with the good taste of the congressman's landscaper.

She and Nicholas walked up to the front door, leaving the animals in the well-ventilated vehicle.

Before she could ring the bell, the door opened.

Congressman Jeffries looked impeccable. His gray hair lay slicked back, not a strand daring to be out of place. His blue eyes remained shuttered and his lips didn't curve into a smile. "Come in." He stepped back and Brooke moved inside. Nicholas stayed on her flank and shut the door behind him. "Thank you for seeing us."

"I apologize for all the delays, but they couldn't be helped. I appreciate your understanding." Instead of going into the reasons for those delays, he simply clasped his hands in front of him. "You said you had a few more questions and I'm willing to do whatever it takes to find Michael's killer. You know that."

"Of course, sir."

Congressman Jeffries led them into a formal living area and toward two navy wing-back chairs. "Make yourself comfortable." They did. Jeffries stood near the fireplace and leaned against the massive mantel. "Now, before you start in on your questions, tell me this, has there been any progress on locating my son's killer?"

Brooke shot a look at Nicholas. "No, sir, not much. We do have some things we're working on, but there's no point in talking about them until we see if they're going to pan out."

He frowned, but didn't push the matter. "What kinds of things?"

Brooke pursed her lips and exchanged a glance with Nicholas. He gave a short nod. "Things like a phone that's linked to Rosa Gomez, your late housekeeper."

"What's so important about that?"

"There's a picture on the phone of a man on the cliffs where she died. The picture was taken the day she died so we're looking for him to bring him in and question him." She could give that much information. The man's face was all over the news so the congressman probably already knew that much.

He snorted and waved a hand. "You're right, you don't have much. What other questions do you have for me then?"

"As you know, we've been looking into everything we possibly can to figure out who would have something against you."

"Yes."

"It seems you and Thorn Industries have a rather close relationship," Nicholas said. He kept his tone mild, but Brooke heard the thread of steel beneath the words.

"What are you implying?" Jeffries asked, eyes flashing.

Brooke opened her mouth, but Nicholas beat her to it. "I'm not implying anything. I'm simply curious about the two bills you introduced that were subsequently passed."

Jeffries's lips tightened.

Brooke picked up when the man didn't speak. "We found it very interesting that those bills allowed Thorn Industries to keep manufacturing a drug with dangerous side effects. And of course that puts more money in your pocket."

"How dare you?" The congressman took a step toward Nicholas, fists clenched at his side, face red.

Nicholas tensed, but Brooke simply watched the man, then said, "We dare because these are facts, sir. Did Michael find out what you were doing? What you were supporting? Did Michael threaten to expose you? Did you get so desperate to keep your secrets that you had to kill your own son?"

Congressman Jeffries gaped at her. Even Nicholas looked a bit stunned at her lack of finesse. But Brooke did it for a reason. She waited for Jeffries's reaction.

And wasn't disappointed.

His red face turned purple. "Unbelievable. My son is dead! Whoever shot him shot me, too. And you dare come into my home and accuse me of killing Michael? Get out. Both of you!"

Nicholas shifted. Brooke met the man's eyes. "Not until you tell us about Thorn Industries. We can keep digging, of course, but if you'll just tell us what we need to know then that'll make things move along a little faster. Which is what you want, right?"

His nostrils flared and the color in his face stayed high, but he gave a short nod. It took him a moment to get his breathing under control. He finally drew in a deep breath and closed his eyes. When he opened them, hard chips of ice stared at her. "Fine. Thorn Industries tried to bribe me in passing the bill. I would never do that. I wouldn't jeopardize my career, my livelihood or my reputation. That would be political suicide."

"Yes, sir, that's true."

"So I told them no. I refused." He gave a halfhearted laugh. "I play by the rules and get accused of murder." The hardness melted. Tears filled his eyes, his shoulders slumped and he dropped to the couch to lower his head to his hands. Sobs shook his shoulders.

Brooke swallowed. Had she gone too far? She raised an eyebrow at Nicholas and he shrugged.

"Sir?" Brooke asked.

He hiccuped and pulled a tissue from the box on the end table. He wiped his face. "I'm sorry. So sorry. But I just miss Michael so much. And your questions…"

Brooke cleared her throat. "Yes, well, I apologize. Sometimes my tongue gets ahead of my brain."

The man nodded. "I miss my son," he whispered.

"Of course you do. I'm sorry for the hard questions. We're just trying to find who did this."

He sniffled and grabbed another handful of tissues. "I know. I know. Michael was a good man. He was a bit of a do-gooder crusader, you know. Nothing set him off like finding out someone was corrupt in the government." He looked up. "That was his big thing. He fought against government corruption." He sighed. "And he didn't care who he made mad. He took on anyone he thought needed taking down or exposed. Anyone." He blew his nose and wiped his eyes. His gaze jumped from Nicholas's to Brooke's. "And because of that, he was killed. No, I don't have proof, but I don't need it. I just know it."

The tears continued to leak down his face. Nicholas stood and Brooke followed his example, her lips pulled into a frown. Nicholas grabbed more tissues and pushed them into Jeffries's hand. "I'm sorry, sir. We'll leave now, but please call us if there's anything else you can think of."

The tears had stopped, but Brooke couldn't deny the agony in the man's eyes. Shame flickered and she had to work to suppress it.

"Of course I'll call," Jeffries said. He swallowed and drew in another shuddering breath. "I appreciate everything you're doing. I know you're working hard. Forgive me for being bullheaded. I just want the people responsible for Michael's death to be brought to justice."

"We do, too, sir," Brooke said. "We do, too."

She and Nicholas left and stood in front of their vehicles. Brooke's phone buzzed and she glanced at the text. "Jonas is at work. Chase is still with him and there's a patrol car in the parking lot."

"Good. He's covered." Nicholas nodded. "Wish we could find his son."

"That makes two of us."

Her phone buzzed again. "It's Gavin."

"Take it."

She nodded and lifted the phone to her ear. "Hi, Gavin."

"Brooke. We need you and Mercy to head over to Brothers Jewelry Store. There's been a break-in at their downtown store. One of the robbers left behind a glove.

DC police asked for K-9 help because of the glove. We want to see if Mercy can track down anything else that might give us a clue who these guys are."

"We're on our way."

Brooke raced to her vehicle, her suspicions about the congressman not satisfied; however, there was nothing to do but head to the other case. Nicholas would write up the conversation word for word and they could discuss it at the next Capitol K-9 meeting. Gavin would be furious with her.

Ten minutes later, she pulled into the parking lot of the jewelry store. An array of law enforcement was already in action. She flashed her badge and Mercy quivered at her side, ready to work.

An officer approached her. "Hey, Brooke."

"Hey, Elizabeth. They've got you out here, too?" Elizabeth Carter, another one of the Capitol K-9 team members. Her border collie, Buddy, sat at her side.

Elizabeth nodded.

"Anyone hurt?" Brooke asked.

"The guard. He was shot in the chest. It's touch and go right now."

Brooke winced. "Okay, where's the glove?"

"The lead detective has it." She rubbed Buddy's ears. "Let's go, boy."

They took off and Brooke turned to find herself face-to-face with Detective David Delvecchio. "You the lead?"

"I am."

"Then let's go."

He held a rubber glove out to her. She popped it over her hand and reached into the paper bag he had in his other hand. Holding the leather glove between two fingers, she let Mercy get a good sniff. The dog's nose wiggled. "Seek."

Mercy took off like a shot to the edge of the road. Brooke followed her at a fast trot, the detective staying with her. "You got this call, huh?" he asked. "They take you off the other case?"

"Of course not. I'm just like you. I work more than one case at a time."

Mercy stopped, went to the edge of the road and into the trees.

"She any good?" David asked.

"One of the best." He glanced at her then back at the dog. "Mercy can find evidence that's left behind. Her nose is super sensitive."

"I know how the dogs work."

"Right." He might think he knew, but Brooke had a feeling he didn't know details. Mercy sifted through the scents all around them and found the one that didn't fit.

"Sorry. I know how they work. I'm not used to working with them, that's all," the detective said.

"It's fine."

Mercy paced, then sat and looked back. Brooke went to her and rubbed her ears. "Good girl."

"What did she find?"

"You have an evidence bag?"

He handed one to her.

With her gloved hand, she reached out and picked up the evidence Mercy had focused on. "It's a pearl earring."

"They came this way then."

"Yes."

"If it was them."

"It was. If the earring had been out here for an extended period of time, its scent would have blended with the surroundings. The fact that she picked up on a scent that doesn't belong says the earring is a new addition to the area."

The detective patted Mercy's head. "Well, you're a good one." Mercy rewarded his praise with a tongue swipe to the hand. Detective Delvecchio looked startled, then laughed. Brooke handed him a bottle of hand sanitizer without a word. He used it and handed it back to her. She smiled.

They made their way back to the road. Brooke led the way, Mercy at her left, the detective on her right. Mercy gave a sudden yelping cry and sat, her paw lifted. Brooke spun. "What is it?"

"What happened to her?" the detective asked.

"I don't know." Mercy held her paw away from the ground and refused to stand. Brooke dropped to her knees. "What did you step on, girl?"

Brooke took the dog's paw in her hand and tried to see, but Mercy kept pulling it away from her. She sighed. "Well, I guess we're going to see Jonas a lot sooner than we'd planned."

In spite of her worry over Mercy, the thought lifted her spirits higher than they'd been all day.

SEVENTEEN

Jonas stood at the window waiting. Brooke had called and said Mercy had been hurt and he'd told her to bring the dog in. His imagination took flight. Had she been shot protecting Brooke? Had Brooke been in danger? His breath whooshed out when Brooke turned in to the parking lot of the office. She flashed her badge at the officers and they waved her in.

Clients had come and gone all morning, eyes wide, curiosity eating at them. Jonas had been vague in his answers to their questions.

Brooke stepped from the vehicle then opened the back door. She lifted Mercy into her arms and staggered slightly under the dog's weight. Jonas went to help, but the officer motioned him back. "We don't want you out here. You'd be too exposed."

Jonas chafed at the constraints. "Then help her with the dog."

The larger officer, who stood about six feet two, took Mercy from Brooke.

"Thanks," she told him.

"Bring her back here," Jonas said.

The officer carried Mercy with ease and gently laid

her on the examination table, then left them alone in the room.

Jonas looked at Brooke. "What happened to her?"

"I think she stepped on something. Either that or she got stung by a bee or—" She shrugged. "I don't know. I didn't think it was that serious, but she wouldn't let me look at it."

Jonas reached for the paw that the animal favored. Mercy whined and pulled away from him. He frowned. "I'm going to have to sedate her."

Brooke sighed. "Fine. She's not going to let you touch her without it, I'm afraid."

He patted the dog's head. "I'll be back in a minute and we'll get you all fixed up."

"Where's Claire?"

He paused at the door. "I told her not to come in today. I just didn't want her in the middle of all the craziness."

"You've been handling the office by yourself all morning?"

"Yes." He gave her a weary smile.

"No wonder you look beat."

"Thanks."

She grabbed his hand. "No. I need to thank you."

"It's my pleasure. I'll be right back."

Brooke let him go this time.

When he returned he had a syringe. Brooke held the dog while Jonas administered the medicine. He noticed her tenderness with her friend, her partner. He also noticed Brooke smelled good. Really good in spite of whatever work she'd been doing.

Soon the drug took effect. Mercy leaned heavily against Brooke and Jonas had to curb his jealousy. He shook his head. Jealous of a dog? He was being ridiculous. "My wife didn't like animals."

Brooke stilled. "Is that why you don't have one at your home?"

"Part of the reason."

"And the other part?"

He sighed. He'd opened the door to the topic, he supposed he'd walk through it. "I didn't want anything to compete with the time I needed to spend with Felix."

"And taking care of an animal would keep you from spending time with your son?"

"I thought it might."

"Or it might bring you closer together."

He glanced up. "Maybe."

"Come on, Jonas, you saw him with those puppies. He was great."

"I know." He did know. "It's something to think about for sure. When he comes home."

"Which is going to be soon."

He shook his head, worry consuming him once again. "I've put him in God's hands."

"No better place for him to be."

"Unfortunately, I keep taking him back, convinced that I can do a better job than God when it comes to Felix." He sighed. "I know that's not true, I've just got to live like I believe it." He nodded at Mercy. "I think I'll be able to take a look now."

Mercy's eyes were closed and a light snore slipped from her. He leaned in to get a closer look at the animal's wounded paw. "Aha."

"What is it?"

"It's not a thorn or a bee sting, but just as painful." He reached for a pair of tweezers, pulled a magnifying glass down over his eye and gently pulled a sliver of glass from Mercy's paw. The dog didn't even move. Jonas held up the piece of glass. "No wonder she was in pain and didn't want to put weight on that foot."

Brooke laid the dog on the table and stroked her head. Mercy stirred enough to give Brooke's hand a lick, then fell back into a doze. Jonas threw the glass in the trash. "I'll clean it and take a stitch. She'll be all right in a day or two."

"I'm glad it was something so simple."

"Yeah. We haven't had much of simple lately."

Twenty minutes later, Jonas had Mercy settled on a blanket in a kennel at the back of the office. He shut the door. "She'll sleep it off and be ready to go in the morning."

"Thanks so much, Jonas."

He looked into her grateful eyes and felt his heart flip over. He curled his fingers into a fist to keep from reaching out to her. Not yet. Not while Felix's whereabouts were still up in the air.

She bit her lip and turned away as though reading his thoughts. "I'll let Gavin know what's happened." She glanced at her watch. "I probably need to get back to my office and get some paperwork done or I'll be spending the night there."

"Go on. I'll take care of Mercy."

"I know you will."

His phone rang as she gathered her things. "Hello?"

"Dr. Parker, this is Officer Davenport. We were patrolling past your house and noticed your front door open."

"What?" he snapped.

At his sharp tone, Brooke looked at him. He told her what the officer said.

She frowned. "Ask him if someone is inside?"

He repeated the question to the officer. "No, sir. We swept the place, but you might want to come home and see if anything's missing."

"I'll be right there."

Brooke drove with precision and one eye on the rear-view mirror. Leaving Mercy behind felt like she'd just cut off her right arm, but the drugged dog would be much more comfortable sleeping it off in the kennel than being transported in the back of the car.

Jonas rode beside her, his heavy frown and brooding eyes reflecting his inner turmoil. "I need to be searching for my son."

"We're looking for him, Jonas. What do you think you could do that the cops aren't doing?"

He shook his head and blew out a harsh sigh. "I don't know. Something. I can't believe he could just disappear like that."

He could disappear like that if he were dead. Brooke kept her eyes on the road and her thoughts to herself. But the more time passed with no word about the teen, the more her mind went to dark places. "Did you try calling his friends again?"

"Yes. I'm sure a couple of the parents think Felix is just a runaway." He tapped his fingers against his thigh. "And I believe he did leave on his own."

"The security video confirms that."

He nodded. "But that doesn't mean he doesn't need help."

"I agree. I think he needs help more than ever right now."

"I'm scared to death the wrong people are going to find him."

"I know." She turned in to his drive. The front door

still stood cracked open and Brooke could see someone standing just inside. The person peered out, then
stepped onto the porch. Brooke figured it was the officer whose empty squad car sat on the curb. He motioned them in and Jonas bolted from the vehicle.
Brooke stayed right behind him, her nerves stretched
tight. Would they never catch a break?

She followed Jonas through the front door and the
officer shut it behind them. "Okay, we've gone through
the house and found nothing damaged, no electronics
obviously missing, but we need you to walk through and
see if there's anything small that's been taken, anything
that I wouldn't notice."

Jonas rubbed a hand down his face. Brooke noticed
the smoky smell had faded almost completely, the big
fans left by the restoration company having done their
job.

Jonas walked through the house and Brooke stayed
behind him. "See anything missing or just not right?"

"Not so far."

They passed through the den, toured the kitchen,
then back into the foyer and up the stairs to the master
bedroom. She waited outside the room, but couldn't
help a curious glance inside. Large oak furniture, dark
browns and beiges and a few red throw pillows on the
perfectly made-up bed. Dark curtains and black rug
on the floor. It definitely needed a woman's touch and
Brooke already had it redecorated by the time he joined
her in the hall.

She gulped and ordered herself to focus on the task
at hand. "Nothing?"

"No." He slipped past her and into Felix's room. It
looked the same as it had the last she'd been in here.

Jonas simply stood in the doorway and looked. She watched him scan the room.

And frown.

"What is it?" she asked.

"There was a sweatshirt tossed over the back of his footboard. Next to the jeans and hoodie." He picked them up then set it back where he found it.

"How do you know the sweatshirt's missing?"

"Because I put it there."

"Maybe Felix moved it?"

He shook his head. "No, he hasn't been back in his room since we moved over to the office. I grabbed some clothes for him after the whole Molotov cocktail and smoke explosion, but it wasn't that sweatshirt and Felix hasn't been here." He rubbed his chin. "Do you have pictures of his room? A cop took pictures the night of the break-in."

"Fiona will have them. She has everything related to the case." Brooke pulled her cell phone from her pocket and hit Fiona's speed dial number.

"Yes, ma'am?"

"Hey, I need the pictures from the Parker scene."

"Coming your way. Any pictures in particular?"

"The ones of the teenager's bed and the clothes on it."

"Check your phone in about two minutes."

"Thanks, Fiona."

"Anytime."

Brooke hung up and waited. Less than the promised two minutes later, it buzzed. She pulled up the pictures and Jonas leaned over her shoulder to see. Her awareness meter shot to the top level. His breath brushed her ear and she swallowed. Why did he affect her so? Even more so than the first time she'd seen him again. Had that just been a couple of days? It felt as though they were picking up right where they'd left off. She shivered and he rested a hand on her shoulder.

"You okay?" he asked.

"I'm fine." She scrolled through the photos, noting the slight tremble in her fingers. She hoped Jonas didn't notice.

"There," he said.

She stopped. "That one?" She pointed to the blue sweatshirt draped over the foot of the bed. Next to a pair of jeans and a gray hoodie. Just like Jonas said.

"That's it. It's missing."

"So while you were at work and the police coverage on your house was minimal, someone snuck in and stole the sweatshirt. Why?"

"Maybe Felix was cold and had one of his friends steal it." He rubbed a hand down his face. "I don't know."

"Or he came back and got it himself."

"I hope so, I pray he did," Jonas said.

It would mean he was moving under his own steam, that he wasn't being held captive somewhere. "You know, the fact that there's been no ransom demand, that's a good thing. If the people who want the phone knew Felix was missing, even if they didn't have him, they might act like they did and demand you give him the phone."

"Or he told them he handed it over to the police and doesn't have it anymore and they have no use for him so they—" He bit his lip and turned away.

Brooke grimaced. She'd thought of that scenario, she just hadn't wanted to say it out loud. "Just in case, let's not let on that Felix doesn't have the phone anymore. I was going to suggest a press conference to announce that the phone had been found and was in the unit's possession, but now I don't think that's a good idea. Not yet. Not until we find Felix and make sure he's not using the fact that he had the phone as a way to stay alive until help can get to him."

Jonas nodded, a sick look on his face. "What if he's already told them he doesn't have it?"

Brooke blew out a long sigh. "Then he might be in serious trouble."

EIGHTEEN

Early the next morning, Jonas hung up with Nicholas after getting an update on the search for Felix. Nothing yet. He turned to grab his jacket when his phone rang for the second time in ten minutes. He glanced at the caller ID, praying for a number he didn't recognize. An unfamiliar number might mean Felix had found or borrowed a phone and decided to call.

But he knew the number and his hopes plummeted. "Hi, Claire."

"I'm happy to hear your voice, too."

He winced. "Sorry. I was hoping you were Felix."

"Of course you were." Her voice softened and sympathy flowed through the line. "I'm sorry."

"No problem."

"Have you heard anything about him? Has anyone found anything at all that might indicate where he is?"

"No, but the officers were out looking all night and I'm staying right by my phone in case he calls again." He sighed. "I was just getting ready to head to the office. Are you already there?"

"I came in. I can't sit at home doing nothing, you know that."

"I know. I don't know what I'd do without you. All right. Is there an officer in sight?"

"Yes. Two of them. Parked right out front. They got here about the same time I did."

"Good. You should be safe enough, then. I'll see you in a few minutes."

He hung up with Claire and started gathering his wallet and keys when he remembered Chase was probably in his kitchen. Jonas descended the steps and found the man sitting at the kitchen table sipping a cup of coffee. "Morning," he said.

Jonas nodded. "Morning."

Chase hefted the mug. "Hope you don't mind."

"Are you kidding? You can help yourself to anything you need or want. I can't tell you how much I appreciate all you guys are doing to find Felix and keep me safe."

Chase's expression relaxed a fraction. "You're welcome. We've had guys out all night looking for him. They want a good ending to this story, too."

"I know. And I know it's probably just all in a day's work for you, but—" He shrugged and grabbed his silver travel mug from the sink. After he filled it with the black brew, he took a sip and breathed in a grateful breath.

A knock on his door pulled Chase from his chair. His hand went to his weapon and he started for the door. "Brooke said she'd come get you this morning, so it's probably her, but we don't need to take any chances."

Tension threaded across Jonas's shoulders. He was ready for this to be over, for his son to be home. To catch whoever was causing the problems and get this burden off his shoulders.

"It's me," Brooke said.

Jonas shifted and set his cup on the counter. Brooke

walked into the kitchen and their eyes met. As always, that special zing whipped through him. He blinked and waved to the coffeepot. "Chase was the hero this morning. May I offer you a cup?"

"Sure."

He filled her cup and handed it to her. "Are you ready to go see Mercy?"

"Absolutely."

"Claire called me. She's there now."

Chase stepped to the door. "I'm going to head back to the office. Let me know if you need anything else."

"Thanks."

Jonas grabbed his keys and headed out after Chase.

"Hey, wait up," Brooke called.

Jonas turned. Brooke was on his heels, holding out his phone. He took it from her with a crooked smile. "I guess I'm a little distracted these days."

"You think?"

Jonas went to his vehicle.

Brooke bypassed him. "Go back on the porch and wait, will you?"

Jonas frowned. "Why?"

"I want to check the car."

Her meaning dawned. "You think someone planted a bomb in my car?"

"I don't know. That's why I'm checking."

Jonas stood on the porch, one hand cramped around his phone, the other around his cup. A bomb? The thought had never occurred to him. He watched her cover the car bumper to bumper. She'd even pulled out a small mirror to check the undercarriage.

Finally she pushed herself up off the concrete drive and held out a hand. "Toss me your keys, will you?"

Jonas narrowed his eyes. "So you can start it and see if it blows up?"

Brooke laughed. "I'm relatively sure it's safe. I don't have a death wish."

"Then I'll start it myself."

"Jonas."

He stepped around her. "No way." He opened the door and tossed his stuff inside and slid into the driver's seat.

Brooke crossed her arms and glared at him.

Jonas met her glare for glare. "Are you sure this thing's not going to blow?"

She sighed. "Yes. I didn't see anything to indicate a bomb. Nothing under the car, nothing under the hood. I'm willing to put the key in the ignition and start the car."

"Then I trust you." Without hesitation he inserted the key and turned it. The car started with a low growl and he realized he still held his breath.

Brooke shook her head and went to her own vehicle. She climbed in and motioned for him to go ahead. He pulled around her and drove the short mile and a half to his office. When he arrived at the parking lot, he noted the police officers and offered a short wave.

Brooke parked and climbed from the vehicle. He could see her tapping her hand on her thigh while she waited on him. She wanted to see her dog and couldn't quite hide her impatience. He led the way into the office, noting she scanned the area in spite of the police coverage. Nothing must have set off her internal alarm. She stepped inside and he shut the door just as Claire came from the back, her brow furrowed.

"What is it?" Jonas asked.

"You didn't turn the alarm system on when you left last night."

"Of course I did."

The woman's frown deepened. "It wasn't on when I got here."

Jonas went to the panel. It was dark.

"Did you leave one of the cages open last night?" Claire asked.

Jonas turned, a ball of dread forming in his midsection. "No, of course not. Why?"

"Because I think one of the animals is missing."

"Which one?" The dread blew up into outright fear as he rushed through the door to the kennel. Brooke stayed right behind. He came to a stop at the open cage.

"Mercy," Brooke whispered. "She's gone."

Brooke blinked, then blinked again as though the act would change the facts. The cage was still empty. "Someone stole her."

"That's impossible," Jonas snapped. "I remember activating the alarm system when I left yesterday. After all the crazy stuff going on, there's no way I would forget that."

Brooke believed him. She spun to find one of the officers behind her. "Can you check the alarm system?"

"Of course." He left and Brooke turned back to Jonas. "This is crazy. Why would someone steal Mercy? It's not like she can tell them what she knows." She couldn't help the sarcasm.

He still looked stunned. And angry. He'd just about reached his breaking point and she didn't blame him. She was pretty mad herself and terribly worried about Mercy. Now she had to track down a missing teen and a stolen dog. She pulled in a deep breath and pinched the bridge of her nose. "All right. I need to think for a minute. And call Gavin." She pulled out her phone as the officer stepped back inside.

"Whoever it was is a professional. The box cover was unscrewed, the phone wire cut first, then the alarm wires cut and the cover replaced. Just to look at it you'd never know anything was wrong."

Jonas reached across the desk, grabbed the phone and pressed it to his ear. "Dead." He slammed it down.

Claire gasped. "I didn't even pick the phone up this morning. I saw the alarm was off and thought you must not have turned it on when you left. I was just going to read you the riot act and—" She pressed her fingers to her lips. "I'm sorry."

"It's not your fault, Claire. Don't beat yourself up about it."

"But—"

"I mean it. Really, I think you should go home and stay there until this is all resolved. I'm going to call my clients and refer them to another vet."

Claire and Brooke gasped in unison. "Jonas, your business will go under," Brooke said.

"Right now, I can't worry about this practice. Mercy is missing. Someone is trying to kill me. I have to find my son." He looked at Claire. "And I don't want to risk putting you in danger just because you happen to work for me."

Claire's gaze bounced between Brooke and Jonas before she finally sighed. "Okay. You're probably right." She bit her lip. "But will you stay in touch? Let me know you're all right and when you find Felix?"

"Of course." Jonas escorted her to the door and Brooke dialed Gavin's number. Her heart was heavy. For Jonas and Felix and for Mercy. Please, God, don't let them hurt any of them. She knew why they wanted Felix—they thought he might still have the phone. That and they thought he could ID the guy he saw in the woods. But why would they take Mercy?

Gavin answered and Brooke drew in a deep breath. "Mercy's been stolen."

"What?" His shout made her flinch, but she didn't back away.

"Someone broke into Jonas's practice last night and took her right out of the cage."

"Any video?"

"No. The wires were cut. Telephone, video cameras, everything."

"Of course they were."

She could almost picture him pacing the floor of his office.

"You've got to find her, Brooke."

"I know. If she can get away from whoever has her, she'll find her way home, but if they've got her tied up somewhere..."

"Okay, we'll put out a BOLO on her. Get her picture on the news and all that. I'll also have Fiona work any angles she might have in tracking Mercy. She has the GPS on her collar. Hold on one second." Brooke held. She heard Gavin shout for Fiona. He came back on the line. "Okay, Fiona's on the computer right now."

Brooke paced from one end of the room to the other.

"Anything?"

"Not yet."

Brooke paced another route. "Well?"

"Working on it, Brooke. Fiona?"

"Nothing like a little bit of impatience," she heard the woman say. Brooke pictured her in a pink flowing skirt, matching Hawaiian shirt with pink flowers, her hair pulled up on her head and held in place with her glasses. "Brooke?"

"Yes, Fiona."

"I can't track Mercy, I'm sorry. The GPS unit on her collar has been removed."

Brooke groaned then pulled herself together. "All right. What now?"

"I want to have a meeting. Let's assemble the team, but tell Nicholas to stay on Jonas. I don't want him un-protected," Gavin said.

"I'll do that as soon as we hang up."

"Hanging up now."

She dialed Nicholas. He answered with a gruff hello. "Hey, I need some more help. Do you think Margaret would release you one more time?"

Gavin was the captain and in charge of the investiga-tion, but Margaret was Gavin's boss and had the final say in where Nicholas was assigned.

"If it's related to catching Michael Jeffries's killer, I think I pretty much have carte blanche."

"Great." She updated him about Mercy and her need to leave. "If you can cover Jonas, I'll work on finding Mercy."

"I'm on the way."

"Thank you." She stopped and thought. "Okay, here's the plan. I'm going to run by my house and make sure Mercy isn't wandering around there. If she got away, that's the first place she'd go."

"Do that. I'll take care of Jonas and see you at the office soon after."

Brooke hung up and told Jonas, "I'm going by my house then on to the meeting. I'll check in with you after. Please text me and let me know if you find Felix."

"Of course," Jonas said.

His anxiety and worry grabbed at her and she just prayed that Jonas or one of the officers found him before anyone else. Because if the good guys didn't find him soon, she had a sinking feeling the bad guys would.

NINETEEN

Jonas watched Nicholas and Brooke exchange a few brief words before she climbed into her SUV and pulled into the street. He said a short prayer for her safety and another for Felix and Mercy.

Jonas swung the door open for him and Nicholas stepped inside. "How are you doing?"

"Hanging in there. Still no word from Felix and now Mercy's missing."

Jonas led Nicholas into the break room and pulled two sodas from the refrigerator. He tossed one to Nicholas, who caught it midair. "Thanks."

"Sure. So what's next?"

Nicholas took a swig and sat in the nearest chair. "We keep digging, keep looking for Felix and searching for a way to outsmart the bad guys and catch them."

They discussed different strategies and possibilities for the next several minutes. The phone rang and Jonas went to answer it. When he returned, he found Nicholas hanging up. "We got a sighting on your son," he said.

Jonas's breath whooshed from his lungs. "Where?"

"Over off Hilton Street."

Jonas frowned. "That's near his friend Travis's house. One street over, I believe."

Nicholas lifted a brow. "You think Travis's been hiding him all this time?"

"I don't know, but I'm going to find out." He grabbed his keys. "Who spotted him?"

"One of the patrol officers. He called for him by name and the boy turned so he feels like it's definitely Felix."

Jonas headed for the door.

"Hold on a second. I'll drive."

"And I'll call Brooke." Jonas donned his vest under Nicholas's watchful eye, then dialed Brooke's number on his way to the vehicle. Her phone went to voice mail for the next two times he tried to call. "She's not answering."

"We'll keep trying."

Throughout the ride to the Fuller home, Jonas dialed Brooke's number. The fact that she wasn't answering concerned him.

"Maybe she found Mercy and is getting help. We'll call her again as soon as we leave here."

When they arrived at the Fuller home, Jonas climbed from the vehicle with Nicholas right behind him. He walked up to the front door and rang the bell. No one answered. He'd called the school to check and see if Felix had shown up, but he was reported as being absent. Travis was also absent. Jonas wasn't surprised.

No one answered the door. He turned to Nicholas. "The parents are probably at work."

"Do you have a number?"

"I have cell phones, not work numbers."

"Let's try them."

Jonas dialed the first number and paced while the phone rang. Just when the thought it might go to voice mail, Charles Fuller answered. "Charles, this is Jonas Parker."

"How are you? Have you found Felix?"

"No, no, we haven't. I'm at your house right now, though. He was spotted not too far from here. Did you know Travis wasn't in school today?"

"What? I dropped him off this morning myself. What do you mean he's not in school?"

Jonas winced at the man's shout. He didn't blame him, though. "I think the boys may be together. If so, we need to find them."

"Does this have to do with all of the trouble you've been having?"

"You know about it?"

"Just what Claire's shared with my wife."

Jonas grimaced. Claire and Hilary Fuller had become friends when she'd brought the Fuller's cat into the office during Jonas's first week of practice. He knew they regularly met for lunch. He shouldn't be surprised Claire would confide in her friend.

"Do I need to come home?"

"No, but do you know where the boys might go to hang out and try not to be spotted?"

Charles paused, then sighed. "No, I can't think of anyplace. Travis doesn't say much. He has his phone with him, I'll give him a call. You can hold this line while I call on another."

"Thanks."

Jonas waited. He glanced at his watch, his impatience building. Finally, he heard the phone click. "Jonas?"

"Yeah."

"He's not answering, but I have software on my computer at home that will allow me to track his phone. I'll be there shortly."

He looked at Nicholas. "Just give me the number, I have a feeling I can get it tracked faster than you."

The man paused for a second, then rattled off the number. Jonas related it to Nicholas and the man got on his phone. He heard him asking for someone named Fiona. "Thanks, Charles."

"I'm on my way home. I'll help you look for the boys."

And pray they found them before the bad guys did.

Brooke drove to her house, praying for Felix, Jonas and Mercy. She pulled into her drive and got out of her car. "Mercy? Girl? Are you here?"

The dog didn't come out from under any of the shrubbery lining the front of her house. Brooke decided to do a perimeter search and walked to the edge of the property then down the side of the house. "Mercy? You here?"

Again no sign.

She had a feeling the search was in vain, but she had to look around the entire area before she would be satisfied. She continued to the back and wound up at the trees lining the back fence. She couldn't help looking up, searching the trees, remembering how easy it had been for someone to climb one and look down into her backyard. She shuddered and moved on until she circled back to her car. With a sigh and a heavy heart, she realized Mercy was either too far away to find her way home or she was unable to get away from whoever took her. Or both.

Brooke decided to make one more pass and check the backyard. She didn't see how Mercy could have gotten into it, but the dog was clever. Brooke opened her front door, stepped inside and shut it behind her. She walked through to the kitchen then pushed open the door that led to the yard. "Mercy?"

Nothing.

Brooke finally decided to give it up. The dog wasn't here. She reached for her phone to call Gavin and grimaced when her hand landed on her empty clip. She must have left the device in her car in her haste to check for Mercy. She stood on the porch for just a moment, thinking. They'd stolen Mercy. They'd stolen Felix's sweatshirt. Why? The two were connected and her mind immediately put it together. They wanted Mercy to track Felix. Of course. She couldn't believe it hadn't clicked sooner. She had to call Gavin. And Jonas.

Brooke stepped back inside the house and reached for the kitchen wall phone. And stopped. Smoke? Not something-on-fire smoke. Cigarette smoke. Stale cigarette smoke.

Someone was in her house?

Her brain scrambled. Had she locked the front door behind her?

No.

She spun, had a flash of something moving toward her head. Blinding pain.

Then blackness.

Jonas, Charles Fuller and Nicholas searched the house from top to bottom with no sign of the boys. They covered the yard area and several officers cruised nearby streets. Jonas prayed one of the officers spotted Felix or found someone who'd seen him. They returned to the house to wait. Max stayed by Nicholas's side, his intelligent brown eyes never straying from his partner.

Jonas looked at the dog, then at Nicholas. "You know,

it's highly likely that if Travis is helping Felix out today, he's been helping hide him all along."

Nicholas scratched Max's ears and nodded. "I was thinking the same thing." He looked at Charles. "Do you have something of Travis's that Max can sniff? Then I can turn him loose and see what he comes up with."

"Of course." Charles disappeared down the hall, then came back with a blue sweatshirt. Nicholas took it and held it out to Max who nosed it. He huffed and snuffled it one more time, then lifted his head.

"I'll take him outside since we know the boys aren't in here. Hopefully, he'll catch the scent and take us on a walk."

Jonas stared. "That's why."

"What?" Nicholas turned.

"That's why they stole Felix's sweatshirt and Mercy. They want to use Mercy to find Felix." He lifted his gaze to lock it on the other officer's. "I've got to get in touch with Brooke."

Brooke rolled and groaned. Something kept nudging her in the ribs while little people drummed on her brain. She winced and tried to sit up, but found she couldn't do it. Her head lay on something hard. She pulled her eyes open, trying to figure out what truck had hit her. The flu? The ringing in her ears finally stopped then started up again.

She blinked. Then blinked again. The fog hovering over her mind lifted when she saw the black-booted feet in front of her face. Squinting against the raging headache and the sudden burst of nausea, she drew in a steadying breath as the memory rushed in. She'd come looking for Mercy. Someone had been waiting on her and caught her off guard.

"You awake?" a gruff voice asked.

She closed her eyes, praying, trying to move her hands. Something held them together. Duct tape? At least they were in front of her. She moved her feet. Not bound.

A harder kick to the ribs. She gasped, opened her eyes and cried out at the excruciating pain that lanced through her head. The room spun, the darkness beckoned.

"Yeah," the voice said. "That's what I thought. Don't pass out on me again or I'll just shoot you and move on. I need information and can't get it if you're unconscious."

Brooke didn't move, didn't breathe. The pain eased a bit and she tried opening her eyes once more. Her gaze landed on her attacker and her training kicked in. Midthirties, strong, sleeveless muscle shirt, tattoo of a scorpion on his right shoulder. A year-round tan, five-o'clock shadow.

The man from the vet's office.

The man Felix had seen on the cliffs.

The man who'd been trying to kill them to get to the phone. "Can't get it if I'm dead either." A spark of something flashed in his dark eyes. Admiration? More likely annoyance. "If you want information, I suggest you quit hitting me," she rasped.

"Guess you got a bit of a headache, huh?"

"A bit."

He moved his weapon about an inch from her nose. "I hit you a little harder than I meant to, but don't worry, it's going to quit hurting real soon."

Fear flickered, but she made sure it didn't show. "What do you want?" she asked.

"The phone."

As he spit the two words, she heard the ringing again and realized it was her cell phone. Not exactly the one he was after. He didn't know that one had been turned over to the Capitol K-9 team. She studied him as she waited for another round of nausea to pass. "I don't have it. Haven't you figured that out by now?"

The man spat. "But you can get it."

"Who killed Michael Jeffries?"

"Wouldn't you like to know?" He laughed and seemed genuinely amused. Brooke tugged at her hands, trying to be subtle, but needing to know how strong and well wrapped the tape was. Another tug. Her hope took a nosedive. She'd need some time to work her way out of the tape. And by the look in his eyes, time was something she didn't have. He shoved the weapon closer. "Now. Where's the phone?"

Jonas kept dialing Brooke's number. And it kept going to voice mail after the fourth ring. Why wasn't she answering? Nicholas seemed concerned as well when she didn't pick up his call either. "I'm calling Gavin."

"I'm going to Brooke's house. She said she was going to check and see if Mercy had come home before going to the meeting with your boss."

"I'll drive," Nicholas said.

They climbed into the vehicle and Max settled himself in his designated area in the kennel. Nicholas shut the door. Worry pinched Jonas and he tried her number once again. He hung up on the voice mail.

Nicholas called his boss and Jonas listened to the conversation. "Brooke's not answering her phone. Is she already with you?" Nicholas looked at Jonas and shook his head. Brooke wasn't there.

Nicholas drove quickly and efficiently, his eyes focused on the road and on his task. Jonas watched the clock. They weren't that far away, but if Brooke was in trouble, every second might count.

"Gavin's sending backup," Nicholas said as he took the next left.

"Will they beat us there?"

"Not likely."

They slowed in front of Brooke's house. Jonas had his door open before Nicholas pulled to a stop. He raced to the front door, then stopped and took a deep breath. He couldn't go bursting in. He had to assess the situation. He felt Nicholas's hand on his arm. The man's face resembled a thundercloud. Jonas nodded and fell back. Nicholas stepped to the kitchen window and peered in. Jonas noted the front door was cracked and knew Brooke was in serious trouble. She would never leave her door open.

Nicholas stepped back and pulled his weapon from his holster. "He's got her tied up in the kitchen with a gun to her head."

Jonas felt his heart stop. The world around him simply froze. Then accelerated at warp speed. "What are we going to do?"

"Wait for backup."

"What if we don't have time to wait for them?"

Nicholas took another look. "We're going to have to create a distraction."

"How?"

"Knock on the door."

"And then what?"

"Get out of the way."

TWENTY

The knock on the door startled her. Her attacker jammed the gun against her head and she winced at the streak of lightning that arced through her skull. "Don't say a word," he growled.

"My car is sitting out front," she whispered. "My friends know I'm here. I'm late for a meeting and they're probably checking on me." She hadn't pulled into the garage that faced the front of the house. She'd just pulled in the drive and come in the front door.

He cursed. She stayed rock-still, her mind spinning. Who was out there? Gavin?

"Brooke? You in there?"

Nicholas. She glanced around for a weapon. The gun at her head was a slight deterrent, but not much. If she didn't act, she was dead. She knew it and the man next to her knew she knew it. But now she was a hostage. He needed her until he could get away. Which she would make sure didn't happen.

She kept her face toward the front door, hoping someone would glance in the kitchen window and be able to see her.

With the door that led to the garage at her attacker's

back, the only way out for her was going to have to be the front door.

"Get rid of whoever it is or they're dead, you understand me?"

"I understand."

"Brooke?" Nicholas called again.

"Yeah, Nicholas, what is it?"

"Are you all right?"

"Yes, late for my meeting with Gavin, but getting ready to head that way." She kept her voice as normal as possible, but speaking up for him to hear her sent pain vibrating through her brain. "I'll meet you there, okay?"

A loud crash ripped through the air and Brooke tensed as the man holding the gun went rigid. "What was that?"

"I don't know. Sounded like glass breaking," she said.

"Get up."

Brooke rose to her feet. The room spun, the nausea brought her to her knees and she fell, managing to roll to keep her head from taking another knock against the floor.

A shot sounded. Her attacker cried out. His weapon skidded to a stop in front of her and he jerked back, blood spreading across his left shoulder. He went to his knees.

She reached out to grab the gun. Her fingers skimmed across the grip but before she could close her hand around it, his palm swept her out of the way and once again, he had the Glock under control. He stood, his back to the kitchen door, the barrel aimed at her head. His finger twitched.

With a desperate cry, she rolled and heard the bullet slam into the hardwood next to her.

Another crash sounded, a scream of fury echoed through the house. Brooke turned to see Jonas come through the garage door, eyes blazing, bat swinging.

A crack and then her attacker's cold eyes closed and he fell to the floor beside her.

Jonas dropped the bat he'd snagged from the neighbor's yard. He had broken the back window then raced around to the kitchen door just in time to see Brooke roll and a bullet slam beside her. Without pausing to think, he'd kicked the door in and swung the bat.

It had worked. She hadn't been shot, but her pale face, bleeding forehead and shallow breaths sent terror spiking through him. He dropped to the floor beside her. "Brooke? Brooke? Are you all right? Open your eyes. Talk to me."

"I'm okay," she said without opening her eyes.

"The ambulance is on the way," Nicholas said as he cuffed the still unconscious thug.

"He's not dead, is he?" Jonas felt queasy at the thought, then stiffened his spine. The man had tried to shoot Brooke and, by the grace of God, missed. He'd been about to pull the trigger again. What else could he have done?

Nicholas shook his head. "He's alive. He'll have a whopper of a headache, but he'll live." Nicholas sounded as though he regretted that fact.

"I didn't want to kill him, just stop him."

"Well, you did that." Officers swarmed the house. Nicholas gave him an admiring nod. "Nice job. A dangerous move, but you did it well." His jaw tightened. "If you'd waited, she would be dead, so I'm not going into all of the ways things could have gone wrong."

"All I cared about was getting to Brooke. I didn't really stop to think about it."

"It's probably best. When you stop to think too much, it slows you down." He gave a Nicholas a smile and the unconscious thug a hard shove. "Wake up, you. Time to rise and shine and do some talking."

Chase and Gavin stepped inside and Jonas could see the intense concern for Brooke and himself. Gavin took one look at Brooke and frowned. "Stay put. I think the ambulance just pulled up."

"Who is he?" Brooke asked. She ignored Gavin and struggled into a sitting position. Jonas reached out to help her and then kept one hand on her shoulder in case she felt dizzy and started to keel over. She swayed, but stayed upright. He looked at the man on the floor, who'd started to stir, and wished he'd swung the bat a little harder.

Nicholas shook his head. "I don't know who he is." He patted him down. "No wallet or anything on him to give us a clue."

"He's starting to wake up," Gavin said. He shoved the man's shoulder. "Nap time is over. We need to talk." The man groaned and blinked. Gavin stood over him. "What's your name?"

"Shut up."

"Got a bit of a headache, I guess?" Brooke snapped.

Gavin pulled his iPhone from his pocket, hooked up the fingerprinting scanner and held it to the guy's index finger. "We'll know in a minute who you are if you're in the system."

The prisoner squirmed and yelled. Nicholas simply placed a foot in the middle of his back and held him down. With his hands behind his back, there wasn't much he could do. Jonas thought the officer was much too gentle.

Gavin looked up. "Damian Sharples."

"Priors?" Brooke asked.

"Oh, yes. A lot of them." Gavin kneeled to look the man in the face. "So, Mr. Sharples. Who hired you?"

"I need a doctor and a lawyer."

Gavin pinched his lips shut. Jonas could see his disgust. He nudged the man. "Where's my son?"

The thug's cold, empty eyes met his. "I don't know."

"You're a liar. Try again." Jonas kept his tone just as chilly.

Damian snarled. "If I knew where he was, he'd be dead."

Jonas drew back. And yet relief filled him. He really didn't know. And Felix wasn't dead. The sighting near Travis's house had encouraged him, but not laying eyes on Felix himself had kept him wondering. Had the officer really seen him? Maybe. Jonas wouldn't feel better until he had Felix back home.

"What about my dog?" Brooke asked. "You're the one who broke in and stole her. I know you know where she is."

"Yeah. I do. Good luck."

Jonas gripped Brooke's arm to keep her from going after the man. She fell back against him.

Brooke allowed the EMTs to bandage her head. However, when they tried to convince her to go to the hospital, she refused. "I know what a concussion feels like and I know what to do for it. I'll be fine."

Jonas disagreed and wanted to protest. He settled for a frown. She wrinkled her nose, but didn't budge on her decision. Jonas chanced a look at her boss, but Gavin simply shook his head and gave a small shrug as though to say not even he could force her if she refused.

Jonas grasped her hand and helped her to her feet. She swayed and he slipped an arm around her and tucked her into his side. "You really should get checked out."

"If the symptoms don't subside in a day or so, I'll go to the doctor. For now, it's just a headache. The priority is finding Felix and Mercy."

"We'll take care of that," Nicholas said. "You need to go home and rest."

Brooke lifted her chin. "Damian Sharples may be in custody, but this case isn't over yet. Felix could still be in danger."

Jonas tensed. "But that guy said he didn't know where he was."

"That guy didn't, but someone else might."

TWENTY-ONE

Once Damian Sharples had been hauled away, Brooke put an ice pack on her head and downed a dose of ibuprofen. She would have preferred something a little stronger, but couldn't afford to feel drowsy. She had a kid and a dog to find.

Nicholas stepped back into the house. "Two officers picked up Felix's friend, Travis. They're waiting on us to come by and talk to him."

"The parents there?" Gavin asked.

"Yes."

"Let's go," Brooke said.

Gavin frowned. "Not you."

"I don't mean any disrespect, Gavin, but I'm going. I can ride with one of you or I can drive myself. It's important. I need to do this." She kept picturing Felix's face at the children's home. He'd opened up there, let go of his attitude and let his true self come out and shine for a bit. She'd seen so much potential in him in that short period of time. And he was Jonas's son. She wanted to see him safe.

Jonas stepped up beside her. "I'm coming, too."

Gavin's face turned red, but he gave a short nod. "We're keeping it informal for now." The color faded from his cheeks and he rubbed his chin. "It actually might be a good idea to have you along, Jonas. They know and trust you."

"That's true."

"All right," Gavin said. "Nicholas, you and Chase head over to the Fuller home. Jonas and Brooke can follow. You guys stay out of sight and let Jonas see if he can get the information from the kid. If he doesn't have any luck, you can step in and put the pressure on."

Brooke walked past Gavin and out the door. Jonas stayed with her. He patted his pockets.

"You didn't drive, remember?" she said.

"Right." He held out his hand and she dropped her keys into it. "How's the head?"

"Hurts like crazy."

"I'm sorry."

She gave him a small smile. "It's all right. You got Sharples with a baseball bat. The fact that his head probably hurts worse than mine gives me great satisfaction."

Jonas climbed in the driver's seat, and Brooke slid into the passenger side. She leaned her head back and gave a small sigh. "I'm just going to keep my eyes closed while you drive, okay? Just follow Nicholas."

"Got it." He cranked the vehicle.

"Do you think Travis will tell you anything?"

"I have no idea, but I think he'll talk to me before he says anything to the police."

Silence fell between them. She could almost hear him thinking. "What is it?"

"Nothing."

"Something." She reached over and grasped his hand, just holding it, relishing the feel of his palm against hers. She'd almost died today. She hadn't had time to process that thought. Now she could feel the shakes start to set in and tried to steel herself against them. She could fall apart later. Right now, she needed to be strong.

He lifted her hand to his lips and pressed a light kiss to her knuckles. She let her eyes flutter open and turned her head to watch him drive. "Something, Jonas. What is it?"

"I can feel you shaking."

"My adrenaline is crashing."

"I could have lost you today," he said. His voice was soft, but she heard the emotion behind the words, the hitch in his breath.

Her heart contracted. He didn't say, *You almost died today.* He'd said, *I could have lost you.* That sentence held so much more meaning than the other one.

She cleared her throat. "I've been in a lot of tight spots, but I'll admit, that was the tightest."

His fingers tightened around hers. "I understand that being in some danger comes with the territory, it's part of your job, but today…seeing you with the gun on your head—" He stopped and she saw his throat work.

"I know, Jonas. I'm sorry you had to see that. To go through that."

He whipped his gaze to hers for a brief moment before looking back at the road. "That's not it. Well, part of it, but seeing that, it brought home a lot of things for me."

"Like what?"

"Like…" He paused and sighed. "Like I want my son back. Now."

"I know." Her heart tumbled to her toes. And that surprised her. She'd wanted him to say something else. Spending time with him over the past week had hit home the fact that she'd never forgotten him—or moved on from him. She gasped.

"Are you all right?"

"Um, yeah. I just realized something, that's all."

"What?"

She looked up. "I'll tell you later. We're here."

Jonas led the way to the door. Nicholas and Brooke fell in behind him. He raised his hand to knock, but didn't need to. Charles opened the door and nodded. "Come on in." He took a look at Brooke's bandaged head. "Are you all right?"

"I'm fine. Just a little run-in with a bad guy and his gun. I'll heal," she murmured.

Jonas stepped inside and made his way into the living room. His heart beat a little faster. If Travis knew where Felix was, Jonas needed to rein in his anger and concentrate on just getting the boy to tell what he knew. Jonas took the couch. Brooke sat beside him. Travis shuffled into the room and slumped onto the wing-back chair near the fireplace.

"Tell them what you know, Travis," his father said. Anger vibrated beneath the surface. Travis's shoulders stiffened and his jaw hardened.

Jonas didn't need the man making things worse. "Travis, I just want to say I appreciate you being a good friend to Felix."

Travis's head shot up before he looked back down at the floor. He shrugged.

"Travis—" Charles stepped toward his son and Brooke rose and walked to the man.

She placed a hand on his arm. "Mr. Fuller, do you think I could have a glass of water?"

The man sighed, not fooled a bit by Brooke's manipulation. "Of course. I'll be right back."

"Thank you."

He left and Brooke returned to her seat with a nod for Jonas to continue.

Jonas cleared his throat. "Anyway, I just wanted to say that Felix really looks up to you and enjoys hanging out with you."

"He's the best friend I've ever had," Travis finally said.

"I know you want to protect him, but I really need to find him." Jonas's throat worked and he had to force the words out. "There are some pretty mean people after him and while we think we have one of them, it's possible the guy was working with someone and that they're still looking for Felix." Travis simply sat with his head hanging, the baseball cap shielding his face. "Travis, will you look me in the eye for a minute?" Travis hesitated, then looked up and Jonas snagged his gaze. The kid was completely conflicted. "If those guys get their hands on Felix, they'll kill him. It's that serious."

The indecision faded and Travis nodded. "And you can keep him safe?"

"As soon as we know he's not in the wrong hands, we have a plan to make sure they know that Felix doesn't have what they want. Once they know that, there's no reason for them to keep coming after him."

"He was afraid you were going to get hurt."

"What?" Jonas sat back.

"That's one of the reasons he took off. He was mad at you for wanting to send him away, sure, but he told me that maybe it was better if he just stayed away from you, then the people who were after him would leave you alone."

Jonas's breath left his lungs. A punch to his solar plexus wouldn't have had more effect than the boy's words. He swallowed and nodded. "I appreciate that. That means a lot to me, that he would do that, but we need to get him home and make sure he's protected. Please, Travis…"

"He's in my neighbor's tree house. Their kids are all grown up and they don't have any grandchildren, so I figured it would be a good place for him to hide out for a while. Just until things cooled down."

Jonas bolted to his feet. "He's there now?"

Travis nodded. "As far as I know."

Brooke laid a hand on Jonas's arm. "Take it easy. If you go charging out there, he might run."

"I won't charge." Jonas headed for the door. He wanted to see his son. He needed the tight ball of worry that had been his constant companion for the past few days to dissipate. And he needed to be able to tell Brooke exactly how he felt about her.

He stepped outside onto the back porch. The woods out back hid a lot. Including a tree house in the backyard of the neighbor to the right. The lack of a fence made for easy access. Heart pounding, palms sweating, Jonas headed for the woods. At the base of the tree, he looked up. "Felix?"

No answer. "I know you're up there, Felix. I talked to Travis. Will you please come down?" If Felix decided to stay quiet, Jonas would have to climb up. He'd placed one foot on the bottom rung of the ladder when Felix's head popped through the window.

"I can't believe Travis sold me out."

Jonas sighed. "He's trying to help you. Like we all are."

"I don't need any help and I'm not going to be sent away. I can take care of myself."

"You don't have to go away. You're not in danger anymore."

Felix fell silent, then his head disappeared. The small door opened and his son came down the ladder, as agile as a monkey. When he reached the bottom, Jonas reached out and pulled him into a hug.

Felix stood there for a moment, then Jonas felt his arms wrap around his waist. "You're not mad at me?" Felix mumbled into his chest.

"Oh, I'm mad, but I'm more glad than mad. So very glad you're safe. You scared me to death, son."

"I'm sorry. I really am. I just didn't want to go away and leave you all alone and not be able to make sure you were okay. Travis kept checking on you for me and letting me know that you were safe."

Jonas sighed and kissed the top of his son's head. "I understand. I'm not saying I'm okay with the way you went about everything, but I do understand."

Felix pulled back and looked up at him. "Really?"

"Really." He thought about the night he'd taken off after Brooke and shook his head. "Love makes you do dumb stuff sometimes."

"Love?"

"Yeah, love." Oh, boy. Yes, love. He cleared his throat. "I love you, Felix, you know that. And I know you were worried you'd brought those guys down on us because you took the phone."

Tears dripped down Felix's young face. He nodded. "I know. I was stupid. Still am, but you know I love you, too."

"Yeah," Jonas whispered. "I know. And you're thirteen. I suppose you're going to do some stupid things over the next few years. Let's just make sure they don't get you killed, okay?"

"Or you," Felix mumbled.

Nicholas stepped up and Brooke was only two steps behind him. "Were you in that tree house when Max was trying to track you?" Nicholas asked.

Felix pulled away from his dad. "Yes."

Nicholas frowned. "I guess Max and I need to do some more training."

Felix gave a small smile. "It wasn't totally his fault. I figured someone would try to track me with the dogs so I changed into one of Travis's shirts and had him drag mine along the ground, then get on his bike and ride with it flapping in the wind. I didn't know if it would work or not, but figured it was worth a try."

Admiration glinted in Nicholas's eyes for a brief moment before he shook his head and looked at Jonas. "Smart kid."

"Too smart," Jonas muttered.

Brooke's phone rang. She answered it and relief crossed her face. She looked at him. "They found Mercy."

"Wonderful."

He nudged his son. "Come on, let's go tell Travis everything's fine."

"His dad's going to kill him."

"Naw, he's mad, but I don't think he'll do Travis any bodily harm. Might ground him for a year or two..."

Felix smiled and wrapped an arm around Jonas's waist as they headed back to the house together. Brooke walked beside them. Jonas reached out and grasped her fingers.

"Now what?" Felix asked.

"Now I go greet a prodigal of my own," Brooke said.

Chase and Isaac met her at her home. Chase opened the back of his SUV and Mercy bounded out.

"Mercy!" Brooke called. She raced over to her friend and partner and dropped to her knees. The dog gave her a sloppy kiss and Brooke didn't even care. Tears filled her eyes and ran down her cheeks. She knew she shouldn't be so attached to the animal, but her heart had been lost from the day they became partners. She looked up at Chase and Isaac. "Where did you find her?"

"Damian's house. He had her tied up in a shed out back."

Felix climbed from the car. Mercy trotted over to him and gave him a wet greeting, too. Felix simply laughed and patted the dog's head. Mercy went to the front door and sat. Brooke laughed. "I guess she wants to go in." She opened the door and Mercy beelined it for her bed in front of the fireplace. She snagged her bone, settled it between her paws and started chewing.

"She's glad to be home," Jonas said.

"I'm glad she's home," Brooke agreed. She looked at Felix. "And I'm very glad you're all right."

Felix looked away then back at Brooke. He gave her a small smile. "That makes two of us."

Chase clapped Isaac on the shoulder. "We've got a meeting in thirty."

Isaac nodded. "We'd better head out."

Brooke frowned. "Is it the whole team?"

"Yes."

"Then I'd better get ready."

"Whoa, wait a minute," Chase said. "That was a hard crack on the head. You're supposed to be taking it easy."

"Says who?"

"Gavin."

She sighed. "I'm fine. I need to be in on the meeting. I'll meet you guys there."

"I'll bring her," Jonas said. He looked at Brooke.

"You don't need to be driving, so we'll just remove that from your list. If you have your mind made up to go, I'll take you."

Isaac clapped Jonas on the back and looked at Brooke. "He knows you. Impressive. You'd better hang on tight to this one."

"Go away," she said, her tone mild.

Isaac laughed.

Jonas looked at Felix. "I guess you're coming with us."

"Ugh. Do I have to?"

Before Jonas could respond, Isaac said, "Why don't I have an officer drop him at his buddy's house and stay with him until we're done with your meeting?"

"Yes," Felix begged. "Please."

"That's fine." Jonas nodded and Felix punched a fist into the air. Isaac made the arrangements and Felix got his stuff together.

After they left, Brooke looked at Jonas and the tender look in his eyes was nearly her undoing. She didn't want to go to the meeting, she wanted to stay home, take some more medication and then snuggle down into Jonas's arms while Felix played with Mercy.

Instead, she drew in a deep breath. "I'm ready when you are."

Jonas led the way to the car and she climbed in. Mercy hopped in the back with Felix. Brooke kept stealing glances at him as he drove, his hands strong and sure on the wheel, his gaze alert as he watched the other drivers. He shot her a glance and caught her watching him. A smile slid across his lips. "You never did tell me what you realized."

"What?"

"Earlier, you said you realized something and then said you'd tell me later." He shrugged. "It's later."

Brooke bit her lip, then stiffened her spine. She'd made a mistake eight years ago. It was time to do things right. "You asked me why I'd never married."

"Right. You said your career was your focus."

"That's what I said. That's what I had convinced myself I believed, too."

"Huh?"

"Jonas, the reason I never married is because—" Did she dare? Her heart pounded and her palms started to sweat.

"Because?"

"Because of the fact that I can't have children, yes, but also because I just couldn't find another...you."

His breath caught and he pulled to the side of the road. "I can't just let you walk into a meeting as though you didn't just say that. You're going to be a little late."

She nodded, shrugged and couldn't stop the little laugh that escaped. "It's okay. I'm always a little late. They expect it by now."

"Tell me what you meant by that last statement."

"I dated a few guys after we went our separate ways. I even got up the nerve to tell one of them that I couldn't have children."

"And he dumped you?"

The leashed violence in the words almost made her smile. She shook her head. "He said it didn't matter, that we could always adopt. He himself was adopted and he'd always hoped the woman he married would be open to going through the process with him."

"Oh."

"I was stunned. I'd already planned my reaction, steeled myself for when he walked away." She spread her hands and blinked back the tears. "And then…he didn't."

"So what was the problem?"

"I realized at that very moment that I didn't love him. I wanted to. I tried. But I just didn't. But his reaction made me sick to my stomach, too."

"I'm confused."

She gave a small hiccupping laugh. "I know. When he said that we could adopt, it hit me that I should have told you. I started playing the what-if game. I nearly drove myself crazy. I told myself I'd hurt you enough and that I didn't deserve you. So, I threw myself into my work and did my best to forget you," she whispered. "But I couldn't. Because I loved you. I've always loved you, Jonas. I've never stopped and I'm so sorry for hurting you and I hope you can forgive—"

He kissed her. He wrapped his hand around the back of her neck and gently pulled her closer. She went still, her brain whirling. Then told it to shut up and kissed him back. An I-missed-you-I'm-so-glad-to-be-back-with-you kind of kiss. When he finally pulled away, Brooke had to concentrate on breathing. Her face felt hot, flushed. "Wow."

"Yeah. Double wow." He blinked, stared at her for a few seconds then shook his head. "Wow." He cranked the car. "Let's get you to your meeting. I'll be waiting outside when you're done and we'll finish this conversation."

"Right."

"And tell everyone that they're invited to a cookout at my house tomorrow night."

"A cookout?"

He shrugged. "For those who can make it. Everyone has really put their lives on hold—some even on the line—for me and Felix. I'd like to do something for you all."

She nodded. "All right, I'll pass the word."

"Oh, and one more thing."

"What?"

"I love you, too."

Fifteen minutes later, Brooke slipped into her chair and ignored the good-natured teasing of the guys. She barely heard them as she replayed the kiss over and over in her mind. The kiss, the words, the look on his face...

Fiona entered the conference room and Brooke shifted into a more comfortable position. The bandage on her left temple made the skin under the tape itch, but she resisted scratching it.

"Do we know anything about the guy we caught at Brooke's house?" Chase asked.

"Not much," Fiona said. "He's got a nice rap sheet that includes armed robbery and assault with a deadly weapon. However, I did find one interesting thing."

"What's that?" Gavin asked.

"He was in rehab for a while. He completed the program, got out and got a job."

"Where?"

"He worked in the janitorial department of Thorne Industries."

Brooke sat up straight as she processed that bomb.

"Which means we can tie him to Congressman Jeffries," Nicholas muttered.

Gavin shot him a dark look. Nicholas didn't look away.

Isaac tapped the table. "So is he talking?"

"No," Gavin said. "Not a word. Said someone called him and asked if he needed some fast, easy cash. He said yes and the person gave him his instructions. He has no idea who the voice on the other end was."

"Of course not," Brooke said.

"But we can tie him to the aide's death. We found Paul Harrison's wallet in Damian's apartment."

"Excellent," Brooke murmured.

"Any word on Erin Eagleton?" Gavin asked.

"Nothing," Chase said, his jaw tight, eyes narrowed. "We'll find her, though."

"It's possible she's dead," Nicholas said.

"She's not dead." Chase's voice rose a fraction and the room went silent. Chase cleared his throat. "Sorry. I just don't believe she's dead or that she had anything to do with the shootings. She'll explain when we find her."

Brooke again noted the hope, the faith in Chase's voice and wondered at his relationship with Erin— who'd been Michael Jeffries's girlfriend.

"Then we need to hope she turns up soon. I'm ready to solve this case. Any more on the internet service provider trackings?" A few weeks ago, someone researching bills introduced by Congressman Jeffries had been tracked to rural Virginia. The research had gone all the way back to his first term.

Chase exhaled and shook his head. "No, nothing since then. If it's Erin, she's gone quiet."

"We've made a statement to the press that we've found the phone and that we're pulling information from it. Hopefully, that will deter whoever hired Mr. Sharples to go after Felix."

"He should be safe now," Nicholas agreed.

"Good," Gavin said. "Now…"

Brooke fidgeted and Gavin's voice faded. Jonas was waiting on her and she wanted to finish their conversation. Hope made her giddy and unable to totally focus on the conversation around her. She just wanted to take a break, to go be with Jonas.

"You okay, Brooke? Do you need to take off?"

She blinked at Gavin's question. She touched the bandage on her forehead. Then stood. "Yes, I think I do." For more reasons than one.

Gavin nodded. "Someone will call you with an update."

"Great." She walked toward the exit then turned. "Oh, you're all invited to a cookout at Jonas's house tomorrow night at five-thirty." She slipped out of the conference room, a smile spreading across her lips.

TWENTY-TWO

Brooke looked around. The cookout was a huge success. How Jonas had managed to put this together so fast, she'd never know. Probably had a caterer for a client who owed him a favor. Burgers and hot dog smoke filled the air and her nose twitched while her stomach rumbled.

Everyone had been able to make the cookout, including Cassie and Gavin, Adam and Lana, Nicholas and even Chase who refused to give up the search for Erin Eagleton. He kept looking at his phone and she knew he was hoping Fiona would have something for him to work with. So far, there was nothing.

All the dogs were in attendance and behaved perfectly in spite of the tempting aromas that drifted past them.

Jonas was dressed in a ridiculous apron that said Real Men Wear Aprons. He kept shooting her secret smiles and she figured she'd never need to use makeup on her cheeks again.

Felix's attitude had changed overnight and he and Jonas seemed to have turned a corner in their relationship. Last night, she'd left them alone to give them time to talk even though she wanted to be with Jonas. He needed to be with his son and she was all right with that.

Nicholas stepped up beside her. "How's the head?"

She touched the bandage she'd just changed that morning. "Still aching, but nothing some ibuprofen and I can't handle."

"I'm glad." He paused and took a sip of his tea, his eyes on Jonas, who threw a football to Felix. "You love him, don't you?"

She sighed. "Yes. I do."

"He's a good man. I approve."

She laughed. "Thanks. That actually means a lot." She sobered. "How's it going with Selena Barrows?"

He shook his head. "She's a feisty one, no doubt about that. She's desperate to find her cousin and pushes me on a daily basis about our progress, but clearly Erin's not too keen on being found."

"Do you think she's still alive?"

"I hope so because I think she's the only one who knows what happened the night Michael Jeffries was killed and his father, the congressman, shot and left for dead."

"Besides the murderer."

"Exactly," he murmured.

She caught Jonas's eye. "Excuse me."

Nicholas smiled. "Of course. I wouldn't want to get in the way of true love."

She punched Nicholas in the arm and made her way over to Jonas. "You don't need an apron, you're not cooking."

"I know, but Felix gave it me for my birthday a couple of months ago and I figured now was a good time to test drive it."

He stole her heart in so many ways. "You're a wonderful dad, Jonas."

He leaned over to place a light kiss on her lips. The crowd faded away. "I love you, Brooke. I feel like I've loved you forever. How do you feel about adoption?"

She blinked. "As you can imagine, I've thought about it a lot. Why?"

"So you've thought about it. Does that mean you're open to it?"

She gave a small laugh. "Of course. Are you?"

"That's why I'm asking. I think you'd be a great mother."

Tears surfaced. She blinked them back. "Thanks, Jonas. I like to think I would."

"So, do you want to adopt some kids?"

She wasn't slow. She caught the meaning behind his words. "I think that would be lovely. One day."

"One day...soon?"

"Possibly. That depends."

"On what?"

"On how soon the father of those adopted kids wants to adopt."

"He wants to pretty soon, I'm sure."

"How can you be so sure?"

Jonas glanced over his shoulder and she saw him wink at Felix who seemed to have a boundless amount of energy. He bounced on the balls of his feet. At his dad's wink, his eyes went wide. He shoved a hand in his pocket and pulled out a whistle. Jonas nodded. Felix blew the whistle. Everyone went quiet.

Felix said, "I have an announcement to make." He looked at Jonas. "Actually my dad has a question to ask."

Brooke looked at Jonas. He swallowed hard and gave

a small laugh. "Okay, maybe I shouldn't have invited all these people because I'm really nervous now," he whispered. "But, oh well." He dropped to his knee and a soft gasp escaped her.

The crowd stayed silent.

"Jonas?"

Indecision flickered in his eyes. "Is it too soon?"

And Brooke knew. She had no doubts. Jonas was the man she would marry. "No, it's not too soon."

His brilliant smile flashed at her. "Brooke, it's been a long time coming, but—" he took a deep breath "—I love you. Will you marry me and fill up our house with Felix and a bunch of other kids from the children's home?"

She didn't hesitate. "Yes," she whispered. "A thousand times yes."

Felix whooped. Clapping and cheers broke out. Jonas lowered his lips to hers and gave her a thoroughly approving kiss. Then he swept her off her feet and swung her around in a circle. When he placed her back on her feet, Mercy bounded over and barked. Jonas scratched her ears and Felix dropped to the ground to hug her. When Felix stood, he looked up at Brooke and gave her a shy smile. "Does this mean I get to call you Mom?"

"You don't have to, but I would be honored for you to call me Mom if it's what you want," she said.

"I want." He blinked rapidly and sniffed, then stepped forward to wrap her in a hug. "Thanks... Mom."

Brooke had to clear her throat before she could speak. And she could only squeak out, "You bet...son."

Felix released her. Jonas looked like he might join in the crying fest, but then people started in on the congratulations and Brooke found her tears gone, laughter taking their place. After a few minutes, she flung herself back in Jonas's arms. "Thank you."

"I should be the one thanking you. You've made Felix and me complete now." He took her left hand in his and slipped a beautiful diamond on her ring finger. "I've had that ring for a long time."

"I don't know what to say," she whispered.

"Say you'll stay with me forever."

She nodded through the tears that had surfaced once again. "I'll stay. Forever."

Another kiss followed another hug, with his arms wrapped tight around her and her head nestled against his healing shoulder.

She sighed and sent up a thankful prayer. She was right where she wanted to be.

Forever.

* * * * *

Margaret Daley, an award-winning author of ninety books (five million sold worldwide), has been married for over forty years and is a firm believer in romance and love. When she isn't traveling, she's writing love stories, often with a suspense thread, and corralling her three cats, who think they rule her household. To find out more about Margaret, visit her website at margaretdaley.com.

Visit the Author Profile page
at Harlequin.com for more titles.

SECURITY BREACH

Margaret Daley

By whom also we have access by faith into this grace
wherein we stand, and rejoice in hope
of the glory of God.
—*Romans 5:2*

To the brave men and women
who are K-9 officers and their canine partners

ONE

Nicholas Cole hurried toward the White House special in-house security chief's office in the West Wing, gripping the leash for his K-9 partner, Max. Two Secret Service agents emerged from the office, wearing gloves and carrying a folder. Both nodded toward him as he entered the room.

General Margaret Meyer stood behind her oak desk, her hands fisted on the tan blotter, a fierce expression on her face, her intense blue eyes narrowing on him. He swallowed hard. He rarely saw her this upset, but tension poured off her.

"Shut the door, Nicholas." The general moved from behind her desk, gesturing toward its flat surface. "This office has been searched."

After following her instruction, he came to attention in front of his boss, having a hard time shaking his military training in the Navy SEALs. "What happened?" He scanned the neat desk and the bookcase to the right, and wondered how she knew.

She straightened to her full height of five feet three inches, her shoulders thrust back. "When I went to get a folder from the bottom left-hand drawer, the stack was out of order. I have a very precise way of arranging everything in here, and thankfully I do or I might not have known someone went through the Michael Jeffries file."

The Jeffries case was an investigation being undertaken by the Capitol K-9 Unit, comprising fourteen cops, soldiers and special agents who looked into important cases and reported to Margaret Meyer, a former four-star general who worked under the president's direction. "Anything missing?"

"No, but it would be easy to take pictures of the papers and evidence the team has uncovered so far."

"What do you want me to do, ma'am?" Nicholas knew the murder of Michael Jeffries—son of the prominent congressman Harland Jeffries, who had been wounded in the attack against Michael—was important to the general, as well as to his unit captain, Gavin McCord. He and the rest of the team had pledged to find who killed Michael and left his father to bleed to death.

"Coordinate with Special Agent Dan Calvert who just left. You're to work with him on this. I want to know who was in my office. It could be the break we've needed on this case. I have Congressman Jeffries breathing down my neck. He wants answers to who killed his son. Not to mention Senator Eagleton insisting his daughter had nothing to do with Michael Jeffries's murder. Those two men have never been friends, and each one has a great deal of political clout."

Erin Eagleton, who'd been Michael Jeffries's girlfriend, was a person of interest in Michael's murder and the shooting of the congressman. Her starfish charm, with her initials engraved on it, had been found at the crime scene. Considering that Capitol K-9 Unit member Chase Zachary had run into Erin only hours before the murder and she'd been wearing the charm, the team desperately wanted to find Erin to bring her in for questioning. They'd been searching for her since Michael's murder. "I noticed Dan carrying a file from your office. Is he processing it for latent prints?"

"Yes, and any other physical evidence he can get. With the Easter Egg Roll today, the White House has been crawling with visitors since early this morning. Dan is going to view the security tapes and no doubt come up with a long list of suspects who had access." She shook her head, a scowl wrinkling her forehead. "Especially with the Oval Office and the Situation Room here in the West Wing being used for the festivities."

A security nightmare in his opinion, but the Easter Egg Roll was a long White House tradition. "When was the last time you opened that drawer?"

"Yesterday evening before I left for a reception in the Roosevelt Room then attended a state dinner for dignitaries from the UN. After that, I went home. I didn't come back here."

"Then we're looking at a sixteen-hour window."

General Meyer adjusted her horn-rimmed glasses. "So you see the problem. The list is much longer than I would like." She checked her wristwatch. "In fact, I need to put in an appearance at the Easter Egg Roll. I know the event is covered by the Secret Service, but I want you out there with Max. My office was breached and the perpetrator could likely be among the guests outside."

"May I inspect your office first?"

She nodded once. "I'll see you later. If you discover anything, find me right away. I want to be kept informed on everything."

"Yes, ma'am."

After the door closed, and he and Max were alone

in the office, he unfastened the leash to his rottweiler and let him investigate. In addition to his usual duties as a guard/suspect-apprehension dog, Max was cross-trained on bomb detection, as an extra security precaution due to their post at the White House.

While Max moved around the room, Nicholas snapped on latex gloves and crouched behind the desk on the left side. He inspected the bottom drawer, then slid his hand back as far as he could under the piece of furniture, feeling for anything that might have fallen and rolled beneath it. Nothing.

Next, he examined a cabinet behind the desk. Underneath, his fingers touched something small. A cufflink? He pulled it out and scrutinized the gold cufflink with a bald-eagle imprint and the initials *VG*. How long had this been there? Did it belong to a visitor or the intruder?

After putting the piece of jewelry into an evidence bag and pocketing it, he continued his search of the office. Ten minutes later, other than the cufflink, he and Max had come up empty-handed.

"Time to go to the party, boy. General Meyer requires our attendance."

His rottweiler turned his amber-colored eyes on Nicholas and gave one bark.

Dressed in his black uniform with the emblem of the Capitol K-9 Unit on each sleeve and over his left pocket, Nicholas exited the West Wing by the West Colonnade and cut across the Rose Garden toward the South Lawn where the Easter Egg Roll was taking place.

For a few minutes he stood on the outskirts of the crowd assembled to enjoy the special party for the young children who'd won tickets by a lottery system. The kids were joined by various government officials, which included the president and his wife, and celebrities. The highlight was a visit by the Easter Bunny, but other costumed characters mingled among the crowd.

He scanned the people gathered, looking for anyone with the initials *VG*. His survey came to rest upon Selena Barrow, the White House tour director, responsible for planning this event. Even from a distance, Selena commanded a person's attention. Tall, slender with long wavy brown hair and the bluest eyes, she was attractive, but what drew him to Selena was her air of integrity and compassion. Since Erin had disappeared, Selena had been relentless in her support of her cousin's innocence, and he admired that kind of dedication.

When a couple with their two little girls stopped to talk to her, she smiled, bent down and spoke to the children. He glimpsed the radiant look on Selena's face. She probably was having as much fun as the kids at the event. Whenever he saw her with children, he got the feeling she must love being around them.

Last year he'd dated a woman who'd wanted half a dozen kids. It hadn't taken him long to know they weren't a good fit. He didn't want to be a parent after the childhood he'd had. His father had certainly not been a good example to follow, and his mother hadn't been much better. He pushed thoughts of his past away and concentrated on the job he had to do today.

Selena would have an updated list of people invited to the party. It might save him a trip to the front gate if he asked her for it. And give him a reason to talk to her.

After slipping her keys back into her jacket pocket, her computer tablet nestled against the crook of her arm, Selena checked the schedule to see which age group of children would be doing the Easter Egg Roll next. Her friend Amy and her daughter were attending this year, and she wanted to cheer for Courtney in the egg roll.

Everything was set up. All the other activities were progressing according to plan—the Eggspress Yourself, the Eggtivity Zone Obstacle Course, the Rockin' Egg Roll Stage and the Storytime Stage with Senator Eagleton, her uncle, reading a Peter Cottontail book. A special appearance by the Easter Bunny would occur at the end of the story.

She watched her uncle entertaining the children sitting on the ground around him, his deep voice expressive, with the right inflection to convey the emotions of the characters. If only things had been different in her past, she and her uncle might have been on good terms. Instead, he barely acknowledged her because of her mother, his younger sister. He was polite but distant and reserved around Selena.

Selena wove her way through the crowd preparing to watch the Easter Egg Roll competition for the three- and four-year-old children. The president stepped into the fenced-off area to demonstrate what they were to do and start the race.

Selena pushed closer toward the activity. Moving quickly through the throng, Miss Chick, one of the costumed characters, bumped into her and nearly knocked Selena down.

Miss Chick, dressed in a feathered chicken outfit, steadied Selena and said, "Sorry. Late for the Eggspress Yourself," and scurried away, the daisy on her large straw hat swaying in the breeze.

Selena turned from watching Miss Chick disappear to continue toward the Easter Egg Roll and ran right into Nicholas Cole. Slowly she raised her gaze to his face, taking in his strong jawline, lips tilted in a grin, his deep brown eyes.

"Where are you going in such a hurry?" His smoky voice with a slight Southern drawl always sent a thrill through her.

"The Egg Roll. To see if everything is going smoothly."

Being at least six inches taller than her five-nine, he scanned the mass of people who tried to get closer to the Easter Egg Roll. "From what I see everything is fine. You've done a good job."

"Thanks, but it isn't over with until this evening. I won't relax until then."

As if she could relax with her cousin missing. Since Erin's disappearance, Selena had constantly asked the Capitol K-9 Unit for updates about Erin's whereabouts, but she'd pestered this man the most because he was assigned to the White House. What was the Capitol K-9 Unit doing to find her cousin? To find the real killer of Michael Jeffries, Erin's boyfriend? There was no way she had murdered Michael. So far, Selena hadn't been successful in proving Erin was innocent, but she was getting closer. She'd been spending her off-hours investigating the cases Michael had been working on as an attorney. Maybe one of them was the reason he was killed.

"I have a favor to ask you." The dimples in his cheeks appeared.

And as usual she melted at the sight of them. He had the most engaging smile. "If I can help, I will." She didn't want to antagonize every member of the unit.

"I need a list of all the people attending today's events."

"All thirty thousand?"

"And the volunteers, too."

"Oh, what's an additional thousand or so. Security has that list."

Now, on top of the dimples, his brown eyes sparkled, luring her to forget she was working. "I know, but I thought you might have it on your tablet. It's important." He tapped the device she held in her hands.

"Only the volunteers. The full list is in my office." She glanced toward the West Wing and realized it was closer than Security. "I can pull it up on my computer for you."

"Please."

"I'd ask you why, but I'm sure you won't tell me for security reasons."

His grin grew.

Maybe if she did him a favor, he would return it and help her concerning Erin. "Let's go. Everything seems to be going fine. If not, I'm sure I'll be notified."

Nicholas looked toward General Margaret Meyer. "I need to tell the general something. Go ahead and pull the list up. I'll be right there."

As Selena headed toward the West Wing, she glanced at Nicholas talking to General Meyer. The older woman frowned, clearly upset about whatever they were discussing. Did it have anything to do with Erin or the murder case? She knew her uncle, Erin's father, was insisting the general's team find the real killer.

Selena walked past the Rose Garden and entered the West Wing through the West Colonnade entrance. When she reached the door to her office, she slipped her hand into her jacket pocket for her keys. Nothing.

They were gone!

She just had them outside. She tried the knob, and it turned as though she'd never locked the door when she left hours ago. She always did. As she eased it open, it was wrenched from her grasp, and Miss Chick, in her yellow-feathered costume, latched onto her arm and dragged her into the office. Before she could react, Miss Chick smashed a vase against her skull. Selena fell backward, hitting the floor as Miss Chick fled.

She started to get up to alert Security, but the room spun before her. She sank back and closed her eyes. The darkness continued to swirl...

"Selena. Selena, are you okay?"

She pried her eyelids up and saw Nicholas's face looming close to hers. Worry lined his handsome features. A pounding in her head quickly reminded her of what had occurred. She tried to rise.

Nicholas clasped her shoulders. "Stay still. I've called Security and the doctor. Someone hit you with a vase." A latex glove on his hand, he held up a shard of a beautiful green-and-pink ceramic vase the president had given her when she'd first come to work as the White House tour director and his assistant.

"Do you remember what happened?"

"Did you see Miss Chick leave?"

Nicholas shook his head. The same costumed characters were hired every year for the event, and Nicholas had to be long used to seeing them all. "Does she have something to do with this?" He gestured to the mess in the office.

This time, despite the throbbing head, Selena propped herself up on her elbows and scanned the usually neat area. "She hit me with the vase and fled." Had she lost any consciousness? "How long did you talk with the general?"

"About five minutes then I came straight here." He spoke to Security through his invisible headset. "Miss

Chick needs to be found and detained." He quickly described her costume. "She attacked Selena Barrow in her office."

Shortly, two security guards came into the room as well as Secret Service agent Dan Calvert. He took one look and said, "Fill me in."

Selena sat all the way up, trying to ignore the light-headedness swarming her. "I came to get the visitor list for Nicholas. That's when I discovered my keys were missing and the door was unlocked. The next thing I know, Miss Chick is grabbing me and yanking me inside then hitting me with a vase. She ran out after that. I don't know anything else."

"Your keys were stolen? Any idea when?" Nicholas asked, helping Selena to her feet and guiding her to a chair nearby.

She eased down, gripping the arms to steady herself. "I know exactly, but at the time I didn't realize it. Miss Chick bumped into me outside a few minutes before you and I talked. I had my keys until then."

Dan directed the security officers to stand guard outside the office. "What keys were taken?"

"To this office, my file cabinets, a storeroom around the corner and my house. I keep my car keys separate in my purse, which is locked in the top left drawer of my desk."

"Was that drawer key taken, too?"

"Yes."

Nicholas peered behind the desk. "Everything has been emptied." Donning a second glove, he moved toward the purse on the floor and held it up. "Check to see if anything was taken. We'll get to the bottom of this."

She took the brown Coach bag Erin had given her for her birthday. All her life Selena had fought for everything she had, so it was nice to have a champion for a moment, especially with all the tension of her cousin Erin named a person of interest in her boyfriend's murder and the shooting of Congressman Jeffries. That day, when they'd met to celebrate her birthday, her cousin had seemed so happy. Just a few weeks later, Michael was murdered…and Erin had disappeared.

Selena intended to help prove Erin couldn't have done it. Erin cared for Michael and wouldn't hurt anyone.

Then why did she disappear the night of the murder?

Selena refused to dwell on that nagging question and instead focused on what might be missing from her purse. She dumped the contents on her lap, her car keys falling out, and went through her wallet, then looked up. "No, everything is here."

The doctor arrived with his black bag. He quickly examined her, asking how she felt.

"My head hurts, but I'm all right. I've had worse headaches than this one." She couldn't leave the White House in the middle of the biggest affair she'd put together.

"Do you have any nausea?"

"No."

He checked the movement of her eyes, then the bump forming on the side of her head. "You'll have a knot, but there wasn't a cut, so no stitches. You should at least go to my office and let me do a more extensive evaluation in case you need to go to the hospital."

"I will later. I want to check and see if anything is missing from my office."

The doctor frowned but nodded. He looked toward Nicholas. "Make sure she does."

"I will."

The doctor turned back to Selena. "If you get dizzy or your vision is affected, blurry, bright-light sensitive, let me know immediately. Please rest as much as possible, and you can take over-the-counter pain meds for the headache. If it gets worse, let me know that immediately, too."

"I understand. If anything changes, I will."

When the doctor left, she swung her attention between Dan and Nicholas. "I want to see if anything has been taken, though Miss Chick didn't appear to have anything on her." Selena had to check a few files in particular to see if they were intact.

"If you're feeling up to it," Nicholas said, "Dan and I need to know that, too." Behind her desk, Nicholas bent over and picked up a straw hat with a daisy on it. "I'm assuming this isn't yours."

"No, it's Miss Chick's."

"Good. I'm going to use it to see if I can find where she went while Dan stays here with you." Nicholas covered the distance to his K-9 partner, waiting near the door.

Taking hold of Max's leash, Nicholas showed the straw hat to the rottweiler, and the dog sniffed it. "Find, Max."

Nicholas and Max disappeared out into the hallway. Previously, when she'd seen Nicholas working with his K-9 partner, she'd always been amazed at Max's abilities. She hoped they'd find Miss Chick—whoever the costumed intruder really was.

Nicholas followed his dog through the crowds and out the door to the West Colonnade. Max headed east, stopping every once in a while and pointing his nose in the air, then charging forward. The dog entered the

Rose Garden and headed to the lawn area bordered by flowering plants and boxwoods. The tulips were in full bloom, adding a brilliant splash among the greenery. Max came to a halt near the cluster of white furniture under a large magnolia tree and barked.

Nicholas checked the area, wondering if Miss Chick had sat here sometime recently. He moved behind two white chairs and inspected the bushes, plunging his hand into the middle. When he grasped a feathery material, glimpsing yellow, he tugged it free.

Miss Chick's costume—discarded.

"Good boy." He gave Max a treat.

He placed a call to Dan. "I found the costume in the Rose Garden minus Miss Chick. Are you still with Selena?"

"Yes. Do you want to talk to her?"

"Yes." When Selena came on, Nicholas asked, "Who's Miss Chick?"

"Just a minute. I'll have to look on my list of employees." A moment late, she answered, "Tara Wilkins."

"When she bumped into you earlier, could you tell if it was Tara Wilkins?"

A long pause—he could imagine her forehead creasing with a frown while her blue eyes darkened—then Selena said, "No, not for sure. Her voice was low and husky, but I'm pretty sure it was a woman."

"When was the last time you saw Tara Wilkins without the headpiece on?"

"When I talked with the costumed characters in the East Wing entrance before the event started. That was seven this morning."

"What do you know about Tara Wilkins? Is she trustworthy? Could she have given the costume to someone so the person could break into your office after the morning briefing?"

"She was Miss Chick last year and did a good job. The Secret Service vetted her as they do for all the people I use as costumed characters for this event, but I suppose it's possible."

"I'll have the police check her residence." He didn't have a good feeling about this.

"I don't see her putting her reputation on the line like that." Selena's worry came through the line.

"One good thing is that all the people who are here are on a list. You don't get in here without going through checkpoints."

"Please let me know what's happening. I'm responsible for the employees I hired for this event."

"I will. Anything missing from your office?"

"No."

"Let me talk with Dan again."

When Dan came back on the phone, he said, "I'll let Security know what's developing."

"Tara Wilkins needs to be found. Her residence checked. We don't have any idea what's going on. I'm not even sure it was Tara Wilkins in the costume, but I'm going to see if Max can follow the scent from the clothing. I'll let you know what I find."

"Good. In the meantime, I'm escorting Miss Barrow to the doctor's office."

Nicholas heard a protest coming from the background, and he smiled. Dan was going to have his hands full getting her to go. "Have fun. I'll check in later."

"Chicken," Dan whispered. "You left me with the toughest job. Anyone can follow a dog around."

Nicholas chuckled and disconnected the call, then let Max smell the yellow feathery costume. "Find."

As Max sniffed the air, Nicholas couldn't get the sound of Selena's voice out of his mind. What he had seen of her around the White House only reinforced the image of a woman dedicated to doing a good job. Did she think she had failed at her job by hiring Tara Wilkins?

As Nicholas followed Max through several areas of the Easter Egg Roll, he scanned his surroundings, wondering if the person who had discarded Miss Chick's costume was still here. If so, Max would find her—or possibly him. He had a photo on his phone of the volunteer who was supposed to be Miss Chick. If she wasn't the one who ran into Selena, then where was she?

Passing the Storytime Stage, Max dodged around the adults and children attending and finally came to a stop at the entrance to the women's restroom on the west side of the lawn.

Was the person still inside?

Nicholas started to look for a female security officer, but before he could, his rottweiler sniffed the ground then the air and took off toward the nearby exit to the event. When Nicholas emerged onto West Executive Avenue, Max halted in the middle of the road then trotted toward E Street. Near the Souvenir Egg Pickup, his K-9 came to another stop then wandered around the area but never picked up the scent again.

"Sorry, boy." Nicholas petted his dog. "She must have gotten into a vehicle. At least we know how she left and an approximate time."

Could that woman also be the same one who had gone through General Meyer's office? The intruder couldn't have picked a better day, with thirty thousand visitors and over a thousand volunteers. He'd have to watch a lot of security tapes to see if he could pinpoint who had ransacked the general's office and who had stolen Selena's keys. And why her keys? To rob her? Nothing was missing from her office.

Was something else going on here involving Michael Jeffries's case? That could be the connection between what had happened in General Meyer's office and in Selena's. Selena was a first cousin to Erin Eagleton—a person of interest in Congressman Jeffries's shooting and the murder of his son. When the Capitol K-9 Unit had begun investigating, Selena had been questioned to determine if she had helped Erin Eagleton disappear. They couldn't find anything to indicate she had assisted her cousin. Yet.

Did someone think Selena knew something? Did she? Had she helped her cousin somehow? He hoped not. He would hate to have to arrest her if he discovered she had.

Security had been breached with the two break-ins —likely by someone who had been at the White House before, possibly a frequent visitor or staff member. This probably wasn't a spur-of-the-moment theft, and he would have to let General Meyer know about this latest development just as soon as he spoke to Selena again.

Max barked, interrupting Nicholas's thoughts.

"Come on, boy. Back to the party." Nicholas shortened the leash as they headed to the White House to find Selena.

A voice came over Nicholas's earbud. "We've found Tara Wilkins."

With Selena's keys in her possession? Or, had someone hurt Tara and taken the costume?

TWO

"Where is Wilkins? Is she all right?" Nicholas asked Security as he neared the White House.

"She was found drugged in the ground-floor restroom of the West Wing. The last time she was seen was in the Situation Room where kids were playing video games. Someone must have caught her in the restroom, and then stuffed her into a stall. One of our Secret Service agents found her. She talked to Tara, but the woman doesn't know who grabbed her. She's with the doctor in an examination room."

"I'm on my way now."

"I let Agent Calvert know about Miss Wilkins. He's already at the medical office with Miss Barrow. He's going to talk with her."

"So am I," Nicholas said to the man who manned the communication in the security office at the White House.

"Since he's working with you on the break-in at General Meyer's office, I'd like him to be included on anything concerning Selena Barrow. There could be a connection between what happened in her office and General Meyer's."

"I agree." Nicholas ended the call and moved inside.

He entered the Diplomatic Reception Room on the ground floor of the main-residence part of the White House. With Max beside him, he crossed the oval-shaped room of pale blue and bright yellow dominating the decor. Over the mantel hung a portrait of George Washington.

The doctor's office was located next to the Map Room off the central hall. When Nicholas went inside, Dan stood near the entrance into the examination area, with Selena sitting in a chair in the reception room.

Nicholas immediately went to her and took the seat next to her. She looked tired and frazzled. He couldn't blame her. It wasn't even noon and a lot had occurred in a few hours. He took her hand. "Are you still okay? No slurred speech, double vision or stumbling." He glanced toward his friend then Selena.

"No. I'm fine. Just angry. Dan said I could talk to Tara when you two finish. She's here because of me. I need to make sure she'll be all right. I want to find out what happened to her. Who did this? In the White House?"

"I understand. I want to find out the same things." His gaze locked with hers. "And I will."

"I appreciate it." Her eyes slid closed for a few seconds before connecting with his again.

Rising, he gestured toward Selena and said to Max, "Sit. Stay." When Selena glanced from his K-9 to him, he added, "I thought he could keep you company."

She petted Max. "Thanks."

Before he could head into the exam room, Dan pulled him aside to a private area. "Security is concerned about the link to the break-in at Margaret Meyer's office, although I'm not sure what the connection would be."

"It could be the Michael Jeffries case. Erin Eagleton

is Selena's cousin. Maybe someone thinks she knows where Erin is. My unit has speculated she might know."

"Maybe Selena is someone you should get to know better." Dan winked.

"Yeah, sure, because Selena will take me to see the cousin she's hiding. If she does know where Erin Eagleton is, do you think she'd let it slip? Selena is sharp. Anyone who can coordinate this event and retain her sanity has to be."

"Personally, I wish they'd drop the tradition. It would make my life as a Secret Service agent tasked with keeping the president safe much easier. I get nervous with so many strangers around here."

Nicholas slapped Dan on the back. "Your life is easy. You usually stand around watching people go by. Not too strenuous, if you ask me."

"I didn't," Dan grumbled as they walked back over to the exam room. He rapped on the door before they entered.

The nurse left as Dan introduced Nicholas to Ms. Wilkins. "I know you can't remember much, but he has a few questions concerning what happened to you."

"I could use your help, Ms. Wilkins. The person who drugged you and took the Miss Chick costume deliberately bumped into the White House tour director to steal her keys, so anything you can tell me will help me find the perpetrator. Please describe what happened and where you were."

The young woman scrunched her forehead and stared down at her hands. "Everything is hazy. I remember leaving the Situation Room and going to the restroom. I was the only one inside. I was surprised because so many people were attending the event, but while I was in the stall, I heard the door opening and someone coming in." Closing her eyes, she lowered her head for a few seconds. "The last thing I recollect is leaving the stall, a sound behind me, then a prick at my neck. Nothing after that until I was found."

"Anything about the person who drugged you. A glimpse? A scent?"

She massaged her temples then shook her head. "My mind is foggy. I…"

"How tall are you?"

"Five feet ten inches. Why?"

"It gives me an idea how tall the fake Miss Chick is." Nicholas removed his business card and handed it to her. "If you remember anything, even if you think it won't help, call me and let me know."

"I will, but I didn't see who it was."

Nicholas rose from the chair. "Thank you, Miss Wilkins. Miss Barrow is outside and wants to make sure you're all right."

"I feel so bad. This was a big gig for me."

"She's only concerned about your welfare." Nicholas left with Dan, and in the reception room motioned to Selena that she could talk with Tara Wilkins.

Selena passed him, giving him a small smile, but it didn't wipe the weariness from her expression. While Selena disappeared into the exam room, he waited out in the empty reception area with Max. Nicholas stared at the closed door.

"I told you Ms. Wilkins didn't know anything," Dan said, breaking the silence.

"I saw Miss Chick approach Selena, and from a distance it appeared the costume fit her well, so the assailant is about the same height. Selena thinks it was a female."

"Is she sure?"

"No, but that will be easy to find out. A male going into a woman's restroom will probably stand out on the security tapes."

"That area of the hallway won't be on tape. It's a dead end, but the hallways leading to it are on camera. So any male seen turning the corner could be going to the men's restroom. It's taken me years to learn every area that's covered and the ones not." Dan grinned. "And then the powers that be change things around."

Nicholas paced the room. "Oh, joy. You and I get to watch hours of tape, and we might come up with nothing."

Dan shrugged. "You know how investigations go. Most take a lot of legwork."

"I've contacted Security about changing the lock on Selena's office and storeroom. Did you check it to see if it was searched?"

"Yes, on the way here, but it didn't appear to have been."

"What did the doc say about Selena's injury?"

"The doctor checked her again and gave her instructions about what to watch for, but he thinks the concussion is a mild one."

"When this is over with, I'm escorting Selena home." Nicholas stopped in front of Dan. "I want to make sure everything is all right. With her head injury and the fact someone has her keys, I won't rest well if I don't see for myself that she'll be okay and safe at her house."

"And that's a great opportunity for you to get closer to her. I can see why you've been with her today. I still think she could lead you to her cousin. They're about the same age. They're related and friends. The things we do for an investi…" Dan's voice trailed off into silence, his eyes growing round as he stared behind Nicholas.

He swung around and found Selena glowering at them, her face pale, her hands trembling.

She charged across the office. "I need to get back to work."

"Wait up." Nicholas gripped Max's leash and hurried after her, the sound of Dan's chuckles irking him.

Selena kept going, her free hand fisted at her side.

Outside the ground-floor entrance, Nicholas caught up with her. "I'm sorry about what Dan said."

She whirled toward him, fire shooting out of her eyes, her jaw set in a fierce line. "Is it true? You've talked to me more in the past couple of months than the whole year before. You can tell your team I don't know where my cousin is, but Erin is innocent. She could be dead or kidnapped and all you think is she murdered her boyfriend. She cared for Michael and wouldn't have hurt him. She wouldn't have hurt anyone."

He let her storm away because what she'd said had a ring of truth to it. He had started talking to her more because of the case. Although there was no evidence to support that she was helping her cousin, he and other members had to follow all leads. He'd learned in this profession to be distrusting and question everything. At this moment, as Selena vanished in the crowd near the Easter Egg Roll, he regretted that aspect of his job.

By the end of the event in the early evening, anger still roiled in Selena's stomach whenever she glimpsed Nicholas in the crowd or thought about him. She liked him—a lot—but overhearing him and Dan talking about her concerning Erin's disappearance, all the feelings she'd been fighting since her cousin went missing had surged to the foreground.

She'd caught a couple of Dan's earlier remarks—his

voice a little louder than Nicholas's—before they'd gone in to see Tara Wilkins and then again later. She hated being the topic of conversation and especially the fact that the Capitol K-9 Unit had suspected her of assisting a fugitive—still did. Not that she wasn't trying to help Erin. She was. But by trying to prove she couldn't have killed Michael. If Selena could gather evidence her cousin hadn't shot anyone, then if Erin was alive and in hiding, she could return. But her greatest fear was that Erin wasn't alive. All she knew—via the Capitol K-9 Unit—was that back in February, an elderly couple in rural Virginia had taken in an injured young woman matching Erin's description, but she'd left a few days later, her appearance dramatically altered. Weeks later, two thugs had terrorized the couple for information on Erin's whereabouts. Who were they? The killers? Bounty hunters?

And where was Erin? Reports had come in last month that someone in rural Virginia was using public computers to research bills introduced by Congressman Jeffries. Could that be Erin? If so, what was she looking for?

One angle Selena was following involved a case Michael Jeffries had been very passionate about. Michael had been working pro bono on a murder case for convicted killer Greg Littleton, a man who Michael believed was innocent. Perhaps the real killer wanted Michael off the case permanently and killed him. Maybe the killer had trailed Michael to his father's house, murdered him there, and when his father, the congressman, appeared, the killer shot him, too.

Lots of maybes and not a lot of answers. Selena hadn't had the time in the past few weeks to work on anything except the Easter Egg Roll, but she had managed to interview Greg Littleton in prison, convicted of murdering Saul Rather. Michael had been fervently working to prove Littleton was innocent. Those who believed in his guilt weren't happy about that. As a crusading attorney, Michael had made himself some enemies.

Now that the Easter Egg Roll was over, Selena intended to devote more time to looking into the Littleton case and any others that appeared promising. Someone had killed Michael Jeffries and left his father for dead—and that someone wasn't Erin Eagleton.

As Selena approached her car in the staff's underground parking, she discovered Nicholas lounging against her white Ford Mustang with Max sitting next to him. How dare he look so innocent with those big brown eyes and cocky grin. He'd removed his ball cap and stuck it in his back pocket. His thick, dark blond hair was cut short but not military-style. Knowing his Navy SEALs background, that had surprised her when she'd first met him last year.

Her anger began to soften as she took in his casual stance, as though nothing was wrong. She quickly shored it up. She would not be used. Her mother had tried to get back in her big brother's graces by using Selena. It hadn't worked. Her uncle had recognized that his sister wasn't serious about not drinking, that all she needed his money for was to support her while she drowned herself in alcohol, leaving her daughter to fend for herself.

Selena had learned one thing growing up. She was the only one who would look out for herself. She ignored Nicholas as she unlocked her car and tossed her purse on the passenger seat.

"Max, what do you do when you're in hot water?" Nicholas said to his K-9.

The sound of the dog's bark echoed through the underground garage.

Selena pressed her lips together to keep from smiling. He was going to charm her. She'd seen him charming the women at the White House, and she wasn't going to buy into it. She'd watched her mother fall for one man after another, thinking he would take care of her.

But her current man had never stayed around long.

He tapped the side of his head with his palm. "Max, what a brilliant idea. I'll try that."

Nicholas sidled along the body of the car until he was half a foot from her right arm. The hairs on it tingled.

"I'm sorry. Nothing I did today had to do with your cousin. I was trying to point out to Dan the error of his suggestion with sarcasm."

Selena squeezed her eyes closed, her heartbeat accelerating at Nicholas's nearness. Finally she turned slowly toward him, backing away a step. "Be honest. Have you ever considered I might have been helping Erin stay hidden?"

"Honestly—yes. I'm not going to lie to you. My team has looked into all the possibilities while searching for Erin, so being a friend and a family member, you would obviously be on that list. And if I was perfectly honest, at first that is why I initiated several conversations with you lately."

She tensed, flexing her hands. "I knew it. At least I appreciate your honesty. Now I need to leave. I'm tired, and I pray I don't fall asleep driving home."

"Then let me drive you to your house."

"I was trying to point out the extent of my exhaustion with exaggeration. I'm perfectly fine to drive myself. I'm not going to fall asleep at the wheel. In fact, with all that has been going on today, it may take hours for me to go to sleep."

He chuckled. "I know that feeling. My body is exhausted but my mind is racing a mile a minute."

She had to fight the urge to respond to his charm. Life lessons from her childhood taunted her. She would never be like her mother, depending on others, depending on alcohol to make it through the day. "This is not going to work." She stepped back again and encountered the open driver's door.

His expression sobered. "Seriously, I would like to escort you home. Someone took your house keys today. You should have your locks changed."

"Believe it or not, I've thought of that. I know how to take care of myself. You should have seen the neighborhood I grew up in. The total opposite of Erin's childhood. My branch of the Eagleton family are the black sheep. I have a locksmith coming to my house in—" she checked her watch "—an hour. I need to be there so he can change my locks, so if you'll excuse me, I need to be going."

"Have it your way." Nicholas moved away from her white Mustang.

When she slipped behind the steering wheel, she inhaled a calming breath and started her car. As she backed out of the parking space, she noticed Nicholas open the rear door of an SUV only three vehicles away and wait for Max to jump into it. She went through the security checkpoint with Nicholas's black Tahoe a vehicle behind hers. When she turned right, he did, too. Her grip tightened as he continued to follow her.

Although she had nearly a full tank, she pulled into a gas station. Nicholas came up behind her.

She shoved open her door and marched back to his SUV. "What do you think you're doing?"

"Escorting you home the best way I can."

Her head pounding, she opened her mouth to give him a piece of her mind, but when she couldn't find the words she wanted to say, she snapped her teeth together, then spun on her heel and stalked to her Mustang. Fine. He could waste his time "escorting her home." That didn't mean she would talk to him or even acknowledge his presence.

As she continued her drive to her house in Arlington, she kept looking back to see if he was still behind her. Although it was too dark to see his face, she imagined his pleased expression for following through with what he'd wanted to do. There was one part of her that felt like a suspect being tailed and another part that warmed when she thought about him trying to protect her from the person who'd taken her keys—for what reason, she had no idea.

In college she'd had her purse snatched on campus when walking back to her dorm from the library late one night. She had been so angry she'd chased after the guy, caught up with him and tackled him to the ground. A campus cop who'd rushed to her aid had lectured her about the risk she'd taken. She supposed it had been foolish, but her reaction to being robbed was automatic. She'd come from a tough area of Washington, DC, and had learned to stand up for herself.

Selena pulled into her driveway and stared at her house, her first, earned by hard work after years of studying and being at the top of her class at school. She was going to prove to her uncle she wasn't like her mother and was willing to work for everything she got. She didn't want a free ride from him or anyone.

Her porch light illuminated the front part of her red-brick two-story home with white trim and green shutters. Hers—as of six months ago. She noticed Nicholas had parked at the curb and exited his Tahoe. He came around the hood. She quickly grabbed her purse, took a spare house key from the bottom of the driver's seat and climbed from her Mustang.

"That's as far as you need to go. You've escorted me home." She waved toward her house. "Nothing is amiss. You can run along now."

He planted his feet apart, crossed his arms and said, "Not until you go in the house to your front window and wave to me. Then I'll leave."

"What if I don't?" the imp inside her asked.

"Then I'll stay here all night."

His determined look drilled right through her. "You're impossible."

"It comes in handy when I deal with stubborn people."

"You think I know where Erin is."

"Do you?"

"No."

"Then I believe you."

"Really?"

"I told you I would be honest with you. I'm worried about you. I think something is going on. It might be connected to the Jeffries case or something else. I don't know. Miss Chick today went to some trouble to get your keys. Why?"

"To rob me?"

"There were a lot richer people there than you."

She lifted her shoulders in a shrug. "Maybe they thought I was wealthy since Senator Eagleton is my uncle. When you catch the person, ask her."

"I will. Nothing was taken from your purse in your office, so it wasn't that kind of robbery. Could the person have been after something—"

"I don't need a protector," she interrupted, remembering all the times she alone had protected herself from the predators in her childhood neighborhood. "I've been taking care of myself most of my life. Go home. Look out for yourself." Frustration churned her stomach.

"Just as soon as I know you're safe inside and the locksmith has arrived."

"Now you're putting more conditions on your leaving."

"What can I say? I changed my mind."

Clamping her lips together, she pivoted and strode toward her porch steps. As she mounted them, the feel of his gaze on her back made her shiver. For most of her life, she had been the only one who took care of herself. What would it be like to have someone who cared?

No! I won't go there. At times, she wasn't even sure the Lord was there anymore. As a child she'd sought refuge in the local church, latching on to the promise that God loved her. But did He? While growing up, she'd been so alone.

Absorbed in thoughts of the past, she unlocked her front door and moved into the foyer. One look into the living room and she froze.

THREE

Selena stared at her trashed living room then, beyond at the dining room and part of her kitchen. What if the intruder was still here? She sidled toward the table nearby and pulled open a drawer. Keeping her eye on the staircase to the right, she felt for her revolver. When her fingers encountered the barrel, she quickly clasped the handle and withdrew it.

"What do you think you're going to do with that?" Nicholas's deep voice sounded from the entrance.

She glanced over her shoulder. "Defend myself. The person could still be in here."

"Put it on the table before someone gets hurt." Nicholas drew his gun.

"I know how to use it."

"I don't care."

She did as he ordered, actually relieved he was here. She must be more exhausted than she thought.

"Now, go outside, open my tailgate so I can call for Max, then you're to stay on the porch while Max and I search the rest of the house. If the locksmith comes, have him wait with you."

Selena nodded then headed to his Tahoe and released Max. She'd been around the rottweiler enough to know he was a well-trained dog. He could be fierce, but she wasn't afraid of him.

"Come," Nicholas said from the doorway.

Max trotted toward her house. Selena followed behind him and stopped at the top of the steps, gripping the post, trying to ignore her headache.

"Check it." Nicholas disappeared with Max into her house.

She lost sight of them when the pair went up the stairs. With only two bedrooms and a bath on the second floor, they were back in the living room within five minutes.

"Do you have a basement?"

"Yes. The stairs to it are next to the back door."

He and Max vanished around the corner into the kitchen. The whole time they were gone, her heartbeat thudded against her rib cage, her breathing shallow. What if the intruder was hiding in the basement? Or there was more than one person? When minutes later, Nicholas and Max rounded the corner and crossed the living room, she sagged against the wooden railing, not realizing until then how tense she'd been while they were checking out her house.

"Does the rest of my place look like the living room?"

"Yes. You'll need to go through your home and let me know what's missing. I'll contact the local police about what happened, but since this might be connected with the White House break-in, I want to deal with it."

"I'll do a walk-through tonight, but I'm too tired to do more than that." The past weeks finally wreaked their havoc on her.

"Why don't you wait until tomorrow. In fact, go to bed. I'll take care of the locksmith, dust for fingerprints since this is tied to a theft at the White House and stay until he leaves. Okay?"

She hesitated, so tempted by his offer.

"I'll make sure everything is locked up." Nicholas's gaze strayed to something beyond the porch.

She swung around and saw Mr. Lamb, the locksmith, park his van behind Nicholas's SUV. "I can't go to sleep until I know the locks have been changed. I want all three door locks replaced even though I only had the front one on the key ring."

"You might also think about getting an alarm system."

"Believe me, I will tomorrow."

After talking with the locksmith, Selena made her way upstairs and changed into a pair of sweatpants, a large T-shirt and slippers. Her feet were screaming pain and demanding she sit, but she was afraid if she did, she would never get up, any surge of adrenaline she'd experienced from the break-in subsiding. After her locks were replaced, she would send Nicholas and Mr. Lamb on their way, do a brief walk-through to check if anything was missing, then collapse into bed with her revolver on the nightstand.

Selena's eyes popped open to a semidark room. A dull ache still gripping her head, she glanced at her digital clock on the bedside table: 7:00 a.m. She rolled over and tried to go back to sleep since the chief of staff had told her to take the next two days off. But after twenty minutes, she gave up.

Thoughts of what the intruder was looking for kept running through her mind. While Mr. Lamb changed the locks, she'd gone from room to room, checking if anything obvious had been stolen, but nothing was missing. Her computer was there but obviously had been handled by the intruder. She'd have it checked to see if something had been added or deleted. Her TV and a few pieces of nice jewelry had been untouched.

After seeing Nicholas out the door and locking it last night, she'd trudged up the stairs, and in spite of being totally drained emotionally and physically, she'd lain awake for another hour until exhaustion must have finally taken over.

Still dressed in her sweatpants and T-shirt, she finger combed her hair—because she didn't want to scare her neighbors—and headed downstairs to fetch her *Washington Post*. Her morning ritual always included savoring the newspaper with her coffee before she started her day. After she prepared the brew and it began to perk, she walked to the front door, opened it and nearly fell over Nicholas stretched out in a sleeping bag against the threshold to her home. She teetered over him.

He reached up and steadied her.

"What are you doing here?" She scanned the porch. "And where is Max?"

He rose, stretching and rolling his shoulders. "I'm making sure you're safe. Max is at the back door guarding that entrance."

"You didn't say anything about that last night. I saw you walk to your SUV."

"To get my sleeping bag." He grinned, a dimple appearing in his cheek. "I did leave your house, but I couldn't completely go. I would have never forgiven myself if the intruder had come back."

She marched past him and snatched up the newspaper at the bottom of the stairs, then retraced her steps. Planting herself in the doorway, she blocked him. "You didn't need to do that. I doubt the person would come back."

"Have you noticed anything missing?"

"That's what you really want to know. Admit it. That was the real reason you stayed."

"Only one of the reasons. I am concerned about your safety." He drew in a deep breath. "Ah, coffee. May I have some?"

She twisted her mouth into a frown, trying to be perturbed at the impossible man. But she couldn't. "One cup. Then you'll leave. I have a rare day off and want to…" What? Relax? Which had been her original plan until someone broke into her house. She glanced at her living room and knew that wouldn't happen until she cleaned it up. The only way she got everything done was to be highly organized; she wouldn't rest until this mess was taken care of.

"Could you use help putting this back the way it was?" Nicholas gestured toward the living room.

She opened her mouth to say no, then chuckled at how ridiculous that sounded. "My mama didn't raise no fool." Actually, her mother hardly raised her at all.

"I take that as a yes."

She nodded. "Come in."

Nicholas entered and shut the door. "I almost forgot. Mr. Lamb gave me the bill." He dug into his pocket and pulled it out. "I didn't want it to get lost in all this clutter."

She'd forgotten all about the bill last night. She'd been too focused on Nicholas prowling her house while Mr. Lamb worked. "Thank you. He would have sent it to me."

"You're welcome."

Pushing some clutter out of her way with her foot,

she padded across the wooden floor to the kitchen and poured two mugs full of coffee. "Let's have it outside on the patio. I won't relax if I keep looking at all this. Besides, Max might want some water. There's a bowl on the counter. Use that to give him some."

"You're certainly a take-charge kind of woman."

At the back door, she peered at him. "It pays to be in my job since so much of it is planning various events for the president. He expects the best from his staff."

Nicholas filled the bowl with water. "Yesterday really showcased your talents. Everyone I saw was having a great time. Even Margaret Meyer. I don't think of her as having a sense of humor."

"Speaking of the general, won't she expect you at the White House this morning?"

Nicholas frowned. "I'll let her know I'll be in later. Dan can start looking at the security tapes."

"Dan is helping you with my case?"

"Yes."

"Why are you on it? I see Dan's role."

He averted his gaze for a long moment, then said, "Another office was broken into yesterday. There may be a connection."

Her face drained of color. "General Meyer's?"

He remained quiet.

"I heard there was a ruckus around her office. You know how rumors can fly around the White House. And you do work for her." Her eyes widened. "If you think there might be a connection, it has to be over the Jeffries case."

"No comment at this time."

She opened the door and stopped. Max, much like Nicholas, was lying down across the entrance into the kitchen.

Nicholas stepped over his rottweiler and put the bowl down on the patio. "Drink."

Selena watched Max saunter to the bowl and lap up the water. "You have to tell him to drink?"

"He waits for commands when we're on the job. When he's off duty, he does what he wants."

On the job? She guessed she was a job to him, especially if he thought she knew where Erin was. She tried to dismiss the thought but she couldn't. It hurt. "I wish I could get the people working under me that well trained," Selena finally said when she realized Nicholas was peering at her with that sharp, assessing look. Her heartbeat accelerated, and she sat in one of the chairs at the glass table.

"That's the result of months of training as well as continual refresher courses." Nicholas took the seat across from Selena.

"He's beautiful. I've never been around a rottweiler until you came to the White House. Does he live at your place when you two aren't on duty?" She had to remember he was probably as distrusting as she was. Most people in law enforcement were.

"Yes. All the dogs in the Capitol K-9 Unit stay with their partners when off duty."

"I've never had a pet even as a child. And now I work all the time, so it wouldn't be fair to leave an animal alone so much."

"I had any pet I wanted."

There was a tone in his voice that indicated there was more to that statement than what he was saying. "So what did you have as a child?"

"A dog named Butch and a horse called Dynamite."

"So you rode, too?"

"Yes, I lived on a farm in Maryland growing up. I'd go riding whenever I could and Butch always followed."

His childhood was vastly different from hers. She'd grown up in Washington, DC, in the area that wasn't technically slums but close. "What did your family grow on the farm?"

"Nothing. They had some horses and that was about it."

"Some? How big was the farm?"

"Two hundred acres. In some people's book it was more an estate than a farm, although Thoroughbred horses were raised there."

"But not you?" Again she sensed an underlying tension in his voice and saw the stiffening of his shoulders.

"The house I grew up in was a mansion. A person could get lost in it. But to me it was only a place to sleep at night." A touch of bitterness laced his words.

Definitely a far cry from where she'd lived as a child. The biggest apartment she ever lived in was three rooms, if you counted a bathroom she could barely turn around in. "You didn't like your home?" she asked before she could snatch the question back. She had no business prying into his past. She told no one about hers.

"It wasn't a home. My family's business was a large import/export company. My parents were rarely there. Their work took them all over the world."

When her mother had been gone, it was because she was drinking and would disappear for days. "You never got to travel with them?"

"No." His mouth snapped closed, and he averted his face, staring at Max sniffing around the yard. "I noticed your flat-screen TV and laptop are still in the house, so what would someone be looking for? Do you have any other valuables?"

"Not much. I've poured all my money into this house. I bought it last year and have slowly been fixing it up the way I want. It's the first place I've really called home." The words slipped out before she could stop them. She quickly added, "I lived in apartments while going to school and my first couple of years working in the White House," as though that would explain why she'd never felt at home anywhere before she'd bought this place.

"That's how I feel about my house in Burke. As a Navy SEAL I traveled a lot and lived on base, but now that I'm working for the Capitol K-9 Unit, I can put down some roots."

"Do you have to do much traveling? I know you come and go at the White House, but I figure you're working on a case."

"Although I'm assigned to the White House, I'm at headquarters for briefings, coordination with other team members, running down leads and training sessions with Max." Nicholas took a sip of his coffee, his gaze connecting with her over the rim of his mug.

"The locksmith changed my locks last night, so why did you and Max stay?"

"It was late when Mr. Lamb left. By the time I went home, I'd probably only get a few hours' sleep before coming back here this morning."

"But you had to be uncomfortable on the porch."

"As an ex–Navy SEAL, I'm used to sleeping on the hard ground. I slept great because I was on your porch. If I'd left you, I'd have worried about you and probably not slept at all. It's traumatic for a person to discover her house was broken into. I wanted to make sure you were okay and whoever did this didn't come back. As I mentioned yesterday, I'd recommend getting a good alarm system today. Mr. Lamb put on sturdy locks, but they only go so far. Having a dog wouldn't be a bad idea, either."

She smiled. "Will you loan me Max?"

"Sorry, we're an inseparable team," he said with a chuckle. "But a dog like Max would be perfect."

Although she'd never had a pet, the idea interested her. "How would I get one trained and as well behaved as Max?"

"He's trained specifically for guarding, apprehending suspects and searching for bombs. You don't need that, but I can help you if you want."

"Let me think about it. I don't want to get a dog if I can't give him the attention he needs." If she accepted Nicholas's help, she would be spending a lot more time with him. That could be dangerous because she couldn't deny her attraction to him.

His dark brown eyes gleamed. "Not all pet owners feel that way. They buy an animal and then ignore it most of the time."

Selena downed the last of her coffee. She could get used to his presence; she needed to end this. "I appreciate your concern last night, but I think I'll be all right today. The break-in was a shock, but it takes a lot to rattle me, so on second thought, I don't need your help cleaning up." She rose. "I'll look into an alarm system since I'm off for a couple of days. But my main concern is righting my house and seeing if anything was stolen. At first glance, nothing is missing, but if that were the case, then why did someone risk breaking in?"

"Looking for something?" He pushed to his feet.

She frowned. "I don't keep anything related to my White House job here. That's why I often stay late at night. I try to leave my work at my office. When I come here, it's my downtime."

"Good way to be. I need to do that more myself."

She started for the back door. "It's probably harder because Max stays with you."

"That's not it. I've never been a person who can just relax and do nothing."

"So no vacations?"

"Not lately. Max and I have gone camping a few long weekends."

"I work hard, but I play hard, too. Maybe I could teach you how if you help me get the right dog." Here she went again. When was she going to learn? His help would come at a price.

"If you decide to have a pet, you've got yourself a deal. Are you sure about not needing any help cleaning up?"

"Yes, I'm sure you have work today. I hope you let me know if you find the person who drugged Tara Wilkins."

"I will." Nicholas turned toward Max. "Come."

His dog trotted to Nicholas's side, and they trailed her into the house. She was again greeted with the chaos, and dreaded the day before her. She released a long breath and realized the only way the cleanup would get done was to start and keep going until she was finished. She wouldn't go to bed tonight until she'd righted her house.

Selena walked with Nicholas and Max to the front door. "Thank you for your help yesterday at my office during the Easter Egg Roll."

He arched a brow. "So my help wasn't so bad, after all."

"Okay. I was a little miffed at you for thinking I'm harboring a suspect."

"A little? I'd hate to see your full-blown anger."

"It isn't a pretty sight, so that's a warning to stay on my good side," she said with a laugh.

"I'll remember that. Let me know if you're missing anything." He gave her a business card with his cell number on it. "Call if you have any trouble—" he cocked a smile "—or if you just want to talk."

"Just so you realize… If I can help my cousin, I will, but I don't know where she is. Erin didn't kill Michael.

He held up his hand before she could say anything else. "I'm leaving. I don't want to get into an argument about Erin's possible part in the murder."

As Nicholas strode away with Max at his side, Selena unclenched her hands, noticing the fingernail indentations in her palms. That man could certainly infuriate her…but also intrigue her. *Lord, give me the patience and guidance to help Erin. Open Nicholas's eyes to the truth.*

Nicholas spent the morning at Capitol K-9 Unit headquarters viewing security video from the morning that Selena was attacked. Next to him, Fiona Fargo, the team's tech wizard, studied video on hallways leading to General Meyer's office.

"Margaret Meyer is a busy lady," Fiona said, pushing her rolling chair away from her desk and twisting toward Nicholas. "This is a list of suspects who could have broken into her office and read the Jeffries case file during your time frame."

Nicholas stared at the fifteen names on the paper. "I want you to check into each one. Give me everything you can on them. Start with Vincent Geary—he's an aide to Congressman Jeffries. The initials on the cuff-links found in the general's office are *VG*. He's my top suspect at the moment. When I leave here, I'm going to pay Mr. Geary a visit."

"Do you want me to investigate General Meyer's secretary, too?"

"Yes, everyone who was in the office during those hours. We have to include everyone. If you find anything suspicious, let me know right away."

As Nicholas rose and stretched his stiff muscles, Fiona asked, "Where's Max?"

"In the training yard. I wanted to give him a little downtime. He's been working a lot lately." Nicholas walked toward the doorway of Fiona's office. "But his playtime is over."

"He's as driven as you are."

"You know how dogs and their owners are."

She shook her head. "Nope. I have cats."

"Don't let Max know."

Fiona smiled. "Oh, he knows. Why do you think he sniffs me every time he sees me?"

"How does Chris's K-9 deal with your cats?"

Fiona's cheeks flushed. "We're working that out."

"Good. He's a good guy. Bye and thanks, Fiona." Nicholas strolled down the hallway. When his cell rang, he expected it to be Dan, who'd been going over security video at the White House, with news about Miss Chick's assailant, but he noticed it was Selena. He quickly answered, "How's the cleaning going?"

"Tedious. I know what the intruder took yesterday at my house."

FOUR

Thirty minutes after calling Nicholas, Selena opened her front door to him and Max. "Come in. Did you break any speed limits getting here?"

"I'm a law-enforcement officer. I know better unless in pursuit of a criminal." He flashed his dynamite smile.

And for a few seconds all the tension and weariness fled Selena as they stared at each other. When Max barked, as though he knew they needed to focus on what had brought Nicholas to her house in the first place, Selena broke eye contact and turned her attention to the dog. "It's good to see you, Max." She petted him and rubbed him behind the ears.

"He isn't going to want to leave if you continue that too long," Nicholas said with a laugh.

She peered up at Nicholas, grinning. "I doubt anyone could sway him from his duties with all his training. I've seen him at work at the White House." She straightened, determined to get down to business. She didn't like the feelings of attraction Nicholas could generate in her. She had to remember he suspected her of helping Erin, and he had a job to do.

She stepped to the side and allowed him to enter, then shut the door. When she swung around, her messy living room, such an alien sight for her, chased away the lightness she'd felt at seeing Nicholas. He was here on business. "I've been working on righting the rooms upstairs. I haven't made my way down here yet."

"Are you sure that your personal computer tablet is missing?"

"I keep it in my bedroom in the drawer of my nightstand on the right. You can't tell from all this chaos, but I'm highly organized and everything has a place."

"The intruder took your tablet but not your laptop. Why? What was on the tablet that wasn't on your laptop?"

She picked her way through the shattered items on the floor, found the couch cushions and put them back where they belonged, then sat. She'd only been cleaning and straightening for a few hours, but after yesterday, she was tired. Usually she could keep going and push through the exhaustion, but not today.

Before Nicholas settled at the opposite end of the sofa, he fixed the two chairs. "For someone who is highly organized, this must be a disturbing sight."

"Yes. Even as a child I kept everything straight. It gave me a sense of control." The second she said that last sentence she gritted her teeth, afraid of what else she would spill about herself. She must be wearier than she realized. She had to remember Nicholas wanted to capture Erin; Selena wanted to free her.

"I wish it were that simple. The older I get, the more I realize we control little in our lives."

"Yeah, I know. Only our attitude and how we respond to what happens around us. But I wish I could control more. Then I would wish this all away, and I wouldn't have to spend my days off cleaning up this mess." As words poured from her, she sat back, amazed she was saying this to Nicholas. What was it about him that made her feel she could trust him? His own words had given her reason not to. She'd remembered what he'd said in the underground parking garage yesterday.

My team has looked into all the possibilities while searching for Erin, so being a friend and a family member, you would obviously be on that list. And if I was perfectly honest, at first that is why I initiated several conversations with you lately.

"I can stay and help. I want to make sure the tablet is the only thing missing."

She bit down on her bottom lip. The temptation to accept his offer was strong.

"Everyone needs help from time to time. Let me help you, Selena."

His calm countenance soothed her, and before she realized what she was doing, she nodded.

"Before we get to work, tell me what was on the tablet."

He wouldn't be happy about what she was about to say, but if that was the reason behind the break-in, she wanted him to know. She drew in a deep, composing breath. "I've been looking into the cases Michael was working on right before he was killed. I think there could be a tie to one of them and his murder."

"Which ones?" His mouth pulled into a thin, firm line.

"There were three that look promising, but one of them was a dead end."

"The Capitol K-9 Unit has been delving into all of Michael's activities, and so far we have come up with nothing, so why do you think two cases are still viable leads?"

"One of them is the Huntington case."

"The man convicted of selling intelligence secrets is guilty. All the evidence pointed to him."

Selena nodded. "But Sid Huntington insists he's innocent, that someone set him up to be the fall guy, and Michael believed him."

Nicholas shook his head. "Michael was wrong. I'm familiar with that case. I went through it when we looked at what Michael was working on at the time of his murder."

"Michael's secretary told me that he was on the trail of a new piece of evidence. He'd been excited about the possible lead."

"But she didn't know what it was?"

"No, and I haven't been able to find out what it was."

"So other than that, Huntington looks guilty to you?"

"Yes." She squeezed her hands into fists. Listening to herself made even her think she was grasping for an answer.

Frown lines grooved his forehead. "What's the other case?"

Selena hesitated. This one involved her uncle, and she'd been putting it off, delving into all the others first because she didn't want to make their precarious relationship any worse. Only in the past couple of weeks had she turned to the Littleton case. "It's another one that Michael was working on overturning the conviction."

"The Littleton case?"

Selena nodded.

"I'm not that familiar with it. Another K-9 officer looked into that one."

"Greg Littleton was sent to prison for murdering Saul Rather. Saul was a young intern for my uncle. He'd been with him only two months."

"What was Littleton's connection to Rather?"

"He was the custodian at Saul's apartment complex." Selena rose. "I fixed some coffee after talking to you on the phone. Do you want some?"

"Yes, please."

She escaped into the kitchen, needing time to decide what to tell him. There was no way her uncle was involved. The intern on her uncle's staff hadn't been there that long. He ranked at the bottom of the office personnel, doing all the work no one else wanted to do. She doubted her uncle had had any dealings with the young man.

"What was Michael Jeffries doing for Littleton?"

The question took Selena by surprise. She spun around, her hand over her heart. "I didn't hear you come in here."

"Sorry. I learned to be silent when I was a Navy SEAL."

She leaned against the counter, the thump of her heartbeat calming. "Littleton had an appeal, and Michael took over the case from Greg's court-appointed attorney. His secretary told me Michael felt the guy botched the case from the beginning."

"Is that why Michael thought Littleton was innocent?"

"The evidence was circumstantial. Greg found Saul Rather's body in the parking lot early in the morning. Minutes before, Greg heard what he thought was a car backfiring. When a tenant found them, Greg was kneeling next to Saul's body. Greg's prints were the only ones on the gun. Greg testified he moved it when he checked to see if Saul was alive."

"That's what he was convicted on?"

"Greg isn't the smartest person. He was shocked at finding a body and wasn't thinking straight."

"So what was his motive?"

"The night before, Saul and Greg had a fight near the apartment's pool. Some of the tenants witnessed it. Saul accused Greg of coming into his apartment and stealing from him. He was going to talk to the management office about firing Greg."

Nicholas scowled. "No one else had a motive?"

"Not that the police could find, but I'm not so sure they looked too hard. With the murder of a senator's staff member, they wanted to close it quickly. I believe my uncle put some pressure on them, too. I don't think he wanted his name in the paper associated with a murder victim. He was up for reelection at that time. This all happened almost two years ago. Greg's been in jail since the crime."

"Greg? You keep saying his first name as if you know him. Do you?"

She turned toward the counter and reached for a mug for Nicholas, filling it and topping off hers.

"Selena, are you avoiding my question?"

Her grip on the coffeepot handle tightened. She put the glass carafe down and passed him his mug. "I have met him."

"When? How?"

"At the end of last week, I went to see him at the prison, and we talked for a while. I used the fact I was the niece of a US senator to have a quiet, extended time to interview Greg and determine if I agree with Michael."

One of his eyebrows shot up. "And?"

"I think he's innocent."

Nicholas took a sip of his coffee. "Why?"

"For one thing, the thief in the apartment complex was discovered not long after Greg was convicted. Michael followed up on that and discovered the items stolen from Saul's apartment were pawned by the man caught, so Littleton was innocent of stealing from Saul. No motive. But the assistant DA said that didn't really prove anything. The threat of being fired was enough of a motive. People have killed for less."

"True."

"There's only so much I can glean from the court records and Michael's secretary's memory. My thoughts and notes of the meeting were on the stolen computer tablet. I'm going back out to talk to Littleton. I know of a couple of witnesses who testified to the argument between the victim and Greg, but there were others who weren't at the trial. I'm thinking about talking to some of those people as well as the others and—"

"Hold it right there." He put up his finger close to her mouth but not touching it. "You are *not* to investigate anything involved in Michael's case, especially now. Have you forgotten someone broke into your house?"

She squared her shoulders and narrowed her eyes at him. "I don't know if your team has really investigated Michael and the possible motives for his murder. If Erin isn't the killer, I think you all believe someone was after the congressman and Michael got in the way."

Nicholas met her intense gaze with his own. "It's more likely that the congressman has made enemies more than his son. Remember he was a victim, too."

"From what I know of the crime, the congressman came outside after his son was killed and he was shot then. That sounds like someone was after Michael, not Congressman Jeffries."

"True. We have to look at all the possibilities." Nicholas glanced away for a few seconds. "What did Greg tell you exactly?"

She frowned. "A lot of what I told you. He gave me some names, but I can't remember all of them. As I said earlier, I'd written them down along with other notes then transferred them to my tablet. That's one of the reasons I need to go back. That, and Greg was going to try to remember any encounters with the delivery boy who was the real thief at the apartment complex."

"Is Littleton the one who told you about the pawn-shop where the perpetrator was fencing the stolen goods?"

"No, I told him. He didn't know anything about it. Michael's secretary told me. It was something Michael discovered a few days before his death. Ask the offi-cer who looked into the case if he even knew about the pawnshop. He might not have had all the information on the case at the time of Michael's murder."

Nicholas stepped closer to her, invading her personal space. "I will. Does that satisfy you?"

She wouldn't move back as was her normal ten-dency when someone came too near. Holding her ground, she lifted her mug and took a long drink of her now-lukewarm coffee. "Until all my questions are answered, no. I'm concerned for Erin, so I will do what I must to prove her innocence."

He thrust his face closer. "Do you want to end up dead like Michael?"

Selena sucked in a ragged breath and backed away. "I told Greg I would come see him again and I intend to. I also asked him to go over the time from right be-fore the fight to when the police showed up. Including if he could remember seeing anyone who wasn't a ten-ant at the apartment complex."

"I'm sure the cops already did that."

"But now he has all the time in the world to go over it. When a person is afraid, he can suppress some thoughts."

Nicholas placed his mug on the counter, putting more space between them while he kneaded his nape. "What if I help you? Will you not do anything without me?"

"Are you going to be open-minded or are you going to try at every turn to persuade me to drop my investigation?"

He paused for a long moment, his dark eyes fixed on her. "I'll be there to protect you and bounce ideas off of. Is that okay?"

"Yeah. Because I'm going to the prison on Thursday and you're welcome to come with me." She wouldn't admit to him that she was concerned after someone had been in her office and her house, picking through her possessions. She kept her journal on her tablet, writing her personal thoughts as well as the developments and questions about Michael's murder and possible suspects. She felt violated all over again, thinking about a person reading through her private thoughts. She shuddered.

"Are you okay? Maybe you should rest. You do have a mild concussion."

She smiled, trying not to think of her journal in someone else's hands. "Is that why my head is pounding? I'd hoped if I ignored it, the headache would go away." She glanced at the kitchen clock. "Time for another pain reliever, and then I need to get back to work straightening up this place."

"I have a suggestion. Why don't you lie down and rest while I at least put your furniture back and straighten some. It might make it easier for you to go through your belongings later."

"Don't you have to work?"

"It's nearly noon, so I'm on my lunch break."

She studied him, his commanding presence appealing at a time when she felt vulnerable. "Fine, if you make sure I only nap for half an hour. I finished upstairs, but look at all this. I've got too much to do, so I can't rest long, and someone is coming at one to install the alarm system."

"That's good he's coming so quickly."

As she made her way to her bedroom, she glanced over her shoulder at Max, at attention, by the front door, then mounted the stairs. She sensed Nicholas watching her from the bottom of the steps, but she wouldn't look back to check. In the bathroom, she swallowed an over-the-counter pain reliever and some water then stretched out on her bed, hoping the tap dancing inside her head would subside. The only reason she'd agreed to his assistance was because she needed her house put back right as fast as possible. The sight of the chaos made her feel exposed and weak. She'd fought hard these past years not to be either.

"Well, Max, it's just you and me to clean this up as much as possible while she's sleeping. She'll probably kick us out once she gets up." Nicholas started at one end of the large living area, returning books strewn near the bookcase. He might not put them back in the right order, but they would at least be off the floor.

As he began picking up items and the small pieces of furniture that were still turned over, he checked for any sign of the tablet. The fact that it was the only thing missing—at least so far—meant this break-in could be tied to the Jeffries murder somehow. Or tied to Michael Jeffries, anyway. Although he didn't believe as Selena did in the connection, he'd been taught to investigate every lead. What if it led to the break the team needed?

Although the Capitol K-9 Unit was working other cases, this one was important to their captain, and therefore the team. Congressman Jeffries had helped Captain Gavin McCord as a child. He owed the man a lot. Nicholas wasn't as fond of Congressman Jeffries, who he suspected might have taken bribes in the past, and Gavin had asked him to withhold judgment until there was evidence that Jeffries was involved in anything shady.

Right now, he had to figure out the connection between Selena's missing tablet and Michael Jeffries's murder. *Was* there something to the Littleton case as Selena hoped? There was the connection to Senator Eagleton, which might be something—or nothing. Selena wanted to prove her cousin was innocent, so she was looking for anything to throw suspicion somewhere else. He wasn't sure what to think, but he did know that someone out there didn't like what Selena was doing. She might not appreciate it, but he was going to hang around as much as he could because he couldn't shake the feeling she could be in danger. What if the person who took the tablet didn't like what he or she found and decided to stop Selena's snooping permanently? What if Littleton was innocent and the murderer knew what Selena was doing? That was exactly what Selena thought might have gotten Michael Jeffries killed.

When Nicholas finished the living room and started on the kitchen, the doorbell rang. He looked at the wall clock and realized it was ten to one. He hurried to the front door, checked who it was through the peephole and let the guy from the alarm company into the house.

"Miss Barrow is upstairs. I'll get her for you." Nicholas turned to Max next to him and added, "Guard."

The man's eyes widened.

"A precaution after what has happened here. Stay right there, and you'll be fine."

Nicholas took the stairs two at a time and knocked on Selena's bedroom door. When she didn't answer, he rapped louder the second time.

She flung the door open, a drowsy look on her face. "You let me oversleep."

"Sorry. I was working and lost track of time. The alarm guy is here."

She rushed into the hallway, finger combing her long, brown hair.

As she descended the staircase, he asked, "How's your headache?"

"Better."

He caught up with her at the bottom of the steps. "Good. I can finish in the kitchen while you talk with the man."

She peered across the room and slanted a glance at Nicholas. "You have Max guarding him?"

He shrugged. "You can't be too careful."

"Yes, you can." She headed toward the man. "Mr. Woods, thank you so much for fitting me in." She held out her hand, and they shook. "My friend is being overly protective. Call Max off, Nicholas."

"Come." After Max trotted to Nicholas's side, he gave him a treat. "Good boy."

While Selena talked with Mr. Woods, Nicholas went into the kitchen and worked, but he kept Max at the door lying down facing her and the alarm guy.

When she came into the room minus Mr. Woods, Nicholas asked, "Is he gone?"

"Why don't you ask Max? He was watching us the whole time."

"I suspect everyone."

"I know you do, me included."

"Not in this."

"Oh, that's nice," she said in a sarcastic tone.

"What do you know about this Mr. Woods? Did you just call anyone in the Yellow Pages?"

"He was recommended by the chief of staff and no doubt the reason he has agreed to come back in an hour with his equipment and install the system today. No thanks to you and Max." She placed her fists on her waist, her lips drawn in a narrow line.

"Okay, I might have been a little overzealous, but I'd rather be that than let anything happen to you."

Her fierce expression and stance relaxed. "I don't have the energy to be mad at you right now."

"Good." He grinned, liking her spunk. "Tell you what. I'll go get us something to eat. I saw a hamburger place not too far from here."

"They have delicious burgers, and I'll take some fries, too."

He started for the front door. "Lock the door behind me. And I'm leaving Max to keep you company."

"We'll try not to have too much fun while you're gone."

Nicholas chuckled as he left the house, waiting to hear the sound of the lock clicking into place. At his SUV he paused and scanned the area. No cars parked along the street and only a couple in driveways. Nothing set off alarm bells.

On Thursday afternoon, Nicholas sat next to Selena in an interview room at the prison while they waited for Greg Littleton to be escorted to them.

"I thought after we see Greg we could grab dinner before I take you home," Nicholas said.

"You haven't been far from my side much except when you had to go in to work. Surprisingly not a lot. You'd think you had these past few days off." She shot him a look. "You haven't been outside my house sleeping like that first night, have you?"

"No, you have a good alarm system and Max for a roommate when I leave."

Which had only been about eight hours the last two nights. "Okay, spill it. I can take care of myself. I have a gun and that good alarm system you mentioned."

"I told my captain about what's going on, and he agrees I need to keep a close eye on you. I can review security tapes from my laptop."

"What have you found about the fake Miss Chick?"

"Not much other than what we already know. The person knew how to avoid the cameras, which indicates a certain knowledge of the West Wing. A slender, unidentified woman, five-nine or ten with long wavy black hair is the person I suspect assaulted Tara Wilkins in the restroom. We're going through the video at the entrances, but we haven't found her."

"A disguise?"

"Probably."

"How about General Meyer's office?" Selena asked, wondering if the same person had broken in there.

"I can't say, but progress is being made. We're narrowing the long list down. But no one fits the description of the suspect in Tara Wilkins's case."

She twisted toward him as the door opened. "You don't have to keep babysitting me. I'm going to work tomorrow now that my house is back to normal," she whispered, then glanced toward Greg shuffling into the room.

After the guard left and took up a post outside the door, Selena gestured toward Nicholas. "This is Nicholas Cole. He works for the Capitol K-9 Unit and has an interest in your case."

Greg looked from Selena to Nicholas. "You mean, someone else believes I'm innocent?"

"I won't go as far as that, but I think there may be more to your situation. Why don't you tell me what happened from the time you and Saul Rather got into an argument by the pool."

While Greg told Nicholas what he had said to her last week, Selena took notes, listening closely to determine if he added anything new. She noticed the weary set to the thin, forty-two-year-old man's shoulders and the tired lines in his face. His skin had a pasty pallor to it, and his brown hair had grayed at the temples. Different from the photo of the man at his trial she'd studied before she'd come to see him a week ago.

As Greg finished, disappointment weaved through her. He'd said nothing new. Nothing new that she could recall, and that was the problem. She couldn't check her notes on her tablet. "Can you tell me the names of the people you remember were with you at the pool that evening when Saul confronted you?"

She jotted down their names, recalling no changes from the last time she'd asked.

"I also remember that Tabitha Miller and a couple of her female friends came out onto her balcony while Saul Rather was yelling at me," Greg said. "I didn't think to mention that before since Tabitha and her friends weren't right there at the pool like the others and only on the balcony for a minute. I tried to visualize like you said to, but that's all I came up with."

She straightened at the same time Nicholas did. Tabitha Miller was an aide for Congressman Jeffries. "She lives there at the apartment complex?"

"Yes, at least two years ago."

Selena jotted down the information, making a note to check and see if she still lived there.

"Did you recognize any of the other women with her? Did they live at the apartment complex?" Nicholas gave her a look that told her to let him do the interviewing.

Selena bit the inside of her cheek to keep from saying anything.

"No to both questions. One of the ladies I'd never seen, but I remember the other had come once before."

"I'm surprised you have such a good memory of who was there." Nicholas lounged back in his chair, taking in Greg's every nuance.

"When a person gets chewed out in front of people, they tend to look around, embarrassed, to see who heard. At least that's my experience. Do you think I'd kill the guy with so many witnesses watching the argument and able to testify to a motive for me to kill him?"

"It's happened before." Nicholas crossed his arms. "Can you think of anything else about that twenty-four hours? Why did you go to the parking garage so early the next morning?"

"I told the police when they picked me up I received a call about a car with a smashed window."

Selena stared at Nicholas. "I didn't know that. I didn't find it in the record. Greg, did your lawyer bring that detail up at the trial? I don't remember it in the court records."

"No one seemed to think that information meant

anything. Just something to cover my tracks. There wasn't a car with a smashed window."

"Do you remember if it was a female or male voice who called you?" Nicholas asked, interest on his face.

Greg thought for a long moment, his lips pursed. "I'm not sure. It was a gruff voice. I think."

Nicholas took out his business card. "If you come up with anything new, give me a call."

"So that's important to my case?"

"It could be. Remember everything and tell us, even if you don't think it's important. It might all fit together. One piece of the puzzle."

For a few seconds Greg's usual defeated expression vanished. "I will. Thank you. Both of you."

Ten minutes later, Nicholas opened his SUV door for Selena. When he came around and slid behind the steering wheel, she asked, "What do you think? We need to go talk to Tabitha Miller as soon as possible. She works for Congressman Jeffries. What if Michael found that out and came over to talk to his dad about her? You see the connection?"

He started the car then angled toward her. "Just because one of the witnesses to the fight worked for Congressman Jeffries doesn't mean there's a connection to Michael's murder. Don't get your hopes up. And you are *not* going to talk to her. I am. Understood?"

"Only if you'll tell me what she says. She fits. She has access to the West Wing and would know its layout. She is about the height of Miss Chick."

"Slow down. When we get back to your house, we'll discuss the next steps." He sliced her a stern look. "The only reason I'm even including you in that discussion is that I'm afraid you'll go off half-cocked, pursuing your own investigation. Even if Michael talked with Tabitha, that doesn't mean anything except he was following every lead and talking to every witness to the fight."

"I hate to see Greg Littleton in prison for a crime he didn't commit. Just as I hate to see my cousin out there being hunted for one she didn't do."

"It must be nice that you know all that for sure. I need evidence to prove it. Not theories and a woman's intuition."

"My, you are cynical."

He stopped at a red light and swung his full attention to her. "And you aren't? I've read your dossier. I know what kind of childhood you had. A tough one."

Surprised, she felt the color drain from her face while her heartbeat slowed for a few seconds before revving up as anger swelled in her. "Tough? I guess compared to yours it was. I wasn't born with a silver spoon in my mouth."

His hands gripped the steering wheel so tight his knuckles whitened. "So I guess we both know the facts of each other's background. For the record, the only reason I looked into your past was because of the case."

"The same reason for me. You were involved in the Jeffries case. I do have a few connections, working in the White House."

He clamped his teeth down so hard that a muscle in his cheek twitched. He made a left turn and kept his focus on the road. Silence ruled for the next five minutes, with Nicholas glancing at the rearview mirror every thirty seconds.

Selena tensed, feeling his alertness spike. "What's going on?"

He swerved across a lane of traffic and took a hard right, the tires screeching. "We're being followed."

FIVE

"Who's following us? Where?" Selena twisted around, looking out the rear window.

Nicholas increased his speed and made another turn. "The white car's coming around the corner. Hold on. We're going for a little ride."

He'd seen that same car when they'd left the prison. Then it disappeared but reappeared a few streets before he stopped at the light.

"Do you think someone followed us to the prison?" Selena kept peering back as Nicholas pushed the speed limit when he finally left a residential area.

"I don't think so. We picked this tail up at the prison." Which made him wonder how. Why? Maybe Selena was on to something about Littleton. This all started after she first visited the man who was convicted of killing one of Senator Eagleton's interns. Everything led back to Eagleton and Jeffries.

He made a quick decision and swerved left onto a side street, then right and accelerated down an alley. Another right followed by a sharp turn, which brought him back to the original street.

"I don't see the car behind us. I think you lost him." Selena straightened in her seat.

"Not for long." Nicholas went down the side street a second time. "We're going hunting. I want to know who is so interested in us."

"Good. We need answers."

He chuckled. "We?"

"Yes, you said we would work together on Littleton's case, or do you want me to do it alone? I will if I have to."

He continued down the side street, searching for the white car. "You drive a hard bargain, which doesn't surprise me. All I can promise is that I'll keep you informed of what I discover concerning Littleton."

"And Erin?"

"I can't, for obvious reasons."

"Because you still think I'm helping her. Is that the real reason you're taking such an active role in *protecting* me?"

Was it? Good question. If he were honest, no. There was something about Selena that attracted him. "It's more complicated than that."

"That's a cop-out."

He spied the rear of a white car turning up ahead and passed the vehicle in front of him.

Selena leaned forward. "Is that our guy?"

"I think so." Nicholas took the corner then pressed down on the accelerator, gaining on the car. "Jot down the license-plate numbers." Suddenly the Dodge shot forward. "I think he knows we're here. Hang on."

Selena dug into her purse and withdrew the pad she'd used at the prison. "I got the numbers."

For the next ten minutes, the Dodge weaved through traffic, ran a stop sign and took Nicholas on a merry chase. He closed the distance between the two vehicles when the white car flew through a light when it turned red. Nicholas slammed on his brakes as a school bus pulled into the intersection.

Selena jerked forward, her seat belt halting her.

Heartbeat racing, fed by the flow of adrenaline into his system, Nicholas eased his tight grip on the steering wheel and uncurled his fingers. "Are you okay?"

"Fine."

"We've probably lost him."

The light flashed green. Nicholas looked both ways then crossed the intersection, heading in the direction the Dodge had gone.

After a twenty-minute search of the surrounding streets, he pulled over to the curb and called Fiona at headquarters. "I need a favor."

"Anything for you, if you promise to bring Max by to see me next time y'all are here."

"I thought you were a cat person."

"I have cats, but I'm an animal lover."

"Same here."

"What do you need? Then I'll give you an update on those videos I've been going through."

Fiona was also going through the same ones he was. Two sets of eyes were better than one. "I have a Virginia license plate I need you to run down for me." Nicholas took the sheet Selena handed him and recited the three letters then four numbers.

"Wait. It shouldn't take long. My fingers are dancing across the keys as we speak." A minute later she said, "I've got it. The owner is Benny Goodwin." Then she gave him the address associated with the license plate.

"Thanks. Will you do another favor for me?"

"I'm already on it. I'll pull up what I can on Mr. Goodwin and call you back."

Nicholas disconnected with Fiona. "I'll have something soon on the guy who owns the Dodge. Do you know a Benny Goodwin?"

Selena shook her head.

"Let's grab something to eat. I want to know about this guy before I pay him a visit."

"Don't you mean we?"

He didn't want to argue with her right now, but he wouldn't put her in danger no matter what she wanted. "Let's check out that café at the end of the block. I forgot to grab lunch before coming to pick you up."

"I'm not going to let you change the subject," she said as Nicholas exited his SUV, scoping out the streets with quaint shops.

If he ignored the question, maybe she would get tired of asking. He rounded the hood and waited for her to climb out of the Tahoe. "I'm thinking a nice big piece of pie. I love pie. Not many I won't eat."

She gave him a frown and marched toward the restaurant ahead of him. Her body language shouted frustration and anger. He didn't care. He wouldn't put her in danger. He would let her help when he thought the situation wasn't risky.

As she entered the café, his cell rang. He noted it was Fiona. "Tell me you have the lowdown on Benny Goodwin."

"When haven't I given you the info you needed? He's a private investigator with an office in Arlington. Do you want the address?"

"You're the best tech support a team could have."

Fiona laughed and gave him the information. "He has a thriving business, from what I can gather, mostly divorce cases."

"Thanks. I won't forget to bring you a chai tea latte and Max next time I come to headquarters."

Nicholas pocketed his cell and headed into the restaurant, a fifties throwback with a jukebox, red booths and pictures of films from that era. Selena sat in a booth with a *Rebel Without a Cause* poster on the wall nearby. He was beginning to think of her as a rebel *with* a cause.

He slid in across from her, opened the menu and spied the waitress coming toward them. "Let's talk after we order."

"What would you two like?" The older woman retrieved a pencil from over her left ear.

"What's your specialty?" Nicholas asked, feeling Selena's glare on him.

"Chicken-fried steak and mashed potatoes with gravy. Also the hamburgers."

"How about pies? We don't have time for dinner." Selena set the menu on the table. "Which is the best?"

"Blackberry is my favorite, but most of our customers order the cherry pie."

"How's the chocolate one?" Selena folded her arms over her chest.

"Good. You can't go wrong with any of them."

"I'll take the cherry pie with vanilla ice cream." Nicholas placed his menu on top of Selena's. "And a cup of black coffee. It smells delicious." That scent fused with baking bread and grilling meat. His stomach rumbled.

"How about you, miss?"

"The chocolate pie would be great with a cup of coffee."

When the waitress left, Selena leaned forward. "I want to go with you to see Benny Goodwin. The name doesn't sound familiar, but I might know him or have seen him around."

"Here. I've got his driver's-license photo." He withdrew his cell and clicked on the one Fiona had sent. "Not a good picture. Looks like a mug shot."

Selena took the phone and studied the screen. "No. He's not familiar. I still want to go with you."

"You're as persistent as the salmon returning home."

She pressed her lips together and glared at him.

"I found out from Fiona that he's a private eye, so I don't see why you can't come with me."

Her eyes brightened. "Really?"

"Yes. After I have my pie. Cherry is my favorite."

"I like cherry, too, but chocolate fits my mood."

"It does?"

"I like to eat chocolate when I'm stressed or frustrated. I'm both at the moment."

"I'm taking you to see Benny Goodwin."

"I think this little bump in our working relationship is an indication of more to come."

He leaned forward, lacing his fingers together, his arms on the table. "You are *not* a law-enforcement officer. I won't put you in danger."

She bent closer to him, their heads inches away. "You are *not* my keeper. I've tolerated your presence in this, but you can't stop me from pursuing my own inquiries. I was doing just fine by myself."

Nicholas ground his teeth together and lounged back. He wasn't going to be drawn into a battle with Selena. "Ah, I see our pie is coming."

She huffed and sat stiffly against the cushion. "I'm thinking of having two pieces."

She was one stubborn lady, but she'd met her match with him.

"Now I see why you let me come. His office is in a nice area. He obviously must be successful at his job."

Selena let Nicholas open the main door to a three-story renovated redbrick house that had been turned into a commercial building. She noticed several lawyers on the plaque of tenants. Smart move on Mr. Goodwin's part. Attorneys often used private investigators.

Nicholas followed her inside but didn't respond to her statement. In fact, through the stop at the diner and the drive to this place, he'd been silent. He wasn't happy with her. Every part of him screamed that. She didn't care. She was the one who had grown up in a tough, gang-infested area, while he'd lived on an estate in Maryland with all his needs met. He hadn't gone hungry or feared every time he'd left his home that he could be shot. She'd done her research on him in the past couple of days. His grandfather had been a senator and had come from a long line of members of Congress. He'd been influential and wealthy—like her mother's family. So why in the world was he working as a cop, albeit in an elite unit handpicked by a former general?

That question taunted her as they made their way to the second floor where Mr. Goodwin had his office. After the interview, she would ask Nicholas. Otherwise it would bug her until she found out. A nasty habit that had gotten her into trouble occasionally.

She approached the private eye's secretary a few steps ahead of Nicholas and said before he could, "We are here to see Mr. Goodwin." Nicholas wouldn't have known about Littleton and the possible importance of him to the Jeffries case without her. The motive for Michael Jeffries's murder might very well be due to Michael's work to set Littleton free from prison and find the real killer of Senator Eagleton's aide. She needed Nicholas to realize she was part of the investigation.

"Do you have an appointment?" the young woman,

probably no more than twenty, asked while smacking her gum. "He's on the phone right now."

Nicholas stepped next to Selena. "No, but you might tell him we're the two he was following earlier today and would like a word with him. Now."

The secretary's eyes grew round, sliding a glance toward her employer's door.

Nicholas showed her his badge. "This is police business."

The young woman jumped to her feet and hurried into Mr. Goodwin's office. When she came back in half a minute, she said, "He can see you now."

"Does that badge always do the trick?" Selena whispered as she made her way to the door.

"Not always. Sometimes it sends a person in flight." Nicholas entered a room with folders and photos stacked on a messy desk.

The older man behind it was hurriedly clearing it off. When he looked up, he said, "I told Betsy to give me five minutes. I was working on a case." He gestured to the papers and pictures spread out before him.

"Does the case have anything to do with following Miss Barrow and me?" Nicholas flipped open his badge and showed it to Mr. Goodwin.

The man's face paled, and he sank into his chair. "There's nothing illegal about driving on the streets. You can't prove I was following you two."

Nicholas took a seat in one of the chairs in front of the desk. "There is when you run a stop sign and a red light. You drove recklessly and almost hit a school bus full of children. That wouldn't look too good on the news."

"You aren't an Arlington police officer. You have no jurisdiction here."

"But I know the chief of police as well as a number of officers in Arlington, not to mention I work at the White House."

Selena hadn't thought the man's face could get any paler, but Mr. Goodwin's did.

"What do you want?" The private detective's voice quavered.

"Why were you following us today?" Selena blurted out before Nicholas could say anything.

Mr. Goodwin remained silent for a long moment then finally said, "I can't break confidentiality."

Nicholas sat forward. "There will be enough evidence to make an arrest once the police review the traffic cam. When I'm finished with you, you might lose your driver's license. How are you going to do your work without one?"

Selena wondered if Nicholas could do that. If she were Mr. Goodwin, she'd believe him because of the hard edge to Nicholas's words and the fierce look on his face.

"This involves the attempted murder of a high-ranking government official."

Selena marveled at how the impression of "don't mess with me" came across loud and clear from Nicholas. Mr. Goodwin shook.

"I don't want any trouble. I was called because you two went to visit Greg Littleton. I'm notified when someone comes to see him, and I follow them to see who they are and where they go."

"Who hired you?"

"I can't tell you."

Nicholas took out his cell phone, rose and leaned over Mr. Goodwin's desk. "I'll give you ten seconds to tell me who hired you. If you don't, I'm calling the police chief."

The private detective blinked rapidly. "I can't…"

Nicholas punched in two numbers.

"I can't get another ticket. Please."

Nicholas pushed two more buttons.

"Senator Eagleton's office," Mr. Goodwin shouted.

Why would her uncle want to know?

"Who hired you? Who set this up?" Selena clenched the arms of the chair.

"I don't know. My secretary took the call and set it up a couple of months ago. Other than Littleton's mother, you are the only one who has visited him. Until today, when he came with you." Mr. Goodwin tossed his head toward Nicholas.

"How do you report to the person who hired you?" she fired another question at the private investigator.

"I call a number and leave a message."

"Don't you think that's strange you don't talk to someone personally?"

Mr. Goodwin lifted his shoulders in a shrug. "Miss, in this job, I've dealt with some strange people."

"How are you paid?" Nicholas sat again in the chair next to Selena.

"Cash, almost immediately after each time I've reported in. The amount varies on how much time I spend finding out who the person is and basic information on them. I won't call the number about today." Mr. Goodwin stared at Nicholas. "Your name won't be mentioned."

"But you have mentioned my associate?"

"Yes. Not long ago." The man turned to her. "Selena Barrow, White House tour director."

Nicholas stood. "Please write down the number you

called and then make a call to it and report that we visited Littleton today."

After Mr. Goodwin jotted something on the piece of paper and gave it to Nicholas, the detective picked up his phone and made the call. He was on the line two minutes, giving the details of who went to see Littleton, then he hung up. "I tried to trace the number once. Prepaid cell phone. I couldn't."

"We're leaving right after we talk with your secretary." Nicholas waited while Selena rose and started for the door. "Keep doing what you're doing. Call me when you receive payment for the tip. I'll need to check the envelope. Don't let anyone know about this chat, not even your secretary."

"I won't. I don't want to lose any business over it. Times are tough and rent is high here."

Out in the reception area, Nicholas smiled at the young secretary and half leaned, half sat on the side of her desk. "Do you remember anything about who set up the account with Senator Eagleton's office a couple of months ago?"

As she continued to chew and snap her gum, the woman scrunched her forehead and tapped her chin with a fingernail with hot-pink polish on it. She finally shook her head.

"A man or woman? This is important," Nicholas said with a slight Southern drawl.

"I think a man… No, wait, a female. I don't believe I got a name."

Nicholas took out a business card and wrote his cell number on the back. "Call me—if you remember anything." He winked and straightened. "Good day, Betsy."

The young woman's cheeks reddened. "I will—" she looked at the card "—Nicholas."

Out in the hallway, Selena rolled her eyes and laughed. "You're a smooth operator, Nicolas Cole."

"It's a tough job, but someone has to do it." He gave her a wink and headed for the stairs.

Back in his SUV, Selena relaxed for the first time since the private detective had started following them. "I have some steaks at home. Why don't we skip going out to dinner? I'm not hungry right now since I ate the pie. I'm sure Max is wondering where we went without him."

"He's probably thrilled. He got an afternoon off."

"Well, not exactly. He's guarding my house."

"True. He's learned to protect his territory. Honestly, I don't think anyone will come back. They searched thoroughly the first time."

"Yeah, I think they got what they were looking for." Selena took in his strong profile and liked what she saw. Not movie-star handsome but definitely heart-stopping when he smiled and his dark chocolate–colored eyes sparkled.

When Nicholas turned onto her street, she broke the silence of the past ten minutes. "So what are we going to do next? Go see my uncle?"

"No." He pulled into her driveway. "I'll look into this lead."

"Have you met my uncle?"

"Once."

"He's a very private man. We may not have a great relationship, but I am his niece." She didn't want Nicholas interviewing him. She couldn't believe her uncle would order her house searched. His method would have been to come see her and demand to know why she was investigating Littleton's case. He'd want to view what evidence she'd collected because Erin was his daughter, and he'd always loved her. He would see she was trying to prove Erin was innocent and might even want to take over Littleton's case. This might be the time she could mend the breach between—

"What's wrong?"

"Nothing. Just thinking about my uncle."

"I don't want anyone to think you're investigating Littleton on your own."

"Okay. Then we go together. I'm conceding Tabitha to you but not my uncle." She'd seen how Nicholas got women to talk. Perhaps he'd be able to charm information out of Congressman Jeffries's aide and find out what she remembered about the argument between Littleton and the murdered intern.

He stared at her as though probing her reasons behind the request. "Why is this important to you?"

For a moment she didn't know if she could tell him, but it was imperative since she had gotten close to Erin. She'd wanted to be part of a family. She was determined to help Erin come back safely, with her name cleared. If her uncle didn't want to have anything to do with her, so be it. She would be satisfied with being close with Erin.

"Selena?"

She angled toward him. "I have a letter from my mother written when she was dying from alcohol poisoning, begging me to give it to her brother and make sure he read it. I'm afraid with the way our relationship is now, he would take it and tear it up without reading. I want to fulfill this last obligation to my mother then I'll be…" She swallowed back the word *free* and averted her gaze.

"You'll be what?" he said in a gentle voice.

"Free of my past. I washed my hands of dealing with my mom's drinking. I refused to see her until the hospital called and told me she was dying. I should have been there for her." What was it about Nicholas that she said out loud something she had been suppressing and struggling with since her mother had died three years ago?

He touched her arm and drew her around so their gazes linked. "I'm sorry. Our past can play with our minds sometimes."

"My childhood wasn't anything like yours."

"Do you think I had an easy time while growing up?"

"Did you go without food for a couple of days at a time?"

He pulled back from her, all feelings wiped from his expression. "I won't play one-up with you. No, my life was different from yours, but it had its challenges."

His blank look, which had chased away the earlier concern, bothered her. "I'm sorry. I know that just because you came from a wealthy family doesn't guarantee an easy life. I haven't walked in your shoes. I shouldn't have judged."

His hands on the steering wheel, his body facing forward, he fixed his gaze on something beyond the windshield. "Let's start over. Is the steak dinner still on the table?"

"Yes, I'll use the microwave to defrost them. I can put a couple of baking potatoes in the oven and make salad."

He sent her that special smile, dimples appearing in his cheeks. "I'm starting to get hungry after that description."

"Let's go. And Max will have a treat, too. These are T-bones, so he can enjoy the leftovers."

"He may desert me for you after tonight." Nicholas exited the Tahoe and met her on the sidewalk to her house.

"I'm beginning to change my mind about having a pet. When this is over with, I want a dog. One like Max. I know you mentioned you'd help me, and I might take you up on it. You're the expert on guard dogs." Before she unlocked her door, she shifted toward Nicholas. "We never settled on me going with you to interview my uncle."

He studied her for a few seconds. "He might not be too happy to see me—us. Do you still want to do it?"

"Yes. I owe Erin. She's the one who contacted me first to meet for lunch. I might never have gotten to know her if she hadn't made that first move after my mom's funeral." She grinned. "And since working at the White House, I've discovered diplomacy. I'll persuade my uncle to help us get to the bottom of all this because I know he isn't personally involved." At least she prayed he wasn't. She couldn't dismiss that someone from the Eagleton office had paid Benny Goodwin to keep an eye on who visited Greg. Who? Why, after he was sent to jail?

"Then okay. You can even initiate the contact to set up a time. All right?"

"Yes. Perfect." She unlocked her front door and hurried to turn off the alarm while Max greeted Nicholas. She glanced back at them and some of her wariness of Nicholas's motives faded as she watched her protector playfully roughhousing with his dog.

"Thank you for seeing me on such short notice, Miss Miller." Nicholas took the seat in front of the desk that Congressman Jeffries's aide gestured toward.

She sat in the one next to him, dressed in an emerald-green pencil skirt, black high heels and a white blouse with cap sleeves. He noticed a matching green jacket hung on a coatrack. Her office wasn't big, but then she was a junior staff member.

"Please, Tabitha." She crossed her long legs. "What brings you to my office?"

"I'm reopening a case and your name came up." He observed her for any reaction to his words, and she didn't let him down. Her pupils dilated. Her body tensed.

"Case? I haven't been involved in any cases."

"It happened two years ago at your apartment complex."

As her forehead crunched, her lower lip stuck out. She brushed back her long, wavy, reddish-blond hair, similar to Erin Eagleton's. "I don't understand."

"Do you recall when Saul Rather, one of Senator Eagleton's interns, was murdered in the parking garage?"

"I wasn't a witness to that murder. I was asleep when it happened, because I remember sirens waking me up. Why do you want to talk with me? I don't know anything about what went down."

He was beginning to wonder if she might know more than she was saying, with the way a defensive wall went up when he mentioned the murder victim. "Did you know Saul Rather?"

"Personally, no. He hadn't lived at the apartment complex but a couple of months, and he kept to himself. I saw him a few times at the Capitol and maybe spoke a handful of words to him. His murderer has already been convicted."

"New evidence has surfaced, and I'm taking a hard look at the case."

"Again, I don't see my connection."

"You and a few of your friends witnessed an argument between Rather and Littleton, the custodian convicted of the crime, the evening before the murder. Do you recall it?"

"Two years ago," she said in a voice full of disbelief. "What do you expect me to remember?"

"What you saw between the two men, your impression of the fight and who else was with you on your balcony."

She blew out a long breath. "No, I mean it was *two* years ago."

"I understand you used to have various aides over to your place after work."

"I used to once a week. Those people would vary from week to week, so to be able to recall the exact ones at my apartment on that particular day is impossible. The only ones I remember who might have been there are the regulars, although even they didn't come every week."

When she didn't elaborate, Nicholas asked, "Who were they?"

"Sally Young, Becky Wright and Janice Neill. We did a lot of things together back then." Tabitha rose. "I'm sorry I can't be more helpful. Saul Rather had a temper. Word had it, he usually held it together during the workday, but once off work he'd speak his mind. That's all I know."

In his gut, he felt she was holding something back. Nicholas took his time getting to his feet, then slowly lifted his gaze to Tabitha's green eyes, dark with— worry? She came to four inches shorter than he was, so she could have fit into Miss Chick's costume. He knew that was a stretch, and yet she was Congressman Jeffries's aide, had been for several years. Could she be connected to Michael Jeffries's murder case somehow? "One last thing, did you go to the Easter Egg Roll?"

"Yes, along with thousands of others. Congressman Jeffries was there as well as a couple of his staff members. Why? What does that have to do with the murder of Saul Rather?"

"Nothing. Just curious." He thought of the cufflinks, with the initials *VG* engraved on them, that he found in Margaret Meyer's office. "Was Vincent Geary one of the aides at the event?"

"No. He had some work to finish up on a bill for the congressman." She walked toward the door. "I'm sorry I couldn't have been of more use to you. I need to leave. I have a luncheon scheduled. Duty calls."

He removed his card. "If you can think of anyone who was on the balcony with you that day or possibly would have been, please give me a call."

Out in the main hall of the office building, he lounged against the wall, waiting to see when she would appear to go to her luncheon. Still no Tabitha Miller ten minutes later. His cell phone rang, and he quickly answered the call from Selena.

"Are you backing out of eating lunch at the White House mess with me?" Nicholas asked instead of saying hello.

"Don't you think after spending most of yesterday together we've seen each other enough?"

"Let's not forget this morning at the White House."

"Yes, you're right. You aren't usually far away. I'm calling to let you know my uncle wants to see me for lunch."

"Okay, I'll be at your office in twenty minutes."

"Don't bother. I'm at the Capitol, waiting for Uncle Preston to meet me. He should be here any minute."

He shoved away from the wall, his hand clenching his cell phone. "What happened to *we* would work as a team and talk to him together?"

SIX

"That's why I'm telling you now." Selena moved to a quieter area of the corridor in the Capitol Building while keeping an eye on the exit from the Senate. "I got a call from my uncle's secretary, telling me he can meet with me when the Senate breaks for lunch. I only had twenty minutes to get over here. When I phoned this morning, I didn't think I would get a chance to see Uncle Preston until next week. Unlike you, I'm sharing. Can you get over here?"

"On my way. Where will you two be?"

"The Senate dining room. Do you know where it is? I know it's hard to find. I could ask my uncle to wait for—"

"Yes, I know its location. My grandfather was a senator. Chitchat until I get there."

"Yes, sir. I see my uncle. Talk to you later." She punched the End button and returned her cell to her jacket pocket while the tall, distinguished-looking man with silver hair walked toward her. Imposing. A neutral expression in place. At least her uncle wasn't frowning.

When a colleague intercepted him, Uncle Preston grinned and his face became lively. She sighed, wishing he would respond to her like that. But every time he saw her he saw her mother. She looked so much like her that she was a constant reminder to Uncle Preston of his sister who had blackened the Eagleton name.

"Hi, Selena. Waiting for Senator Eagleton?" Carly Jones, her uncle's chief of staff, asked.

"Yes, we're supposed to have lunch. Do you need to talk to him?"

"Just for a moment about a bill coming up for a vote." Dressed impeccably, with short brown hair, Carly stepped closer and lowered her voice. "I heard there was some trouble at the Easter Egg Roll. I didn't stay long. Too much that needed to be done. What happened?"

"I'm not at liberty to say, but everything has been taken care of." She wasn't going to tell Carly about the break-in and Miss Chick. Her uncle's chief of staff hardly ever talked to her unless she wanted something. Carly was what she called an information gatherer, going from one person to the next to see what she could glean. That might be helpful to her uncle, but Erin had learned to keep her distance and so had Selena.

"I'm glad. I see the senator is free. I won't keep him long." Carly quickly left to catch Uncle Preston before he reached Selena.

She tried not to stare at Carly and her uncle talking, but something his chief of staff told him didn't make him happy. He was still frowning when he approached Selena.

"Our lunch will be short. I need to talk to another senator before the vote on a bill this afternoon."

"I understand. Do you need to reschedule?" Suddenly she didn't want to talk to her uncle. Growing up listening to her mother talk about him, Selena had become wary of the man by the time she was a teenager. According to her mom, he could be ruthless and cold, and so far, not much she'd witnessed had changed her mind. She hadn't let the thugs in her neighborhood scare her, but Uncle Preston did.

He checked his cell phone then shook his head. "No, I'm tied up for a while, and you said this was important concerning Erin. Let's go in, and I'll ask for a table in a quiet corner. You haven't heard from Erin, have you?" He started down the hallway that led to the dining room.

She understood his desire to find out anything concerning his daughter, but there was a small part of her that wished he'd want to spend time with her because she was his only niece, not because of information she might give him concerning Erin. "No, I wish I had. Nicholas Cole will be joining us in a few minutes. He's a member of the Capitol K-9 Unit, and we've discovered information that might help Erin."

Her uncle slowed his step. "I'm not a patient man nor do I like surprises."

"I promised Nicholas we would talk to you together."

Silence fell between them until they were seated at a table in front of a large window. He'd informed the staff he was expecting one more person to join him at his table.

"I knew Nicholas Cole's parents and had heard he was working at the White House. I saw him once there. He looks a lot like his father. Are you friends with him?"

Heat seared her cheeks. She rarely blushed, but her uncle got her to. She didn't know her father, and there were times as a child she used to think of Uncle Preston as her father. She even found a photo her mother had and took it to keep. Her mom never missed it. "Yes," she finally answered, realizing she did consider Nicholas a friend. She could talk to him a lot easier than to most people.

"Ah, I see him coming this way."

Selena glanced at Nicholas, strolling under the huge chandelier, its light reflecting off the golden walls. He paused a moment at a table with two senators, shaking their hands and saying a few words before bridging the distance to the table. She knew he came from wealth, but not until she'd seen him in this environment, as though he belonged, did she realize how different their backgrounds were.

Nicholas took the chair near the window, so he faced the diners in the large room. "It's good to see you again, Senator Eagleton."

"I was just telling my niece I knew your parents. And I was a congressman when your grandfather served in the Senate from Maryland. Any interest in going into politics?"

Nicholas picked up a white napkin and placed it in his lap. "I'm enjoying my job and don't see a reason to change."

After the waiter took their orders, her uncle sipped his water then said, "Selena asked me to wait until you arrived to find out why she needed to talk with me. You're here, so why the urgency?"

"We're investigating a lead in Saul Rather's murder."

Uncle Preston's eyebrows hiked up. "Greg Littleton was found guilty. Case closed."

"We're not so sure he's the one who murdered your intern," Selena interjected.

Both men looked at Selena, and she tensed her shoulders. Surprise filled her uncle's face while Nicholas's mouth tightened into a hard line.

Nicholas cleared his throat. "Greg was convicted on

circumstantial evidence and some of it has come into question of late. We were at the prison to interview Greg yesterday, and when we left there, someone followed us. We confronted the private detective and discovered you or someone from your office hired him to keep an eye on any people who visit Littleton."

Uncle Preston's forehead furrowed, but he didn't say anything until the waiter set their orders in front of them and left. He stared for a long moment at his poached halibut with saffron nage, then looked Nicholas in the eye. "Who was the private investigator?"

"Benny Goodwin." Nicholas picked up his braised short-rib sandwich and took a bite, watching for any kind of reaction from her uncle.

Popping a sweet-potato fry into her mouth, Selena saw her uncle's jawline harden and his eyes glint. The scent from her crab-cake sandwich churned her stomach.

"First of all, I don't know what this has to do with my daughter. Second, I don't know a Benny Goodwin. I've never used him for any kind of work. If he told you I hired him, he's lying."

"Could someone on your staff have hired Goodwin without your knowledge? When he's paid, it's cash and the private detective has never seen a person associated with the request." Nicholas returned her uncle's intense regard.

"I guess it's possible. I certainly know I don't hire anyone and pay in cash, for accounting reasons. But why would someone from my staff do that?"

"To keep track of what's going on with Littleton because they have something to lose if evidence is uncovered to prove his innocence." Nicholas reached under the white tablecloth and clasped Selena's hand.

She was sure her distress was evident on her face. Her uncle had that effect on her. She wasn't like her mother and had for years wished he would acknowledge that. Her family was small, and she wanted some connection with the few she had. It was lonely being a loner all of her life.

"What does this have to do with Erin? Not that I don't want an innocent man, if he is, exonerated." Uncle Preston shifted his attention from Nicholas to her.

Nicholas squeezed her hand, as if to say she should take this question.

"When Erin went missing, I was determined to find a way to clear her name. I looked into Michael Jeffries's personal life and couldn't find anything that would be a motive for murder. That's when I decided to investigate his professional life. I knew Michael had a couple of current cases he was working on, and I decided to see if anyone connected to those would have a reason to kill him. Erin didn't."

"Of course, my daughter wouldn't," her uncle said in a raised voice, then snapped his mouth closed as a few people glanced their way.

Selena's grip on Nicholas's hand tightened. "Michael and she were good friends, and she never indicated any problems between them to me. If nothing jumped out with the current cases, I was going to work back from there. Littleton's case was badly handled by his court-appointed attorney. The more I dug into the evidence, the more I'd come to believe, like Michael, that he was innocent."

Uncle Preston's stern expression relaxed, and slowly his features transformed into a pleasant look. "You never said anything to me about that or sought my help," he said to Selena, as though surprised by that fact.

She released Nicholas's grasp and straightened in her chair, her gaze fixed on her uncle. "You'd made it clear you didn't really consider me a member of your family, but Erin accepted me from the beginning."

His eyes, so like Erin's, flared. "I deserved that." He blew out a long breath. "Not knowing if my daughter is alive or not has made me take a good hard look at myself. I've been pushing the police to discover the truth, even hired my investigators, but you went out and did something yourself. I haven't been the father I should have been...or the uncle to you."

Selena dug her teeth into her lower lip to keep her jaw from dropping.

"I've been reconsidering how I treated you the last couple of months, so when you called me to ask for a meeting, I rearranged my schedule to see you right away. I could have asked you for any news you had about Erin over the phone. I knew I couldn't put off telling you how I felt, and I wasn't going to do that by phone. My stubbornness has kept me from forgiving your mother, and she is dead. I could never condone her lifestyle, but she was my only sibling. I should have been better than what I was."

Selena blinked the tears away. She wouldn't cry in front of her uncle or Nicholas. She'd learned when she was young to hide her real emotions. "I didn't condone my mother's lifestyle, either. I left home as soon as I could. I couldn't help her if she wouldn't help herself." She stared at her uneaten sandwich. This conversation had thrown her past front and center. Foremost, she regretted that there was nothing she could have done to help her mother and now it was too late.

"I'm sorry. You should have felt you could come to me. I cut you off as though you were your mother, and now I have a daughter running away from the authorities when all your mother did was make a social spectacle of herself."

Nicholas cleared his throat, drawing their attention to him. "Should I leave?"

She said, "No," immediately, with Uncle Preston's two seconds behind hers.

Her uncle checked his watch, flashing her a smile. "Let's eat. They serve good food here." He cut into his halibut. "And if I can help either one of you in this Littleton case or anything else that can prove my daughter innocent, I will."

As Selena took her first bite of her crab-cake sandwich, she couldn't believe how well this conversation had gone. She'd prayed to the Lord to help her concerning her uncle, and she'd finally received an answer. *Maybe You* are *listening to me. Thank You, God.*

Nicholas escorted Selena back to the White House after their luncheon with Senator Eagleton. "Do you think he's telling the truth? Do you think he's had contact with Erin in any way?"

Selena tossed her purse on the desk in her office then swung around toward Nicholas. "We don't, as you heard, have a close relationship, but I think he is telling the truth. Erin wouldn't put her father at risk. She was always conscious of his political career. Before all this happened, there had been talk of him running for president. Now I doubt he will." She propped herself against her desk and grasped its edge. "What did Tabitha Miller have to say when you interviewed her?"

"She couldn't remember much about the day Littleton and Rather argued by the pool or which congressional aides were on her balcony with her. In other words, she was a dead end."

"Did you believe her?"

"I don't know." He kneaded the side of his neck. "Not so much about not remembering specifics about the day or people, but when I asked her how well she'd known Saul Rather, she said hardly at all. Yet there was something in her body language that made me doubt her. For just a second she touched her nose and averted her gaze."

"I don't remember any gossip about her from two years ago, but I do know she flits from one man to the next. Anyone who can better her standing in Washington. I think I even heard some chatter about her going after Michael. But you know how reliable rumors can be."

"There could be truth in that one. I'll do some checking." Nicholas closed the distance between them.

"More likely she saw Michael as a way to elevate her position on the congressman's staff. That doesn't mean Michael went along with that."

"I'm glad the senator gave us permission to investigate his staff members to see if we can find anyone who would have hired Goodwin. What I wish I could really do is access their financial records, but we don't have enough for a warrant at this time. Maybe later."

"Follow the money trail?"

"It often pays off." He locked gazes with her, being drawn even nearer by the glittering blue of her eyes. Listening earlier to the senator talking to Selena about their nonexistent relationship, he'd caught regret and vulnerability in her eyes. He'd been in the same situation with his parents, wanting a relationship that never materialized. He prayed Selena and her uncle could repair their familial bond. "What are you doing this afternoon?"

"I have several meetings. One of those with the president. How about you?"

Her spicy scent surrounded him, roping him to her. He inched forward. "Interviewing a suspect concerning the break-in of General Meyer's office."

"I'd ask who but I know you. Mum's the word."

"We have a few leads from going through the security videos, nothing solid, but that doesn't mean we won't narrow the suspect list down to a few."

"And then keep an eye on them," she said with a grin.

His heartbeat began tapping faster against his rib cage. She had a great smile. "I'll make a law-enforcement officer out of you before this is over." He couldn't resist plunging his fingers into the thick waves of her hair.

Her eyelids slid partially closed, and she shivered. "Not me. You can have the job. Look what has happened with my one attempt at investigating."

Holding her head framed between his hands, he leaned toward her until he was a breath away. "True. You'd better leave that to me." Then he brushed his lips across hers, lightly, teasingly.

Now his heartbeat hammered maddeningly within his chest. The urge to sweep her against him and deepen the kiss overwhelmed him. He started to, when a rap at the door echoed through his hazy thoughts.

Selena reacted by pushing away from the desk, stepping to the side and breaking their contact, her hair mussed where he'd held her. She started for the door.

"Wait."

She turned toward him, and he ran his fingers through her strands to neaten them.

"There. I wouldn't want any tongues wagging around here about us. I'll let the person in on my way out." He winked and sauntered toward the door. "See you later today."

He peered over his shoulder as she greeted one of the president's staff. He wanted to kiss her properly. He'd choose a better place next time.

Earlier today, he'd found out when Vincent Geary would be in his office this afternoon. He intended to have a talk with him about the gold cufflink he'd found in General Meyer's office the day of the Easter Egg Roll. He'd discovered they had been purchased at a Washington, DC, jeweler last Christmas by the congressman as a gift to each of his male staff members. Jeffries's aide had been dodging his calls and attempts to interview him. He was determined Geary wouldn't today.

Twenty minutes later, he sat across from the congressman's aide in his office. "I'm glad you could meet with me on short notice." He intentionally hadn't set up an appointment with Geary after the two times he'd tried and been given the runaround.

The tall, slender, dark-haired aide with equally dark brown eyes lounged back in his chair, his elbows resting on the arms while his fingers formed a steeple. "What can I do for you? Is this something to do with Congressman Jeffries's son's murder? I'd love to tell him that you are close to arresting someone. Erin Eagleton, perhaps."

"This concerns something different. General Meyer discovered someone had rifled through her files the morning of the Easter Egg Roll."

His eyebrows beetled together. "How can I help you?"

"After the break-in, one of your cufflinks was found

under the general's console behind her desk." He'd taken a photo of the piece of evidence and gave his cell phone to Geary. "Is that yours?"

"It looks like it."

"You hadn't been on her calendar that day or the day before. How did your cufflink get there?" Nicholas scrutinized him for any small indication he wasn't speaking the truth—not that his gut feeling would ever hold up in court.

"I have no idea unless it's been there since the last time I met with the general in her office, which was last week. Later that day, I noticed I'd lost it."

"And you didn't backtrack and check to see if someone found it? I understand it was a special gift from the congressman."

"No. I'd been quite a few places that day."

Although Geary's expression seemed relaxed, when Nicholas had first mentioned the cufflink, his left eye had twitched twice and his mouth had tensed slightly before Geary maintained control over his reactions. Smooth. "Did you say anything to anyone about losing it?"

"I had a dinner meeting with the congressman. I might have said something to him. If it was under a console, the cleaning staff could easily have overlooked it. Will I be able to get it back?"

"When the investigation is over."

Geary frowned. "I've missed wearing them. I suppose I should be glad that at least you found the missing one, and I'll get it back sometime in the future."

Nicholas started to rise but stopped. "Oh, by the way, why were you at the White House the evening before the Easter Egg Roll? In the West Wing." Geary had been one of many caught on camera near the general's office.

The aide's mouth firmed into a scowl. "I attended a reception with the congressman in the Roosevelt Room before the state dinner. I've done nothing wrong and resent the accusation."

"What accusation?"

Geary glared at him but remained silent.

Nicholas stood and extended his hand for Geary to shake. He finally did and the clammy feeling confirmed to him that the aide had been lying. But he didn't have any hard evidence to prove it—just years learning to read people.

Geary accompanied him into the hallway and Nicholas felt the aide's eyes on him as he strode toward the elevator. When the doors swished open, Congressman Harland Jeffries exited. With his hair graying, his tanned features stood out even more.

He spied Nicholas and said, "Weren't you here earlier today?"

"Yes, sir." Nicholas shook the man's cold hand. "I needed to see Vincent Geary. He mentioned losing one of his initialed cufflinks that you gave him at Christmas. He felt bad about losing it."

The congressman looked at a spot behind Nicholas. "It seems I remember him telling me he lost one somewhere."

"When?"

"Frankly, everything has been a blur for me with all that has happened. I don't remember exactly."

The elevator doors opened with the down arrow lit up. "Thanks, Congressman." Nicholas stepped inside and punched the button for the lobby. His gut instinct told him Jeffries was hiding something.

When he headed out of the building, his cell phone

rang. He saw it was his captain, so he found a quiet area to answer the call. "What's going on, Gavin?"

"A woman who reportedly looks like Erin Eagleton was spotted spying on Congressman Jeffries's house. I need you and Isaac Black to go check it out."

For Selena's sake, Nicholas hoped it *was* Erin—it meant her cousin was alive. But finding Erin would also mean bringing her in for questioning and grilling her about the night of Michael Jeffries's murder. Was Erin the killer?

Nicholas pulled up in front of Congressman Jeffries's mansion, parking behind Isaac Black, a Capitol K-9 Unit member who used to work for the CIA. With Max on a leash, Nicholas approached Isaac, a tall, muscular guy with dark brown hair and eyes. Abby, his canine partner and a beagle, wagged her tail and greeted Max.

Nicholas scanned the large home. "I understand from Gavin that a neighbor, Mrs. Applegate, reported a woman who fit Erin's description was outside the congressman's house, looking in the windows. Jeffries is at the Capitol and is aware that we're going to search the grounds. He mentioned his gardener works today and may have seen something."

"I'll interview the gardener while you talk to the neighbor. I'm going to do a walk-around and see if I can find him."

"I will, too, after I talk with Mrs. Applegate. Are you having Abby sniff for a bomb?"

"As a precaution." Isaac glanced around. "If it was Erin skulking around, why would she come here? For what purpose?"

"I don't know. And we don't know if it *is* Erin. I

agree we take every precaution and check everything out. We don't need the congressman killed, too."

With Max beside him, Nicholas made his way to the palatial house to the right of the Jeffries's mansion. A petite woman with graying hair, dressed in jeans, a blue shirt and straw hat, opened the door. "I'm here to see Mrs. Applegate."

"I'm she. Please come in, Officer."

"Max is my K-9 partner. He is very well behaved. May I bring him in?"

"Of course. I love dogs."

Mrs. Applegate led them to the living room. Nicholas sat in a wingback, while she sat across from him on a couch. The casually dressed lady was in stark contrast to the elegant surroundings. "Please tell me what you saw earlier. You reported seeing a woman trespassing on Congressman Jeffries's property at around two o'clock."

"Yes. I don't wear a watch when I work in my gardens, but I'd just gone back out after a short break to work on my roses, my prize flowers. If you come back in three or four weeks, they'll take your breath away."

"What I saw of your flower beds is beautiful."

Mrs. Applegate beamed. "Any artist loves to hear that. Anyway, I was outside working when I saw a woman in glamorous, big black sunglasses, just like Erin always wore, looking in a window of the congressman's house. She had a silk scarf wrapped around her head like from an old Grace Kelly movie. I assumed it was Erin because the few times I saw Michael and Erin arriving at the congressman's house in a convertible, Erin wore a scarf just like that to protect her beautiful, long curly hair. Anyway, she didn't look like anyone he has working for him. I'm familiar with his staff and gardeners."

"How tall do you think she was?"

"Five-seven, five-eight."

Nicholas knew from previous meetings with the Capitol K-9 Unit that Erin Eagleton was five feet eight inches tall. Forensics had noted that the murderer was, too.

"Of course, I can't be certain it was Erin Eagleton, but I know from watching the news that she's been missing ever since Michael was killed, so I called it in immediately." Mrs. Applegate shook her head. "Such a tragedy about Michael. I was on vacation in Paris when the murder occurred."

"You said she was wearing sunglasses, but did you get a look at her face, features such as her nose and mouth?"

"I only got a brief glance at her face, and I didn't have my eyeglasses on, but because of the sunglasses, scarf and her general height and build, I thought the person was Erin."

Nicholas nodded. "What did you see the woman do?"

"She ducked down when the gardener came around the side of the house, then hurried away, running off in the opposite direction."

"Will you come outside and show me exactly?"

"I thought you might say that. I'm ready to go. Anything to help Harland. Poor man. Losing his son like that. Harland is always checking on me, especially if he hasn't seen me in my gardens in several days."

As they walked from the house and around the side toward Jeffries's property, she told Nicholas stories of how much the congressman had helped her. Nicholas had to admit that the man was a study in contradictions.

Kind to some, like his captain. Jeffries had even started a foster home on his property. But that didn't mean the congressman wasn't corrupt. Nicholas kept thinking about Jeffries's ties to Thorn Industries, a shady pharmaceutical company that he'd said had tried to strong-arm him with bribes he refused to take. Nicholas wasn't so sure Jeffries hadn't taken those bribes. But again, he couldn't prove anything. Without proof, his captain didn't want to hear a word against Jeffries.

Mrs. Applegate stopped near her rosebushes, which were beginning to leaf out. She pointed to a large window on the right side of the mansion with bushes under it. "That's where I saw her. You know, now that I think about it the woman looks similar in style and build to Tabitha Miller, too—she's one of Harland's aides—but there wouldn't be any reason for her to be skulking around the congressman's house."

He envisioned the woman he'd interviewed earlier today. She was around Erin's height and had that same glamorous style as Erin. Nicholas could easily imagine her in huge black sunglasses and a silk scarf keeping her hair from being blown around in a convertible. Could Tabitha be the woman Mrs. Applegate had seen? Mrs. Applegate was right when she said Tabitha wouldn't have a reason to sneak around. The congressman's staff would admit her inside.

No, it made more sense that it was Erin. But why had she come? What was she looking for?

A few minutes before seven, the last of the meetings over, Selena was ready to go home. Nicholas had left a text telling her he was going to Congressman Jeffries's house and might be a while before he was finished. All she wanted to do was go home and collapse. Halfway through her second meeting she'd felt all the exhaustion from the past weeks' frantic pace physically and emotionally catching up with her. Her two days of rest hadn't turned into any rest at all, not with the break-in at her home and the visit to the prison.

She gathered her purse and work tablet and headed for the underground parking lot. As she strolled toward her car at the far end, she thought of all the things she needed to do.

Her cell phone chimed. Nicholas. "Are you done for the day?" she asked him.

"Yes, I've left the congressman's house. Are you heading home?"

"I'm nearly at my car."

"You need to wait for me. Remember, I follow you to and from work."

"I fell asleep at my desk. I imagined my bed and thought that might be a better place to sleep. I'm going to have to finish some work at home. I don't usually do that."

"I'm not far from the White House. Wait. I'll feel better."

"Okay," she said and gave him her precise location. Nicholas said something, but she couldn't hear over the sound of a motorcycle behind her and heading toward the exit. She raised her voice. "I didn't hear you. Just a sec until the bike passes." She twisted toward the motorcycle.

All Selena saw was a person dressed totally in black, closer than she realized. The biker slowed to a stop and reached out toward her, snatching her work tablet.

"Don't." She lunged toward her attacker to grab the tablet back.

There was a flash of metal, then something sharp cut

into her arm. She was knocked back against a car behind her. Slamming into its bumper, the air swooshing
from her lungs, she sank to the pavement as the biker
revved the engine.

SEVEN

The sound of a motorcycle, Selena crying out "Don't!" and a thud chilled Nicholas to the core. He pressed down on the accelerator. "Selena. Selena, are you okay? What happened?" he shouted, sure she'd dropped her cell phone.

The seconds ticked by agonizingly slow.

Then Selena came on the line. "I was attacked… and stabbed—"

"Are you hurt?"

"My arm's bleeding."

His heartbeat pounded. "Listen to me. I'm calling Security. I'm four minutes away." He turned on his siren, "Make that two minutes."

He called Security, giving details of where Selena had been attacked and asking them to shut down the exit from there and send medical help. Now he was only sixty seconds away. He approached the tunnel to the underground parking, his heartbeat thundering in his ears. He saw a black motorcycle speeding past him, its driver dressed in black, and wanted to give chase. He'd heard what sounded like a motorcycle in the background when talking to Selena, but he didn't know if that was the assailant on the bike. Looking through the rearview mirror, he called local police and reported the license number, though, and where it was headed.

He was the first on the scene, parking his SUV near Selena and hopping from his car. She sat against a vehicle's bumper, looking dazed, a stream of blood oozing between her fingers clasped over the wound. It ran down her arm. As he rounded the front of his Tahoe, several White House security officers jogged toward them.

She looked at him as he knelt next to her. "Selena?"

"I'm okay…a little stunned. Black motorcycle," she said, trying to take a breath. "Rider all in black." That was all she could get out before needing to close her eyes for a moment.

If only I'd gone after the bike, Nicholas thought. But getting to Selena had been more important. "He passed me on the way in—I called in the police. Medical help is on the way."

She glanced at her arm. "No ambulance…just need… stitches."

She spoke almost as though she had disassociated herself from the incident, but she was having trouble forming sentences. "Did you hit your head again?"

"No. Just had the—" she blinked "—breath knocked out of me." She inhaled deeply. "No—cracked ribs."

"Don't move. I'm talking to the officers then I'll be right back."

Before he stood, she added, "He took my…work tablet."

"I'll let security know."

Please let her be okay, he thought as adrenaline had him moving when all he wanted was to stay by her side.

Selena felt shell-shocked more than anything. Her arm barely hurt, but she saw the blood coursing down it in spite of clasping the wound. While Nicholas spoke with the three men in a low voice, she tried to think of something in her car she could use to stop the bleeding. Her mind refused to function properly. She couldn't string a coherent thought together. Probably blood loss affecting her.

One of the men, trained as a paramedic, stooped next to her with a first-aid kit and began working on her wound while Nicholas pointed toward the exit. He moved to a knife on the pavement and instructed an officer to bag it. She'd felt the cut but hadn't seen the knife, just a flash of metal.

After that, Nicholas strode to his SUV and released Max. While a bandage was being wrapped around her arm, Max sniffed the air and set off, following a trail from the direction the motorcycle had come from.

She began to tremble, chills streaking through her. Pain finally leaked into her mind, demanding attention.

Watching Max come to a stop at a narrow parking spot in the underground garage, Nicholas noted the space would easily fit a motorcycle.

He gave Max a treat. "Good boy. Now all I need to figure out is whose bike was here. Looks like more security video for me." He tried to think of White House staffers who rode a motorcycle to work. He'd get a list and start questioning them. They usually knew who else was a biker. He checked the camera; the area wasn't in direct line of sight but the approach was. He would find the owner if the local police hadn't caught him already.

His priority now was to get Selena to the ER to have her wound taken care of and to make sure she wasn't injured anywhere else. Adrenaline could be masking something else.

He and Max jogged back to the crime scene. The paramedic-trained security officer had finished bandaging her. Still sitting on the pavement, she turned her head slightly and looked right at him. There was an ashen cast to her skin and she shook. As he neared her, he noticed the pool of blood next to her as though a vein had been cut.

"Open my passenger door," Nicholas said to the paramedic working on Selena. "I'm taking her to the emergency room."

Nicholas squatted next to her and lifted her into his arms. Cradled against him, she gave him a weak smile. He carried her to his Tahoe and settled her onto the front passenger seat.

"Thanks," she said to the paramedic then Nicholas while supporting her arm against her trembling body. Shock was setting in.

Nicholas leaned over and buckled her in then took off his jacket and covered her. Selena reclined back and shut her eyes. "Hold on. It won't be long." As he rounded the back of the Tahoe and put Max inside, he motioned to another White House security officer. "Take care of the crime scene, and notify Dan Calvert about what happened and that Miss Barrow's work tablet was stolen. Put a rush on the knife. I want to know if there are any fingerprints on it."

"Will do."

The security officer with paramedic training looked at Selena then back at Nicholas. "She'll be all right once she gets stitches."

"Thanks for taking care of her."

He hurried around the driver's side, slid behind the wheel and started the engine. As he went over a speed bump, he glanced at Selena and found her gaze glued on him.

"Okay?" he asked as he slipped into the flow of traffic.

"I'll live."

"You scared me back there. Do you remember anything about your attacker?"

"It happened so fast. I'm starting to get my bearings."

"Good. You need around-the-clock protection."

"You can't do that and continue to work."

"Yes, I can, especially when General Meyer hears."

Selena drew in a deep breath "I'm planning another event for the president. I don't have time to take off. He just told me about it today."

"I see you're beginning to feel more like yourself. Arguing every detail with me."

"I'm not arguing. Pointing out the hurdles in your plan. I want you to find the person who took my tablet. I assume the Miss Chick impostor, the person who ransacked my house and the motorcyclist are the same person."

"Agreed. What was on the tablet?"

"Information pertaining to my job. For instance, most of the plans for the Easter Egg Roll. So I need you working."

"And I need you alive." As he spoke, he realized how important Selena was becoming to the case—to him.

As he pulled into the ER, he decided he would talk with the captain about this. He needed another team member to help him. He felt this was all tied to the Jeffries case. *If we find who's after Selena, we may be apprehending Jeffries's murderer.*

* * *

Spending most of the night in the ER wasn't Selena's idea of fun, but finally Nicholas pulled into her driveway as dawn began to pinken the sky. She yawned.

"You need to get some rest." Nicholas opened his door. "Stay there. I'll help you."

She ignored his instruction and climbed from the Tahoe as he came to the passenger side, frowning. "I tolerated you carrying me to the car at the crime scene and at the ER, but I caught a catnap on the way here and I'm fine." Actually, she did more than tolerate it. She cherished the strong feel of his arms around her because for a brief moment in the garage, she realized how close she'd come to being seriously injured.

"Twenty minutes isn't sufficient sleep." Nicholas released Max from the back of the Tahoe.

"About my Mustang. You should have driven me there to pick it up."

"Not until you've rested like the ER doc said. You lost quite a bit of blood last night. Max was worried."

She chuckled. "But not you?"

"Yeah, me, too."

Selena paused and bent to pet Max. "I'll be good as new by tomorrow, boy. Will you tell your partner that?"

Max barked.

She straightened too quickly. The action of leaning over caused the yard to spin. She closed her eyes and got her bearings before she climbed the porch steps. When she looked at Nicholas beside her, she knew he hadn't missed her bout of light-headedness. Slow and easy or he would declare her an invalid. And she did need that sleep.

Inside the house, she placed her purse on the table by the door. Before she went to bed, however, she wanted to know what he'd discovered about her assault. "You haven't said anything about what happened last night. What does White House Security know?"

"There were a couple of fingerprints on the kitchen knife used in the attack. One that they could match."

"Who?"

"Vincent Geary."

"Why would he be interested in the Littleton case? That's what the assault has to be about. This all started when I began digging into it."

"Good question and one I will be asking him. I'm having him brought to headquarters for me to interview."

She whistled. "You mean business bringing him in."

"I want to take him out of his comfort zone."

She thought back to the scene in the underground garage. "I think the biker had on black gloves."

"I still need to know why Geary's fingerprints are on the knife."

"So when will you be leaving?" She started for the stairs.

"As soon as my replacement arrives."

Stopping, she glanced over her shoulder. "Who?"

"Brooke Clark. She's a fellow Capitol K-9 Unit member."

"Couldn't you just leave Max? He's great company."

"I called my captain last night, and he'd already heard from General Meyer. You are to have protection. That comes from the president and Senator Eagleton."

"My uncle?" She slowly rotated toward Nicholas, who covered the space between them.

"Yes. They were both at the same gathering last night, and when they heard about the attack, they insisted you be protected, especially after what happened at the Easter Egg Roll. The president was not happy about your office and the general's being compromised. I have a feeling heads will be rolling if we don't come up with answers. Soon. That's from the general and the head of the Secret Service. Someone in our midst isn't playing nice."

"My body can attest to that. No cracked ribs, but I'm going to have bruises. In the past week, I've had more physical contact than when I was growing up with gangs all around."

His eyes twinkled, and one corner of his mouth lifted. "Are you sure I can't help you up the stairs?"

"I'm not even going to answer that."

As she mounted the steps, Nicholas's chuckles floated to her. If she was truthful with herself, she was glad for the protection. That thought took her by surprise. She would never have admitted that in the past. What was it about Nicholas that made her so easily persuaded?

"I'm being framed. First the incident with General Meyer's office and now this." Vincent Geary's face reddened with anger, one hand clenched on the table in the interview room at headquarters.

Nicholas took the chair next to Geary, not the one across from him. He wanted to invade this man's space, make him squirm. "Then explain your fingerprints on this kitchen knife." He held up the evidence bag with it inside, its carved ivory handle distinctive.

Geary's eyes widened. "My fingerprints are on it because it's mine. I have a whole set of them on my kitchen counter. Where was this found?"

"In the underground parking garage at the White House. Used in an attack on Selena Barrow."

"The tour director?"

"Yes, and the president has taken a personal interest in this situation."

The red flushed from the aide's face. "When did the attack happen?"

"Last night at seven. An assailant riding a black motorcycle snatched her tablet from her and stabbed her then fled. The bike was found this morning and your fingerprints were on the gas tank and side of the seat."

Geary's mouth dropped open. "That's impossible. I have an alibi."

"What is it?"

"I was meeting with Congressman Jeffries and several other members of Congress, including White and Langford, at his house."

Nicholas slid a pad toward him. "Write their names down, and I'll check it out."

"I've never ridden a motorcycle."

Nicholas rose. "If you want to prove that without any doubt, I would suggest you hand me your cell phone until I return. I wouldn't want you to call your boss and get him to vouch for you."

Anger flooded his face again. Geary dug into his pocket and slapped the cell phone into Nicholas's outstretched hand. "Congressman Jeffries is above reproach. He has a stellar reputation."

"Anyway," he said, hardly agreeing with that assessment, "it's not easy to dispute fingerprint evidence."

"I don't know how, but someone planted those fingerprints."

Nicholas exited the interview room and headed for his Tahoe, making a call to Brooke Clark to see how things were going at Selena's. He hoped she was still asleep. "Anything happening there?"

"The grass has grown a millimeter since you left an hour ago." Laughter filled Brooke's light voice.

"Funny. Is Selena still asleep?"

"Yes. Do you want me to call you when she wakes up?"

He could still hear the smirk in her words. "No. Just keep her safe, but don't tell her I said that."

The next call he made was a carefully worded one to Congressman Jeffries's home; a butler assured Nicholas that Harland was home. Then Nicholas texted Isaac Black, asking his fellow K-9 Unit member to immediately interview Senator Langford to verify Geary's alibi. Isaac texted back that he was on his way.

As Nicholas drove to Jeffries's home, he thought about the case. The problem was that whoever was behind this was a frequent visitor to the White House or someone who worked there; because it wasn't easy to get inside otherwise and know the layout so well to go undetected.

When he was admitted into the congressman's study, Harland Jeffries was sitting on a couch reading a book.

He peered at Nicholas. "Come in. I hope you've found the woman who was lurking around my house earlier. Clare Applegate was very concerned for me."

"Yes, she was." Nicholas took the seat across from Jeffries. "Did you find anything missing, disturbed inside or outside?"

"Not that I or my staff can tell." Jeffries closed his book and laid it on the end table next to him.

"I understand you've had cameras installed outside since Michael's murder. Was anything suspicious on them?"

"Yes, the woman was caught on tape, but I couldn't see her face."

"Like she knew the cameras were there?"

"Yes."

"Who knew about them?"

"The security company who put them in and my staff. It wasn't a secret but not a well-known fact, either."

Nicholas relaxed back in the overstuffed chair. "Are you aware that I talked with Vincent Geary yesterday in connection with the break-in of General Meyer's office?"

"Yes, and I already protested to the general. He would have no reason to do that. I understand his cufflink was found at the scene. Someone could have placed it there anytime or he lost it when he was in the office on business for me."

"He was brought in today for questioning in another matter that occurred yesterday. Selena Barrow was assaulted in the underground parking garage at the White House when she was leaving work."

The congressman frowned. "What time?"

"Seven last night. Geary's fingerprints were found on the weapon, as well as the motorcycle used during the attack."

His frown evolved into a furious expression. "What's going on here? There's no way he could have been in two places at the same time. He was here at seven and didn't leave until nine. The culprit can't be him."

"How do you explain the fingerprints?"

"Someone stole the weapon from his house."

"On the motorcycle?"

The congressman waved his hand in the air. "I don't know. It's your job to figure it out. He's being framed. You need to be out there looking for the real assailant. If you don't want to take my word, check with Congressman White and Senator Langford about Geary's alibi. They'll tell you the same thing."

"We are right now. Do you know anyone on your staff that might do this? You said yourself your staff knew about the additional cameras outside."

"I can't imagine anyone on… Wait, Tabitha Miller has been calling in sick a lot lately. In fact, she left work yesterday afternoon and didn't attend the meeting last night at my house. She said she was getting sick." Jeffries rubbed his nape. "I don't know. She probably was, but she's been acting strangely the past couple of months."

Tabitha's name sure came up a lot in this investigation. Nicholas stood. "I appreciate you taking your time to discuss this."

The congressman shoved to his feet and walked with Nicholas to the front door. "Of course. I don't want to see a good man's name damaged for something he didn't do. I understand you feel the same way. I heard you're looking into the Littleton case. I'm glad. My son was working on that and believed him innocent."

"I only want the guilty to go to prison."

As he strode to the Tahoe, he glanced back and saw Jeffries looking at him out the window. The congressman said the right words, but Nicholas couldn't bring himself to trust everything he said. Call it a gut feeling, but he couldn't shake it. He slipped into his SUV. Now to talk to Congressman White.

Her throbbing arm dragged Selena from her dream of lying on a beach reading a book as the sun blanketed her in warmth. When she opened her eyes to her bedroom, reality washed over her, especially when she touched the white bandage around her left forearm. She glanced at the bedside clock. She'd slept for three hours. Her stomach rumbled its hunger.

Slowly she rose and descended the stairs to the first floor, wondering if Nicholas was back from talking with Vincent Geary. She couldn't understand Geary being behind the attack unless he was somehow involved in the Littleton case. She'd only talked with him on a few occasions.

At the bottom of the steps, she peered into the living room and spied a strange dog—a beautiful golden retriever, lying on her floor. A petite woman with short dark hair and blue eyes, carrying a mug, came around the corner from the kitchen.

She smiled. "I'm Brooke Clark, babysitter extraordinaire."

The laughter in her gaze enticed Selena to grin and reply, "I'm Selena Barrow, but then you already knew that. I could say I'm a victim extraordinaire, but I'm not owning up to that title."

"Would you like coffee? I took the liberty of making some."

"Sure, but even more, I want something to eat. How about you?"

"Starving. I was thinking of sending Mercy on a rescue trip to the nearest fast-food joint."

As she followed Brooke into the kitchen, Selena peered back at Mercy, who had perked up at the mention of her name. "She's beautiful. What's her specialty?"

"Retrieving."

"That makes sense given her breed." Selena opened the refrigerator door. "I have the makings of a turkey-and-cheese sandwich."

"Sounds great. Nicholas called not too long ago to say he's on his way back here."

"I'll make him a sandwich, too, and if he doesn't eat it, we can split it. I'm hungry enough. I haven't eaten in almost twenty-four hours."

Five minutes later, Selena gave Brooke a plate with her lunch then took a seat next to her at the kitchen table. "Did he say anything about the case?"

"It looks like Vincent Geary is innocent. He has an airtight alibi."

"But the fingerprints?"

"Not his. They were planted in both places. Fingerprints can be transferred, and there's evidence of that occurring when they were closely analyzed."

"Why would someone frame him?"

Brooke shrugged. "If we knew, we'd probably know who was behind the attack."

"Do you think the assailant is also Michael's killer?" Selena picked up a potato chip and popped it into her mouth.

"It would be great to solve both cases."

"And Erin could come home." *If she's alive.* She wished she knew for sure her cousin was alive even if she only saw her from afar.

"Nicholas said you believe Erin is innocent."

"She's family and I know her. She wouldn't kill Michael. Like Vincent being framed for my assault, things might not appear as they really are."

"True. I've seen that in other cases."

"What's Nicholas like at work?" The grin on Brooke's face made Selena want to take back the question. "Forget I asked that. I've seen him on the job at the White House. He's thorough and intuitive."

"He doesn't take anything at face value. That's why when Vincent Geary insisted he was innocent, he had the lab go back and analyze the fingerprints under a microscope, a more thorough analysis."

So Nicholas was the right law-enforcement officer to help her prove her cousin wasn't guilty. At least it sounded as if he had an open mind. He did with Littleton. That gave her hope. "I'm grateful he's been around lately."

"He's a good guy to have on your side."

She was beginning to see that, even though years ago she'd promised herself she would stand on her own two feet—be totally independent. She saw what happened to her mother, and she didn't want to go down that road. Ever. Her drinking and constant need for love from the wrong men had driven her to an early death. It saddened her because her mom had had such potential at one time.

Chimes echoed through the house. Selena started to rise to answer the front door, when Brooke hopped to her feet and said, "Stay here. You shouldn't go."

Selena stood, her body taut. When Brooke let Nicholas into the house, Selena leaned against the edge of the table, releasing the tension. Brooke and Nicholas talked in low voices.

"Okay, you two. If it's about my case, I'd like to know what's happening. I was the one attacked. Remember?"

Nicholas lifted his head and snagged her with an intense gaze, his expression grim. "I was telling Brooke that we're back to square one since I've ruled out Vincent Geary."

Brooke turned toward Selena. "I insisted on coming back tonight since Nicholas hasn't gotten any sleep. I'm reminding him that he can't stand guard twenty-four hours without consequences."

Selena straightened and folded her arms over her

chest. "I agree. In fact, I insist. I can always complain to General Meyer."

Nicholas scowled. "Going over my head won't win points with me."

Selena laughed, the action shedding what stress she had left. "Brooke, I like your suggestion. One person can't do it all." She zeroed in on Nicholas. "You need to sleep without worrying about protecting me."

"Good. I'm glad we got that settled." Brooke called Mercy. "We're leaving, but I'll be back at nine. I have a dinner date with my guy." Her face lit with a huge grin.

"If you need to, come a bit later." Nicholas opened the door for his team member. "I don't want to interrupt your plans."

"Jonas will understand. And tomorrow morning, I'd better not see you until nine. The captain said we're to work together."

Selena sat as Nicholas locked the door after Brooke and Mercy left. "I'm going to church tomorrow at ten. This is my Sunday to help with coffee hour after the service." She gestured toward a plate. "I made you a sandwich."

He joined her at the table with Max lying on the floor between their chairs. "Tell me what happened this morning."

As he ate, Nicholas recalled the interview with Vincent then told her about checking the aide's alibi. "I'm not convinced Vincent isn't messed up in the Jeffries case somehow."

"What do you think of Harland Jeffries? I know my uncle isn't a fan of his. They've been political rivals through the years."

"I'm not a big fan of Jeffries, either."

Reaching for her coffee mug, Selena stopped in mid-motion. "Why aren't you? He has a long list of public service. He's actively involved in All Our Kids foster home."

"Speaking of the home, Max and I usually volunteer on Sunday afternoons. Would you mind going with us tomorrow? If not, I can cancel this week."

"No, don't. I love kids. I'm involved through my church with various activities when my schedule allows."

"Max enjoys the children, too. That's when he gets to play. All service dogs need playtime. So much is asked of them when they're on duty."

She sipped her coffee, watching Nicholas finishing his sandwich. "You look tired."

"Going a night without sleep is no big deal. When I was a Navy SEAL and on assignment, sometimes I had to catch sleep whenever and wherever I could. Once I slept on a rocky ledge halfway up a mountain. One wrong move and I'd have been dead in the ravine."

"You can take a nap. Max will protect me. That and my gun."

"No. If I sleep now, it will throw me off for tonight. Brooke is right about taking shifts, and then on Monday I can work the case while you're at the White House, if you promise not to leave the West Wing without me."

"I promise, after what happened in the parking garage." She covered his hand on the table between them. "Thank you for being there so quickly. I think if I hadn't turned and stepped back, the motorcycle would have run me down. Several of the staff members have bikes, and I didn't think anything of it when I heard it coming."

"Then why did you turn?" He clasped her hand between both of his.

"I don't know. A gut feeling. I just did." Either way,

she thanked God she had. "Let's not discuss the case tomorrow. Give ourselves a day of relaxation with the children."

"That sounds like a good game plan. I sometimes do my best detecting when I'm not focused on it."

He pushed to his feet and drew her up against him with his arms entwined around her. Her pulse rate accelerated. Every time she got close to Nicholas her feelings shifted inside her. After seeing her mother go through man after man, she'd vowed to remain single. She didn't want to repeat any of her mom's mistakes. So much heartache. She'd had enough in her childhood to last her a lifetime.

And yet, when Nicholas framed her face between his large hands, she melted into him, her legs quivering. She tightened her uninjured arm about him and peered up at him. A golden light twinkled in his brown eyes, pulling her to him as though they were tethered with invisible ropes.

He cocked his head and slowly inched his mouth closer to hers. The rapid beating of her heart filled her chest, making breathing difficult. She wanted him to kiss her.

EIGHT

Nicholas claimed her lips in a deep kiss. She fit perfectly in his arms. He didn't want to let her go. And yet he had to. He was protecting her. He needed to keep his emotions contained for both their own good.

Ending the kiss, he backed away. "Sorry. I shouldn't have done that. I have a job to do and that isn't part of it." If he said it enough, he might believe it.

She turned away, gathering up the dishes from the table. "I understand completely. Frankly, I don't have time. That's one of the reasons I keep things casual between me and anyone I've dated."

"So you're career focused?"

"Yes, aren't you?"

He nodded, but he didn't like her response. She loved children. She should be a mother. And that was another reason to keep his distance. He would never have children even if one day he married. His role model left a lot to be desired. All he knew was a cold, callous father who only warmed up around his wife, and a mother who only cared for her husband.

Selena brought the dishes to the sink, when chimes, like bells ringing, resonated in the silence between them. She washed off the plates while he strolled to the door, checked the peephole and then let in Senator Eagleton.

"Selena, you have a visitor."

"I'm not expecting…" Her voice faded as her gaze connected with her uncle's. "Have a seat, Uncle Preston," she said, gesturing toward the living room "I wasn't sure you knew where I lived. I haven't been here long."

The senator didn't move. "I can't stay long, but I wanted to make sure you were all right after what happened last night. I was assured you would get protection." The tall man glanced at Nicholas. "Are you it?"

"Part of it. Brooke Clark will be here at nights."

"Good. Someone isn't happy with you, Selena. Two attacks in less than one week." He looked right at Nicholas, saying, "I expect the best from you," then rotated toward the door.

"Wait. Why did you come all this way and only stay a minute?"

"I told you—to make sure you were all right."

"You could have called." Wonder sounded in her voice.

"I needed to see you with my own eyes. I know how tough you can be, and I wanted to make sure."

Selena swallowed hard. "Are you certain you can't stay for some coffee?"

Her uncle's expression softened. "No. I have a meeting in an hour, and I can't keep the vice president waiting."

She crossed the room. "Thanks for coming."

"I'll call you about having dinner or lunch away from the Washington scene."

"That'll be nice." Selena waited in the entrance until her uncle climbed into his town car.

Nicholas came up behind her and clasped her shoulders, feeling the tension beneath his fingers. He kneaded her muscles. "It looks like he's trying."

"I hope so. I don't want to close that door because when Erin returns, I want to have a family relationship with her, which also includes her father. She loves him."

"But you don't care about him?"

"I don't know. When I was young, I used to think of him as a father figure since I never knew my own. After a while, I realized what was really going on between him and my mother. I couldn't forgive him for disowning my mother, therefore me." She released a long breath. "I'm trying to do what the Lord wants us to do. Forgive and move on. I'm closer but not there completely. We don't have a big family. How could he turn his own sister away? His only niece?"

"Did your mom tell you why?"

"No."

"Why don't you ask him, then?"

Selena shut the door, threw the lock in place and then leaned back against it. "I just might do that, but I'm almost afraid to know."

"You? I thought you weren't afraid of anything."

"Everyone has fears. If they say otherwise, they're lying."

"What else are you afraid of?"

"The usual." She shoved off the door and headed toward the kitchen. "How about you?"

"Same answer—an evasive one."

"Okay, rats." She shuddered. "When I was a kid, I woke up with one on my chest staring at me. I haven't been able to shake that fear."

"Turning out like my father. My mother and making money were all he cared about."

"With the job you have, helping others is one of your priorities."

He chuckled. "True, but then I have my inheritance stashed away."

"I keep forgetting you were born with a silver spoon in your mouth."

"Good. It's not something I tell a lot of people."

"Then why me?"

"You're easy to talk to."

She tapped her chest. "Me?"

"It has to help you in your job. You work with a lot of people when you set up events."

"I didn't start out wanting to do that kind of work. I sort of fell into the job when I was an assistant for the president's chief of staff. When he went to the White House, he asked me to come along and work for him. When the job of White House tour director came up, the president asked me to take the job. He'd liked what he'd seen me do."

"My commanding officer knew General Meyer, and when I left the service, he recommended me for a position with the Capitol K-9 Unit. He knew how I felt about animals."

Selena began loading the dishwasher. "Would you change anything about what you did?"

"Not one minute. How about you?"

"No. I love a challenging job and mine is definitely that."

As they exchanged stories of their work, Nicholas realized just how easy Selena was to talk to. He'd shared more with her than most, especially in such a short time. It must be the close quarters while he guarded her.

* * *

On Sunday afternoon, Cassie Danvers greeted Selena and Nicholas in the foyer of the foster home, protected by a high fence, a security system and a guard with a dog. Selena thought of her own house and realized she had the same things except the high fence. All Our Kids foster home, which Harland Jeffries had founded on his property, was temporarily located in a safe house. On the night of the murder at the congressman's house, a child's mitten had been found near the crime scene and determined to belong to one of the foster children. None of the kids would admit to being out that night, though. The home, housemother Cassie Danvers and the children had all been targeted by the killer or accomplices, so All Our Kids had been relocated to this secret residence out in the country. Nicholas had received special permission from his captain to bring Selena along, but she'd had to wear a blindfold during the drive.

Cassie outstretched her arm toward Selena. "I'm glad you could come. Gavin told me you're the White House tour director and planned that fabulous Easter Egg Roll for the children."

Selena shook the hand of the petite woman who ran All Our Kids Foster Home. "Gavin?"

"He's our captain," Nicholas answered.

"And my fiancé." Cassie pointed into a great room. "They're waiting for Max. Oh, and you, too, Nicholas."

"Thanks, Cassie. I know who the real star is in this team." Nicholas took Selena's hand, and they entered an area filled with all kinds of toys and children.

"The kids don't want for a thing. I think Gavin is spoiling them—and I know Harland Jeffries also often orders toys for Gavin to bring over—but who am I but the manager," Cassie said with a laugh.

First Brooke and now Cassie, happy and making plans to marry. Love was all around Selena. A secretary in the West Wing announced a few weeks ago she was getting married, too. That was good for some people—just not her.

A boy about six or seven jumped up and rushed toward them. "Max, you're finally here." He threw his arms around the rottweiler. "I've missed you."

More kids started crowding around.

"Tommy, let others greet Max, too," Cassie said to the child with sandy-brown hair and blue eyes.

The slightly built boy backed away, mumbling, "Sorry."

As the other children petted Max, Selena moved to Tommy, who stared at the floor. "Max is special, isn't he?"

The boy lifted his head and nodded. "I wish I could have a dog like him."

"I'm Selena, Tommy." She knelt down and whispered, "I'll tell you a secret. So do I. Max is wonderful."

Tommy grinned, showing one of his missing teeth. "I just lost this." He pointed at his mouth. "I got a whole dollar for it. Cassie gave it to me." He dug into his jeans pocket and pulled it out. "All mine."

Selena's heart cracked, and all she wanted to do was hug the boy. She could remember, when she was growing up and got anything, how special it was, especially one Christmas when a charity gave out presents. She got a doll. She still had it.

"What are you going to do with the dollar?"

"Save it. I want my own bike, not one I have to share with the others."

After the children lavished attention on Max, Nicholas motioned them to the far side of the large room. "Are you all ready for a story?"

Several said yes, while others cheered.

Tommy hurried toward the group.

Cassie came up beside her. "I would never have pegged Nicholas as a storyteller, but he is. I think it surprised him when they all asked him to tell them a story after he'd read a book to them." She slanted a look at Selena. "I admit I'm surprised you received clearance to come here to the safe house."

There was a wealth of questions in Cassie's voice, and her gaze assessed Selena. "He's been ordered to guard me."

The manager's eyes widened. "Why?"

"I've been attacked twice, and my home and office have been burglarized"

"I assume it involves the Jeffries case if the Capitol K-9 Unit is involved."

Selena nodded. "I'm Erin Eagleton's cousin. Like the Capitol K-9 Unit, maybe the attacker thinks I know where she is." Now that she'd said it aloud, she realized it was a real possibility. *Or the attacks were tied to the Littleton case or both.*

"Do you?" Cassie asked with a twinkle in her eyes.

Selena chuckled. "No, but if I did, I wouldn't be telling the captain's fiancée I did." She panned the group of children—their expressions were intense while listening to a story about the White House. "Have they ever been to the White House?"

"No."

"I'd love to give them a tour. I can make the arrangements."

"I'll take you up on that when the Jeffries case is settled and the murderer is in jail."

"Perfect." The loud clapping drew Selena's attention back to the children and Nicholas.

A few kids threw their arms around a grinning Nicholas. He would make a great father. Not one of the children hadn't responded to him.

"I'm glad we got away from the White House for lunch," Selena said a few days later as Nicholas pushed her chair into a white-clothed table at a popular restaurant nearby. "The West Wing has been busy this morning with meetings"

"I saw your uncle." Nicholas picked up the menu.

"I did, too. He even stopped and talked to me before he met with the president. Congressman Jeffries was there, too. Did you find out anything about who was peeking into his house?"

"Dead end. The shoe print was a woman's size, but only one camera caught her back. She was wearing a silk scarf, and besides, we know from the elderly couple who took her in before she disappeared again that Erin changed her hair color and style. Whoever it was made a point to disguise herself."

"But from the tone of your voice, you don't think the woman is Erin," she said as the waiter appeared at the table.

Nicholas waited until after they had ordered before replying, "No. I can't see why she would be at the congressman's house. I would think that would be one of the last places she would go."

"You've got a point."

"If I spot Erin, I'll let you know."

"And then you'd watch me like a hawk to see if she contacts me."

He pointed at himself, grinning. "Who, me?"

Out of the corner of her eye, Selena spied Carly Jones, Tabitha Miller and a couple of other aides to the senators and representatives at the White House. "It looks like we aren't the only ones escaping for lunch. Did you ever find out who was at Tabitha's that day Greg Littleton had an argument with Saul Rather?"

"Tabitha could only give me three names of who attended her get-togethers, Sally Young, Janice Neill and Becky Wright. Sally couldn't remember if she was there that day. But Becky Wright confirmed that Tabitha had shown some interest in Rather. That was why they were out on the balcony, since he was swimming. I think she was the one on the balcony with Tabitha."

"What about Janice Neill?"

"I haven't been able to track down Janice, who no longer lives in the area. It seemed those three were the regular attendees. I'm looking into how far Tabitha's interest in Saul Rather went. The problem is, the incident was almost two years ago."

The waiter delivered their iced tea, and Selena took a long drink. "I hope we can prove Greg didn't kill Saul. From my research into the case, I believe he's innocent."

"Perhaps Janice will have a better memory of what happened that day at the pool."

"So three regulars at these weekly get-togethers at Tabitha's with others occasionally dropping in."

Nicholas touched her hand, compelling her to look at him. "Don't sound so defeated. I know this is a long shot, but if Littleton didn't kill Rather, then we need to see who used the man as a scapegoat. I'm looking at the court records and police evidence with the mind-set Littleton is innocent."

As their lunch arrived, Selena watched Tabitha and Carly leave together after the other two aides. Outside in front of the large plate-glass window, the two women faced each other and, guessing from their expressions, the exchange wasn't a pleasant one. Did the animosity between Eagleton and Jeffries carry over to their staff?

While Selena enjoyed her spinach salad, she said, "I'd love to go back to the All Our Kids Home this weekend, but my uncle wants me to come to lunch on Sunday. I don't want you to cancel going to the home because you're protecting me. Could we go on Saturday instead?"

Reuben sandwich in his hands, Nicholas put it on his plate. "Yes, if you don't mind being blindfolded again?"

"Not one bit. Things have been calm the last few days. Maybe the person who attacked me and trashed my house realizes I don't know anything."

"Don't count on that. You need to stay vigilant. We haven't been able to figure out who the person on the motorcycle was. There were no one else's fingerprints on the knife, and on the bike the only other prints belonged to the owner who, like Geary, had an airtight alibi. He was in a staff meeting with the press secretary."

"I especially want to see Tommy again. There's something about him that draws me."

"We've all tried to get Tommy to open up."

"About what?" She forked some salad and slipped it into her mouth.

"There's evidence one of the children from the foster home could have possibly witnessed Jeffries's murder. Tommy denies he is the one, but he's been having nightmares about a bad tall man with white hair."

"Harland Jeffries?"

"We talked about it, but his hair is gray, he was shot, too. The gun was never found at the scene of the crime.

So where is it? Also a car was sighted speeding away from the house. Tommy's description of the man in his nightmare still leaves who it is inconclusive. Too vague. Lots of men have white hair, and it might not have anything to do with happened at Jeffries's estate."

Selena rubbed her chin and thought a moment. "Tommy would have had to sneak out at that hour to have witnessed the shootings. Most kids won't admit that."

"Cassie has stressed to the children no one will get into trouble if the one comes forward. Still nothing."

"But you think it's Tommy?"

"Yes. He has been upset a lot and withdrawn. Brooke worked hard to help him open up, but he's just too scared."

"Except around you and Max."

"That's because he loves dogs."

"A kid after your own heart."

His eyes crinkled with a big smile. "I used to go once a week when it was on Jeffries's property, but I didn't know Tommy well. I've been trying to get closer to the boy, and I have, but not enough for him to trust me."

"What if he really isn't the one?"

"Cassie is on the lookout for anything that indicates it could be someone else, and I'm getting to know all the kids even more than before."

Selena tapped her forefinger against her chin. "You know, this getting to know a person better in order to get information sounds like a familiar pattern of yours."

His tanned face deepened to a red shade. "You want to find out the truth as much as I do. And I really believe if Erin contacted you, you'd let me know."

Under his straightforward stare, she shifted in the chair, wondering if she would. And that question plagued her the whole way back to the White House. Would she turn in her cousin if given the opportunity? She didn't have an answer. She didn't trust many people. Could she trust Nicholas to look out for Erin's best interests?

At her office door, Nicholas's cell phone rang. He quickly answered it and frowned, turning away from her.

When he hung up and looked at her, she asked, "Was that about Erin? The case?"

"Yes, there has been another sighting—at the Capitol Building—of a woman in sunglasses and a silk scarf over her head who fits Erin's height and build. I'm meeting Isaac there to check it out. Remember, I'm your ride home."

"I'm not going to forget that." She watched him hurry away.

On Saturday at All Our Kids, Nicholas finished another one of his stories about a brave little boy who came forward and admitted he'd eaten all the candy. Then he told another one about a special zoo with unusual animals in it.

Again Selena marveled that he could keep their attention, especially Tommy who sat near Max and petted him.

At the end, Nicholas looked at the children. "Now what I want from you are what do the animals in the zoo look like."

Selena and Cassie passed out paper, pencils and markers for the group to begin.

As the children started working, Cassie turned toward Selena and Nicholas. "I hope you'll stay for an early dinner."

"I'd love to," Selena said before Nicholas had a chance to voice his answer. She'd found a place she could donate some of her free time and wanted to get to know the children better.

For the next half hour, she and Nicholas walked around the room, helping different children with their pictures. At six, Cassie announced dinner and sent all the kids to wash their hands.

"It's not fancy. I hope you like macaroni and cheese." Cassie walked with Selena and Nicholas to the big dining room with two long tables. "Gavin was supposed to be here, but he was delayed and will be late."

As the kids filed into the room, the girls sitting at one table and the boys at the other, Cassie checked their hands before they sat.

Selena positioned herself at the boys' table and said to Nicholas, "I think we should mix things up. Don't break too many hearts this evening." She winked at him and sank onto her seat.

Nicholas leaned down and whispered, "The same goes for you. I'm not sure how much I'll be able to contribute to the conversation if they talk about dolls, boys."

"I disagree. You should be able to give them great advice."

He headed to his place at the girls' table, and as he sat, they all giggled. He turned red and sent her a glare.

She ignored him, and after Cassie blessed the food, Selena scanned the boys on her right then on her left. At the other end of the table, a chair was empty.

"Is someone missing?" Then Selena realized there was, and it was Tommy. "Where's Tommy?"

The guys looked around, then the oldest near her shook his head. "He was with us in the bathroom."

"Could you go make sure he's all right?"

A tall, skinny boy jumped up and rushed from the room. He returned five minutes later and announced to everyone, "Tommy is gone."

NINE

Everyone in the dining room went quiet.

Nicholas shot to his feet. "Thanks," he said to the boy who'd checked the bathroom. "You should eat your dinner before it gets cold. I'll check the house." He kept his voice calm while his thoughts raced with possibilities of where the seven-year-old could be.

The first place he headed was the security-system controls to see if it was on. Cassie had told him that when they were in for the night, she immediately turned the alarm on. If a child tried to go outside or someone attempted to break in, it would go off. When he inspected the box on the wall, he noticed it was still on.

Then Tommy should be in the house.

Selena came out of the dining room. "I'm helping you look. Cassie has gone to get her assistant, Virginia, from the kitchen. She'll stay with the children while Cassie starts with the downstairs."

"Good. Someone needs to be in the dining room to keep the kids calm. Although Cassie's assistant is a bit high-strung and might not be the best person for that, but we need all the help we can get. We'll search Tommy's room he shares with four other boys then work from there."

"Virginia seems so nice." Selena ascended the stairs with Nicholas.

"She is and great with the kids, but she worries a lot and can get dramatic."

In Tommy's bedroom, three sets of bunk beds were along the walls, four beds made while one was messy and another had only a bare mattress. As Selena inspected the top bunk and then under the bottom one, Nicholas opened the closet and inspected anyplace a boy would hide.

"Nicholas, the window is open."

He backed out of the closet and peered toward Selena, who had opened the curtains. She started to raise the window up the rest of the way, when he said, "Don't. If someone came in here and took Tommy, there may be prints."

Without touching anything, Selena studied the sill. "I don't think that's it. There's a sheet tied at the side." She held the drape totally back to show Nicholas one end was tied to a nearby bunk bed.

From the door with the curtains shut, it hadn't been obvious. Using a ruler he'd found on a desk, he painstakingly lifted the window without touching it with his fingers then leaned out. "There's only one sheet. He made it to the roof of the back porch." Nicholas pulled back and rotated toward Selena. "I'm going outside with Max. Continue to go from room to room, and if you or Cassie find Tommy, call me on my cell."

"Where's Max now?"

"In the great room. I was letting him rest." He started for the door. "I'm calling Gavin. We may need more team members with their dogs."

Nicholas left Serena to examine the rest of the rooms on the second floor. He made his way downstairs to

Cassie, still in the dining room, and whispered to her what he was going to do and to have Gavin come as fast as he could with any of the team nearby.

Cassie turned a worried face up at him. "Anything else?"

"Check the rooms downstairs," he said as Virginia Johnson entered from the kitchen with a grim expression on her face.

The boy nearest Cassie chimed in, "We can help."

Nicholas scanned the children, some afraid, others concerned. "I'll find Tommy. The best thing you all can do is stay here and follow Cassie's and Virginia's directions."

"Tommy was upset when we went to wash our hands," David said.

Nicholas nodded. "Thank you for that information," he said to the child. "Cassie, can you get the jacket Tommy wore today when they played outside?"

She hurried from the dining room and returned a minute later. Her hand shook as she gave him the coat. She walked with him to the great room.

"I didn't want to say this, but I'm sending the guard inside after I talk with him. He'll lock the door and turn the alarm on as a precaution." He called Max and put the leash on him.

Pausing on the front porch, he waited until he heard the lock being clicked in place. He waved to the security guard with his dog and jogged toward him, Max trotting next to Nicholas. "I think Tommy sneaked out. I'm going to check the grounds, but I'd feel better if you were in the house until I figure out exactly what happened."

"How long ago?"

"No more than fifteen minutes ago."

"I've been on the front and left sides of the yard. I didn't see anything and Gus didn't indicate he was concerned about an intruder."

"He probably wouldn't since he's used to the kids. Tommy used the back porch. I'm not sure how he got down from there yet."

"I know. There's a trellis with climbing roses on it. If he's determined, he could have used that."

Remembering the knotted sheet, Nicholas headed for the vehicle. "He is."

"I don't see him getting over the fence with the barb-wire on top, but he could hide in the woods at the rear of the property."

"Thanks." When Nicholas grabbed his flashlight from the Tahoe, then rounded the side of the house, he glanced at his watch. About another hour of light left. It was April, but the nights got chilly.

When he reached the back porch, he zeroed in on the trellis and found broken-off stems, and one thorn had blood on it. Fresh.

Nicholas let Max inhale the child's scent on the jacket then said, "Find."

Max sniffed the air and took off toward the woods, the area heavy with foliage. Nicholas could imagine a small boy crawling into the dense vegetation and hiding. But why? Did something scare him?

Max delved into the underbrush. Pausing every once in a while, his K-9 partner smelled the air then took off again. The forest became darker with a canopy of leafing trees above him.

Nicholas turned on his flashlight and yelled, "Tommy. Max is worried about you. Where are you?" Over and over he repeated the plea for the little boy to show himself.

Max stopped at a big bush, sat and barked.

"Tommy, are you in there?"

Silence.

"Everyone is worried about you."

A faint sound of sobs drifted to him. Nicholas knelt, parted some branches and shone the light into the dimness.

Tommy lifted his tear-stained face. "I can't go back." His words quavered as the green leaves did in the breeze.

"I thought you loved being here."

"Not anymore."

Nicholas's lungs seized his next breath and didn't release it for a full minute. "Did something happen today at the house?"

"I don't want anyone I care about being hurt. I'm not brave like the boy in your story." Tommy sniffled and knuckled his eyes.

"No one is going to get hurt. We won't let it happen."

"I'm fine. I'm staying right here, hiding." Tommy scooted back toward the oak tree the underbrush butted up against, determination evident in his crossed arms and his lower jaw jutted out.

"Okay." Nicholas twisted toward Max and said, "Stay." Then he crawled between the branches, fully loaded with leaves, and squeezed his body next to Tommy. "If you don't go, I won't, either. Here's your jacket in case you get cold." He held it out to the boy.

Tommy snatched the coat and quickly donned it, then went back to hugging his arms against himself.

"Is it okay if I call and let everyone know you're safe? Cassie is mighty worried. So are Selena, Virginia and all the kids."

"Kent doesn't."

"Your bunk mate?"

"Yeah. He makes fun of me crying. Says I'm a big baby."

"When did you cry?"

Tommy dropped his head, staring at the ground. "This morning."

"What made you cry?"

"The bad man."

"Did you have a nightmare?"

Tommy nodded his head several times.

"He's coming for me. I can't let him hurt anyone. I lost…" His bottom lip trembled, and he twisted away so Nicholas couldn't see his face.

"What did you lose?" he asked in a soft voice, wanting to hug the frightened child.

"Everyone I love."

"Who?" Nicholas touched his arm.

"Mommy. I don't have a daddy. I don't have nobody." He swiveled his head toward Nicholas, his eyes shiny. "Then Mr. Mike was killed. He was nice to me."

"How do you know Mr. Mike was killed?" He must be referring to Michael Jeffries.

"I saw…" His eyes grew wide. "Cassie told us." He lowered his head.

"Tommy." Nicholas waited until he had the boy's attention. "Did you sneak out of the home when Mr. Mike was killed?"

A long silence filled the air. An owl screeched nearby, and Tommy threw himself at Nicholas. The child clung to him. Slowly the boy's shaking body relaxed.

Nicholas hurt for Tommy. If he had witnessed the murder, the trauma would give anyone nightmares, especially a young child. "Tommy, I can help you, but you need to tell me. Did you sneak out of the house that night? It was cold. You would have needed a coat, hat—gloves."

The boy tightened his hold on Nicholas.

"Did you? You aren't in trouble. In fact, you can help the police find the bad man." He needed to call Selena and let her know he'd found the child, but he didn't want to stop Tommy from telling him what the team had been trying to get the boy to say since Michael's murder.

Tommy buried his face in the crook of Nicholas's arm.

"You know, Tommy, I lost my parents when I was a child. It was hard on me. They died in a small-plane crash in another country. I don't have much family, either."

The child stirred and pulled back in order to look at Nicholas. "You're alone, too?"

"God is always with me. He was when I was a child, too. When I was upset or sad, I turned to Him. When something troubles me, I give it to the Lord."

"I pray to Him every night." He drew away. "Are you sure He listens?"

"Yes."

"Then why am I still having nightmares?" Tears welled in Tommy's eyes.

"Maybe you're trying to remember something that's important. Talking about it can help. Have you sneaked out like tonight before?"

Tommy nodded, one tear released to slip down his cheek.

"Tell me about it." Nicholas held his breath, hoping the child would voice his fears.

"I wasn't stealing the gloves. I was only borrowing them."

"Whose?" The child's blue glove found near the crime scene at Harland Jeffries's house?

"David's. He was sick and couldn't use them. They were brand-new and my favorite color. Blue. I lost one. I'm having bad dreams 'cause I did." More tears ran down his face. "I'm bad."

"No, you aren't, Tommy. You were only borrowing them."

"I wasn't gonna be gone long."

"What did you do when you sneaked away? How did you lose the glove?"

"Bad. Bad." The child kept shaking his head.

What was he referring to? What he did? The man in his dreams? "No, you aren't."

"Bad man. He hurts people."

Was he talking about the man who had tried to get inside the original foster home on Jeffries's property? Or someone else? Michael Jeffries's murderer?

"What did he do, Tommy?"

"Nothing. I don't know." Fear gripped Tommy. He scrambled away until the tree trunk halted his progress again. He hugged his arms to him and began rocking. "I've got to get away."

"Come, Max." The rottweiler scooted under the bush until he wiggled his way to them.

"Max is here. You are okay." Nicholas spoke in a soft, soothing tone, giving Tommy time to calm down. "No one is going to let anything happen to you or the other kids. Nothing has at this home. You've been safe."

"Yeah."

"I'm calling to let everyone know I found you. Cassie and the others will want to know you're okay."

As though sensing the child was troubled, Max snuggled close to Tommy, who began petting him.

Nicholas called Selena's cell. When she answered, he said, "Tommy's fine and with me. We'll be back soon."

"Your captain and Isaac Black arrived a few minutes ago. Isaac is outside with the guard. He was going to walk the perimeter of the fence. You might see him on the way back. Gavin will let him know about Tommy."

He lowered his voice. "Everything all right there?"

"No problems, except the kids are all concerned about Tommy."

"See you soon." Nicholas slipped his cell into his pocket. "Ready to go back? Your friends are going to be glad to see you."

"Kent isn't."

"He might be. They were worried. Ready to head back?" he repeated.

"Yeah. Can I lead Max?"

"Sure. He always loves playing with you."

Nicholas made his way out from the underbrush and waited while Max and Tommy crawled out. They started toward the house, Nicholas shining his flashlight to illuminate the path. Out of the woods, Nicholas glimpsed Isaac and his beagle, Abby, emerge from the trees near the fence line.

A few minutes later, the front door opened and Cassie scooped Tommy into her arms. "Don't do that again. You scared me. Promise me?"

"I won't."

Cassie plucked a leaf from Tommy's sandy-brown hair. "First, the children want to see you, then you can go into the kitchen and eat some dinner. Virginia saved you a plate. After that, a bath and bed."

Tommy moved inside, and the kids swarmed around him, all talking at once.

Cassie turned to Nicholas. "Thanks. I'm so glad you were here when it happened."

"So am I." He spotted Gavin, escorting Tommy toward the kitchen, the leash to Max still in the boy's hand. "He's scared the bad man from his dream will get him. Will hurt you all. He's upset that Kent is making fun of him crying when he wakes up from a nightmare. I don't know if that had anything to do with him leaving tonight or not. As you're aware, he's very fragile right now. He almost told me about the bad man. He did admit he sneaked out and lost one of David's gloves. He feels guilty about that."

"At least that's a step forward. I'll talk with him. Put his mind at ease about the bad man. I wonder if the man is the one who shot Michael and Harland or if he's the one Tommy remembers from the attack on the original foster home."

Nicholas frowned, remembering when that happened. "We can't let anyone know that Tommy was the boy who dropped the glove near the murder scene."

"I'll see what I can do to get more from him. Gavin will help, too."

"Where's Selena? We need to leave. I know it's getting close to bedtime for the kids."

"She's upstairs helping to get some of the young girls to bed first."

"I'll go fetch her." He rotated toward Isaac. "Thanks for coming out here in case we needed to put out a larger-scale search for Tommy."

"No problem. Lately it seems like I've been on a few wild-goose chases."

"Yeah, I heard about the Erin sighting."

"A dead end like the one at the Jeffries house. Gavin

wants me to do a perimeter search even if Tommy was found, so Abby and I are getting back out there."

Nicholas ascended the stairs to the second floor, hearing a few giggles coming from the young girls' room. He paused in the doorway. Selena stood in the center of the room while the three girls' gazes were riveted on her. One child had her hand over her mouth, trying to contain her laughter.

Selena held up her hand, palm outward. "Honest. When I rose from that mud puddle—no, more like a muddy river—I was covered from head to toe. I even had to wipe it out of my eyes so I could see. That'll teach me to try following the big kids when they didn't want me to." She glanced over her shoulder. "I'm going to have to leave. Tommy is safe downstairs, and it's getting late. From what I understand, it's *way* past your bedtime."

As Selena went to each of the girls, she tucked them in then kissed them on the forehead and said, "Good night."

Nicholas could envision Selena as a mother. She'd told him she loved kids, and it was obvious when she was around them. Why wasn't she married, with children of her own?

He backed up as Selena came to the doorway and flipped off the overhead light. Two night-lights remained on, though. Then she stepped into the hall and closed the door shut.

A loud sigh escaped her lips. "I haven't done that in years. As a teenager, I used to help working mothers and often put their children to bed."

"You haven't lost your touch. Ready to leave?"

"Just as soon as I see Tommy with my own eyes.

There are times I see him, and he's so sad. Breaks my heart."

"I know. Mine, too. But nothing can be done until this case is over." Especially for Tommy. He was a witness to something that happened at the congressman's house. What, he didn't know. But the child was in danger until everything was settled.

"He's probably still eating. Max is with him, so I need to get him."

At the bottom of the staircase, Selena angled toward him. "The children had fun today. I'm glad this incident ended well."

The kindness and concern in Selena's expression touched Nicholas, reminding him again what a special lady she was. He lifted his hand and brushed a stray strand of hair from her forehead. Her blue eyes—the color of a calm sea—captured him and held him enraptured until he heard a cough. He looked over her shoulder and caught Gavin in the entrance to the dining room, a gleam in his eyes, Max next to his captain.

The moment of connection evaporated, and Nicholas wished he could bring it back.

"I figured you needed Max." Gavin bridged the space between them and gave Nicholas the leash. "I hope tomorrow is uneventful. We all need it."

"I set up a meeting with my uncle. Nicholas is going with me to my uncle's estate, so I don't know how uneventful it will be. I intend to ask him all about Saul Rather."

"I might need combat pay. See you Monday, Captain." Nicholas guided Selena toward the exit, wishing they could have one day off from the case.

The closer Nicholas came to the Eagleton estate in

Maryland, the more shallow Selena's breathing became. The past few months, her uncle and she had been tap-dancing around each other. She wanted answers today about Saul Rather and also about her mother, and didn't intend to leave until she got them. If her uncle had something to hide concerning Saul, she needed him to come clean because every lead on the Littleton case was coming up empty.

"Are you okay?" Nicholas asked as he pulled up to the redbrick mansion with a small porch with white columns.

"Yes, or I will be when I get this over with."

"It's his loss if he doesn't swallow his pride and accept you into the family wholeheartedly."

She tried to smile but couldn't maintain it more than a second. "I know that here—" she tapped her temple then splayed her hand over her heart "—but not here. As a little girl I would dream of being saved by a knight in shining armor like in fairy tales. I used to think my uncle might, but after a while, I realized there was no such things as a knight coming to rescue a damsel in distress. I began to look at life realistically. Then I met Erin and we became good friends. Suddenly that dream of my uncle being in my life started haunting me." A constriction in her chest expanded, and she sucked in several deep breaths.

Nicholas ran his hand down her arm and captured her hand. Cold. Sweaty with her fear, this would be a death to her dream once and for all. "Remember, I'm here for you."

She moistened her dry lips and swallowed to coat her parched throat. "And I appreciate that. I need to do this. For years I denied I cared about my family. I need to put an end to my dream one way or another." This time she smiled into Nicholas's beautiful deep brown eyes. "Let's get this over with."

After retrieving Max from the back, Nicholas joined Selena on the walkway and started for the mansion, clasping her hand again as though to tell her she wasn't alone. She knew the reality. She'd always been alone.

A maid admitted them into the house, the foyer huge, elegant and opulent, reminding her of the family her mother had come from. "Senator Eagleton told me to show you to the gazebo. He has lunch set up there."

Selena, with Nicholas by her side, followed the young woman to a long veranda that overlooked a beautifully landscaped yard, full of flowers already blooming. She saw the gazebo at the end of a brick walk nestled in front of a stand of towering oaks and maples. "I know my way."

After the maid excused herself and returned to the house, Selena faced Nicholas. "I need to talk with him alone first. This conversation has been years in the making. I'll call your cell and you can join us. I won't say anything about Saul Rather until then."

"I understand. I'll stay here until you let me know otherwise."

Selena leaned over and petted Max, the feel of the animal comforting beneath her fingers. Then she descended the steps.

As she strolled toward the gazebo, she admired the different colors of tulips, other flowers she didn't know the names of and the cherry blossoms on a few trees scattered around the gardens. Tranquil. A place to commune with God's creation. Although unsure of the conversation she would have with her uncle, she began to relax with each step as if the Lord walked with her.

She mounted the steps to the gazebo. Her uncle

stood, and as she came toward him, he moved forward, uncharacteristically clasped her by the arms and drew her to him.

The sound of a gunshot blasted the moment to shreds.

TEN

Nicholas paced the veranda, his attention switching between Selena and her surroundings. Her uncle hugged her. The sight gave Nicholas hope she would work everything out with the senator.

The crack of a gun going off hit Nicholas as though he had been shot. But the noise came in the direction of the gazebo and the stand of trees nearby. Two hundred yards away.

Clenching Max's leash, he flew down the stairs to the path, and instead of taking it, he raced through the immaculate flower beds—the most direct route to where Selena and the senator were. He scanned the area then returned his focus on the gazebo.

His heart beating a mad staccato, he pumped his legs harder while pulling his Glock from his holster. When he reached the gazebo, he prepared himself for the worst. One or both were dead.

Selena swiveled her head toward him, her eyes dilated. "It came from there." She pointed to the thick trees twenty feet away from them. "When Uncle Preston collapsed against me, I saw a black movement over there. I called 911. Go."

"I'll be back." Nicholas jumped over the shrubs on

the perimeter of the small woods, Max's leash in one hand, gun in the other.

He spied evidence of trampled ground and a broken stem on a young plant. "Max, check it." When the rottweiler latched onto a scent, Nicholas said, "Find."

Giving Max a long leash, Nicholas jogged behind his K-9 zigzagging the diameter of the stand of trees. A motorcycle starting up reverberated through the woods. When Nicholas came out the other side, he caught sight of a bike zipping away on the road in front of the senator's estate, a person all in black seated on it. Max yanked on his leash, wanting to go after the assailant. He was too far away for Max to catch up with him, even if the K-9 managed to get over the six-foot-high chain-link fence.

"Stay."

Nicholas took out his cell phone and called the police and headquarters. By the time he talked to Isaac, he'd climbed the fence and reached the place where the bike must have been. "No license plate visible. An older Harley chrome and black. I informed the Maryland state police and they are coming. The senator was hit, but I don't know how serious. Selena is with him." He studied the ground nearby. "There are tire tracks and shoe prints. Looks like boots—small size—maybe nine."

"I'm coming. I want to get copies of the evidence, too. Who was the target?"

"I don't know. I'm going back to talk with Selena and, hopefully, the senator."

After he scaled the fence, he petted Max and gave him a treat. Nicholas made his way to the gazebo by way of the perimeter of the woods. He didn't want to disturb the evidence any more than he already had chasing the shooter.

When he returned to Selena, her uncle was alert, scowling, while she held a white handkerchief pressed into the upper left side of his back. Nicholas noticed there was no exit wound.

She glanced at him. "The ambulance is on the way. They should be here by now, but I don't hear any sirens."

The senator clutched her forearm. "This won't keep me down. I'll be fine in no time."

"Not until a doctor sees you and takes the bullet out of you."

If the bullet had gone through the senator, Selena would have been hit, too. The thought chilled Nicholas. Who was the target? Was this a second attempt on her life or was someone after the senator, too?

Selena paced the hospital room, checking every few minutes to see if her uncle had awakened yet. After his surgery earlier to repair the damage the bullet had done to his shoulder, he'd been brought to his room, where he would stay at least overnight, possibly a couple days. He told her again he would be fine and for her to contact his chief of staff about what happened, then he'd fallen asleep. Carly Jones was downstairs right now letting the gathering press know what had occurred at the Eagleton estate.

Finally exhausted from the stress and worry, Selena collapsed on a small couch and leaned her head back against the wall. She was safe. Her uncle was safe now. A police officer stood guard outside the door. She closed her eyes and tried to wipe her mind clear.

But the memories of earlier inundated her. Her uncle coming toward her, stepping in front of her and hugging her. And because he had, he'd been shot. *Instead of me*. The realization that *she* might have been the target iced the blood pounding through her veins. She shuddered and wrapped her arms across her chest.

She'd known it in the back of her mind and had refused to acknowledge the possibility until now. This had to do with her looking into the Littleton case. It had all started then. She'd been investigating Michael Jeffries since Erin's disappearance and nothing had occurred until she'd gone to visit Greg in prison. Who had she made nervous enough to try to kill her? Had she discovered something and didn't know it yet? She needed to delve into the files she'd collected—at least the ones she still had. Some were gone, the files on her stolen personal tablet. She'd tried to rack her brains to reconstruct what she'd found, but with everything happening, she hadn't completely.

When the door opened, she straightened, tensing in spite of the fact her uncle was guarded. Everything was making her jumpy. She relaxed when she saw her uncle's chief of staff, a well-dressed woman with short brown hair and brown eyes.

Carly entered, glanced at her boss in bed and frowned. "The press can be brutal. They kept wanting to know if this had anything to do with the attempt on Harland Jeffries." She plopped into the chair near the couch.

"What did you tell them?"

"The truth. No one knows the motive behind the shooting, but the police are working on the case. The reporters want answers instantly."

"So do I." Selena breathed deeply, trying to calm her rapid heartbeat.

"Where's your handsome bodyguard?"

"Who?" Selena asked, knowing full well to whom Carly referred.

"Nicholas Cole. Who else? Do you have another gorgeous man following you around?"

"He's on his way. Should be here any moment." Then she hoped Carly would leave. She didn't care to socialize right now. With Nicholas she didn't feel the need to fill the silence with chitchat.

"The senator's shooting has caused quite a stir on Capitol Hill. I've been handling calls all afternoon and evening. I finally forwarded my calls to another aide. He'll let me know if there is anything critical I need to take care of." The woman relaxed in her chair, stretching her legs out as though she was settling in for the night.

"You don't have to stay. I'm his closest family member here. I'll call you if you're needed. I prefer he have quiet when he wakes up. No worries about work."

Carly's eyes grew round. "But—but…" She looked long and hard at Selena and didn't move to leave.

The door to the room opened, and Nicholas came inside.

Carly's gaze swept between Selena and him, then her uncle's chief of staff rose. "I'll leave you two alone." When she flounced toward the exit, she passed so close to Nicholas she nearly brushed up against him.

"What's wrong with her?" Nicholas asked when Carly was gone and took the chair she'd been in.

"I'm staking my territory. Since Erin isn't here, I'm stepping in as his nearest family member. I'm doing it for Erin—" her gaze shifted to her uncle "—and for him. If it hadn't been for him, I would have been shot."

"Do you think he saw something and did that to save you?"

"I don't know, but I'd like for a little while to think my uncle loved me enough to try to save me."

"I know he can be a hard, demanding man, but when we had lunch last week, I didn't get that sense from him. In fact, I think he was acting a bit awkward, as if he didn't know what to do with you."

Love me. Accept me. Those words slipped into her thoughts unexpectedly and caught her off guard. She'd always thought of herself as tough, a loner who needed no one.

"Selena?"

She focused on Nicholas only feet from her, a man who had been there for the past couple of weeks, and realized she cared for him—beyond a friend. Maybe she was just vulnerable right now, with what was going on.

She cleared her throat and swallowed hard. "Sorry, thinking about today. Did you get any leads from the crime scene?"

"Tire tracks from the motorcycle. I think the bike was picked up at an intersection on that road close to I-95. The police are looking for it, but I wouldn't be surprised if it was stolen, like the one in the underground parking garage. The person was dressed all in black like the other one."

"The same attacker?"

"It makes sense, but how did he know the senator was in the gazebo, and if you were the target, that you'd be there at that time."

"Followed us?"

"I didn't see any motorcycle or someone following us and, believe me, I checked a lot on the trip to your uncle's." His forehead creased. "No, I think the shooter was waiting."

"Which probably means I was the target, or he would have shot the senator earlier."

"Although we need to consider both options, that's

my thoughts, too. It had to be someone who knew you were meeting with your uncle."

"I've been thinking. These assaults are tied to the Littleton case."

"You're probably right." One corner of his mouth tilted in a half grin. "I'm not going to let him have another chance. I'm pulling Isaac's help in on the Littleton case. We need to find that aide who was at Tabitha's the day Littleton had the argument with Rather at the pool. Janice Neill might remember who was there that day since the others didn't."

"We can't count out them, but maybe Janice will be able to help. Have you found out anything about Tabitha and Saul?"

"They went out but weren't dating at that time. The few people I talked to said there was no indication it ended on a bad note."

"I wonder who ended it."

"According to two busybodies at the apartment complex, Tabitha, so what would be her motive for murdering Saul?"

"Okay, if she wasn't rejected, maybe Saul was harassing her. From what I hear about her, she isn't a wimp and wouldn't take much from anyone."

"Don't you think she would have told her friends at the time?" Nicholas asked. "Sally, Janice or Becky?"

"Probably. I don't see her being quiet about it."

"I'm still looking into her, especially her whereabouts when certain incidents went down."

"Does she have an alibi for the time I was run down in the garage? The person riding the bike could have been a female. It happened so fast I'm not sure about much other than the attacker was dressed all in black with a dark motorcycle helmet."

"No alibi. Claims she was home alone, and I will be asking her about today, too. What I saw was from a distance as the shooter went over the fence. The person was a smaller man or a bigger woman."

"That fits Tabitha. I know there's no love lost between my uncle and Harland. What if she was dating Saul to get information about Uncle Preston's activities? Someone hired the PI to report on the visitors to Littleton. Lots of questions, no answers."

"Maybe Tabitha was using Saul. She wouldn't be the first here in Washington." Nicholas sat forward and grasped her hands. "How are you holding up?"

"I'm okay."

One of his eyebrows lifted. "Are you?"

"I'm not one of those women who fall apart at the sight of blood."

"Men do, too."

She sent him a small smile. "What I'm trying to say is I'll be okay with time. It was traumatic, but sadly not my first time to hold a person who had been shot."

"When?"

"A good friend in high school angered a gang member in the neighborhood and was wounded in a drive-by shooting." Talking about that sunny day when she'd turned sixteen brought back a rush of memories. The fear of her friend dying. Jasmine clinging to her until the paramedics arrived. The blood that covered Selena and trying to scrub it off her and feeling as if she hadn't succeeded.

Nicholas gave a low whistle. "Did your friend live?"

"Jasmine did, but she basically lost the use of her left arm." The tears she'd refused to shed when it happened surged to the foreground. She swallowed over and over, but they still wanted their release after all these years.

"Did the gang member go to prison?" Nicholas moved to the couch and sat beside her.

"No, he was killed in a shootout." The words came out in a hoarse stream as tears ran down her cheeks.

Nicholas slipped his arm around her and pulled her against him. He held her while she cried, wetting his shirt. His quiet support reinforced her growing feelings for him, but everything was such a mess. She felt as though she were on a merry-go-round that would never stop and was picking up speed, the world flying by.

"My childhood was very different from yours, but I've had my share of caring for a wounded buddy while waiting for medical help to come or in some cases until he died. War isn't for the faint of heart, and it sounds like you lived in a war zone while growing up."

"My home wasn't in the thick of things, but some of my friends lived in the middle of it. I'd been visiting Jasmine that day."

"I'm—sorry," her uncle murmured in a raspy voice.

Selena pulled from Nicholas's embrace and twisted toward the bed. Uncle Preston's eyes, half-open, were fixed on her. She rose and went to him. "How are you doing?"

"I've had—better days. Water. Please."

Selena poured some into a plastic cup and helped him drink. When he finished, he relaxed back on the pillow, his eyes closing.

Nicholas approached her. "Why don't I go get you something to eat and bring it back here, unless you want to go with me to the cafeteria downstairs."

"No, I need to stay in case he wakes up again. I want him to see a friendly face." *And find out why he said, "I'm sorry."*

While Nicholas was gone, Selena sat in the chair

close to the bed. She wanted to be right there when her uncle awakened again. How much had he overheard of the conversation with Nicholas about Jasmine?

Not long after that incident, she'd paid her uncle a visit because her mother had insisted Selena be the one to ask him for financial help. She'd watched Uncle Preston and Erin from a distance but never approached them. She couldn't bring herself to do it. He'd rejected her mother's attempts, and Selena couldn't take it if he rejected her. That was the day she'd resolved she would rise above her circumstances and prove to the world— to her uncle—she was a worthy person. She didn't realize until later that in the Lord's eyes she was worthy no matter her circumstances. Once she'd figured that out, her fight to prove herself changed. She'd wanted to make a difference in people's lives. As the White House Tour Director and assistant to the president, she'd found a way to influence policies that benefited the huge number of people and groups who wanted to visit the White House and also plan special events like the Easter Egg Roll for children.

Her uncle stirred, but his eyes remained closed. Selena reached out and touched his hand. He could have died today without knowing Erin's fate. She was going to do all she could to get Erin back safely and cleared of any suspicions concerning Michael Jeffries's murder.

"I'm going to make sure Erin comes home soon," Selena whispered, coating her dry throat.

Her uncle squeezed her finger and rasped, "We both will."

"Do you want some more water?"

"Please." His eyes slowly opened and latched onto hers.

She felt his stare as she poured some liquid into the

cup then brought it to his mouth, holding him up to drink. When he indicated that he had had enough, she put the water on the bedside table then turned toward him. "Anything else?"

He nodded slightly, swallowing hard. "Your forgiveness."

Her heartbeat slowed. She never thought she would hear her uncle say that to her. Maybe he didn't know what he really was doing. "For what?"

"For letting my relationship with my sister..." His eyes slipped closed.

No! Please finish what you're saying.

Her uncle looked at her again. "Affect ours."

She wanted to understand why he had. What did her mother do to make him turn away from her? She pressed her lips together. This wasn't the time to talk about it, but she would later.

"Did they catch...who shot me?"

"No, not yet, but they're following several leads. Did you see anything?"

Silence dominated for a long moment, then he took a deep breath and let it go slowly. "Not much. A flash of black. It happened fast. I tried..." Again he shut his eyes.

"What?"

"To protect you."

Emotions clogged her throat, and she tried to fill her lungs with oxygen-rich air. "Thank you," she said in a hoarse whisper. *I don't care about the past. I forgive you.* But she kept those words inside, not quite ready to openly admit her need for a family.

"I wasn't going to let you get hurt...again."

She smiled and took his hand between hers. "Do you

know who knew you would be in the gazebo or that I was visiting?"

"If I'm at my estate, I usually eat my lunch at the gazebo on Sunday."

"It's gorgeous, as are your gardens. Who knew about me?"

"My staff." He frowned, his eyes drifting closed. "I think…that's all."

She waited to see if he'd say anything else, but he didn't. He'd fallen asleep again. Selena slipped her hands from his and rose, stretching. Then she began pacing once more, pausing at the window to look out at the darkness descending. Where was Nicholas?

Before coming to the hospital, Nicholas had taken Max to Selena's house. He was glad he had because he would stay with Selena tonight in the senator's hospital room. He didn't want her alone that long, even with a guard on the door. He couldn't shake the sensation that she had been the target today. Before heading into the cafeteria, he stepped outside, where cell reception was better, to call Isaac to see if he'd discovered any clues to who was behind the shooting.

"Anything new?" Nicholas asked Isaac when he answered, inhaling the welcomed fresh air without the scent of the hospital infused in it.

"The motorcycle was found, stolen like the other one and left abandoned."

"We need to check and see if anyone involved in the case has ridden a bike. This attacker wasn't a beginner, not from what I saw the night of the garage assault or today."

"I'll have Fiona run a check in the morning. I just came from talking with Tabitha Miller. She doesn't have an alibi. She says she went for a drive. I had to wait until she showed up."

"When?"

"An hour ago."

"Did she say where she'd been? That she'd stopped for gas, something we can check?"

"She said she drove to Solomons Island where she walked along the pier. She didn't stop for gas or to eat. I'll do some checking on traffic cams and see if I can verify her whereabouts, at least her car's whereabouts."

"I'm surprised she didn't eat or stop somewhere." In the distance Nicholas saw someone who looked like Erin with a black wig on walking toward the hospital entrance. He took a few steps in that direction.

"That's what I thought. I can't rule her out yet."

The woman stopped, stared at him then whirled about and ran toward the parking lot. "I've got to go." Nicholas pocketed his cell and gave chase. If it was Erin and he could catch her, a lot of questions could be answered.

ELEVEN

Selena checked her watch for the tenth time in half an hour. What if something had happened to Nicholas? He should have been back by now, even if the cafeteria was crowded.

The sound of the door swishing open made her tense at the same time that relief flowed through her. She pivoted toward the entrance. The sight of Nicholas with a tray full of food made her sag and ease down on the sofa, her legs trembling.

"It's about time. I was thinking all kinds of things happened to you."

"Sorry, but I thought I saw Erin and chased her." He set the tray on a table and pulled a black wig from his back pocket. "I didn't catch whoever wore this, but if you can get a shirt from Erin's place, I'll run a test with Max tomorrow. My plan is to let Max sniff one of Erin's shirts, then I'll hide the wig and command him to find it. If the scent of Erin's shirt leads him to the wig, it was Erin at the hospital earlier."

"If it was her, at least I'll know she is alive."

"We'll see if your uncle will help us tomorrow, unless you have a key to her home. I'm having Isaac pick the wig up and see if Forensics can pull hair with DNA from inside it."

"I don't have a key to Erin's place, but I'm sure my uncle will give you access." Selena removed the covers over the food and drew in a deep breath. "I'm so hungry. I could eat cardboard right now."

"Save some for me. I'll be right back."

"Where are you going now?"

"To get an evidence bag from my car for the wig."

Selena was halfway through a club sandwich when Nicholas returned with the bag. "If you don't hurry, I might eat your food, too."

He put the bag with the wig inside on a vacant chair and settled next to her on the couch. "The woman I chased earlier got away in a cab, but I couldn't see its number. Isaac is running down taxi pickups in the area. Maybe we'll be able to find out where she was dropped off."

"Don't sound so excited. If it was Erin, she's innocent."

"She needs to come in and tell her side of the story. It might help us make sense of what's been happening. If she was the one out in the parking lot, that means she heard about her father being shot. General Meyer made sure it hit the news big-time that it was touch and go with the senator."

"So you were hoping Erin would try to see her father?"

"Yes."

"Why didn't you tell me?"

He dropped his gaze.

"Nicholas?"

"I didn't want you to worry. The guard at the door knew, and a plant on the floor was here keeping an eye out for her. Also hospital security and another guy in the lobby."

"If I didn't know better, I would think you planned my uncle's shooting."

He glared at her. "I'll forget you said that. You do know me better than that."

"Yes, but think about what Erin is going through right now. Not knowing how her father is doing."

"We'll update the press first thing tomorrow morning. I'm sure she won't come back after seeing me."

"How does she know you?"

"Remember, my grandfather was a senator and an acquaintance of your uncle's. I saw Erin at several events and we spoke a couple of times. She knows I work for the Capitol K-9 Unit."

"Do you believe my cousin is innocent of Michael's murder?" Steel ran through her voice because she'd thought he'd gotten past the idea that Erin was guilty.

Nicholas twisted toward her. "Why is she running? Why doesn't she come forward and explain what happened?"

"Because the real killer is after her."

"Then we can protect her. She should know that."

The food in her stomach solidified. She rose and towered over him, anger churning in her gut. "I think you should leave before I say something I'll regret."

"I'm *not* leaving. I'm guarding you." When she continued to glare at him, he said, "I didn't say she was guilty. I think she's in trouble. If she didn't kill Michael and shoot Harland Jeffries, then I agree she's running from who did. She most likely has information we need to solve the two crimes. That's why I want her to come in. She may need to be protected, too."

The appeal in his eyes tore down her defenses. She

sank onto the couch next to him. "That makes sense. Then why are you helping me with the Littleton case if you don't think she murdered Michael?"

"Because you riled someone when you starting delving into the case. Did Michael, too, and that's what got him killed? Even if that isn't the motive for Michael's murder, I want justice served for Littleton—if he's innocent—and to find out who really did murder Rather. But even more than that, you're in danger. If something happened to you, I wouldn't be able to forgive myself for turning away from you when you needed me."

His declaration soothed any remnants of her earlier anger. "Then we're going to continue looking into the Littleton case?"

"Yes. We know the person has access to the White House and knew that you were going to be at your uncle's today. Also, someone on Eagleton's staff hired the PI to keep tabs on Littleton's visitors."

"That's still a long list. People in this town talk. It wasn't a secret we were meeting. I think I mentioned it to several at the White House."

"Who?"

"For one, Ann, General Meyer's secretary. One of the president's secretaries and the nurse who was on duty the day of the Easter Egg Roll. So from there, no telling who heard. We were talking about our plans for the weekend."

"In other words, anyone possibly in the White House or who visited recently."

"Yes. I never considered someone was outright trying to kill me. I thought the incident in the garage was solely for grabbing my tablet for information like the one I had at my house. I was excited my lunch with my uncle might lead to a reconciliation. Ann and I are good friends, and I was telling her, when others joined us. For that matter, I'm sure General Meyer knew."

"So since the whole world knows, it's futile to match the list of people at the White House when you were attacked in the parking garage with the ones who knew about the lunch date?" Sarcasm laced his words.

"No, go for it. It will probably take a few people off the list."

His eyes gleaming, he chuckled. "You still have some of your sandwich to finish. I don't want you to say I didn't feed you while I was guarding you."

With her appetite back, Selena finished her meal, comforted by the fact Nicholas sat next to her. He obviously thought that the shooter had intended to kill her, not the senator, confirming her own suspicions, which meant Erin could soon be able to come home—if Selena could stay alive long enough to find Saul Rather's real killer. That person could be the murderer of Michael, too.

The next afternoon Selena entered her uncle's hospital room after returning from the White House with some work she had to attend to. She wanted to be near if Uncle Preston needed her, and his chief of staff as well as General Meyer had insisted on it, especially when they weren't sure who the assailant was and if the person was attached to the White House.

"Where's your young man?" her uncle asked, sitting up in bed, alert and ready to go home.

"He brought me up here and is leaving to get his dog at headquarters and to check in with his captain on any developments in the shooting yesterday. Has your doctor been in yet to release you?"

"Not soon enough for me. Probably in the next hour. Sit. I have something to talk to you about."

His serious expression set off alarms for Selena. She made her way to the chair by the bed and eased down onto it. "What's wrong?"

"You ask that question when someone tried to kill one of us yesterday? I'm worried about your safety."

She hadn't expected him to say that. The fact he was concerned encouraged her that their relationship would develop over time. "I'm worried about yours, too. You've been hurt. The doctor said another inch over, and you would have been seriously wounded."

He waved his hand in the air as if that didn't mean anything to him. "I want you to stay with me at my house. My town house in Washington, DC, has exceptional security, better than my estate. Carly had a consultant looking at it this morning to beef up anything needed to make it top-notch. I'll be staying there until my home in the country is as secured."

"I appreciate the offer, but my home is fine, especially with Nicholas or Brooke there." There was a part of her that wanted to jump at the chance to get to know him better immediately, but her cautious side caused her to hesitate. Any true change in their relationship had to come naturally if it was going to last.

"I won't be able to rest like I should if I'm constantly worried about your well-being. With Erin's disappearance, that's all I've been doing. Don't make me have to with you, too. Please." That last word almost seemed torn from him.

Selena clamped her lips together to keep from grinning. He probably wouldn't appreciate it.

"Besides, I want your Nicholas to find my daughter.

I know she's alive." He laid his hand on his chest. "I know it in here. I heard you and him talking last night."

"You eavesdropped on our conversation?"

Her uncle smiled. "Not exactly. It was my room, and you two were sitting there talking."

"You could have let us know."

"In my defense, I was going in and out of consciousness, but I heard enough to know you believe the Littleton case could prove Erin is innocent of killing Michael and shooting Harland. I'll help you two any way I can. All day I've been thinking about those months Saul Rather was an intern on my staff."

"Did you remember anything that might help us?"

"At the young age of twenty-three, he was a Casanova. I may be busy, but I try to keep up with what my staff is doing."

"One person we know he dated was Tabitha Miller, an aide for Congressman Harland. Anyone on your staff?"

"I frowned upon that, but it didn't stop him from flirting with all the ladies."

"With Erin."

"He tried, but she wasn't interested. So you see, you'll have unlimited access to me if you stay at my DC house." His grin grew.

"Okay. Fine. Nicholas will be coming, too. He's been guarding me." And something told her he wouldn't turn it over to her uncle and his staff.

"It will be interesting to see how he's changed since he was a boy."

She wondered if this was the time to approach him about her mother, but as she was thinking about how to phrase the question, the doctor came into the room.

"Good. It's about time. I was ready to go home hours ago."

As her uncle and his doctor talked, Selena wrestled with even saying anything to Uncle Preston. Should she accept that he was changing his attitude toward her and not delve into why he'd turned away from his only sibling? What if she didn't like what he told her? She was trying to forgive her uncle for his coolness toward her. She didn't want anything to ruin that. Their relationship was so fragile she didn't know if it could weather his reasons.

Nicholas paused at the entrance into the den at Senator Eagleton's town house and enjoyed watching Selena working on a laptop concerning plans for a big event at the White House in celebration of the Fourth of July. He'd noticed when she was thinking seriously she often twirled her hair. At the moment it was entwined around her finger, and her facial features were set in concentration, her forehead knitted.

Suddenly she glanced up from her computer screen and looked right at him. "How long have you been there?"

"A couple of minutes. I was debating whether to bother you or not. Then you took the decision out of my hands." He moved into the room and settled near her on the couch. "I've got Max fixed up in the kitchen. He's met the guards at the back and front doors. I wanted him to be able to roam freely through the whole house."

"When this is over with, he's going to need a vacation."

"I totally agree. I'm going to take him camping in the Blue Ridge Mountains for a long weekend. Have you ever gone camping?"

"Me, camping? My idea of roughing it is a two-star hotel."

He studied her then burst out laughing when he saw the mischief in her eyes. "Not you. I know the area where you grew up. Camping would be a step up."

"On a more serious note, I don't like camping because you're vulnerable to all kinds of creatures, especially bears."

"That's why Max goes with me. He's a great warning system."

"That's what I love about Max. I feel safe with you and him here. I have a lot to do between now and the holiday, and it helps to be able to fully concentrate on what I need to accomplish."

"I hope you aren't going to open the White House to the public as you did for the Easter Egg Roll."

"Not the building, but the grounds will be used extensively. Besides, you can't see fireworks very well inside."

"You've got a point there." He wondered if the case would be solved by then. He hoped so. Erin was important to Selena, and he was discovering what was important to Selena was to him, too.

"Did your uncle talk about this Saturday night?"

"No, when he came home yesterday, he went to bed. Since he woke up this morning, he hasn't rested with the parade of folks coming to see if he's all right. It wore him, out and I finally persuaded him to rest."

"On Saturday, even more people will be coming to see him. Before Carly left earlier, she told me about this fund-raiser your uncle is hosting at his estate Saturday evening. He insisted on going forward and forbade Carly from canceling the party. She thought it might be too much for him."

Selena shut her laptop and set it on the coffee table in front of her. "And she's right. I'll say something to him. Maybe he can postpone it a couple of weeks. He isn't up for reelection anytime soon. Who's he raising money for?"

"One of his favorite charities, supporting our returning veterans and their families. Eagleton Foundation gives a lot to the charity. It's a good cause."

"So you want him to have it only days after being released from the hospital?"

Nicholas held up both of his hands. "I didn't say that. But if he does have the party, he doesn't have to be there the whole time. I know the guy that heads Wounded Heroes. He can manage without your uncle there."

"What about the security at the party?"

"If he doesn't postpone it, I'll work with your uncle and Carly on that. You aren't to worry about it."

Selena started to pick up her laptop.

Nicholas stopped her and drew her toward him. "No more work today. You hardly got any sleep the past couple of days."

"That couch in my uncle's hospital room wasn't comfortable. But it was better than the chair you were sleeping in."

"Sleeping? That's a stretch for what I was doing. More like resting my eyes. Too much noise for me to sleep. You know, hospitals aren't that quiet in the middle of the night."

"That's why my uncle insisted on coming home right away. He said he'd get more rest here than at the hospital."

Nicholas wrapped his arms around her and tugged her against his chest. "How about you? You need to take care of yourself."

She tilted her head back and looked at him. "I have you to do that. Isn't that part of being my protector?"

The teasing note in her voice captivated him. He loved seeing this fun side of her. He leaned her back against the arm of the couch, his mouth hovering above hers. Caressing her hair, he couldn't resist anymore the strong urge to kiss her. His lips touched hers. All his feelings toward her swelled to the surface.

He pulled back a few inches, their breaths mingling. "When this is over, we need to talk."

Her dreamy expression slowly faded. "When what is over?"

"Me having to protect you. The last thing I should do is kiss you." His words sobered him, and he straightened.

She sighed. "You're right. I'm never going to get my work caught up with you hanging around."

She infused humor into her voice, but deep in her eyes, he glimpsed concern. Selena wasn't used to depending on anyone else. From what she'd said about her past, it had become a necessity to do everything herself in order to accomplish all she had. He understood that. In many ways, he'd raised himself as Selena had done, just under vastly different circumstances.

He noticed her looking at her laptop sitting on the coffee table. "Is that your way of telling me to get lost?"

"Not too far. You are my protector, at least in General Meyer's and the president's eyes."

"How about yours?"

"I'm not sure. You confuse me."

He'd expected her to say yes or no. "How?"

"We're different in so many ways but the same, too. We should have nothing in common, but I'm discovering we do have a lot. We're both workaholics and enjoy our jobs. We grew up alone although there were many people around us. We both love Max." A smile brightened her eyes. "What's not to love about Max?"

"You're straightforward and so am I. And you like coffee the way I do—black and strong. And I believe we've shared things with each other we don't usually tell others."

"Your faith is strong. I saw that when we went to my church. When I thought I might have lost Erin, I began to question God. I'd wanted a relationship with my family, and Erin and I were becoming close like sisters. Then she vanished. I fought so hard my whole life and that hit me hard. Now I see I need to give it to the Lord. The only thing I can control are my actions and attitude. I can't control what's happening with Erin. It's ultimately in His hands. I need to trust Him."

Nicholas cupped his hand over hers. "Trust is hard to give to another, even the Lord, especially for people like us. But you're right. Ever since I left home, I've been running from my past. I turned my back on my family and although my parents are dead, I have neglected what they left behind. I haven't been home since I left years ago. I have caretakers watching over the estate, but it could be in ruins and I wouldn't know."

"You said once you grew up in Maryland. Is it near my uncle's place?"

"About thirty minutes away."

"Then I hope you'll take me to it one day. I want to see where you grew up."

"Only if you will show me where you lived." He didn't know if he'd want anyone to go with him and he was pretty sure Selena wouldn't want him going with her.

She opened her mouth but closed it and averted her

gaze for a long moment. Then she turned and said, "A deal."

"Really?"

"Yes. I think where we grew up will always be part of us. Like you, I haven't gone back to the neighborhood since I left. Of course, I'm sure the landlord didn't take care of where I lived like the caretaker did with your estate." One corner of her mouth tilted.

Suddenly their conversation took on a lighter tone, and he was thankful for that. Selena had a way of getting him to say and do things he usually held back. "Did you talk to your uncle about getting an article of clothing from Erin's house?"

"Yes, and in fact, he gave me the key. I forgot about it when I started working." Selena dug into her jeans pocket and pulled it out. "When are we going? I'm anxious to know if it was Erin at the hospital. Uncle Preston is, too."

"We're not going. I'm sending Brooke tomorrow morning. We'll know something shortly after that. She'll bring the wig, which the forensics lab ran their tests on today. They found hair, the color we were told Erin had dyed hers, but DNA couldn't be pulled from the strands. So no confirmation that way."

"I know in my heart it was her. I can't answer for the other sightings. Erin would be drawn to the hospital to see about her dad."

"Maybe the senator was the target, after all. What if someone was trying to lure Erin out of hiding?"

"The real person who killed Michael and wounded the congressman? Hmm. That makes sense. So does that mean you don't have to follow me around?"

He chuckled. "Nope. We don't know for sure who the shooter was targeting, but we do know you were assaulted in the underground garage. You're stuck with me."

"I guess it could be worse," she said with a laugh. "Now go so I can work another hour or so until dinner." She shooed him away.

"I guess that's my cue to walk Max around the yard. He needs to go outside."

At the entrance into the room, he sent her a woebegone look that only made her laugh more.

The next morning, in the glassed-in back porch, Selena stood at the floor-to-ceiling window and stared out at the gorgeous day. This was as far as she would go to enjoy it. Since the glass was bulletproof and several guards patrolled the grounds, Nicholas had agreed she could work here and enjoy the blooming flowers from a distance. She wanted her life back, but that wasn't going to happen until Nicholas discovered who had come after her.

"I see you've found my secret retreat. This is one of my favorite places at my town house, even in the winter."

Selena rotated toward her uncle standing in the doorway, his arm in a sling. Some color had returned to his face since the shooting. "How are you doing today? You slept in."

"Better. By the time of the party this weekend, I'll be back to my old self." He glanced down at his bandaged arm. "Except for this. My doctor wants me to use the sling for the rest of the week, but I'm ditching it for the party."

"Are you sure?"

"I don't want people to see me as a victim."

She knew that feeling. She hadn't, either. That was

why she'd worked her way through college. "I know you don't have to run for the Senate anytime soon, but your sling could give you the sympathy vote."

He frowned. "No, the only way I want people's votes is the straightforward way, that my stand and platform are similar to what they want. In my youth, I made some bad decisions because of how something would appear to my constituents. Image was important. When Erin was splashed all over the news, I didn't care about what the voters thought. All I wanted was my daughter back safe, but we still don't know if she is alive. That is my reality check." Her uncle slowly moved toward her. "I think we need to talk."

"Yes." She waited until he took a seat on a white wicker love seat with green cushions, then she sat in the nearby matching chair. She resisted the urge to place her hand over her heart as if that would stop it from beating rapidly. "What do you want to talk about? The Littleton case?"

"No, but I want you to know that I had Carly check into my staff members to see if someone in the office hired that private investigator, Mr. Goodwin, to track the comings and goings of anyone who visited Littleton in prison. So far, she can't find anything. No money was used from my funds."

"It could be someone not in your office. The private investigator never met the person."

"That's what I think, but that's not what I want to talk about. The case is in good hands with Nicholas and you. I owe you an explanation of why I disowned your mother."

She didn't know if she wanted it now. They had taken steps to build a relationship. She didn't want anything to destroy that. "You don't—"

"Yes, I do," he interrupted, his mouth twisting into a hard line. "I don't know what your mother told you, but I didn't totally kick her out. She left with part of her inheritance from our parents that wasn't tied up."

"She did?" All she could remember her mother talking about was how she'd left with only the clothes on her back.

"Yes, and she blew through the sizable amount in three years. That's when I denied her access to the rest because I was the executor of my parents' will. There were stipulations she had to meet before she would get any more of it. One was she would stop drinking and would go into rehab. On the surface she pretended she was trying, but within a week had left. She finally refused and started openly taking drugs with the alcohol."

For a second, Selena closed her eyes, hating to see the pain in his expression mixed with disgust. She'd fought that for years—feeling sorry for her mother, then so upset she couldn't stand to be around her.

"The last straw was when she made a spectacle of herself at a huge game-changing fund-raiser for my first campaign for a congressional seat. I lost a lot of my funding and support. The following month I lost the race by a narrow margin." He locked gazes with her. "I reacted with anger and told her I never wanted to see her again. That was the last time I did. I was—still am—stubborn."

"What did she do?" She remembered how many times her mother had embarrassed her and she'd been so mad that she finally ran away at seventeen. Although she had seen her mom some in the years afterward, she had never forgiven her for her actions.

"She got drunk at a function with investors and started a brawl that escalated and the police were called.

The photo of her handcuffed, looking drunk, was all over the news for several days. Then she turned right around and shoplifted, again for attention because she had the money to pay for the clothes she took. She was sick, but I didn't know what to do for her anymore. She refused any help from me and wouldn't see a therapist."

Selena dropped her gaze to a spot on the floor between them. "She didn't want to stop. I think all she lived for was her next drink or fix. I couldn't watch her destroy herself, so I can understand how you felt."

"I knew we couldn't have any kind of relationship until I told my side of what happened. When I saw you, I saw her and I couldn't get past that, even though Erin kept telling me you weren't your mother." He cocked one side of his mouth. "Did I tell you I'm a stubborn man?"

She laughed. "Yes, but I figured that out on my own."

"I'm also blunt. Where do you and I stand?"

"You're my uncle and Erin's father. And to be blunt myself, it's easier to forgive you than my mother."

"I know. She had such potential, but she became friends with the wrong people who used her until she had nothing left. In the past years, I had been keeping tabs on you when Erin told me about meeting you at your mother's funeral. It didn't take me long to realize you aren't like my sister. You may look like her, but that's where the similarities stop."

She dipped her head. "Thank you. I worked hard not to be. If I learned anything from my mother, it was what I wouldn't do."

The chimes of the doorbell rang.

Her uncle looked toward the doorway. "I hope that isn't more people wanting to see how I'm doing."

"You mean, you don't love the attention?"

"Not one bit. I need the rest instead."

Selena spied Nicholas in the entrance with Brooke beside him. She smiled at Brooke. "It's nice to see you again."

"Hey, how about me?" Laughter danced in Nicholas's eyes.

"I already saw you earlier. Brooke, this is my uncle." She swung her attention to him. "She helped Nicholas protect me after the break-in. Mercy is her K-9."

Brooke crossed to Selena's uncle and shook his hand. "I brought the wig and a piece of clothing from Erin's house."

Her uncle's expression perked up. "To see if it was her the other night?"

Nicholas took the paper sack and removed two pieces of clothing—a blouse and a jacket. "Did Erin wear these much?"

"I know the jacket was her favorite. I don't know about the blouse," her uncle said.

"I got both of these from her hamper, so she had worn them before she went missing."

Selena stood and looked behind Nicholas. "Where's Max?"

"In the kitchen until I've hidden the wig, then I'll bring him in here to find it."

After Nicholas put the wig in a cabinet in the corner, he left and a moment later returned with Max. Selena held her breath as Nicholas took out the clothing and had his dog sniff it. She glanced at the anticipation on her uncle's face that mirrored how she felt. If Max didn't seek out the wig, then it wasn't Erin who'd been wearing it.

TWELVE

A band tightened about Selena's chest as she watched Max sniff the air then put his nose against the tiled porch floor and make a beeline for the corner where the cabinet sat. He pawed the wooden door on the left side where Nicholas had stashed the wig. He moved to his K-9 and opened the cabinet. Max stuck his head in, sniffed then barked several times.

"Good boy." Nicholas gave his partner a treat and removed the wig. When he turned toward her, a grin spread across his face. "It has been confirmed. The person wearing this wig wore those clothes."

Relief flooded Selena. She twisted toward her uncle. "Erin is alive!"

He grinned. "Praise God." He sank against the back cushion on the love seat. "Now all we have to do is find her and prove she is innocent. She won't be safe until we do."

"I agree, Senator Eagleton. We aren't sure who was the target when you were shot. It could have been Selena, but there's the possibility you were the intended victim to lure your daughter out of hiding. It almost worked." Nicholas handed the sack to Brooke.

After she left, Uncle Preston said, "I'd been wondering that, too. And if Selena was the target, it's probably because she's looking into those cases Michael was working on."

"All I know is that your niece's snooping has stirred up a hornet's nest."

Petting Max next to Nicholas, Selena chuckled. "I'm glad to oblige."

"So what's next?" her uncle asked, rising from the couch.

"We have a lead on an aide we've been looking for." Nicholas swung his attention from her uncle to her.

"Good. Please keep me apprised of the investigation into my shooting and Saul's murder, too."

"Yes, sir."

Uncle Preston walked slowly toward the doorway into the main part of the house. "Now to find some coffee and my newspapers to read. Work does not stop because I'm injured."

"I'd like Max to go with you, if that's all right, sir."

Her uncle glanced over his shoulder with a somber expression. "Just so long as he doesn't talk while I'm trying to read." A grin spread across his face.

When her uncle had disappeared from view, she laughed. "I know Max has many talents, but so far talking isn't one."

"Max thinks he does when he barks. It's good to see your uncle kidding."

"Yes. We had a good talk about my mother. I realized I could forgive Uncle Preston, but I still haven't been able to let go of my anger toward her. Do you think it's because I might be able to have a relationship with my uncle, but since my mother has died, I can't with her?"

"Do you think that's it?"

"Answering my question with one of your own isn't any help."

"Think about it. You were estranged from both of them and not because of anything you did." Nicholas stepped closer, clasping her hand. "So why are you still mad at your mom?"

"Because I can't talk to her and tell her how I feel. She's gone."

"But you can still tell her how you feel. Nothing is stopping you. Let it go."

"Have you let your past go?"

He tilted his head to the side. "I'm working on it."

"I guess I can say the same thing." She peeked around Nicholas. "Now that we're alone, were you referring to a lead on Janice Neill's whereabouts?"

"Yes. Isaac has left for a small town in Delaware to interview her."

"Why aren't you?"

"Because I'm not leaving you and your uncle. He'll call me as soon as he's finished the interview. We've hit a dead end with the other aides that went to Tabitha's the day Saul Rather and Greg Littleton got into that argument. Brooke told me when she arrived earlier that the stolen motorcycle I saw fleeing the Eagleton estate was found—at Tabitha's apartment's covered parking. It had been parked there for days. When the custodian who took Littleton's job realized it didn't belong to a tenant, he reported it to the police. We'd already talked to the owner earlier about it being stolen and ruled out the man for the shooting. I think someone is trying to frame Tabitha as well as Geary."

"Like the first one in the underground parking garage. Why a motorcycle not a car?"

"In a chase, they can go places a car can't. It does

mean the shooter is a practiced motorcyclist since he or she feels comfortable using it as a getaway vehicle, so we've added that information to cross-check against the suspect list."

"Any word on the break-in of General Meyer's office?"

"We have a short list of suspects, but no concrete evidence to make an arrest."

"What's your gut feeling about who did it?"

"Vincent Geary. There's something about the man that doesn't feel right. And I could see him wanting intel on the Jeffries case."

"So you think he had something to do with Michael's death?"

Nicholas rubbed his chin. "Maybe, or he just wants to know all the latest for the congressman."

"But Congressman Jeffries would be filled in on the investigation."

"There are always pieces of information held back, even from a victim in the crime."

She set her fist on her waist. "So what are you holding back from me on my attacks?"

He smiled, his dimples appearing. "Nothing. I know better. Besides, you're the best one to help me with this, and I know you aren't involved in your attacks."

"You trust me?"

"Is there a reason I shouldn't?"

"No." The fact that Nicholas—who didn't trust easily—did trust her spread a warmth through her body.

He inched even closer. "So if you see or talk with Erin, you would tell me?"

"A few days ago I wasn't sure, but I am now. Yes, I would."

"What changed your mind?"

"You."

His arms slipped around her. "You trust me."

"Yes."

The softness in his eyes held her roped to him. She didn't want to move from his embrace. "Thank you." He dipped his head toward hers, paused and pulled back. He took a step away, releasing her. "You're a distraction. When this is over, I'm going to kiss you properly."

Although disappointed, she laughed. "I'm going to hold you to that."

Later that afternoon, Nicholas hung up from talking with Isaac and turned toward Selena sitting beside him on the couch. "We have a few more pieces of information to help us."

"What did Janice Neill say?"

"We have some more names of regulars at Tabitha's weekly get-togethers, and Janice is pretty sure most of them attended frequently that summer. Nancy Jackson, Carly Jones and Adele Carpenter."

"Nancy still works for Senator Langford, and Carly Jones and Adele Carpenter work for my uncle."

Nicholas smiled. "Also, Vincent Geary stopped by a couple of times, as well as Adam Hansom, an aide for Congressman White. Both White and Langford were Vincent's alibi for the night of your attack in the parking garage."

"How is this going to help us? It's just more names to add to a list that seems to be growing." Selena massaged her temples.

"Are you all right?"

"I have a headache, but I'll be fine." Selena sighed. "So it seems we need to find out who rides a motorcycle."

"Exactly. Fiona will cross-check all these names with any history of biking."

"Maybe we're grasping at straws."

"Sometimes it's the little things that trip someone up."

"That'll be a lot of digging into a person's past."

"That's Fiona's expertise—getting information."

"Are you going to interview each one?"

"No, I'll send Brooke, except for Carly and Adele who work for your uncle. I'll ask him to request they come to the house."

"I'll give a call to the office and tell Carly that my uncle wants to see her and Adele."

"You think they'll come?"

"Why do you want to see Carly and Adele?" Senator Eagleton asked from the doorway into the den.

Nicholas told him about Tabitha's get-togethers after work and why he wanted to talk to both women.

Scowling, the senator took a chair across from Nicholas. "I'll do it if you'll let me know what they say. I don't understand why who was at Miss Miller's is important to the Littleton case."

Nicholas leaned forward and rested his elbows on his thighs. "A handful of people witnessed the big argument between Littleton and Rather, which became important in the trial because it gave Littleton a motive for killing Rather. We've checked out the ones who testified at the trial, but Littleton remembered looking up to Tabitha's balcony and seeing three women watching Rather accuse Littleton of stealing from him."

"Did Littleton rob Saul?"

"No, the real thief was caught a few months after Littleton's trial with a few of Rather's items in his possession. The man confessed but had an alibi for the time of Rather's murder."

"What about the couple who testified against Littleton?" the senator asked. "I remember their testimony, particularly the wife's, was damaging about how angry Littleton was when Saul accused him."

"I talked to Mr. Quincy," Leaning back, Nicholas stretched his legs out. "His wife was visiting her sister, but he told me that she had a tendency to exaggerate the facts."

Selena sat forward. "Why didn't he say anything at the time of the trial?"

"He was afraid she'd get in trouble."

Selena frowned. "Then why did he tell you that the fight between Littleton and Rather wasn't like what his wife had said?"

"Remorse. He felt Littleton was red with embarrassment, not anger, at the pool. It has been bothering him."

"What did Tabitha say when you interviewed her?" Selena took a composing breath.

"She remembered the fight but didn't pay a lot of attention to Littleton, only Rather."

"How about the other two ladies on the balcony?"

"She couldn't remember who else was there except Becky Wright, who couldn't give me much more than what Tabitha did."

Senator Eagleton picked up the phone on the end table and called his office.

Selena moved closer to Nicholas and whispered, "Michael made a note to talk with Mrs. Quincy after speaking with her husband. That was the day he died. Do you think he told Michael the same thing?"

"I'll call and ask Mr. Quincy. I have his number in my notes." Nicholas left the den as the senator wrapped up his conversation with Carly. He retrieved what he needed and found a private place to make the call.

"Mr. Quincy, this is Officer Cole of the Capitol K-9 Unit. I have a question about what you told me about your wife's testimony."

"Just a minute. She's here, and I don't want her overhearing me."

Nicholas heard a sound like a door shutting.

"Okay. I'm outside and can talk. You do remember you promised me my wife wouldn't face any repercussions concerning her testimony."

"Yes. What I need to know is did you tell Michael Jeffries the same thing when he came to see you about your wife's exaggeration of what she saw?"

"It was just my opinion and I made that clear to Mr. Jeffries, but yes, I told him. He seemed excited by what I said. I wanted to tell the court I thought Greg Littleton wouldn't have stolen from anyone at the apartments. I never got the chance to say it. The DA cut me off."

He wasn't as familiar with the trial transcript as Selena, so he asked, "Did the defense ask you to elaborate about Littleton's character?"

"No."

"Thanks." Nicholas pocketed his cell phone and returned to the den.

"Carly and Adele are on their way," the senator said. "I'm going to run through some details for the party this weekend with Carly, so talk with Adele first. Neither lady has given me any reason to suspect them of this crime. Murder? That's hard for me to believe."

Nicholas sat next to Selena. "Tell me about Saul Rather. What kind of intern was he?"

"He was driven, very capable at his job and would have probably gone far in politics. When I interviewed him for the internship, he told me he hoped one day to run for office. The only drawback was that he was a ladies' man, and we've seen how that can get a politician in trouble."

"Did you ever see him with Tabitha Miller?" Nicholas asked.

Senator Eagleton firmed his lips and stared at the floor for a minute. "I think she came to the office one time not long before he was killed. I saw them when I left to go to the Capitol. They were arguing, or at least Tabitha wasn't happy with him." He tilted his head. "You know, I wouldn't have thought about that if you hadn't asked."

"Did he ever flirt with members of your staff?"

Selena's uncle grinned. "If she was a woman under forty, he flirted."

The sound of the doorbell filled the house.

Nicholas rose. "I'll send Carly in to see you while I talk with Adele."

When Nicholas came into the foyer, Max stood waiting for him. His K-9 greeted every visitor. Nicholas opened the front door to allow Carly and Adele into the house. "Senator Eagleton will speak with you in the den, Ms. Jones, while I talk with you, Ms. Carpenter."

Adele stiffened. "Why?"

"I have a few questions concerning the Jeffries case." Out of the corner of his eye, he could see Carly lingering by the entrance into the den down the hall. He gestured toward the living room a few steps away.

Adele went ahead of him, shaking her head. "I don't know anything about that case. I never even met the congressman's son."

"I understand." He waved his arm toward a chair

while he sat in the one across from her. "Have you ever attended a get-together at Tabitha Miller's after work?"

"Sure. I was a regular a couple of years ago, but lately I haven't. What's this got to do with Michael Jeffries's murder?"

"Two years ago in June, did you go to one?"

"I'm sure I did. I usually went with Carly once or twice a month back then."

"Were you there when an argument broke out between two men outside by the pool?"

Her forehead knitted. "Yeah, I heard one huge fight. I even went to the balcony and peeked out. Tabitha and Becky were watching. I really wouldn't call it an argument so much as Saul Rather screaming at some man. I'd never seen Saul go off like that."

"What did the other man do?"

"He was totally uncomfortable. He kept looking around as though searching for a way to escape."

"Did that man say anything to Rather? Shout back?"

"He just said he wasn't the one, then tried to calm Saul down."

"Did the man look angry?"

Adele closed her eyes for a few seconds. "I don't think so and certainly not like Rather."

"Who else was at the get-together that day?"

"I can't remember specifically except Tabitha, Becky and Carly. Sometimes different people came and went. In fact, a couple of times before Saul was killed, he went to Tabitha's get-togethers but not that day."

"How did the argument end?"

"Saul finally just stormed off." Adele relaxed against the chair and crossed her legs.

"When you went back inside, did you all discuss the incident?"

"Yes. We often ended up talking about the latest gossip. Carly was surprised at Saul's anger, too, so he became the object of our conversation that day."

Nicholas rose and handed her a business card. "If you remember anything else about that day, please contact me."

She pushed to her feet. "Saul's murderer was caught and convicted. Why the interest now?"

"I can't comment on an ongoing investigation."

Adele snapped her fingers. "You don't think the building janitor killed Saul."

"I didn't say that."

"You don't have to," Adele said, a satisfied expression on her face as she exited the living room.

When they entered the den, the senator finished up with his chief of staff. "So the security will be upgraded by Saturday?"

Carly nodded. "They've been working all week. I'll go out Friday and check it over with the supervisor of the project."

The senator looked at Nicholas. "Do you need to talk with Carly?"

"No, sir. I got what I needed from Ms. Carpenter."

Frowning, Carly glanced between her boss and Nicholas. "What did you need?"

"Some information about a fight between Saul Rather and Greg Littleton by the pool the night before Rather's murder. Ms. Carpenter told me she was the third person on the balcony watching the exchange." Nicholas observed Carly intently.

"Oh, I remember hearing about that fight. Adele told me Saul laid into the other man." Carly stood and turned toward her boss. "If that is all, Senator Eagleton, we need to return to the office."

Nicholas escorted both women to the door then locked it after they left. When he looked toward the den, Selena emerged and came toward him.

"Did she give you anything to help the case?" Selena asked.

"Possibly. She confirmed that Littleton wasn't really angry but uncomfortable by the scene Rather created. I'm beginning to see why Michael was interested in the case. Something doesn't feel right here."

"But you don't know what?"

"No, but if we can prove someone else had a better motive, that'll be a start. I'd like to go back and talk to Littleton, but I don't want to leave you."

She stepped closer, her scent wafting to him. "I'll be fine. This place is secure. You can even leave Max to protect me and Uncle Preston. Remember, I'm capable of taking care of myself. I brought my gun with me."

"I should have frisked you for weapons," he said with a chuckle. "I'll go to the prison on Friday and then check the security at the estate."

"You don't trust Carly's assessment?"

"You know I don't trust easily. I want to see it with my own eyes."

She pressed against him, smiling up at him. "But you trust me? Remember before you answer, I have my gun upstairs."

Laughing, he gave her a light kiss on the forehead. "I think you know the answer. You're at the heart of my investigation. Usually my only partner is Max."

She moved back. "I'll take that as a compliment."

On Friday, Selena met Carly in the hallway at her uncle's town house. Uncle Preston had asked Selena to let his chief of staff know he was on the back porch.

After Selena did, she asked, "Had Nicholas arrived at the estate before you left?"

"No, was he supposed to? I thought he was staying here all the time."

"Usually, but he had to interview someone and decided to go look over the security on the way back."

"I'm surprised he didn't have the person he's interviewing meet him here like Adele and me."

"He couldn't in this case." Selena removed her cell phone from a pocket and headed down the hall. "I'll just call him and see where he is."

Selena went into the living room before punching in the numbers. With the sheers pulled closed, she stood at the window, a security guard with a dog making his rounds. When Nicholas answered, she asked, "What did Greg say? Anything new that might help us."

"Actually, yes. He remembers hearing the sound of a motorcycle when he walked toward the parking garage right before he found Saul's body. He didn't think too much about it because he figured the motorcycle was on the street. No one at the apartment complex had a bike."

"So a motorcycle shows up again, this time at the crime scene. Interesting. How's Fiona coming with the list of people at the White House who've ridden a bike?"

"Slowly, but she's diligently working on it. If the information is out there to find, she'll find it."

"How's Greg? Holding up?"

"He says he's okay, but I don't think so. I should be back soon. I'm finishing up at the estate. Everything seems all right, but I wish the senator would postpone this fund-raiser until the case is solved."

"Which one? Michael's or Saul's?"

"Both. See you in a little while."

As she disconnected with Nicholas, she thought she

heard a sound in the foyer and turned. When she walked to the entrance into the living room and checked the entry hall, she didn't see anyone. Maybe it was Max or her imagination?

She hurried to the porch since her uncle had wanted her to be present as he and Carly were discussing tomorrow night's party.

"Oh, good. We can start now," her uncle said as she took a seat. "I was telling Carly that you'll be my hostess. Erin usually is, but…" His voice trailed off into silence as he looked away.

Surprised by the statement, Selena thought she might have heard wrong. "Hostess?"

He returned his gaze to her. "With all that's been happening, I've forgotten to ask. I hope you will."

"Well, sure. What do I need to do?"

"After we greet everyone who has shown up, I usually move around the room. When it's for the Eagleton Foundation, I actively solicit donations, but in this case there will be others doing it for the Wounded Heroes Organization, so we won't be the only ones."

"Good, because if I had to depend on working as a saleswoman, I'd probably starve," Selena said.

"Me, too," Carly added.

For the next hour they discussed the different aspects of the fund-raiser, from the food to the A-listers attending. When they had finished, Nicholas showed up in the doorway to the porch, Max beside him.

"Did I miss anything?" he said with a smile, his gaze finding Selena's.

"I'm playing hostess tomorrow," Selena said, a part of her uncomfortable taking Erin's place next to her father. "I'm going to be helping to get donations for

Wounded Heroes. I'll need to read up on the charity so I can answer questions."

Nicholas winked at her. "I'll help. I'm a big supporter of the organization."

"Oh, great. You can be my first donor. Bring your checkbook tomorrow night."

Carly rose. "How did the security look at the estate?"

"Good. It will be hard for someone to get inside without being invited."

"I'm glad. That's what I thought." Carly turned to Selena's uncle. "I'll be waiting for you at the estate. See you all tomorrow afternoon."

As Nicholas escorted Carly to the front door, her uncle uncrossed his legs and sat forward. "You looked worried about something. I should have asked you to be my hostess in private. That way, you could have declined. I don't want you to do anything that'll make you uncomfortable."

"I'm fine. I'm used to big receptions. No, I was just thinking Erin should be here doing it."

A look of sadness captured her uncle's expression. "So do I."

Feeling as though she'd intruded on her uncle's grief, Selena peered away and caught sight of Nicholas returning. He believed in Greg's innocence. It wouldn't be long before she would convince him Erin was innocent, too. Selena sent him a smile. For all her independence, what would she have done without his help?

After changing into a royal blue cocktail dress and matching high heels she was wearing to the fund-raiser, Selena descended the stairs to the first floor at her uncle's mansion fifteen minutes before the guests were to arrive. Although Carly had probably already checked on the food, as the hostess, Selena felt it was her duty to make sure it was what her uncle wanted.

Handsome in a tuxedo, Nicholas stepped into the large foyer and stared at her as she came downstairs. She gripped the wooden banister to keep from falling because his intense gaze made her self-conscious. Her knees weakened. Dressed as he was, she realized how well he fit into this wealthy environment, whereas she'd had to overcome her nerves and keep repeating that she was good at her job.

With her gaze glued on him, Selena knew she had to put some distance between them. She was becoming too dependent on Nicholas. She looked forward to seeing him, to what he said. And when he wasn't around, she missed him. *I am not my mother. I don't need a man to complete me.*

At the bottom of the steps, Nicholas came up to her, letting his attention move down her length slowly before returning to her face. "You look beautiful."

Memories of her mother and various men paraded across her mind. She forced a smile and pushed the thoughts away, but she couldn't totally dismiss them. "Thank you. I needed that. I'm getting nervous. As the White House tour director, I'm usually behind the scenes and very comfortable with that."

"It's your turn to shine and believe me, you will."

Maybe she could request someone different than Nicholas to guard her and her uncle. Brooke wouldn't threaten her piece of mind. Scare her like Nicholas did. She started to say something, when his cell phone rang.

"It's Fiona. I've got to take this."

"That's fine. I'll be in the dining room."

Did she have any good news for them? Earlier, Fiona had made her way through almost three-fourths of the list that Nicholas had given her and, other than Vincent Geary, she couldn't find anyone who rode a motorcycle. She knew Vincent had an alibi for the evening she was attacked in the parking garage. How about the day her uncle was shot? She knew that Nicholas would check out his alibi for each occasion where a bike was used. But that didn't mean someone couldn't have hired a person to do the job. Vincent was on the top of Nicholas's list for breaking into the general's office, which made him a prime suspect in her eyes. And the most damaging piece of evidence against him was that he had lied to Nicholas about being able to ride a motorcycle.

She walked around the buffet layout in the dining room, stopping to make sure there was a serving spoon for the artichoke dip. After the party tonight, she could talk with Nicholas about someone else guarding her. Or better yet, she could persuade her uncle to request Brooke. Chicken. That wasn't like her, and that scared her even more.

She spied Nicholas coming toward her, his features set in grim lines. "What did Fiona find out?"

"Tabitha Miller used to ride a motorcycle in high school and even race off-road. I called Isaac to bring her in to headquarters and interview her."

"What about her alibi for Sunday when my uncle was shot?"

"What if someone else was in her car or she and Vincent Geary worked together. They both work for Congressman Jeffries. They could have known what Michael was working on." Nicholas glanced at his watch. "I'll have to worry about this later. Isaac will handle Tabitha. We need to get through this evening without any problems. It's showtime. Ready?"

"Yes, Uncle Preston is in the living room. I think the downstairs of my house is smaller than his living room."

"Perfect for these kinds of large parties but harder to keep an eye on the whole room at once." Nicholas offered her his arm and escorted her to her uncle, who stood next to Carly in the foyer just outside the living room.

Her uncle grinned at her. "Our first guests have arrived. I appreciate your being here."

"Good. Just remember that when I insist on you leaving the party before you wear yourself out."

Her uncle harrumphed.

"I owe it to Erin to take care of you."

Before he could say anything else, the first guests came into the foyer. For the next hour Selena met hundreds of people, some she knew from her job. Names swirled around in her mind, and she tried to keep everyone straight. Many of them knew Nicholas, and he ended up greeting people while he stood beside her.

As Carly left, her uncle turned toward her. "Now the fun part starts, persuading these guests to fork over money to a good cause."

"I don't think it will be too hard. They came to the fund-raiser."

"We need to split up." Her uncle headed toward a group of senators.

She looked at Nicholas. "I want you to stay near him. If you think he's overdoing it, please let me know. I'm going to talk with General Meyer."

Nicholas watched her uncle across the room. "Not without me."

"Afraid of what I'll find out about you?"

His gaze zeroed in on her. "Yes," he said in dead seriousness. When he chuckled, his eyes sparkled. "No, I'm afraid of what you'll tell her."

Selena winked at him. "You should be."

For an hour she went from one group of guests to the next, pleased by the number of pledges she received for Wounded Heroes. Every once in a while she found her uncle and Nicholas in the crowd. Both were talking to the people around them. She enjoyed watching them.

When she moved into the dining room to make sure everything was flowing smoothly with the food, Congressman Jeffries approached her.

"I've heard about all the problems you've had lately," he said.

She didn't know what to reply. She knew of Nicholas's suspicions the congressman wasn't what he appeared to be, but everything she'd heard about him was good. "Nothing like what some wounded soldiers have when returning to the States. I hope you'll support a good cause," she chose to say rather than talk about the case.

He chuckled. "Preston has already hit me up, but I have no problem giving more." He took out his checkbook and made another generous donation. When he gave the check to Selena, he smiled. "Your uncle and I might disagree on some issues, but I'm glad you're here to make his life easier."

When he left, Selena stared at his retreating back. She could see why the congressman was so popular.

"Ma'am, I have a note for you," a waitress said next to her.

She looked at the woman then took the note. "Who gave this to you?"

"A man in the living room."

"Thanks." As the waitress disappeared in the crowd,

Selena read the message. *Meet me in the library. Good news. Nicholas.*

The handwriting looked similar to what little she had seen of his. Maybe the good news was about Isaac's interrogation of Tabitha Miller. This might be the best time to talk to him about Brooke taking over the protection detail. She headed back into the foyer, looked around for Nicholas, and when she didn't see him, started down the hallway to the library.

He wasn't there, either. She scanned the room again. She began to back into the hallway, when she felt a prick at her neck. Everything twirled before her eyes and darkness fell.

THIRTEEN

Nicholas panned the crowd in the dining room where he'd seen Selena heading fifteen minutes ago. When he didn't find her there, he glanced around the large foyer. Where was she? She wasn't in the living room. Maybe there had been a problem with the food, and she'd gone to the kitchen. As he made his way there, he asked a couple of security guards if they had seen her.

A guard near the hallway that led to the den, restrooms, office and library said, "She went down the hall about ten minutes ago."

"Do you know where?"

"She turned at end of the hall, which only leads to the library. Do you want me to look for her?"

"No, I will. Did anyone else go to the library?"

"No. Just Miss Barrow."

Maybe she needed quiet time. He could certainly understand that. Nicholas strode toward the library. When he went inside, he found an empty room and the window open. His gut clenched.

He hurried to the window and looked out. When he examined the sill, a royal blue swatch of fabric riveted his attention. Selena wouldn't leave without letting him know—at least willingly and especially out a window.

His blood iced. He needed Max.

He spun around and rushed into the hall, stopping at the end to talk to the guard again. "Are you sure no one else went to the library?"

"Yes, sir. I note where everyone goes when they walk past me. Right now one woman is in the rest-room. That's all."

"Put out an alert that Selena Barrow is missing. I want everyone to be on the lookout for her."

Nicholas made his way to General Meyer near the dining room. "Ma'am, I think someone took Selena from the library. I'm going to track her from there and see what I find."

"I'll handle everything here. We're going to lock down the party and gather everyone into the living room."

"Because of all the precautions, if someone took Selena, it probably was one of the guests or staff."

"I know. I'll take care of this end."

As General Meyer gathered some of the security guards and began to corral the guests and servers into the main room, Nicholas pushed through the crowd and retrieved Max in the kitchen. He put a leash on the rott-weiler then hurried upstairs to get an article of Selena's clothing. In the library, Max sniffed the blouse she'd worn earlier, found her scent by the door and followed it to the open window.

Not wanting to damage any evidence on the window, he hastened to the nearest exit and had Max pick up the trail outside below the window. His K-9 tracked Selena's scent to an empty spot in the parking area. One of the security protocols he'd put into effect before the guests arrived was for the guards to note who parked where.

Nicholas spied a guard with a clipboard and asked him, "Did you see this car leave?"

"No, sir. It was here about fifteen minutes ago."

"Who parked here?"

The guard checked his list. "Carly Jones."

"What was the license plate and make and model of the car?" He'd told the guards before everyone arrived to add that information down on their list.

The man gave him the information.

Nicholas placed a call to Fiona, who he hoped was still at headquarters. On the fifth ring she picked up.

"You must have been reading my mind. I finished the last person on the list minutes ago and was going to call you."

"This is an emergency. I need you to send out a BOLO on this car and its driver, Carly Jones. I believe she's kidnapped Selena from the party. Tap into traffic cams in this area. I need to know where she is taking Selena."

"It's not like the city has traffic cams in a lot of places."

"I know. I need something to indicate where to find Selena. Anything." Desperation edged his voice, and he didn't bother to mask it. He had to find Selena unharmed. He'd never forgive himself if he didn't.

Selena slowly felt sensations—the feel of leather against her cheek, a musty smell that roiled her stomach and the sense of moving. Was she in a vehicle? She tried to move. She couldn't. Rope dug into her wrists, which were tied behind her back, and bound her ankles.

She inched her eyelids up. Darkness surrounded her, but she could tell she must be in some kind of SUV. Suddenly it went over an obstacle, and she bounced.

"Sorry about that. The road is getting a little rough."

Carly?

She decided not to say anything, but she continued to try to assess what was happening.

"Playing possum?" Her uncle's chief of staff cackled. "I know how long what I gave you would last. I want you to know what's going to happen to you since you've ruined my life. I've given your uncle the best years of my life and then you start snooping."

"What are you talking about?" Maybe playing clueless would get her some answers.

"Ah, so you are awake. We're almost there."

Where was *there*? Selena lifted her head to see what she could make out in the dim light from the dashboard. Another bump sent her to the left, and she hit her head against something she thought was—a stick—no, a handle.

With her arms behind her, she couldn't reach it to see what it felt like. She scooted and rocked until she managed to sit up on the backseat. "Where are we?" She needed information and the only one that had that was Carly.

"We're on I-95. Once I dispose of you, I'll make my escape. I have it all figured out, and if I can't escape, you're going to be my bargaining chip." Carly exited the highway. "But I don't think I'll have a problem. I've got a boat ready to take me wherever I want to go if I couldn't stop you from looking into Saul's death. Why didn't you leave it alone?"

"Did you kill Saul?"

"Duh. Yes. He tried to blackmail me. I wouldn't allow that. He should have known that. If I take bribes to sway the senator's point of view, then I wouldn't think twice about protecting my cash cow."

"Cash cow?"

"My job. Once I made chief of staff and became indispensable to the senator, I started planning ways to make money. There are a lot of lobbyists out there that have no problem paying for a vote, but with Senator Eagleton, that wasn't going to happen. One of the few men of integrity. So when I was paid off, I used any means I could to persuade the senator the way I needed. I worked hard for that money and no one was going to take it away from me."

"And that worked?" Selena tried to figure out where they were, but it was pitch-dark. From the headlights she glimpsed thick woods on both sides of the country road.

"About eighty percent of the time. Enough for me to stash a couple of million over a three-year span."

Selena squinted her eyes and kept her gaze trained on the landscape out the window. If she could manage to get away from Carly, she needed to know her whereabouts. "How did Saul find out?"

"He overheard an exchange with one of my best clients. He was going to blow the whistle on both of us if I didn't pay him." Carly pulled off the country highway onto an unpaved rougher road. "Even if they find this SUV, I'll be long gone by then."

"How? Walking?"

"Oh, no. I've got a motorcycle waiting for me."

"So you attacked me and shot my uncle?"

"Yes. No one asked me for an alibi. I had one for one of the times just in case. I took a lesson from Saul and blackmailed a client to provide it." Carly went off-road and parked. "Time for the next part of my plan." She exited the front seat and opened the back door nearest Selena. "I'm untying your feet, but don't try to get away.

I have a gun and won't hesitate to use it, especially when I think of all the trouble you've caused me."

The interior light illuminated the weapon Carly stuffed in her pants' waistband. When had she changed? What time was it? "Where are we going?"

"To your grave."

"The SUV is stolen?" Nicholas asked Fiona on the other end of the phone call.

Everyone in the dining room quieted. The area had become the command center for the manhunt for Selena. The guests had left and law-enforcement officers were arriving. The senator had called in every favor he could think of to get as much help as possible.

"The vehicle doesn't belong to Carly Jones," Fiona said in a voice full of concern.

"But I've seen her driving it the past week."

"She stole it from one of her neighbors who is still on vacation to throw us off. I have a call in to them in Bermuda. The hotel said they went to dinner. They are checking to see if the couple is in one of their restaurants. As soon as I hear from them, I'll let you know. In the meantime, we are searching a ton of traffic-cam footage to see which way Carly went when she left the estate."

"Thanks. I know you are doing what you can. The general has computers being set up in here." When he hung up, he realized everyone was waiting for him to report what he'd discovered. "As you heard, the vehicle wasn't registered to Carly. It's her neighbors' SUV, and they are out of the country, so it hadn't been reported stolen."

"Can it be tracked?" General Meyer asked.

"Don't know. Fiona will find out. In the meantime,

we look the old-fashioned way. I'm grateful for traffic cameras. They might be able to spot the car and track it."

Nicholas noticed the senator backing out of the dining room. His pallor concerned Nicholas. They were going to find Selena. He wouldn't rest until they did, but he didn't want her to return to find her uncle sick.

Margaret Meyer's gaze moved from Nicholas's to the senator's and back. "Go talk to him. This has got to be a reminder of when Erin disappeared. I have everything under control in here."

"But what if—"

"I'll let you know," the general interrupted, "if we find the car on one of the roads. In fact, we've got too many people on this. We're stumbling over each other." Then she turned away and went to speak with Dan Calvert and a few other Secret Service agents, who were there at the request of the president.

Nicholas found Selena's uncle in the living room, the furniture still arranged as it had been for the fundraiser. He stood in front of the fireplace, staring at an empty grate as though a fire was blazing.

"Sir, are you all right?"

Senator Eagleton lifted his head and peered at Nicholas with eyes full of sorrow. "I can't go through this again. Erin is still missing. What if we never find her or Selena?"

Nicholas approached the older man, whose hands shook until he finally stuffed them in his pockets. "We will find both of them. I won't stop looking until we do. This time we know about the getaway vehicle and the person who took Selena. She only had a ten-or fifteen-minute head start before we started searching."

"I should have known Carly was capable of this. I trusted her with everything."

"And your knowledge of Carly can help us. Think about your conversations with her, especially in the last months. Is there a place she might go to hide? It could even belong to a friend."

The senator returned his gaze to the empty grate, his shoulders hunched forward. "I don't know. Maybe. I can't think." He glanced at Nicholas. "I've seen how you and Selena are. You care about her—she's more to you than just another assignment. How can you be so calm?"

"Because I have to be. I refuse to think we won't rescue her. The Lord is with her, protecting her until I can get there." In that second, he realized he loved Selena, and all he could do at the moment was put her in God's hands.

"But life doesn't work that way." The senator kneaded his nape. "What if…"

"Sir, I can't let worry take me down, or I won't be ready when I need to be." He laid his hand on the senator's shoulder. "Sit down and let's go through conversations you've had with Carly. How about the last vacation she took? Where did she go? What does she like?"

He thought a minute then replied, "The water. She always goes to the beach. In fact, a friend of hers has a boat."

"Do you remember where? Who she was talking about?"

"I don't know. I can't remember."

"Close your eyes and think back to when she told you about the boat."

Nicholas slipped into the chair across from Selena's

uncle. There were so many marinas in Maryland and Virginia.

"It's not coming."

"Give it time. Relax. Don't force it." He'd used this technique many times in the past with witnesses. He prayed it would work this time. But he was struggling to keep his doubts from surfacing.

Lord, I need You. Give me peace to do what I need to do.

The general sat forward, snapping his fingers. "Virginia Beach."

"Okay. We can investigate the marinas…"

The general appeared in the entrance to the living room. "The SUV pulled off I-95 at Exit 152 near Prince William Forest. We think she's headed toward Highway 234."

"That's a big area." Nicholas rose. "But we can get the team down there and begin searching for the SUV. At least it's something to do and a start."

"Yes. I've called Gavin, and he's mobilizing the team."

Nicholas strode toward the foyer where Max was. "We're on our way. I'll call Gavin, and maybe before I get there, Fiona will know if the vehicle can be tracked."

"I'm coming with you," the senator said as he stood.

Nicholas paused. "No, sir. I'm taking the helicopter that brought some of the White House Secret Service agents here. To put it bluntly, you'll slow Max and me down. I'll call you when I know something. Sir, see if you can remember the name of the person with the boat. Then we can locate the marina. If this is a dead end, we'll have that lead." At least Selena's uncle wouldn't be sitting around, waiting. He had something to do.

"I'll have a highway patrol officer meet you at the

152 exit." The general gestured for Nicholas to leave. "I'll keep you company, Preston."

Nicholas exited the house with Max, and in minutes he was in the air, heading for the national forest. He pictured the last time he'd seen Selena before she'd gone to the dining room. Their gazes had linked across the expanse of the living room. At that moment it had been tough to keep his professional facade in place. All he'd wanted to do was be alone with her.

In the dark forest, the only illumination Selena had was the flashlight Carly wore on her head. In one of Carly's hands she held her gun and in the other a shovel. Selena stumbled over something in the middle of a trail and went down on her knees. Without the use of her arms, which were tied behind her back, she barely caught herself from falling forward."

"Keep moving. We're almost there. Remember, if you try anything, I'll shoot you in the leg to keep you from escaping and then drag you to the spot I made for you."

Selena contemplated "trying anything." Maybe someone would hear the shot and investigate. That might be her only chance. The darkness could be used to her advantage. As she ran through one scenario after another, Carly grasped Selena's arm, causing her to stop, then shoved her into the underbrush on the side of the trail.

"This way. A couple of hundred yards and you'll meet your fate."

"The police will come after you. Why not run now? Leave me here. No one is around. I'm lost. I won't find help before you get away."

Carly laughed, a chilling sound in the cold air. "Sure.

Do you want me to untie your hands first?" She used the handle of the shovel to poke her in the back. "Move!"

When Carly's light shone on a spot a few feet away, a small clearing, Selena knew they had arrived. In the middle there was a pile of dirt.

Another nudge with the shovel and Selena came out of the thick forest. Carly illuminated the area. The sight of a hole in the ground about the size of a body sent a wave of panic through Selena.

As Nicholas climbed from the helicopter near where a highway-patrol officer waited at Exit 152 off I-95, his cell phone rang. Seeing who was calling, he quickly answered it. "Did you find anything, Fiona? I'm almost at the forest."

"Yes. The neighbor called me back and gave me the information to track his SUV. They had a tracking device put on it when they bought it."

"And?"

"I know where the car is parked right now. Off Highway 234 on an unpaved road, not for public use. I've got a forest ranger heading there to open the gates in case they aren't. You'll probably be there before him. I imagine Carly somehow opened them because the SUV isn't far past the second gate."

"Thanks. Let the captain know, so whoever is already here can head toward the area. Max and I will track them from the SUV." *Unless they're in the vehicle.* That thought made him rethink what he should do. "How far from the second gate?"

"It's hard to tell exactly, but not far."

He shook hands with the highway-patrol officer and climbed into the front seat with Max in the back.

"Nicholas, you'll pass an RV campground," Fiona

continued. "The turnoff is about a half a mile farther on your left."

"I'll let you know what I find." Nicholas ended his call with Fiona and relayed the information to the highway-patrol officer.

"I know that road. It's Spriggs Fire Lane," the Virginia state trooper said and pulled onto Highway 234. "It's not too far."

Fifteen minutes later, wearing night-vision goggles, Nicholas exited the patrol car, put Max on his leash and walked through the second open gate, leaving the officer to coordinate the others who would arrive shortly. He spied the SUV off the road. Gun in hand, he approached the dark vehicle and searched it to make sure Carly or Selena weren't around. Empty. He wasn't sure if he was relieved or not.

"Your turn, Max." Nicholas gave his dog the blouse to smell. "Find Selena."

Selena stared into the hole at a coffin.

"Get in it. I'm giving you a chance to be saved if they get to you before the air runs out. You're my bargaining chip." Carly waved the gun at Selena. She stared at the woman, realizing that she wouldn't see Nicholas again. She cared for him more than she ever had another. These emotions stirring in her were so different than anything she'd ever experienced. She wanted to explore them more in depth.

"I said, get in the coffin. Now."

"No."

"That isn't a choice." Carly charged Selena so fast it took her by surprise.

Carly contacted with Selena and sent her flying down into the pit. Her head hit against the side of the coffin and her sight blurred. Before she could scramble from it, the top slammed down while the darkness spun. A loud thump struck the wooden casket as if Carly had jumped down on top of it. Quickly, Carly hammered against the lid to keep it shut, causing shock waves of sound to thunder through Selena's mind.

I can't lose consciousness. Please, Lord, help me. Somehow.

FOURTEEN

A crashing sound echoed through the trees up ahead. Max kept going forward through the thick vegetation. Nicholas tried to speculate what the noise was, but he finally pushed it away and focused instead on getting to Selena before she was killed.

Through the eerie green of his view, he saw Carly jump into a hole. He increased his pace as much as he could without making noise. He needed to surprise the woman and prayed Selena was alive in the hole, the length of a grave. A pounding sound reverberated through the air. A few yards ahead of him, Max flew out of the underbrush toward Carly, her head visible above the ground.

"Get her," Nicholas shouted, lifting his gun.

Carly screamed.

When Nicholas planted himself at the edge of the grave, his weapon aimed downward, he found Max's mouth clamped around Carly's arm with the revolver. She lay on a coffin, a hammer by her feet.

"Get him off me."

"As soon as you let go of the gun."

Carly complied, and the weapon fell between the

coffin and the dirt wall. Max was between Carly and the gun.

"Max, loose it. I've got her, boy." His K-9 partner dropped Carly's arm. "Where is Selena?" he demanded of Carly. "In the coffin?"

Flat on her back, Carly glared at him.

"Find Selena, Max."

His rottweiler scratched at the coffin at the same time Nicholas heard banging from beneath Carly. "I'm in here. Help."

"I'm here, Selena. I'll get you out." Then to Carly he said, "Climb out and lie facedown on the ground. One wrong move and I'll sic Max on you with no regrets."

Carly followed his order. As soon as the woman was lying on the ground, he pulled out his handcuffs and secured her.

"Guard her," Nicholas said then lowered himself into the hole, took the hammer and pulled the nails out of the wood.

When he lifted the lid, Selena launched herself into his arms, shaking against him.

He had so many things to say to her, but that would have to wait until Carly was taken care of. He gave her a quick kiss then climbed from the hole and turned to help Selena out of her grave.

He stared into her beautiful features. "How are you?"

"I have one killer headache. Carly pushed me in and I hit my head, but that's nothing now. You saved me."

"I was only doing my job." He took out his cell and couldn't get reception. "We need to walk back to the Tahoe. There's a highway-patrol officer with a radio. You need medical attention."

"I'm fine. Really. And the best part is, I know why Carly killed Saul Rather. Greg will be freed soon."

* * *

The prison door opened, and Greg Littleton appeared in the exit. He looked around, saw Selena and Nicholas and waved. Bag in hand, the freed man hurried toward her and Nicholas. The sight of Greg's smile made her heart sing.

Selena watched as Greg cut the distance between them. "I can't believe this day is finally here. This is the best feeling."

"I agree," Nicholas said.

Greg stopped in front of Selena with a huge grin on his face. "I'll never be able to thank you two enough for what you did for me. I tried to convince everyone I was innocent, but no one would listen." He took Selena's hand. "Until Mr. Jeffries, then you."

Selena gave Greg a hug. "I'm so glad the truth finally came out."

"How did you two solve the case? I've heard some of it on the news." Greg swung his attention from Selena to Nicholas.

"It was mostly Selena. She got Carly Jones to tell her why she killed Saul Rather."

Greg's forehead furrowed. "Why would the woman confess to you?"

"Because she was going to kill me and she wanted me to know why." Selena glanced at Nicholas. "But he saved me." In the coffin, as Carly had hammered it shut, all Selena could do was pray and give in to the Lord. She wasn't going to get out of her situation without help, and Nicholas was the help the Lord had sent her. *Thank You, God.*

"As Senator Eagleton's chief of staff, Carly had been accepting bribes for several years and Saul found out," Nicholas explained to Greg. "He was blackmailing her, so she killed him. When she heard about the argument the evening before between you and Saul, she used that to frame you. Saul was meeting her for his first payoff, instead she shot him and fled as you came into the parking garage." Nicholas smiled at Selena. "She wouldn't stop digging deeper even when Carly came after her at the Easter Egg Roll and in the White House underground parking."

"She was desperate toward the end and tried to shoot me at my uncle's. Instead, he was wounded. That's when Carly decided to leave the country with the money she'd accrued from the bribes she had taken."

"But she went after you first?"

"Yes, she wanted me to pay for ruining her scheme."

Nicholas clasped Selena's hand. "Can we give you a ride, Greg?"

Greg panned the area. "Thanks, but my mom should be here. We're going out to celebrate." His face lit up. "Ah, I see her coming."

"Greg, my uncle would like you to come visit him. He wants to offer you a job at his estate as groundskeeper."

"You're not joking?" Greg asked in a stunned voice.

"No." Selena gave him a piece of paper. "Call that number when you're ready."

"Thank you. Tell him I will." Greg shook Selena's hand then Nicholas's, then headed for the nearby Chevy and hugged an older woman waiting by the car.

Selena's throat clogged, and she swallowed several times before saying, "I'm glad I could finish what Michael started with the case."

"Come on. I've got one more place to go." He tugged her toward his Tahoe.

"Where?"

"A surprise."

As Nicholas headed toward Maryland, Selena relaxed, thinking about the whirlwind past few days since Carly had been arrested for Saul Rather's murder. "At least we found one murderer. I'd hoped Carly had killed Michael, too, then Erin could come home."

"Carly had an airtight alibi with a dozen senators able to verify her presence at a small party your uncle had given."

"And she was there the whole time?"

"Yes. Believe me, I went through her alibi, wanting to tear it apart. I couldn't. Neither could Isaac or Gavin."

Selena sighed. "Which leaves Erin where she was—a suspect."

"I'm not going to rest until the truth comes out. But I need you to promise to stop doing your own investigation. I can't go through the past few weeks again." Nicholas pulled up to a gate and pushed a remote control.

The black iron gates slowly opened. "I thought we were going to my uncle's."

"No, I told you I would bring you to my childhood home and that's what I'm doing."

Selena sat forward, looking out the windshield at the white-brick mansion with a long veranda across the front of the house and tall, massive columns. At least four chimneys thrust up toward the sky.

"This isn't that far from my uncle's."

Nicholas parked on a circular driveway near the massive double doors that led inside. "Actually, this place is closer than I realized. Probably no more than twenty minutes away." He opened his door and climbed from the Tahoe. "I want to show you the place."

She slid from the car as Nicholas rounded the hood. Was this his way of saying goodbye because neither she nor her uncle needed to be guarded anymore? The physical threat was over, and now she faced a different kind of threat. When she was praying to the Lord to be saved from Carly, she'd realized how she really felt concerning Nicholas.

"Why do you want me to see this?" she finally asked Nicholas, who paused and stared up at the front of the house.

A neutral expression descended, as if he was struggling to hide any emotion. "Because I needed to let my past go in order to move forward."

Move forward? Where? Doubts assailed Selena. "Have you forgiven your parents?"

"Yes. I can't change what happened, but I can put it behind me once and for all. I'm going to sell the place. This isn't me, but it will be perfect for someone else. I want some family to enjoy it the way it was meant to be enjoyed."

Her heartbeat thumped against her chest. "So you don't see you having a family one day?"

He shifted toward her and clasped her arms. "On the contrary, for the first time I do see me having a family—with you. That is, if you'll have me."

For a moment no words came, as if his declaration had robbed her of coherent thoughts.

"I know we haven't been together long, but I hope you'll give me a chance." Concern lined his face.

She flung her arms around him, pressing her body against his. "Yes. It's not the quantity of time we've been together that is important, but the quality of time. I know I should be scared of my love for you, but I've realized I'm not. You understand me."

He framed her face with his hands and peered down at her. "And you understand me."

"For years I was determined never to be like my mother. She had to have a man around. If she didn't, she couldn't function. I know I'm not ever going to be like her because I have for years lived a happy, content life." She looked into his beautiful eyes, full of love. "But you've changed that. If I went back to the way things were before I got to know you, I wouldn't be happy and content as before without you. There was a time I would have been scared about that. I'm not now. When I needed someone, God sent you."

He leaned down and touched his lips to hers. "I love you, Selena." Then he deepened the connection, his arms entwining her.

The feeling of forgiveness toward her mother and of finally being free of her past spread through Selena as she poured all her love into the kiss.

* * * * *

"I have your new identities." US marshal Jonathan Mast
sat across the table from Julia in the hotel where she and
her children had been holed up for the last five days.

The Luchadors wanted to kill William so he wouldn't
testify against their leader. As much as Julia didn't trust
law enforcement, she had to rely on the US Marshals and
their witness protection program to keep her family safe.
No wonder her nerves were stretched thin.

"We're ready to transport you and the children,"
Jonathan Mast continued. "We'll fly into Kansas City
tonight, then drive to Topeka and north to Yoder."

"What's in Kansas?"

Jonathan pulled out his phone and accessed a
photograph. He handed the cell to Julia. "Abraham King
will watch over you in Kansas."

Julia studied the picture. The man looked to be in his midthirties with a square face and deep-set eyes beneath dark brows. His nose appeared a bit off center, as if it had been broken. Lips pulled tight and no hint of a smile on his angular face.

"Mr. King doesn't look happy."

Jonathan shrugged. "Law enforcement photos are never flattering."

Her stomach tightened. "He's a cop?"

"Past tense. He left the force three years ago."

Once a cop, always a cop. Her ex had been a police officer. He'd protected others but failed to show that same sense of concern when it came to his own family. The marshal seemed oblivious to her unease.

"Abe is an old friend," Jonathan continued. "A widower from my police-force days who owns a farm and has a spare house on his property. He lives in a rural Amish community."

"Amish?"

"That's right."

"Bonnets and buggies?" she asked.

He smiled weakly. "You'll be off the grid, Mrs. Bradford. No one will look for you there."

Don't miss
Amish Safe House *by Debby Giusti,*
available February 2019 wherever
Love Inspired® Suspense books and ebooks are sold.

www.LoveInspired.com

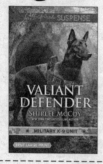

Love Inspired®

Save $1.00

on the purchase of ANY
Love Inspired® book.

Available wherever books are sold, including most bookstores, supermarkets, drugstores and discount stores.

- ✂

Save $1.00

on the purchase of ANY Love Inspired® book.

Coupon valid until March 31, 2019.
Redeemable at participating retail outlets in the U.S. and Canada only.
Limit one coupon per customer.

52616176

5 65373 00076 2 (8100)0 12404

LISCOUP08184

Love Inspired®

**Inspirational Romance to
Warm Your Heart and Soul**

Join our social communities to connect
with other readers who share your love!

Sign up for the Love Inspired newsletter
at **www.LoveInspired.com** to be the
first to find out about upcoming titles,
special promotions and exclusive content.

CONNECT WITH US AT:

Facebook.com/groups/HarlequinConnection

 Facebook.com/LoveInspiredBooks

 Twitter.com/LoveInspiredBks

LISOCIAL2018